Born and educated in Sydney, Australia, Titania Hardie is the highly successful author of distinctive non-fiction books and the children's series, *The Frangipani Fairies*. Best known for her television appearances on This Morning with Richard & Judy and The Paul O'Grady Show, Titania is a serious student of esoterica. She has first-class honours degrees in psychology and English, and was awarded the Chatterton bursary for post-graduate study at Bristol University, where she is currently completing her MA on the Romantic Poets. *The Rose Labyrinth* is her first novel. Titania lives in Somerset with her husband and daughters.

The ROSE Labyrinth

TITANIA HARDIE

A Quadrille book

First published in Great Britain in 2008
by HEADLINE REVIEW
An imprint of HEADLINE PUBLISHING GROUP

First published in paperback in Great Britain in 2008
by HEADLINE REVIEW

7

Cataloguing in Publication Data is available from the British Library

ISBN 978 0 7553 4457 4 (B format)
ISBN 978 0 7553 4745 2 (A format)

Typeset in Adobe Garamond by Avon DataSet Ltd, Bidford on Avon, Warwickshire

Printed and bound in Great Britain by Clays Ltd St Ives plc, Bungay, Suffolk

Headline's policy is to use papers that are natural, renewable and recyclable products and
made from wood grown in sustainable forests. The logging and manufacturing processes
are expected to conform to the environmental regulations of the country of origin.

HEADLINE PUBLISHING GROUP
An Hachette Livre UK Company
338 Euston Road
London NW1 3BH

www.headline.co.uk
www.hachettelivre.co.uk

For my husband, Gavrik Losey,
who is my peace whenever the Tempest blows.

In great contests, each party claims to act in accordance with the will of God. Both *may* be, and one *must* be, wrong. God cannot be *for* and *against* the same thing, at the same time.

– Abraham Lincoln

\+ ELOHIM + ELOHI +

ADONAI	4	14	15	1	ZEBAOTH
	9	7	6	12	
	5	11	10	8	
	16	2	3	13	

\+ ROGYEL + JOSPHIEL +

'Vexilla Regis prodeunt inferni
verso di noi; pero dinanza mira',
disse 'l maestro mio 'se tu 'l discerni'.

PROLOGUE

St George's Day, April 1600, At an Inn on the Road to London

A snow-bearded, elderly man is seated at the head of a refectory table, close to a fire, with his head bowed. He grasps a dark, shiny object in the slender fingers of his right hand. Blooms of Rosa Mundi – white petals streaked pink-red – carpet the table in front of him. Thus, all those who are seated at the trestle know that what will unfold here is secret, a marriage of the spirit and the soul of everyone present, and the birth of something unique, which they await: the Philosopher's Child. Against the bubbling din of other inn patrons behind closed doors in adjacent rooms, they are hushed, waiting for his words. A door softly opens and closes, then a sudden shuffle of feet around him intrudes into the silence. A note from a servant, who has entered largely unobserved, is put into his fine hands. This he reads slowly; his high forehead – surprisingly smooth for a man of his years – creases into a dark frown. After a long moment, he looks at every face in turn, gathered around the long table. Finally he speaks, his voice hardly more than a vesper.

'Some little time ago, in the month of lights, Signor Bruno was burned at the stake in the Campo de' Fiori. He had been given forty days to recant his heresies: that the earth was not the centre of this world, that there were many such suns and planets beyond our own, and that the Saviour's divinity was not a literal truth. Monks offered him a crucifix to kiss in repentance of his errors, but he turned his head from them. As a demonstration of mercy, the clerical authorities placed a necklace of gunpowder around his head before they set the fire – to hasten his end. They also nailed his tongue fast to his jaw to stop him from talking.' He raises his eyes to each of his dinner companions, and takes some moments to speak again.

'For some of us, then, the thread now begins to unravel, and another journey starts here.' His eyes rest on one man, sitting hunched over a tankard just to the left of the head of the table at the opposite end. His neighbour is nudging him, whispering to him, alerting him to the gaze of the speaker, which has settled on him alone. Both men stare, quite locked together, until the younger allows a half-smile to soften his features, prompting further quiet words from the senior man.

'Is there a way,' he asks, in a stronger cadence now, 'to use all the fierce endeavours of our wit, to keep his thoughts of love, and universal harmony, as fresh as dew? May it ever be that Love's Lost Labours can be Won?'

1

A blackbird's song broke into his uneasy dreams, but the shutters on the cottage windows were still tightly closed.

Will had arrived late, the faded September twilight long gone, but the moon had been bright enough to find the secreted house key among the geraniums. He woke now in panic in the darkness, strangely disorientated, though a tiny shaft of light was trying to force its way in. Without his noticing, morning had come.

He leaped from the bed in a rush, and worried at the window catches. The wood had swollen in the rainy weather, and the shutters stuck for a moment before his fingers understood them. Then instantly he was bathed in intense light. It was a perfect early autumn morning, the low-lying mist already pierced with sunshine. The myrrh scent of roses came in with the light and the moist air, blending with the distinct note of French lavender from a hedge somewhere below. Such bittersweet memories stole in with the smell, but at least they restored some sense of calm and drove the haunting faces that had crowded his dreams from his mind.

He had forgotten about the immersion heater last night, but he was desperate to shower off the dust from yesterday's long ride from Lucca. He found the cool water refreshing, sorry only to lose the heat that might have eased the stiffness in his body. His Ducati 998 was definitely not a touring bike: it was like a tetchy supermodel. Breathtakingly quick, absurdly demanding yet exhilarating to ride, it suited Will's humour and eccentricity to perfection; but over long stretches without a break it was uncomfortable, if he were honest. His knees had been cramping a little in the leathers late yesterday, but he shrugged that off. You had no business riding such a bike if you were faint-hearted.

His face in the mirror confirmed his mother's view of him as 'an angel a little fallen'; he resembled an extra in a Zeffirelli film, he thought, his jaw-line outlined with dark stubble. He laughed with shock, recognising that at this moment the look would unsettle even her. There was something manic in the face laughing back at him, and he knew he hadn't kept the demons of his journey from getting a little too close to his soul.

He pared – rather than shaved – away the growth of several days, and wiping soap from the razor he suddenly noticed a slightly faded rose which had dried perfectly in an old ink bottle by the sink. Perhaps his brother, Alex, had brought someone there in the last couple of weeks? He had been so immersed in his own thoughts lately, he hardly knew anyone else's movements. He smiled, intrigued at the idea.

'I'll call him early this evening,' he said aloud, surprised at the unfamiliar sound of his own voice, 'once I get to Caen.' The ferry wasn't leaving until nearly midnight; but right now, he had things he wanted to do.

In the serene morning light of the kitchen he started to relax for the first time in weeks, losing the disturbed, fugitive feeling he'd found shadowing him recently. The smell of apples in the orchard spilled through the open door – bringing the comfort of the thirty-one autumns he'd enjoyed before this one. He'd run from everything and everyone, but it felt good that he was coming home. He rinsed the blood-red wine stain from the glass left from last night, and threw what was left of the French loaf into the oven to encourage it for a few minutes. He decided to check the bike, as he barely remembered how he'd parked it: all that had kept him going during those last grinding miles at speed from Lyon was the thought of refuge, breaking into the pungent Meaux brie he'd packed in his rucksack, with a baguette, a glass of his father's St-Emilion, and bed.

Outside, everything was disarmingly peaceful. There was a late flush of wisteria scrambling over the front of the cottage. Apart from superficial signs of neglect betrayed by an uncut lawn and unswept path, the house didn't reveal the family pain that had shaped its solitude for many months. Following the sudden and terrible loss of Will's mother from cancer late in January, no one had appeared to want to visit it. Easily accessible on any three-day weekend from their home in Hampshire, this had been her space, her escape, her joy to paint and garden in; and her ghost haunted every corner even now, in broad morning light. His father was grieving quietly and saying little, working as hard as ever to avoid thinking too much; and Alex seemed somehow to cope with all events without letting others in on the depth of his feelings. But Will was proudly his mother's son, emotional in his response to life and passionate in his relationships. And here, in her enchanted space, he missed her.

His eyes swept the short pebbled lane from the road to the door, but nothing exceptional caught his attention. The emptiness was almost an anti-climax – but a welcome one. It seemed that no one knew, or cared, where he was – at least for now. Unconsciously his fingers toyed with the small silver object suspended from a short chain around his neck, suddenly closing on it possessively. Then he headed towards his mother's rose garden. She had spent more than twenty years gathering a collection of old blooms, in homage to the great rose growers, that would have looked perfectly at home in Malmaison. She had painted them, embroidered them, cooked with them; but if they noticed she was gone, they whispered it to no one. Set into the fountain among the beds was a bright mosaic tiled with broken china, which she had made herself when he was small. It was a spiral with a motif of Venus, patroness of roses, in the heart of it. It exerted a magnetic pull on him.

Vaguely noting that the sunshine-yellow bike was grimy with the miles, but perfectly safe in the shade by the house, Will retraced his footsteps. The smell of good coffee brought him back to the present as he went into the kitchen. He ran his hands through his untidy curls. His hair was clean and already dry from the warm air, but badly in need of a cut.

He'd better do that before Alex's birthday lunch on Sunday: things were frosty enough between his father and him already, without his looking quite so vagrant. His fairer brother, with straighter hair, was always neat and untangled, but after more than a month in Rome Will had started to resemble a local. And that suited him; he preferred to blend in wherever he could.

There was no butter, but the warm bread was good smeared with jam from his mother's last batch in the pantry. He was licking his thumb when a postcard on the dresser took his eye: unmistakably her handwriting. 'For Will and Siân', it began. He reached for it. When could she have written this?

For Will and Siân. Try to rest for a few days. There's some venison in the chest freezer – can you make use of it? Be sure to check the knot garden for me. See you at home over Christmas – D x

Last November, it must have been. He and Siân had spent most of that year quarrelling, finally splitting up late in the spring, but strife had dogged them at least since his birthday in August last year when her unceasing demands for commitment had convinced him that it would be better to abandon the idea of a week in the house in Normandy together. Siân had no other friends there at the time, and without much French she was thrown back entirely on him, which he doubted their relationship could take at that moment. So they had never come and collected the note, walked in his mother's healing garden, nor eaten a last supper in the Pays d'Auge.

He smiled now to think of her: three months on the road had softened his anger. She was so strikingly unusual – not to everyone's taste, but thus, somehow, doubly so to his, and he suddenly felt an unanticipated longing for her physically, as though aware for the first time of the blank space beside him and in his heart. But setting passion aside – the passion that had been the nucleus of their relationship – he knew he had been right to end it. Their love was springtime, and the skies had changed. He was not forgiving and pragmatic like Alex, nor always a finisher of what he started, and he could never be the husband she wanted – the achiever, the man to shop with on Sundays at the Conran Shop, the lover who would sell his Ducati and buy a Volvo. Having declared a passion for his wildness, she had sought from the beginning to tame him. He was happy to cook for her, make her laugh, sing to her, and make love to her as no one ever had; but he knew he could never dissolve his personality to silence the strong political opinions he held, which always led to violent arguments with her mindless girlfriends and their docile partners. Ultimately he couldn't inhabit her safe – and in his view, bland – world. He was committed to experience life, whatever the cost.

He flipped the card over. It was the Great Rose Window at Chartres. His mother had painted it often, from inside, from out. She loved the light through the glass – the way it almost stung your eyes with its brilliance, penetrating the gloom.

He toyed with his mobile for a moment. It was now

charged and, without taking his eyes from the image on the card, he texted his brother.

> Have at last invaded Normandy! U've been here l8tly? Sailing from Caen 23.15 tonight. Will call you B4. Much to ask U. W

In one smooth motion he slid into his leather jacket, pocketed the phone and secreted the postcard against his chest, right next to the treasured document that had sent him spinning into Italy for the summer on a frantic research quest. He had started assembling some of the answers he'd come looking for, but a continuum of questions seemed to be opening up even now around him, and a sense of mystery deepened. He stepped into dusty boots and swiftly closed the house, depositing the key in its hiding place. He didn't even chamois down the bike, just pulled on his helmet, took his gloves from the tank bag, and swung into the saddle. He'd need fuel for the seventy or so kilometres to Chartres.

2

19 September 2003, Chelsea, London

Lucy blinked in the stark equinox sunshine, which was filtering through heavy leaves. She was sitting under a mulberry tree of impeccable lineage at the Chelsea Physic Garden, pleased just to be there. The tree was fruiting, and a heavy scent permeated the air. She'd felt better this morning, and her doctors had cautiously agreed she could go for 'a gentle walk', to pass some of the time that they understood seemed so strangely suspended for her, as long as she rested often. She had walked a little too far really; but she wouldn't tell them that, and anyway, it was so good to get away from the confines of the building, where your feelings and emotions were common property, and just have some private time alone with her thoughts. These days were a miracle, and she planned to be out in them as much as possible.

Patiently awaiting a heart operation too serious and

potentially dangerous to think deeply on, and ready for transfer to Harefield at the first sign that it might be possible, she felt today newly alive, thrilled by the beauty of autumn. Keats was right: autumn was the season England did best. She was lulled by the moan of bees and lawn mowers and by a child somewhere, and especially the absence of traffic noise.

And she was contemplative and surprisingly hopeful on this bright September morning, reading from a well-thumbed volume of John Donne's poems: 'A Valediction: Forbidding Mourning'.

As virtuous men pass mildly away
And whisper to their souls, to goe,
While some of their sad friends doe say,
The breath goes now, and some say, no:

So let us melt, and make no noise . . .

28 March 1609, On a Bend in the River, Close to London

An old man is dying in a fine, rambling house on the Thames. He has followed Signor Bruno's fate carefully. He is a friend – a fellow philosopher and scholar, a man of learning and wisdom. He may be the only other soul alive who is privy to the same extraordinary secrets as Bruno. Elizabeth, the great Queen, had been like his goddaughter and held him in trust for many years, called him her 'eyes' –

though she too has not very long since gone to her grave. Her successor is the dour Scottish king who is fanatical about ghosts and demons, afraid of anyone who can by any means challenge his authority. The old man has laid low at this, formerly his mother's house, for several years now.

It is an unusually foggy night just after the March equinox. Lanterns bounce back off the mists as a boat pulls steadily up the river from Chelsea to Mortlake on the rising tide. A shrouded figure stumbles on to the pier in the half-light, and makes its way to the door. Ushered in by an upright little woman of uncertain years, the young man flies to the privy chamber of his old master. Candles flicker and almost die from the haste at which he enters.

'Ah, Master Saunders,' his words are spoken softly. 'I knew you would come to me, though I was hesitant to demand this task of you. Alas, no one else can be trusted.'

'Your Grace, I am sorry to see you this way. Are you wanting me to help prepare you for this last long journey the angels have spoken of to you?'

The old man manages a grim, ironic laugh. 'Journey? Aye, I have lived long enough: I should in truth be on my way. Listen carefully to me, Patrick. I am certainly dying, and time is measured. I cannot answer the questions I know you will wish to ask, but I myself ask that you listen.'

The words come between increasingly short gasps, which only partly reveal the effort they must cost the old man now to speak out.

Slowly he continues: 'Next to the three caskets you see here beside me, there is a letter penned by my own hand, which will make clear anything you don't at present understand. At any moment we will receive three visitors who will perform an operation at my request. Please, do not fear for me, but wait while they are here. When all is ended, they will give you these three chests. Follow my instructions to the letter. Do not deviate, I implore you. It is my last wish, and such a thing is beyond the scope of my dear daughter, Kate. You know it is a lifetime's thoughts that go with that wish.'

Three silent, cloaked figures enter the chamber, and close around the man. A rolled leather case opens, revealing surgical instruments. One fine-gloved hand reaches to the old man's wrist, measuring his pulse. They wait. At last, she nods.

No tear-floods, nor sigh-tempests move . . .

The delicate, gloved hand, now bloodied, encloses the still-warm heart of Dr John Dee in the leaden-topped casket. The other two, one of gold, and the other silver, are gathered up and given to the now bewildered Patrick Saunders, who sweeps them together with the letter and a precious gift of books, departing in shock.

19 September 2003, Chelsea, London

Lucy heard the sound of an aeroplane overhead and, looking up with the trace of a smile, returned from her daydream. The skies had changed suddenly; and what was only a drop of light rain quickly became heavier. She left the tree under the inadequate cover of the poetry book. The muses would hopefully protect her. In the moist air, the fluid movement of her body in her oyster silk skirt and cream lace shirt made it appear as though she'd melted into an impressionist painting, and was about to dissolve.

Her pager rang: it was the Brompton Hospital. She had to get back urgently.

3

I have a will to be what I am, and what
I will be is only what I am.

The mysterious script had come to the younger brother with the modest silver key in a side-letter to his mother's will. Family tradition decreed they should be passed from mother to daughter but, having only sons, she had agonised in her last weeks over what to do with these funny, seemingly valueless objects that had been handed down for generations. As the elder, Alex should perhaps have been the recipient in the absence of a daughter, yet Will was *one* with her somehow, and though she genuinely loved her boys equally, she kept returning to the feeling that Will was the rightful recipient. The document seemed to say as much.

When Alex had married she had waited for a granddaughter: that would have solved everything. But the impossible demands of a high-pressure job that meant he was rarely at home had brought his marriage sadly to a close, and he had no daughter to show for it. And Will. Well, she knew better than to wait for him to start a family. He was talented, loving, warm-hearted and irascible. Women were inevitably drawn to her younger son, to his tousled good looks and his sheer physicality. Both of her boys were good sportsmen, both played cricket in the village, but Will might have played for the county if he'd chosen. A dangerous middle-order batsman, he square cut fours and hoisted sixes in an ungainly but effective manner; and bowling to the other team's tail he was adept at the art of reverse swing, laughing as they prodded one way while the ball cut back in the opposite direction. He was talent-spotted a few times, but refused to put in the necessary hours of practice, wouldn't commit his summer. He'd play for love if his day was free, but never for money, and never so anyone would depend on him – that was Will.

She had thought Siân might get her way after all and push him to the altar. Siân was so fiery and attractive, determined, and ready to settle. She had just turned thirty, and time wouldn't wait for ever. Perhaps one day Will would have a little girl – and knowing the sensitivity that lurked behind his outward masculinity, it would be a daughter he would father, his mother felt. Whatever it was the key gave access to, it must have surely been meant for Will's daughter: and he would hand it to her. Yes, she'd trust to time and Siân's single-mindedness, and leave the key to Will. She'd penned a note, and put it with the key and the single ancient leaf of vellum in a huge envelope:

For Will, when he is something, or someone, that he is not now.

And she'd said not a word more on the subject, even when they bid each other goodbye in her last hours.

Will had inspected his talisman as though it were a jewel, turning it in the light, looking at it in an array of moods: over a port, late at night; in the demonic glare of his dark room; in the freezing January wind, right after his mother's funeral; in the Valley of the Temples in Agrigento; and again in his tiny allotted space in the reading room at the Vatican, where he'd spent days searching the archives for the murky history of the Campo de' Fiori. Such an emblematic object, a key. What lock did it turn? The lock it had fitted seemed to have vanished with time, lost in a spiral of years. He didn't even know, he realised, who had first left it. He knew nothing really about his mother's family; his normally mild-tempered father refused flatly to talk about the subject.

I am what I am, and what I am is what you will see.

His mind rehearsed these closing words over again while he covered the last miles along the B road to Chartres. He knew the whole sheet by heart, and easily managed the impressive feat of focusing on the necessary road skills while contemplating the text on the aged parchment, which he had photocopied and carried with him inside his leather jacket all the summer long. Even in the heat in Sicily he'd clutched the jacket to him, rather than be parted from the precious legacy, and the small key found a home on a chain around his neck where, he'd decided, it would remain until death, if necessary. He had tried explaining his need to understand so much more about his inheritance to others, but he knew that even Alex felt it was becoming a worrying obsession. His elder brother, of course, would have approached the whole enigma very differently, fitting any conjectures into the spaces between his work, his research paper and his close relationship with his young son. Nor could Alex have disappeared to Europe for the summer because of his other commitments. But Will was a different man, consumed with a desire to know what it all meant, and unable to give his full attention to anything else until he'd solved this riddle of the sphinx and found the lock that was home to the mysterious key. His own sense of identity seemed caught up in the puzzle, and it was not the rumours of the key securing 'the most precious treasure of our family' that were the lifeblood of his quest. He wasn't interested in gold or jewels, but wondered what had been so important to his family's sense of secrecy, for them to guard this object – for ever and an age, it must have been.

Will was a freelance photojournalist, and well connected. A long-time colleague, now his closest friend, had become intrigued over a beer and offered some help, taking a fragment of the parchment to a cousin at Oxford who could do the carbon dating. At least they'd know the approximate age of the paper. Will had been clicking off photos in the Greek Theatre in Taormina on a blistering mid-June day when the text appeared tantalisingly on his phone:

Samples tested x 2. Both conclude it's probably late C16.
Any interest? C U Sept. Simon

Interest, indeed! What happened in the Campo de' Fiori – the so-called Field of Flowers – in the late sixteenth century? This was only the very first reference on the document and, quick as he was at crosswords and anagrams, he had no idea how it might fit in with the key. After weeks of travel and research he'd begun to piece some thoughts together, but his mind was still whirling with the myriad facts that might – and as likely might not – be relevant. He'd spent the last day in Rome emailing back to himself photographs of any places that seemed of possible relevance, as well as pages of data about the political climate in Rome during the sixteenth century. He'd ordered a library list from Amazon to be waiting for him at Alex's. He wondered about the Cenci, about Bruno, and Galileo. He'd have to peruse it all again at leisure, but it was taking his feet along some strange alleyways, past grim hooded figures in a kind of courtly dance. He'd thought of it as a 'merry dance' more than once, and when the alleyways dead-ended he was often left with an eerie, unsettled feeling. Rome could entice you to look over your shoulder sometimes, even when there was nothing but paranoia waiting behind you.

Despite the limited long-distance vision from under his visor, he could see the impressive mirage that was Chartres Cathedral floating above the flat plain from miles away. Approached at speed, its sheer magnitude was suddenly upon you; he could imagine how a medieval pilgrim must have felt dwarfed into insignificance, and he realised that this amazing image of the great church dominating the landscape – its many personal associations – would never lose its magic for him.

Will now propelled himself round a corner and dropped to street speed. The steering instantly felt heavy again and he concentrated in order to ride smoothly through the maze of medieval lanes. He'd twice stalled the bike while learning her idiosyncrasies, and she was petulant if you didn't give her due attention. Slipping through the restricted zones as though he belonged there, he ignored the invitations to park in a designated site and glided towards the spires. The rumble of his Testastretta engine broke the cloistral quiet of the town as he cruised through the Place Billard and along the Rue des Changes. He sidled up to the kerb at the south side of the cathedral, and hooked out the kickstand in a pay-and-display area. It must have been nearing noon, and the powerful aroma of *moules marinières* and French onion soup from a bistro just opposite reminded him that he must eat something after his visit. There had been a long space between proper meals.

He glanced up at the familiar sight of the two unequal spires, then his helmet was off in a gesture of knightly courtesy as he walked under the shadow of the impressive west portal. While his eyes adjusted to the womb-like darkness, his ears picked up the whispers in different corners and in different languages from various tour groups, as the flocks all stared open-mouthed at the beauty of the stained glass above his head. But although this was what Will thought he had come to see, his gaze was immediately distracted by a sight he didn't ever remember noticing in the dozen or so times he'd come into the cathedral over the years. Many of the chairs were removed and Will's eyes drank in the enormous black and white circle of marble stones, inlaid in the paving of the great Gothic nave, between the pillars. Splashed with the odd jewel-bright colours from the glass, the maze breasted the whole of the width of the huge church. In the centre a girl was standing with eyes closed, but he could clearly see the flower shape that marked the middle of the pattern. He must have walked across it towards the altar many times, and never looked down to see it.

Nearby there was a young French girl informing her tour group about it, in good English and at a respectful volume. He smiled: a student with a summer job.

'Well, this is the famous Chartres labyrinth, and labyrinths as you will know are very ancient. They are in so many different countries; but when you are seeing it here inside a medieval cathedral like Chartres, this pagan symbol is obviously invested with a strong Christianised meaning. We know there was one also inside Auxerre Cathedral, in Amiens also, and in Reims, and Sens, and in Arras. All of these were taken away because they were not understood by the people in the seventeenth and also eighteenth centuries. We understand the clergy were disturbed by the people who were walking them! But here this one is the best preserved . . .'

Will was hooked, and he edged a little closer. She smiled in mid-sentence, well aware that he was not one of hers; but perhaps his genuine appreciation of her knowledge was translated through his smile at her, and she carried on without missing a beat.

'. . . and it dates from around the year 1200. Can you regard once again the western Rose Window of the Last Judgement behind it here, which we have just been looking at. It is from around 1215, remember? As you can see, the labyrinth almost mirrors the size and distance from the door on the ground as the rose is above the door. This demonstrates the idea that to trace the labyrinth path on the ground is a step on the stairway to the upper world. It is 16.4 metres wide at the biggest point between the pillars, and you will remember this is the widest Gothic nave in France. If you walk the whole path, like the medieval pilgrim, it is more than 260 metres. It has been referred to as "the Journey to Jerusalem", and we understand that pilgrims possibly walked it on their knees as a kind of penitence. You see, on the maps of the time, Jerusalem was marked as the centre of the world, and for many believers even today the Last Judgement is strongly bound up with prophecies about Jerusalem and the great Temple. Now, if you will please follow me, we will go to the Adam and Eve Window.'

As she turned with her hand up for them to follow her, Will touched her gently on the arm. '*Mademoiselle, s'il vous plaît; je n'ai jamais vu le labyrinth comme ça – je ne l'ai aperçu jusque ce jour . . . Comment est-ce que c'est possible?*'

She was not offended by the intrusion. '*Les vendredis, seule! Chaque vendredi entre avril et octobre. Vous avez de la chance aujourd'hui, n'est-ce pas?*' She laughed warmly, and was gone with her sheep.

The girl who he had seen walking in it was just now completing her full circuit of the labyrinth, emerging from the centre with her eyes wide open. She looked slightly flushed.

'Excuse me, it's open only on Fridays, did she say? Gosh, that was lucky for me then. I came today because it's the fall equinox. From today, feminine energy becomes dominant again, until spring.' She was American, fresh-faced and unreserved, and she too smiled at Will. 'You should do it, walk it, it's amazing. This is a good moment, and the light's perfect. I had to wait ages till it was clear of people. You should go for it now.'

Will nodded. 'OK, thanks. Thank you.'

He felt oddly shy. He was not a religious man – well, not in any conventional way. He had certain spiritual ideas, sensed we didn't comprehend everything there was to understand; but essentially, he didn't buy the whole virgin-birth thing, and he definitely wasn't one to wear whatever ideas he had about his soul on his sleeve. But he found his feet moving without his authority as they traced the route to the starting point.

Yeah, OK, he thought. I shall too. Only on Fridays . . . he smiled to himself . . . *and* it's the equinox. This last was an ironic afterthought. He was amused – though not judgemental – that it was such a special day for this rather sweet girl.

There was just one entrance, and he started forward, three paces towards the altar, and then it took a left turn into a beautiful curving path that looped right back on itself. He had to watch his feet at first to follow the direction carefully, because it wasn't all that wide. He noticed he was following the light-coloured path, and that it was pricked out by the dark border. He was symbolically treading in the light and avoiding the dark.

Cradling his helmet closer to him, his eyes closed a little, he began to tread without such a heightened awareness of his feet. The second loop took him almost to the centre; he thought it would suddenly culminate at the flower shape. But the wondrous path coiled back on itself in a short series of bends, like a beautiful snake, until there was once again a great swooping curve that took him near the centre and then right out again, into another quadrant. He gave himself to the feeling: his eyes were drawn up to the intense colours that dappled his face from the window on the south side. He paused for a second and took in the picture: a man emerging from the gateway of a walled city, with a cobalt glass background; then, in the roundel, a man stealing behind him and pulling a sword from its sheath, with a fabulous ruby-coloured background. This man was wearing green, and was beautifully drawn, while the man in front of him wore a blue robe and carried a yellow cloak over his shoulder. The red, the blue and the yellow hues all fell upon Will's face as the equinox sunshine, approaching noon, slanted through the glass. Will felt light-headed; the experience was unexpectedly intense and moving. He laughed slightly self-consciously, and warned himself about roads to Damascus.

No one else was walking. They had generously given him some space, it seemed, though he was dimly aware of a few faces following his movements with surprise. He didn't care though, and enjoyed instead the sensations of his face moving from the light to the dark, and back again; and his feet tracing shorter paths and then sweeping into longer ones, turning him back and forth, as if in a sophisticated game of blind man's bluff. The mantra from the document began again in his head . . .

OUR TWO SOULS THEREFORE

All that was ablaze in the Field of Flowers! Pluck forth a bloom, and think on what has been; on centuries of betrayal, and pain, and misunderstanding . . .

Will's feet wandered along without seeing properly. Only the single page was in his mind, and he touched his jacket as he continued walking and rhythmically tapping out the maze . . .

I am what I am, and what I am is what I am. I have a will to be what I am, and what I will be is only what I am. If I have a will to be, I will to be no more than what I was. If I was what I am willed to be, yet they ever will be wondering what I am or what I ever was. I want to change the Wall, and make my Will.

That I am that same wall, the truth is so.
And this the cranny is, right and sinister,
Through which the fearful lovers are to whisper.

Each pair adds up to every jointed piece; the bottom left is a square; bottom right is a square; top left is a square; top right is a square. The heart is a square too.

WHICH ARE ONE

And I am halfway through the orbit. And if you take half of the whole and make up pairs to equal me, you will soon use up all of the pairs.

Now, look no further than the day. My alpha and my omega. Make of these two halves a whole. Take the song of equal number in the old king's book. Equal number of paces forward from the start. Equal number of paces backwards from the end – omitting only the single exit word. Amen to that.

I am what I am, and what I am is what you will see.

Count on me very carefully.

ENDURE NOT YET A BREACH, BUT AN EXPANSION

Will's head had at first felt heavy, and now was growing light. He was unaware of the looks he drew – from a young boy holding his mother's hand, an older lady who took off her glasses to watch his steps without any hint of rudeness or alarm, and from a vivacious redhead, who'd stopped chatting to her girlfriend, and found she'd become fixed on this devilishly beautiful man. A priest watched him, nodding acquiescently, and a man behind the pillar on the north side also seemed mesmerised by Will's whole experience. He clicked off a digital picture of the man in the maze.

And Will's feet danced lightly, his words like a rosary: 'I have a will to be what I am . . . If I was what I am willed to be . . .'

He had reached the middle of the labyrinth, and his face was full west, the Great Rose Window straight above him.

Eight bright angels watched him from the larger petals of the inner rose, sitting in pairs between an eagle, a winged man, an ox and a lion. Will was exhilarated. He hadn't suddenly undergone a religious conversion, but he marvelled at the effect of the steps, the light, the sounds inside the great church and his own psyche, which felt ecstatic. And, more amazing still, he understood something in the message on the sheet, next to his heart, which he hadn't seen previously. *He* was Will; his destiny was to uncover the home of the key, and be initiated to its meaning and its treasure. It would happen, without him forcing it any further, quite passively perhaps.

He took six strong steps out of the centre, where a plaque bearing Theseus and his vanquished Minotaur had once been pinned upon rivets that were still visible. He swivelled to the left, and caught the unmistakable perfume of roses – like an exotic attar. His feet paced on, and as he came to the 180 degree turn, he thought to see what or who had wafted the fragrance; but it was nothing, no one. He turned again towards the east, and the scent came again, with a sensation of the liquid movement of fabric, but it was a trick of the light and his giddiness, and he was able to complete the labyrinth without a soul interfering.

Almost breathless, he walked straight from the heart of the labyrinth in the nave to the rear of the altar, to the Lady Chapel; and here he lit a large candle – well worth the two and a half euros, he decided. He felt his mother here with him, watching him, and he quietly mouthed: 'I am now what I was not then.'

He strode from the cathedral through the north porch,

and his feet felt nothing of their contact with the floor, nor was he aware of a shadow slipping from the murky light behind the pillar.

4

The rain eased, and for the first time since leaving the Physic Garden, Lucy slowed her footfall. Her pager beeped again, but the hospital had been a lonelier place than usual this week, and she was not yet willing to terminate her freedom. Besides, she'd done this before – scurried back to her doctors from one part of Chelsea or another only to find there was a false alarm. Twice in this last fortnight, in fact. Perhaps this time would be different – though a part of her almost hoped she might have to wait. Until he was back.

She sauntered up Flood Street for a block, then her feet chose a path to the left along St Loo Avenue. She knew she was going a little out of her way, but after an uncharacteristically good summer the trees were already turning golden and she loved the leafy avenues around this area, where the old Tudor manor house had stood and a garden had been planted with mulberries by Princess Elizabeth herself in the early 1540s. They were still flourishing a few streets away, near Cheyne Row. And just here, Chelsea Manor Street was serene. She took a road to the left into Phene Street, past the pub that was getting busy with the Friday lunchtime regulars: she remembered hearing about Dr Phene's 'good idea'. He was accredited as the man who had thought of planting trees up and down the street. The idea caught Queen Victoria's imagination and then took off across Europe. Well, so the story went; it might be apocryphal, but there were still a few fine trees in the pretty pub garden to testify to his vision.

She prompted a wink from a thirty-something man with an appealing, impish grin who was walking into the pub, and she smiled at the compliment. So she couldn't be looking all that bad then. She felt like a waif, but she still had strength despite her physical fragility and, even if her ego had failed to notice recently, she raised high brows from low brows wherever she walked. She'd just been too ill and preoccupied to care.

As she neared the immense block that bounded the hospital she felt a sharp thrill: she was tempted to do something really naughty and not go in – like a child playing truant from school. All of her days were in a spin: time for her stood in a separate place outside the real world, so that she constantly felt like Alice falling the wrong way up the White Rabbit's hole. Nothing seemed real, and she had to force herself to make a mental note of what day, what month, what time she was inhabiting. One hour blended with another; she'd gradually read her way through Wordsworth, J. M. Barrie and some Schopenhauer – more books on a diversity of subjects than at any time in her life – to help her think deeply. The quilt she was patchworking slowly grew; but everything else seemed as though it happened in slow motion. Outside, there was a memory of another life; and just now she wanted to stay in the midst of that energy and not to return to her cloister. But that would be so unfair to the astonishing team of people who were looking after her. Attending one of the leading cardio-thoracic hospitals in the world – one that was at the fore-front of so much pioneering technology – she had expected to witness a vibrant performance of clashing egos and a polite lack of engagement with the seriously ill patients; but the opposite was true. Mr Azziz was one of the most extraordinary people she had ever met, and however busy his surgeries or appointments, he frequently dropped in on her to chat informally, asking her dozens of personal questions and demonstrating real interest in who she was. Sister Cook was all business on the outside, but wonderfully personable once you knew her; and Dr Stafford never left for the evening without calling in on her and sharing anything with the merest shade of humour that had happened in the hospital that day. With no real family of her own to speak of – and those few relatives she had far away in Sydney – they had adopted her and seemed committed to keeping her smiling as far as possible. They were so keen for her to recover, so determined that she would get through it. Self-doubt wasn't allowed, they applauded her courage, and she absolutely couldn't disappoint their faith in her.

An ambulance was at the entrance with its rear doors open: nothing unusual, and yet she shuddered in the sunshine. 'Transfer to Harefield Hospital, love. I'll bet it's you we're waiting for.' He smiled at her kindly, as though holding the reins of Pegasus who would fly her to the moon. She tried to return his enthusiasm, but she suddenly felt very small and alone, and not in the least romantic about the course that lay ahead. The line at her mouth was thin. The great front doors swallowed her.

The Phene Arms was heaving with people starting their easy weekend a few hours early, wanting food, so Simon went through to the garden to look for more space. The weather had dissuaded most of the patrons, but he checked a bench with his hand to see how wet it was, then chose a touch-dry table that had been fairly sheltered under a tree. He sipped his beer, and scribbled off a postcard with a Union Jack on it: 'Welcome back. You must have noticed the lines from *Midsummer Night's Dream*? But what does it mean . . . ? Is there a secret garden with a key into a wall . . . ?' He hadn't had time to complete what he wanted to write when a tall, slender figure wearing a white trench coat over fitted designer jeans appeared through the doorway. He pocketed the card secretively.

'You're such a Spartan, Simon.' Siân folded her coat and put it on the seat to combat the damp.

'Good to see you, hottie.' Somewhat self-consciously he used the name he always called her by to try to maintain a friendly tone without it being mistaken for any hint of flirtation, to settle his mild anxiety about meeting a mate's very sexy 'ex' for lunch. Her signature scent was like a room full of exotic lilies and jasmine, and she oozed sensuality. He did feel a bit guilty. 'You look like a danger to the parish today. What's been happening?'

'Work's been totally manic; loads of jobs. After so long away from the action, it's a good feeling to hit a period of frenzy. I've been through a lot, but at least my bank balance is looking healthy again. Everyone I've ever worked for seems to have called, which is great. I got a few days in the Seychelles styling a commercial last week – took my mind off things entirely.'

Simon was a gritty, hard-news journalist, and though he travelled often for work, he never got assignments that took him to exotic A-list locations like the Seychelles. 'I'm sure you went under sufferance?' he asked her with exaggerated irony.

She laughed, and he was pleased to see her looking so sassy and strong, not at all weepy – which he'd been worried might be the case when she'd called to ask him to meet her. He knew very well Will was due back tomorrow and his mind had been flying through a list of possible favours she might be about to demand. But she seemed in control.

'It's strange, isn't it? I didn't push myself when I was with Will . . . seemed to go completely into autopilot. I always thought my work annoyed him a bit, so my career took a nose-dive. But you know, I'm a good stylist. I don't mind the hard work, and if the job's interesting it kills the time. It's no sacrifice.' She giggled and tidied her perfectly applied lip gloss with a finger. 'Even if it means adjusting the model's décolletage for hours – which is what I was doing in paradise last week. But they paid me well for it. God knows, I need the money now I'm on my own.'

'Mm. But you're positively smouldering, Siân. Something beyond work must be going right?' He felt encouraged to find out the lie of the land. He was Will's mate, and his loyalty rested there, but he couldn't help liking Siân, certainly noticed her considerable attributes, and he wanted to see her survive the heartache of a bad break-up. Will wasn't an easy man to be in love with, and he was sure his friend would want to see her move on and be happy again.

Siân looked down at her Chablis, and answered the glass. She was unsure how Simon would take this, but she did want to talk about it – wanted a friend of Will's to tacitly give his approval. 'There is someone new, sort of . . .'

Simon nodded for her to continue. She was now laying her head against the inside of her arm; the body language was invitingly coy. She continued without consulting his eye. 'Not sure where it might go; but he's quite special, really very sweet. Not my usual vodka and tonic, maybe, but fascinating. I still can't quite make him out. He's just got back from America – from the East Coast, I think, but he's been studying somewhere in the Midwest, like Kansas. He's doing a part-time research degree in something or other – very clever. Cute style, too – almost preppy. Blond – not very up-front. Very different from Will, in spite of their relationship.'

Simon was caught off guard. She communicated – in a flash, with a mock demure look – a picture that was much more full-on than he'd expected. He was surprised to find himself offended. Will was demanding, yes; even difficult sometimes, but in a league of his own. Uniquely himself, a copy of no one. He'd always believed Siân knew this too; and here she was selling him a new lover's credentials. A bit low, he thought, but he said what he didn't truly mean from a long habit of finding good manners when they were needed. 'As long as you're happy, Siân; I think you deserve that. You got through the break without losing your dignity or your cool. Don't rub it in Will's face, though – unless you want to see if he's jealous?'

'Simon . . .' She hesitated in a way that was completely foreign for someone who had Siân's confidence. 'He's . . . I was just saying . . . related to Will . . .' She swallowed some wine while Simon tried to decide how he would cope with the idea, suddenly flooding his mind, that she was somehow going to tell him she had started seeing the blonder, rather intriguing Alexander. What appalling taste. But Alex wouldn't let this happen, surely? Would Siân be his type? No, don't be absurd; of course, she'd already said he was an American, hadn't she? What a ridiculous leap of the senses, he thought, and winced unconsciously. Who was it then?

'Calvin is a cousin of Will's. At least, they've never actually met, but his mother and Will's are cousins.' While she tried to untangle the branches of Will's mother's family tree, Simon relaxed and could hear properly again; his heart was no longer pounding against the casing of his brain. He didn't care about this – and it wouldn't bother Will either. Strange, even a bit kinky perhaps? Yes, it was a little on the kinky side – but it was unquestionably better than putting on Mahler's Fifth and opening a vein. His mind picked up her commentary again.

'. . . And when he came to London to study this summer, he wanted to look them all up. Apparently the cousins exchanged Christmas cards and the odd letter, but not much more; and when Diana died early this year, and Calvin's mum couldn't make it over for the funeral, Calvin thought it would be the right thing to pay them a visit, and to say sorry in person – you know. It's the kind of well-mannered thing he does. And the funny part is, he knocked on my door, and Will had already gone off to Italy, and Alex was away lecturing in some country or other . . .'

Simon was nodding again, blood had returned; Will could handle this.

'. . . And he asked so much about Will, so much, Simon. And I found myself talking. To someone totally new. All about him, for hours. Days even. And it was surprisingly cathartic. I cried, and he comforted, and the rest is human nature. "Modern knight with good CV and old-fashioned values seeks damsel to rescue from her bruised ego." Not in the least original, but welcome in the flesh.'

Simon laughed out loud, but without him using words, she couldn't decide the meaning.

She scrutinised his expression. 'Do you think Will's going to mind?'

Simon challenged her. 'Do you want him to?'

She didn't quite answer, and said, 'I suppose he's not the ideal person to get involved with, but the heart seems to have a mind all its own, you know.' She looked at him entreatingly. 'And mine was broken, Simon. I've been numb since last Christmas, tears most nights until Calvin showed up at the end of June. I just tried not to do it too publicly. There'll never be another Will, I know very well. But what choice do I have? None but to get over it. There was some painful stuff between Will and me last year that nobody but Alex knows about. Will's never going to forgive me. I just don't want my motives brought into question. I didn't choose his cousin to annoy anyone. I think it's just that fate chose us – threw us together. Calvin says he's never given his heart away: and perhaps he won't with me. But it feels . . .' She broke off. She had no way of explaining how it felt.

Simon was impressed with her honesty; and the navy-blue eyes and coppery curls made her an irresistible Pre-Raphaelite *femme fatale*. 'Siân, I think it's fine. Will's a big boy, and even though I admit we all probably do like to be grieved over for a while, he's a generous human being. Maybe he'll even like this guy?'

She smiled gratefully at him. She couldn't imagine Will giving Calvin five minutes of his time. He was too careful with his clothes and his image, too closed to people, in a way that would drive Will mad; but she appreciated Simon's efforts, and she was glad it was out in the open.

'Let's order some food.' Simon gathered up the empty glasses to go for refills, and she touched his arm.

'My treat, Simon: I'm in funds, remember?'

She was happy. As usual, she'd got what she'd come for.

5

The vast chains rolled back, and the great doors heaved open. The huge white interior of the *Mont St Michel* was still packed with an assortment of vehicles, in spite of the fact that it was late September and most of the family tourists had long since passed through, returning to schools, jobs and the routines of home and hearth. The usual clutch of juggernauts, the run of questionable antique dealers and VAT dodgers, a few French couples and some university students yet to resume the new academic year were crossing to Portsmouth for *le weekend*; and there were a number of expensive cars – with and without dogs. The immaculate, dark blue, Rome-plated Lancia Fulvia caught Will's eye. He'd seen a few of them on the continent, a classy restyling of the sixties model. What a classic beauty, he thought, with its slim tinted windows and low sweeping lines. Quick, really quick – the kind of car Will would love to have, maybe when he was older. For now, the Ducati would carry him swiftly through the last stage of his long journey home, where he was desperate to be.

The sharp morning air reminded Will that autumn was showing signs of coming earlier to Britain than Normandy. A watery sun was breaking through the sea mist, but the temperature was still cowering. Taking his gloves from the tank bag and checking his passport was under his leather jacket, he pushed the bike off the stand and flicked the engine into life. He kicked into first gear with his foot and let the clutch out delicately. He was a little tired: he rarely slept well on overnight crossings, even when he took a Commodore-class berth, as this time. But his mind had been racing all night, ever since Chartres in fact, and he couldn't come to terms with all of his thoughts, discoveries, ideas that had been forming and pressing on his mind. He couldn't think about it all again now: he'd wait until he could talk to Alex and then, he hoped, make some sense of it all.

Gently now, Claudia, we'll be home soon, he thought almost aloud, as he manoeuvred the nervous beauty over the slippery bumps on the metal boarding ramp and down toward Customs Control. The duty officer held out his hand for him to stop. Will unzipped his jacket, pulled out his passport, and as he handed it across he lifted his helmet. The agent glanced briefly at the likeness between the man and the passport and nodded him on.

Will settled his weight in the saddle and considered the route home. Motorway around Southampton to Winchester, A34 north. He'd come off near Kings Worthy, country lanes to Barton Stacey, down the hill and over the bridge on the Test by the trout farm, then on home to Longparish. Momentarily he pondered whether to take the

A34 all the way, to Tufton, then Whitchurch. But that was an accident black spot, with reckless local traffic on a Saturday. No – the back lanes reminded him that England had beauties of her own alongside the sunflowers and poppies of Tuscany, the lavender swathes of Provence, and the farms and pargeted buildings of the Pays d'Auge. There'd certainly be fog along the river at this time of the year, lying all along the valleys until the sun had a chance to burn it off. Which it would – in the next few hours. Unexpectedly he felt homesick; he was longing to see his father and his nephew and hug them, and to have some quality time with Alex in an hour or so. Then they could all enjoy a drink at the pub later over lunch. What the hell, he decided. Taking the scenic route meant he could burn some gas and the law wouldn't bother him. There was a cow crossing before home, but he was in no hurry. God knew what time Alex would be arriving, though – perhaps not until later in the day. Will let out a soundless sigh, knowing he could do with someone there to soften the dynamic with his father.

He pulled up quite suddenly, and tried his brother's mobile once again. 'Sandy, where in the world are you? It's Saturday, for God's sake. Did you get called in late for an emergency? You're still on shift, I suppose, as your phone's switched off. I've left messages everywhere.' Will felt a wave of disappointment. As he thought about the unanswered calls and texts he realised Alex was probably stuck at the hospital, and he was impatient to talk to him. He tried not to sound too demanding. 'I'm heading for The Chantry now – Dad hasn't answered, but he might not be up or he's gone for the papers. Can we meet at the pub on our own for a while later?

You won't believe what I've got to tell you, but I can't say in front of Dad. Please come down today; I need your mind alone. And, if not today . . .' He stopped, not wanting to explore that option. 'Please, ring me, would you, when you get this?' Then, almost as an afterthought, 'Do you know where Mum's Bible is? The really old one? OK, later.'

The thought of the stream gliding through the woods with the shafts of sun cutting it, like long fingers through the ice-white mist, appealed to Will's romantic side. His mind had been in freefall since noon yesterday, and he needed the calm of the river. As he crossed the A30 he noted another car had turned in behind him, and he pulled away without effort. He passed under the A303, and the road rose again before dropping along a slow bend to the valley floor, and home.

This was home more than ever at the moment. He didn't have a new flat of his own in London yet, and he'd let Siân remain in his old flat, having paid the three months' rent for her first when they'd split a few months before. A lot of his material self was still there; he'd have to sort things out more permanently and get a London base again. He couldn't keep crashing at Alex's place. But although his home was in Hampshire, had always been here along with his darkroom and his books and most of his music, there were wounds that hadn't healed with Henry, his father, since the loss of his mother. He'd run away in June, from Henry and from Siân; he had to face it now and clean up all his relationships.

The autumn sun was now up, slightly over his right shoulder to the south-east, but as he breasted the hill he saw the valley below shrouded in a thick blanket of fog that the sun had not yet touched. 'Season of mists' was putting it mildly; 'blanket fog' was more like it, he thought – if more prosaic. From his vantage point on the bike, the road bent steeply downwards in a gentle curve, disappearing in a wall of swirling white topped with yellow where the sun touched it. Will swiftly dropped the bike to a lower gear to radically reduce speed. As he did so, the white cloak embraced him in a bright luminous light, reducing his vision to a few metres in a matter of seconds. It was like being in the Chartres labyrinth again. He smiled quietly to himself as he stared into the mist from inside his helmet. He knew the route like the back of his hand: at the end of the hill the road crossed a bridge, then straightened past the fishing lake and on to a second bridge, passing some cottages further on and then into the village at a T-junction. An easy right towards their own end of the sprawling three miles of Longparish brought him to the house that had been in his mother's side of the family for centuries, and he wanted to get straight into her books and her garden.

The atmosphere brought her near to him now. She used to call these fogs 'river sprites'. He remembered the white-outs, descending very suddenly at day's end when he was younger. It could occur in minutes, sometimes, at either end of the cricket season. The fog would fall so fast that the batsman might quite suddenly see the ball appearing out of the mist as if by magic. Those days ended early, with a more prolonged session than usual at the local – appropriately called The Cricketers – as it was almost impossible to drive far until the fog had lifted. His mates usually stayed to dinner, and his mother spread sleeping bags around in the attic.

His mind crashed back to reality with the roar of a car engine accelerating on to the bridge just behind him, and a flash of lights. Something seemed to tear the handle bars from his grasp. The bike veered sharply to the left, driving its front wheel into the iron railing along the bridge-head that he'd known was coming. With a nauseating wrench, the fairing around Will's knees broke and he was thrown over the handle bars, goring his leg badly as he cleared the barrier rail headfirst, and then falling the fifteen feet or so into the River Test below. Despite the searing pain in his leg, he was relaxed as he fell, worrying more about the Ducati than his own injuries. The sun through the fog cast astonishing shards of prismatic light through his mind, as he tumbled seemingly endlessly. Some idiot had overtaken him on the bridge. Didn't see him, probably. He certainly hadn't seen or heard anyone.

As his instincts had told him to roll forward when he realised the bike was going, he'd landed quite tidily in the very clear water on the back of his head and shoulders. Still conscious, and preternaturally calm, he momentarily registered the beauty of the pebbled bed as he lay in the freezing stream that ran rapidly away. It had a surprising slurping current, and was of a fair depth for a relatively small river. He was angry, but relieved to be able to feel all of his limbs: he was clearly not too seriously harmed except for the vicious throb in his thigh numbed by chill water. His helmet hadn't come away completely, which he understood was a blessing, and he was aware enough to realise he should pull himself to the bank quickly or he would drown where he lay, in water deep enough for the purpose. The fierce determination of the river always impressed him, and it inspired once again his last reserves of strength as he dragged his body partially out of the water and on to the thin incline of the bank. He had enough clarity to recollect that he was only a mile or so from home before he suddenly felt nauseous and giddy, and slumped forwards, passing out completely. In an icy dream, he heard the voice of an American girl telling him to 'go for it', and Alex's voice: 'Sorry, can you leave a message after the tone . . .' then the scream of the bike's engine, like some demon lover's wail.

Just beyond the end of the bridge, the blue Lancia was waiting. The door opened, and the tiny jewel-red warning light on its edge lit up. A fine pair of hand-made shoes at the end of a pair of grey flannel trousers descended from the car, accompanied by the figure of a man in a camel coat. The form advanced towards the moaning bike, and a gloved hand dislodged the throttle from the ironwork on the bridge and fiddled with the key. In the profound silence that followed, the rustling of Will's tank bag seemed deafening. He opened it quickly and examined its contents. A dog at a farm somewhere along the road started barking furiously. Ignoring the sound, he walked over to the end of the bridge and around the barrier fence towards the point where Will lay, still half submerged in the icy stream. There was a film of steam above the water, where the air and water temperatures collided. Visibility was very limited. With his foot the man rolled Will's inert body on to its back, and started to bend over him. Safe in the knowledge that the mist was obscuring them from any observer, he ignored the sound of someone stirring in a cottage, perhaps two hundred metres away in the whiteness. But then voices could be heard a little nearer, above the sound of a barking dog.

Now the man straightened quite sharply and retreated towards the Lancia. The engine purred quietly, the rear light flickered bright red for a second, then the car merged into the heavy shroud.

6

Will laughed aloud. It sounded hollow inside his head, but he felt like Dante as he passed from Purgatory to Eden. This celestial being, crouched now beside him on the slope of the river bank, had such a clear voice, so piercing, like Dante's angel. *l'angel cantava in voce assai piu che la nostra viva*, he thought, 'more piercing and clear than ours . . .'

'Will?' she repeated. She tried not to be hysterical, but Melissa thought at first that he was dead. She was confronted with a dilemma: should she risk moving him and possibly damage his spine, or leave him in the freezing water? She called frantically backwards down the lane in the direction towards her cottage. His eyes were lolling, not focusing at all, and he was laughing incoherently. The signal from her mobile kept dipping: the damned fog. Now she was connected with 999, arranging an ambulance, listening to advice about the victim's position, answering questions about his neck, describing his blood loss, the severity of his leg wound. She couldn't control her voice, she knew; she was scared she'd do the wrong thing; but she mastered the situation as best she could, put her coat over him, and tried to look calmer than she felt.

Why is she so worried? he thought. He took in the details of her face: one of Raphael's putti, perhaps, more than a grown angel; her gentle touch, and the warmth that spread over him from her coat. He heard words like 'sinews' and 'tourniquet' and 'hypothermia' and, strangely, 'head injury'; but that was an eternity away from his own experience. He was floating freely – vaguely aware of the red spreading through the little pool of water near to him, like wasted claret – but feeling no pain, no concerns, content and serene. Shafts of colour made an extraordinary kaleidoscopic journey through his mind, like his grandmother's emerald and ruby necklace when he was a child.

Sirens wailed around him. He shrank from them instinctively, and suddenly felt this was not a place he wanted to be. He thought of leaving another message after the tone.

The figure in a light olive jacket and faded denims looked almost relaxed as he placed a briefcase and a carrier bag from FAO Schwarz on the floor and an overcoat on the low table, then slipped into the seat beside them. The business lounge was surprisingly full, but Alex had picked a spot where he could make some calls without disturbing those bent at their laptops.

He looked at his watch, and felt it was now a bit late to be calling Anna in England to confirm his arrangements about picking up their son next morning; but he wanted to try his father once more in spite of the hour. He hit the speed dial and waited: then was a little thrown to get the answering machine again. It was a Saturday night, and Alex had expected to find his father still sitting up, talking to Will.

He frowned a little, and left a second message in a quiet voice. 'Dad, I've no idea if you got my earlier message – my mobile isn't roaming properly here and I can't pick up my own voicemail. But assuming you did, you'll know the conference overran last night and we never made the flight. A few of us stayed with one of my colleagues at his house in New Jersey for the night, but I'm at Kennedy now and the flight's on time. Sorry for the changes, but I'll still make lunch tomorrow. I had a call from my secretary so I have one small detour to make to Harefield; but the car's at Heathrow and I'll get Max from Anna's on the way down. We'll be there by noon.' Alex broke off for a moment, sorry not to be able to talk to a person instead of a machine. He smiled, and slightly changed the tone of his voice. 'Hey, Will, I think you got back today or yesterday, and you two are probably out for a late dinner? See you both tomorrow. Max and I have missed you. Save me a glass of good wine! Sleep well.'

Alex had stayed wide awake, hoping to have a quick word with his brother; but now he noticed exhaustion was threatening to overwhelm him. He'd been on the go for four unbroken days with late social nights, and he dreaded the overnight flight. He couldn't sleep on planes, from an ingrained habit of being a light sleeper at work. Long years of night shifts and eighteen-hour days as a houseman had permanently inured him to deep dreams, and he only ever dozed, listening out for every noise. But he was grateful for the comfort of a business-class seat, and the food and movies would be something of a substitute for proper rest.

Nor had today been his own to unwind in, though it was usurped by a well-meaning biochemist who had given Alex and the other doctors a taste of the fall in and around Ridgewood. It wasn't at its best yet but was still lovely, appreciated by the whole group after three days of notepads, water bottles and film clips in a conference room without natural air or light. The trees and the company were genuinely friendly, and he'd still had just enough time to grab a cab to Fifth Avenue and pick out a gift for Max at Schwarz's legendary toy store. He could slow down tomorrow, walk through the quiet village past the cricket field with its thatched clubhouse to the parent-friendly pub his mother had preferred, where they would celebrate the eve of his thirty-fourth birthday.

They were an all-male contingent for the first time in years. He'd wondered if Siân might join them, just to see if there was any remaining hope for her with Will. But his father had said, rather oddly, that she hadn't replied to his invitation – it was unlike her to be so bad-mannered. Alex understood she was waiting for Will to ring and ask her himself, but that wouldn't happen. He'd also thought Anna might come down. They had been divorced two years ago, but were still fairly close, and she fitted in with Alex for Max's sake. But she wasn't coming either, for reasons of her own.

And still the hardest thing was his mother's absence. She was a kind, unjudging rock, held them all together through strife and pain, took no sides. His father coped quietly, worked as hard as ever – a country barrister with a good heart and held in respect by everyone. But he avoided talking about the life he had to get used to alone. At first, Alex and Will had tried being there more often, but if it made any difference to their father, he never told them. Someone from the village cleaned; his father did the garden at weekends; but the fire was snuffed in the hearth. And a bit of fire had gone from all of them, Alex thought.

Tomorrow there'd be laughter. Will would be back, and that was never dull. No dramas though, Will, please, Alex thought, and he laughed quietly to himself as he collected up his bags and coat to make the walk down and clear security. He and Max had grown used to having Will at the flat in London for a couple of months, and it would be so nice just to have a gentle day.

He must have dozed off. When Will woke there were figures moving around him in a sombre dance, like performances of tragedies at the Globe Theatre that closed with a macabre Bergamasque. He thought about the angel's coat – like the stained glass in Chartres, the figure being set upon, and then given a cloak. He wished he could remember what it meant, but he'd forgotten so many Bible stories – apart from their significance in art history, which was one of his passions. Even then, he was better on his classics than the numberless Bible tales adorning all those tiny churches. He remembered Santa Fina in San Gimignano, and Santa Lucia in Sicily; but he tangled nightingales and cornfields with Samaritans and prodigals. For some reason all of those disparate images meant something to him just now.

Light streamed through a door as it opened, and he heard the angel's voice again. She was talking to another person whose voice was soft, male, halting – possibly accented? The door closed and all was quiet. A lot of fuss, thought Will. Everyone tiptoeing around me. He wanted to touch the key around his neck, just to be sure it was safe; but oddly, his arm wouldn't obey his command. They've drugged me, he realised – bloody Alex's tribe; so he refused to worry about it. He tried to address the form quietly moving around him, to ask where he was and what had happened; but the words were lost on his lips. No sound issued from them. The frustration might have annoyed him, but he felt so unworried and unhurried, so he simply let his body sink into the cloud of white bedclothes, and his mind race at will. At Will.

His father's voice was beside him – when did that happen? – talking gently. That made Will smile, inwardly at least. He was speaking with the other being in the room, oddly unaware that Will was listening intently, though the words made little sense. He was still thinking in Italian (or was it French?) and he couldn't concentrate on what his father was asking. He was instead drenched with an impression of Sicilian sunshine, the smell of lemons, the taste of the delicious wine grown on Etna; and most satisfyingly, the boat trip he had taken to Fonte Ciane, the lush clumps of papyrus rising from the water. A beautiful Sicilian girl had gone with him – no, she was from Tuscany – as they were the only ones waiting for the boat to appear, even though it was high season. The day was scorching, they had shared their supplies of water, bread and fruit with each other and with the boatman. Her thick black curly tresses, hanging lower than her waist and scented like citrus blossom, floated out over the water on the warm wind. He told her, in desperately inadequate Italian, how he could imagine dolphins swimming about in her wavy hair; and she explained to him in Italian mixed with English the story of the nymph who was pursued by Alph, the ancient river, escaping his passion only with the aid of Artemis, who turned her into a spring. But the river had caught her in a last embrace, and the water turned brackish with their salty union. It had happened right here, she'd said. He hadn't been sure if this was an invitation to a salty embrace, or a warning not to inflame the wrath of the goddess, but the day was utterly perfect in every sense. He would carry something of its scent, of its unexpectedness, and its chaste sensuality, to his last hour.

Henry Stafford's long fingers came up involuntarily and took refuge in his grey but still thick head of hair, as though he wanted to hide himself. 'We quarrelled. It was so senseless.'

'Mr Stafford,' the woman in a white uniform beside him suggested, 'don't go over the negative things. This is so unhelpful, really, for either one of you. Just talk to him: we never know how much they take in when they're in a coma; but our understanding is that hearing is the last thing to go. He's aware of things you and I can't begin to fathom – on a plane quite beyond us. I'm a great believer in that.'

'He wanted to know about his mother's family, about this silly key.' He stared into his palm. 'I never liked talking about it. I'm a rationalist – unapologetically, I'm afraid. He spent the summer away – had gone off in a passion, unhappy with me. Today was his homecoming. I wanted to talk to him tonight, and discuss his mother. She was such an extraordinary woman, wiser than any of us. And of course he just misses her. We all do. Why couldn't I just tell him what he wanted to know?'

Ruth Martin was wiser than almost anyone herself; and years working in the Intensive Treatment Unit had taught her to listen to the family. They needed whatever assurances she could give, much more than the patients. The last CT scan hadn't looked good, but she wanted to give the father something to help him through these next dark, uncertain hours. 'Whatever it was, just tell him now. He's a captive audience, and yours is the voice he'll most want to hear.'

But the only voice Will heard was his own, so loud in his ears that he was sure he was shouting at his brother. '*Sandy, quel âge auras tu demain?* You are a Virgo, aren't you? Like Astraea. The last of the divine race to leave the earth . . .' Will couldn't collate the information, but he pressed on and climbed the mountain. There was a plume of smoke hovering over the caldera. It was exhausting work; but he wanted to see the view from the top, wanted to touch the volcano's power. He thought of Demeter scouring Etna for her daughter: he must tell her he'd found her. Where had he read 'If your soul wants to be in India, to cross the ocean, in a moment it can be done'? He couldn't find its source. His mind searched through the great hard drive that was his memory. It was Bruno: he saw the face. He neared the top of the mountain, and the air was not sulphurous, as he anticipated, but clear and scented of limes and grapevines. And a rose.

Shh! His father was speaking to him, but the words

seemed to take shape for a second, then fragment. Someone else's words were drowning them out. 'Living beings will not die, but like composite bodies they are merely dissolved, like the dissolution of a mixture rather than death. If they are dissolved, it is not to be destroyed but renewed. What after all is the energy of life?'

Henry Stafford had the feeling his son wasn't hearing him, but he spoke on. 'And he was a great man, that I know. His interest in metaphysics was not the only thing in his life worthy of comment. A great mathematician, a scientist, translator. A spy who might have worked for Walsingham – the first to call himself 007, it's been suggested. He had the best library in England. But remembered as Queen Elizabeth's astrologer, someone who conversed with spirits – or tried to. And I have not much patience with that. But your mother was more flexible; we just didn't talk about it. My wish – and she complied. Whatever there is in that genetic mix of yours, Will, John Dee certainly contributes much of its richness, brilliance, and probably some of your mysticism. I believe the key opens something that belonged to him.' Ignoring the equipment that made his son seem far away and out of touch, Henry had seized Will's hand on the cover-sheet. His hair was tidy and trimmed, his face tanned and handsome – yet he looked frighteningly colourless.

Will may have heard him; he wasn't sure. He was standing, all at once, in a parallel moment, in the centre of a labyrinth, with the smell of roses blissfully overwhelming him, light streaming over him: and, at the same time, on the top of Etna's core, the air pregnant with citrus scents, flatter light, heavy heat. *Kennst du das Land, wo die Zitronen blühn?* he thought: Do you know the land where the lemon trees bloom? What a mistake he'd made. How much time he'd wasted, never learning the whole of any one language, just bits and pieces – never enough for an intellectual conversation with someone from another time and cultural space. How else could you see the world through someone else's eyes, if you couldn't complete an important sentence? The word was everything, he understood.

'Dodone. Delphi. Delos.'

He saw a triangle in his mind's eye; and then looked closely at the pattern on the hilt of the little key. There was a pearl upon it, in the centre of a spiral. Why hadn't he ever taken proper notice of it before? He looked down at his hands, which were grasping something warm and leathery. A dark, old book. He turned it over. His eyes had trouble focusing on the title, lettered in gold. 'Ah. The Old King's Book.' Inside the front cover was inscribed: 'Diana Stafford', above her drawing of a stag and a triangle.

A tear escaped from his father's eye, and he offered no apology for it.

Will floated in a scented sea of light. His sense of humour was still with him. It seemed like Paradise but designed by Muji – all white and uncluttered and beauteous. He willed a great heavy hand on his father's shoulder, and intellectually connected with the touch somehow. He spoke, though his lips were stone: 'Ah! but those tears are pearl which thy love sheeds, And they are rich, and ransom all ill deeds.'

Henry Stafford picked up the large envelope near the bed, closed his hand over the key, and left the room with its soft exhalations of machinery.

'Melissa, please let me drive you home? It's been a long night, and you've been kind to stay . . .' His voice trailed off, and the young girl put a firm hand on his shoulder.

'Thank you.' She said no more. It was nearing midnight, and they were both exhausted in every sense. She knew Mr Stafford a little; her mum occasionally did some extra typing for him. On this night, however, they'd travelled miles together. They were newly forged friends of old.

The run home from Winchester Hospital, where Henry had brought his sons to be born and his wife to die, would take about twenty minutes. They both needed sleep now. And Henry would be glad of Melissa's silent presence.

His grey BMW was the last car but one left in the visitors' car park. Unbelievably, someone had parked him in. A blue Lancia had pulled in halfway across the entranceway, obviously in an emergency. Henry preferred to manoeuvre back and forth rather than find someone who must be suffering a distress of their own, so it took them several minutes before they were clear of the hospital.

7

The over-uniformed officer at Passport Control reminded Alex that 9/11 had cast a long shadow. Gun, cap, and wooden face, the official scrutinised him as if he represented the entire terrorist threat to the USA. Lights flashed and a computer whirred. The officer's eyes narrowed suspiciously. Then benignity was restored, Alex's passport thrust back into his hand without comment beyond the obligatory, 'Have a nice day.'

Alex's attention was markedly elsewhere, already in the lecture he would give his students on the current thinking on cell communication. He found himself moving to security absent-mindedly, placing his briefcase on the belt, moving to the scanner, following another passenger through the ritual: he was hardly aware of his physical actions. Something was bleeping. A man behind him, immaculately dressed, three or four places away, hadn't taken his eyes off Alex. Now other heads were turning.

To Alex, the whole dreamlike sequence was surreal, his

brain and physical motions partially paralysed with fatigue. Then the harsh voice of authority suddenly broke through the moment. 'Empty your pockets, sir', and Alex realised he was being addressed. 'Put your change in the dish and try again.'

Alex understood the officer was affecting a New York ironic sense of humour, which he was sure the man didn't truly feel. Without alarm he was reaching deeply into his overcoat pockets, producing a fistful of coins in one hand and a small plastic bag containing a paperback in the other. The officer was taking the bag, glancing inside, showing it to a colleague, then indicating simultaneously that Alex should place his coins in a tray next to the book. He added his mobile.

'*Extraordinario, este libro*,' the second officer seemed to have murmured, so inaudibly that Alex was almost sure he hadn't spoken at all. He looked up quickly; and for a tiny moment it was as if they were sharing a personal secret. Then all sounds were on alert, a harsh flat beep assaulted the air, and the first officer, stony-faced now, invited Alex to do it all again. Alex returned through the scanner, and was still watching the second officer with a quiet smile, when a flash of awareness made him suddenly produce a fountain pen from the inside pocket of his jacket.

'That'll be the offender, yes-siree bob.' The main officer had the look of a satisfied FBI agent who has just closed an important, life-threatening case. 'I'm afraid we'll have to relieve you of this, sir.'

A din was erupting around the scanning equipment, other passengers grumbling about the delay. From the most detached perspective, Alex was aware that he was shrugging, not quite apologetically. His mother had given him the pen years ago, when he got a place at Cambridge, and he wasn't going home without it.

He made eye contact with his interrogator, and somehow smoothed over the rising tension. 'I'm very attached to it. Could we ask one of the crew to take it for me, let me collect it at the other end?'

The officer was nonplussed, and inspected Alex's name engraved on the pen. 'That's highly unconventional, sir. But I consider it a peaceable suggestion. Let's see what we can do.' He handed the offending item to his colleague, who had been smiling drily and subtly communicating assurances to Alex for a heartbeat. Now he took the detail of his flight to arrange things, and was suddenly giving back the other items, making real contact as he handed Alex the book.

'*E muy metafísico, sí?*' Alex was wishing his Spanish was stronger, but the officer was delighted to have any answer in his language, and nodded gently. 'It's a long flight, and I've seen the films. This will be better company.'

The officer passed over a receipt for the pen, nodding him on. The whole incident had surely not occurred. But the odd humanity of the encounter had touched Alex, and strangely, he was aware that he hadn't even thought much yet about the book that had forged this transient bond – never mind really knowing what it was about. *Extraordinario*, indeed.

He was still pondering the book and the pen when the crisp English tones of the stewardess recalled his attention. Alex reached for a blanket to combat the tiredness that was making him feel the chill, and stared at the little volume in clear plastic. It had been thrust into his hand by a very sympathetic, clear-speaking South American doctor, just as he had been driven away from the conference on his way to stay in Jersey. 'This may give you an insight into the madness of trying to find the difference between spirituality, and reality. Have a good trip home: and *buena suerte*.' She had touched his arm warmly, and then vanished.

He had pocketed the book in its bag in his overcoat, without a proper thought for it, and closed the car door on that world for the time being. Now, as he sank into the generous seat, he turned his attention to *One Hundred Years of Solitude*.

> Many years later, as he faced the firing squad, Colonel Aureliano Buendía was to remember the distant afternoon when his father took him to discover ice.

Crunch. The opening lines captivated his imagination. He heard the author's voice in his ear; such was the power of Gabriel García Márquez. He would never have thought to buy the book; what excellent happenstance. Now here he sat, a captive audience with only time.

The stewardess smiled at him obligingly, and offered him the menu and a drink as they reached cruising altitude. 'I have your fountain pen, Dr Stafford. How very traditional of you to use one. Hardly anyone can write properly any more!' She laughed and showed her lovely white teeth. 'I'll return it to you as soon as we reach Heathrow and clear the plane.' She proffered champagne as a goodwill gesture. 'I'm amazed, actually, that they agreed to your suggestion. It must be your air of English tranquillity.'

Alex grinned like a schoolboy, declining the champagne flute but accepting the *truite amandine* on the menu. He returned to the pirate, Francis Drake, who had destroyed Riohacha in the sixteenth century unwittingly changing the lives of the people Alex was about to meet on the page. Dinner came; he ate; and read on. A colleague behind him was snoring softly.

There was something compelling in the style of writing. Fatigue rose around him like a great protective blanket. He dozed, as was his wont, reawakening, and reading more, pausing to think about the details and complexities of the book, comparing it to aspects of his own family's life. Entirely another world, and yet connected. The galleon in the middle of the rain forest: Will, forever on his questing, Quixotic journeys. The woman who was too beautiful to be placed in a grave in the earth, who was magically taken up to heaven wrapped in the bed linen she was hanging out to dry. Intangibly like his mother. The fable-like quality of the subject matter was made real by the narrative style. Alex was sure Will would have read this book, and loved it; he had seen it among the piles of his life that cluttered his own London flat now. His brother had not an investment to his name, but endless shelves of intellectual property, music – on disk and sheet music – books to the ceiling, first edition Penguins that Siân had threatened him about so often, perhaps one time too many. Not at all a good idea to ask him to choose between 'me or those awful, grubby books' – she had given up on tying them into beribboned piles on the shelves to offset their drab appearance. Alex knew better than she which way the choice might go, although now he could sympathise with Siân, given the sprawl they caused. He looked forward to talking to Will about this book, though – wished he could do so now: he knew that the raw emotion and fantasy would have attracted Will. But a fresh realisation was born. Although Alex and his brother were two sides of the same coin – Father's elder son, and Mother's younger boy – Alex knew there was a deeper level in his own being that he had not truly explored, just as there was a serious side to Will that he did not like to expose. He lamented the tendency well-meaning parents and friends have to typecast their progeny. 'Alex is so steady, hard-working, a real logician. He'll make a wonderful doctor. An impossible act for his brother to follow. Will? He's just a dreamer, can't spell a word, head always in a book. Plays the piano like Chopin. But God knows what he'll ever achieve – he never settles to anything.' Will had traditionally laughed off this kind of comment, saying he'd 'rather have been George Sand'. But it must have hurt inside, just as it rankled with Alex that he came off – according to this binary opposition – as ever dependable and by correlation a little unexciting. Their mother knew better and fought familial opinion. 'They are intelligent, inspirational men, both of them. Let's wait and see how they use their hours on this earth.'

Alex needed some sleep, realising his mind was wandering. This thought was accompanied by a darker one: is everyone all right? This last threatened the quietude of his night hours, but he dismissed it as the product of exhaustion. His father and brother had probably quarrelled over dinner, and Alex would have to turn up as usual as the peacekeeper. The sun had kept pace with the pages, and rose in an arc above the purple line of cloud before turning white. The moon just as suddenly paled, and vanished in the sky over the ocean. Is this merely the speed of the plane against the direction of time? Alex mused. He dozed briefly; read on again; and finally folded the cover with the comment that '. . . races condemned to one hundred years of solitude did not have a second opportunity on earth.' Which begs the question of redemption in heaven, thought Alex.

He and Will had sometimes debated such philosophical questions when not arguing whether Gary Sobers or Ian Botham was the more complete cricketer. He had forgotten that part of their relationship. Interesting, the depth of thought they had shared when they were boys; but Alex realised he hadn't been much help on the subject of immortality when their mother died. He could see his brother now after the funeral, a cigarette propped in his mouth while he thundered angrily through Chopin's emotive Fantasy Impromptu. Dreadful habit that he'd resumed while their mother was ill: thankfully he'd given it up again since. And his music too, it seemed.

What had changed? Only time really – especially Alex's absurd lack of it. Will had coaxed him to open up about the pain of his failed marriage to Anna; tried to talk a little himself about the sadness of his break with Siân. But Alex wouldn't, couldn't, make the time for these confidences any more. Each of them exercised their own avoidances, though their intuition of each other was occasionally enough support. Oh, Will, I have missed you – even if you are a pain in the arse a lot of the time, Alex thought, and tried to pull his brain back to reality. He was sure this nostalgia for his younger brother's company would fade as soon as he spilled noisily across Alex's calm Chelsea space again. Within a week Will would have taken over his kitchen, insisting on doing the cooking and dirtying every pan in the process. He laughed quietly and stared at the back cover of the book.

'Cabin crew: ten minutes to landing.' The stewardess touched his shoulder as she helped him pull his seat forward, and picked up the last remaining glasses from the tables around the cabin. Moments later the familiar thump came as the wheel locked into place, and Alex felt the huge plane slip nervously sideways like a show horse dancing as it approached a jump; it straightened, dropped gently to the ground, and galloped down the runway, until the noise of the reverse thrust broke the spell and he was home.

Given the mass of humanity that spewed from the many overseas flights at this hour of the morning, Passport Control was remarkably cheerful and civilised. 'Good morning. Thank you, sir. Welcome home, Dr Stafford.'

The stewardess found Alex in the baggage hall. 'You'll want this. Mightier than the sword, and all that!'

She flew on past him as the pen that had written so much of his history appeared in his palm. He hadn't time to thank her. Alex switched on his mobile as he waited for the bags to come through. He had seven messages. With fast-track clearance, a wonderful perk with the superior class of flight, he was wheeling his luggage away as his world froze: 'Alex, it's very serious about Will, I'm afraid. More than I knew in my last message. Please, please call me as soon as you get this. I'll certainly need your advice.' His father's voice was hoarse.

He let two more messages play out before he stopped them off, taking him deeper back into time as the earlier calls came up after the latest one. His face was gaunt as he ran from the terminal building.

'16.43: Do you want to shut down?'

'Do I ever!' Jane Cook blurted out. She clicked 'Yes' and closed her laptop. She sat at her desk, slowly picked up the phone, then put it back on the cradle. She put off calling her little girl for the moment. She was so late – beyond late – that she couldn't face another apology just now. Well, at least someone would benefit from the hours of extra time she'd put in, she thought.

Most of this particular job had been set up on the assumption that the donor would not recover. Sometimes the work went for nothing, but it did reduce the time between death and receipt, which was vital. The second phase of the job could now fall into place if everything went according to plan. Poor Lucy had already had one letdown in the last forty-eight hours: everyone marshalled, only to find that the heart wasn't up to it – a second-tier organ, which had sounded good, but ultimately didn't make the grade. She didn't want that to happen again now.

As many as forty people would be involved before the operation was completed, and at this stage there were still a great many unknowns. The spate of calls and emails she had just finished had told Senior Nursing Sister Cook that the helicopter's ETA was approximately ten minutes from now. The push of another button on her phone confirmed that the heart should be here in a further fifteen to twenty minutes after landing.

The Heart Transplant Co-ordinator checked her watch. A little over an hour and twenty minutes would have elapsed from the time that the first surgeon had harvested the organ from the donor and transferred it to its special transportation container for its arrival at Harefield. Not bad, all things considered. This was not strictly the best way of dealing with organ movement, but no mobile life-support system had been available to move the donor complete, so the heart had been harvested in situ and the organ moved to London. The team had performed with punctilious dedication, as always. People knock the NHS, Jane thought, not for the first time, but where else in the world would you get all of this on the health service?

Being a Sunday, the anticipated twenty minutes around Heathrow airport shrank to less than fifteen. 'Very nearly perfect,' was the team leader, Senior Cardiac Surgeon Mr Amel Azziz's, only comment as he checked out the organ and test results. 'Not at all bad,' he had added with a satisfied countenance. 'God', as he was known among the staff in private conversation, had pronounced in his laconic manner that he was in his heaven, and all was right with the world. Jane knew that Lucy King would be safe in his hands.

'Tissue matches, blood types all look significantly better than we have a right to ask. I presume everything is in place, so I can go and scrub up.' He looked at Jane over the rim of his half-glasses, and she was pleased to have pleased him.

'Unless you have a problem that I should know about?'

'Not at all. Everything is in order, sir.' The epithet was only half teasing. She had long ago earned the right to call him by his given name, but she liked 'sir', or 'himself' when she was talking about him affectionately to others.

'Of course it is, Jane. I have complete faith.' His eyes twinkled at her. And of course it was. After all, wasn't she the best co-ordinator on any team? That was why she worked for God. And she thought the world of him, professionally speaking, but she would never let him know as much. And in his turn, he knew beyond all certainties that she would never let the side down. Every detail had been taken care of, from the moment the donor had been declared dead from a massive brain haemorrhage. The scan showed no activity, and the life support was left in quiet symphony with the spirit, whatever that meant. That had been hours ago. As the donor had carried a card, there had been no question about going ahead: although the next of kin, who had been at the hospital at the time of death, had also signed the consent forms. Copies of everything were already in the files and on the computer.

The phone went again, drawing her back to her station, demanding attention. This time the call took Jane by surprise. Everyone and everything had been called, checked and double-checked. So this could only mean a hitch. Azziz made eye contact with her, a question inflecting them. She nodded reassurances at him, belying her real reaction. 'Damn,' she thought out loud, censoring her worse language in front of the doctor when she realised the single word had escaped her.

Her family would not see her for dinner any time tonight. 'Another working weekend, Mama,' little Sarah had said. 'When do I get to see you, I mean really see you?' She had wrapped her arms around her mother's neck and wouldn't let go when she came to say she was off early this morning. People with families shouldn't take on these jobs. Jane barely stifled the thought, then turned to the job at hand in the blink of an eye, with total professionalism.

She ended the call with a finger on the pulse, got a new dial tone, and phoned out in the same motion. 'Hello there, James. Can you fill in for me at once?' She nodded a few times to herself, once to Mr Azziz, said, 'Oh, that's grand,' and put the handset down. She rolled her eyes. 'That was a call we could have done better without,' she explained to God, the Irish inflection in her voice helping her to sound upbeat. 'I thought he was on call – according to my paperwork – but we've had no success contacting your preferred immunologist. Apparently he's a day late getting back from a conference. His secretary can't locate him – although she insists he was rostered off for his birthday today. Anyhow, Dr Lovell will fill in for us – he's still in the building and will be here in five minutes, and we won't need him for long.'

Jane Cook personified efficiency, and communicated control to the transplant surgeon. Secretly, she was irritated. She was working over her weekend and wouldn't get home to her family for a nice, cosy Sunday lunch. An extra day away on the firm, do you mind! No one would say 'boo' to a consultant. Birthday or not, if you're on call, you're on call. Jane had images of a glass of fine wine in a smart country pub with the family all there, mobile switched off thoughtlessly. But she smiled at the world, and congratulated herself that everyone on her team was a top dog.

Azziz read the thought staining her brow like a cloud blotting the moon. 'Well, I think we might excuse Dr Stafford on high days and holidays, don't you? These trials only wrong-foot mortals, Jane – never you. Never do you lose the thread.'

She was completely soothed by Azziz's charm and confidence in her. Never mind indeed, James Lovell was a first-class doctor, and was already at hand. All she had to do was tell the patient about the change. She didn't think that would be a problem. Mr Azziz was probably not all that happy, she realised, but he'd live with it. He liked to have the people he knew and trusted around him, and he liked to be a little dependent on Alexander Stafford. The Sphinx, he called him. 'May not always say much, but he sees absolutely everything and knows more than he will tell you,' he had once confided to Jane about him, although he knew she would have been more comfortable with the said doctor if he had been more obviously exuberant – and more easily understood. She was prone to mistake his slight reserve for unexpressed criticism of others, which Amel knew was unjustified. 'He's a calm and rational young man, but never in the least judgemental of other people's ideas and foibles. I like him.'

Anyway, thought Jane, right now they'd have to do without their all-knowing 'Sphinx'; he was either in somebody's airspace or had gone incommunicado for his birthday. There was nothing more she could do for the next twelve hours, so she would get some food and a little rest.

She was on standby, 'just in case', and couldn't go yet.

'Don't worry, Jane. I'll tell the patient myself.' It would disappoint her, though – just how much, perhaps he alone knew.

He made a short detour en route to the theatre. 'Lucy, you look especially lovely today. Now you are in my hands, and Allah's, for the next few hours.'

She smiled through the haze of her pre-med, and looked softly haloed with her jet hair against the pillow framing her pale, Romanesque face. There was no light, no shadow, and her features seemed almost erased – and Mr Azziz was considering that her appearance seemed far too surreal for someone who had been fighting a treacherous disease and was now on the point of life-changing surgery.

'I can manage it,' she spoke with surprising strength, 'being a guest of yours and Allah's for a few hours.'

But the surgeon recognised a glimmer of fear behind the outward confidence. 'We are going to go somewhere magical together, all of us now.' He looked at Lucy as though she were a highly intelligent child. 'Dr Stafford, I am very sorry to say, can't be with us for the present. It seems to be his day off, and he is nowhere to be found, or perhaps he has not yet come back from his trip – otherwise, I know it was his intention to come in and support you, and he would want to do so. But I have checked the tissue matches myself this time; and we additionally have Dr Lovell just for today. You will have Dr Stafford back the day after tomorrow at the latest – and you won't know a great deal about it before then.'

Lucy felt thoroughly flattened at this news. She had so much respect for Dr Stafford, and she had come to the realisation this week that she had grown to rely on him being somewhere around her. He was the gentlest soul she'd ever met; and she would rather not make such a journey into the dark unknown without his particular lightness of being there in the room. But her thin veil of energy was mistaken for the effects of the pre-med by everyone except Mr Azziz, whom, like Alex Stafford, no subtlety escaped. He smiled and patted her thin hand.

Jane Cook thought him amazing as he almost imperceptibly assuaged any sudden doubts about the operation Lucy might have harboured. His seemingly serene bearing gave a level of reassurance to everyone, staff and patients alike. It made them believe that in his hands nothing could go wrong, in spite of the dire warning that had to be given to each patient before they signed up. Amel, more than any other surgeon Jane had worked with, was special.

She'd call Sarah after tea. Her dad had taken her to the park this afternoon; it looked lovely outside in the late afternoon, and all the rain from the past week had cleared away. She picked up the pile of files from her desk, and headed for the wards.

As they squeezed her hair into a cap and loaded her on to the trolley, Lucy glanced – without truly focusing – on the hazy colours of her patchwork. This was the life she had stitched together over the last few months, ever since she had brought Chagas' disease back with her from Colombia. She was twenty-eight, and looked nineteen with her illness; but she took every day as it came like a wise old crone. She had patched a story in gem-bright colours or pastels as the mood dictated, for weeks on end. Her huge tired eyes rested briefly on the last piece she'd done: a heart on the wing rising towards the tiny sliver of moon, in a night sky. She meant it as a reminder of her mother flying away when she was little – a flight from which the mother had never returned, and the child never recovered. It was a sea-change in her life. But now, in the nebulous space she occupied with the anaesthetics taking hold of her, she saw the winged heart in a new light, about herself, which she hadn't contemplated before. Her lids gave up, and folded her into a divine sleep.

8

Lucy sensed his presence, even before she opened her eyes. He had a smell that was apart from anything else in the hospital – vetiver, or bergamot, she thought. She smiled with her eyes still tightly shut for a moment longer, then she opened them and spoke.

'I'm sure I'm looking better than you've ever seen me today.' Her voice was thick, and didn't sound at all like her own. She was in the intensive care unit, and ached in parts of her body she'd never been closely acquainted with, but she saw in Alex's amused eyes that she'd found the power to convey some irony. And despite the bruising, and wires, and brutal incisions, she felt pleasantly sleepy.

'You look pretty good for eight or nine hours of surgery.'

His voice was clear and gentle as usual, but tired, she thought. And she knew that what he'd said wasn't true: she knew without asking that she looked as wounded as she felt. But Alex himself was reassuringly calm looking at her. Peeping from behind a sterile mask, she noticed his eyes were devoid of their usual brightness, but they were doing their best to engage with her.

He moved closer. 'Besides, you'll get no sympathy from me. I thought I'd find you up and on the treadmill today. My secretary got an urgent message to me that your operation was scheduled for last Friday. I can't believe you'd have wanted to delay it – or have second thoughts? What happened?'

She tried to speak to assure him she hadn't got cold feet, explain why the postponement had happened. But he smiled and stopped her with a finger up to his lips 'Don't worry – your throat still hurts from the tube. I'll get the whole story from Mr Azziz. Just tell me if you're all right.'

Lucy slowly found her voice again, and she wanted to speak to him. 'I wish I could say.' She took her time, trying to throw off the effects of the heavy painkillers that made her so deeply drowsy. 'I'm trying to give you an intelligent answer. Discern what's in my brain.' She was like a cat, stretching after sleeping too long near a fire. 'Oh, and my heart. I forgot that . . . Today's my birthday, the first day of a new life.'

'Well, perhaps that was the early hours of yesterday, when the operation was over. Many happy returns. And mine was yesterday too, so you see, we share one.'

Lucy smiled with slight confusion. 'A nurse told me your birthday was Sunday – that you were in the country for lunch.'

'The true day was yesterday though, September the twenty-second.' Alex couldn't begin to tackle 'Sunday in the country'. 'Are you still tired from the sedation?'

'I've slept long, haven't I? Have you been here for some time?' Her words were soft but quite distinct. She moved her neck a shade, though it had a tube in it; and she noticed he had a book and had been in the single chair. That was unusual, as he was always rushed off his feet. Another masked face came in and recorded something on her chart, which Alex then took over from her. She was aware, as the door opened, of the wonderful fragrance of jonquils – narcissi. Where were they, and where had they come from in September? Had Grace arranged them?

'I wanted to be here when you woke up.' Alex had been occupying himself with her notes for a moment, waiting for the sister to depart. 'Mr Azziz asked for me to check things before your surgery, and I couldn't get here. I felt I'd let you down – although I can see you've managed annoyingly well without me.' He joked easily with her, and it had the desired effect of raising a warm smile. 'I did put my head in late last night, but you weren't waiting up for me.'

'Even doctors are entitled to a birthday lunch. And I've lost Monday. Anyway, you've been in the States?'

'I'd have come straight from lunch for you, Lucy. Something . . . just . . . came up. My family needed me.'

Alex's voice betrayed a momentary loss of surety; and it confused her. What he'd just said had contained a compliment, and also a riddle. But the space between the two closed quickly when he replaced her chart and looked at her again with clarity.

'I've checked your medication and glanced at the tissue report and obs. I haven't seen the notes from your surgery yet, but I'll catch a word with Mr Azziz or Mr Denham about you today. It seems like serendipity. It's not the heart you were originally coming in for, I gather, but a better one, possibly. Two suitable matches in as many days? You're lucky.'

Lucy felt like she'd been through a terrible car crash, in truth; the drugs didn't quite mask the top of the pain. But despite her dislocated sense of self, she strained to read something in Alex Stafford's face that wasn't usually there. She couldn't discover it; couldn't entirely recognise the stranger who had chased away his usual peace and quiet strength. Nor could she attempt bravado: she wasn't physically up to it, and was tiring quickly. But she did her best.

'Don't worry about the rest of the world today. I'm not going anywhere. You need one of these,' she said, pointing at her drip, 'and to get yourself to bed. I've never seen you look so exhausted. You obviously had a rough trip.' Even through the ether of her drug-induced reverie, and despite the cloth hiding most of his face, she saw sharply that he hadn't slept for, perhaps, a few days. He was a handsome man with nicely chiselled features, and always kind. The nurses loved to chat about him. But he looked ghastly today – his green eyes red-rimmed. Not a man you'd bring home to tea.

'All right.' He laughed, and was grateful for her perceptiveness. 'I may look in tonight, and tomorrow you should be back in the step-down ward. I'll join up with Mr Denham then and we'll go through your antibiotics with you, what we need to do to prevent infections after your surgery.' He adjusted her cover-sheet. 'Is there anything you'd like?' He was in charge again. The mask between the man and the doctor had slipped only for a second. 'You're on nil by mouth for a day or so, so no roast beef and Yorkshire pudding just yet.'

Lucy was a vegetarian, which he knew well; but the joking idea sounded strangely like the comfort food her aunts used to give her as a child, and welcome. 'Nothing now, thanks. Could I have some lemon tea tomorrow? I'm craving it.'

'Mm. Good choice. You need a taste for decaffeinated now.' He showed approval. 'No dairy's good, Lucy. I imagine the dietician will be in to see you late tomorrow. You're no stranger to low fat, I know. Don't forget low sodium now too. And the prednisolone raises your glucose level, so we'll be monitoring your blood sugar very carefully.'

'And I can't eat grapefruit, either, because of some drug or other.' She was teasing him; he'd told her all of this before, and she'd listened to him very carefully.

'Sorry! Not everyone holds on to these things. It's a lot to take in.' Alex laughed genuinely, and was glad of the sound. 'Yes, grapefruit is banned because of the cyclosporin. But you studied ballet for years, didn't you? I don't think you'll give us trouble with your eating habits. And you could put a little weight back on.' Lucy was still painfully thin.

'Good morning to you, Lucy King. Well, it's gone noon, actually.' A masked Mr Azziz had appeared silently at the door in a sterile white coat, rather than his familiar blue. 'Do you feel as though you've travelled to the Emerald City and returned with a new heart and the courage of a lion?' Every word was so succinctly pronounced that it gave him a permanent tone of beneficence.

'Good afternoon, dear Doctor-Wizard. I feel . . . strangely

mellow.' Lucy was sunny with the attention from her two favourite people in the building. It dwarfed the sense of physical hiatus she was experiencing. Light filtered through the small window in the intensive care unit, becoming prismatic, like the colours in her patched quilt. A message from the goddess of the rainbow, perhaps, that she was on her way back towards life. She said with surprising control: 'I have had a dream past the wit of man to say what dream it was.' The words presented themselves.

Alex and Amel Azziz looked at her very seriously; then the senior surgeon smiled, and turned to his immunologist.

'Dr Stafford.'

Alex was instantly aware of unspoken sympathies. From Azziz's look, he knew everything.

But he said simply, 'Good to see you. Come and have a word, when you've a minute.'

Alex just nodded, and the surgeon turned back to Lucy. 'Well, now. I will leave you to get some more rest. I think you can come out of the Intensive Treatment Unit tomorrow morning – you look far too well to be in here! But take things gently; you have been all around the world, in a manner of speaking. I'll be in my office, Dr Stafford.' Though his words to the two of them had been characteristically unhurried, his physical self now vanished like an apparition, the door wafting the flowery scent again.

'Those flowers outside in the hall, the fragrance. So distinctive. They're narcissi.' Lucy had returned her attention to them. 'Do you know if a friend left them for me? I can't understand how they can be there. Spring jonquils in autumn? Although they used to come out under my bedroom window in the middle of winter, in Sydney.'

'You've a good nose! They come from Liberty's florist. They always have things out of season. They're just a small apology for missing the show. You can't have them in here, but I'm pleased you like them. They're a token of a new spring, Lucy. They can follow you back to your room in a day or two. Now I must let you stop talking and get more rest. I'll try and come back – unless I'm called to the other hospital.'

And he too was gone. Lucy thought over the significance of him buying her the flowers, and she laboured through the haze of her drugs to understand why it meant so much to her. Was that a bit out of the ordinary? But she cautiously retreated from this dangerous zone. She was his patient; he was just one of her consultants. He was exactly as charming and kind to every patient, which she knew very well. He'd brought her room-mate, Mrs Morris, a book last week, and a senior nurse a Cymbidium for her birthday the week before. And Lucy rarely risked her feelings for anyone, in any case. If she weren't in control, she'd walk the other way. But she let her senses swim in the scented air, in a dreamlike web of semi-sleep, at the end of a rainbow.

The mood in the flat seemed sombre and heavy, but a light breeze moved the curtain in front of an open window. It was an incongruously beautiful late September day with sunshine streaming in, and the fragrance of some white peonies placed on the piano carried to Siân, inert on the couch. She covered her ears as the phone rang again and Calvin, coffee mug in hand, quickly crossed the floor from the small kitchen to answer.

'Hello? Look, I'm sorry. Thanks for your condolences. I'll tell her you called. She's just not up to coming to the phone yet.' He listened for another moment and then interrupted the caller. 'Yes, if you want to know the arrangements for Friday, you could call his brother.' Calvin reeled off a phone number and said goodbye in record time.

Siân's blotched face looked up gratefully. 'You're sweet to handle all this for me. I'm so sorry. I can't believe it's knocked me this hard. How does word get out so fast?'

'Sure it's hit hard. How long were you guys together? You don't lose someone you were involved with so closely for years and just shrug it off, you know.' He passed her the coffee, then grabbed his coat and keys. 'Look, I'm going to the store to get you something for lunch. A little hot grilled chicken, some salad?' He looked for a reaction, but she hardly heard. He picked up the card that had come with the peonies and placed it in her hands to remind her: 'Don't forget Will's brother wants you to call him.'

He was nearly through the door when his mobile phone rang.

'God, can't they leave us alone for a day or two?' Siân's patience snapped. She wanted to concentrate on her own emotions, not be burdened by the exhausting sympathies of her friends. That was too much. You cancel one day's work, and suddenly the world knows your business. She'd shut off her own mobile; but all sorts of well-meaning colleagues had tracked down Calvin to ask after her. But as he answered he shook his head at her, indicating it was for him, and waved goodbye, closing the heavy door behind him.

*

'This is a strange business.' His voice was lowered, and he increased his pace to clear the front of the sprawling Victorian building without being heard. These residential streets off the square were too quiet. 'First my cousin dies. Then his father's house is broken into. Did you have anything to do with that at all? The break-in? I understand we all want information, but it's God-awful timing.'

'I know, Calvin.' The person at the other end refused to let his emotions rise. 'I have no idea about it. I'm putting all my faith in your success, and so is Professor Walters.'

'Don't worry, Guy. I'll get control of the key. It'll be back with his father now. I'll hang in close here, and see what I can learn. But let's at least be respectful.'

'Don't let us down, Calvin. The papers we believe the key will take us to are going to be highly sensitive. This is our chance to know the whole picture. And I'm getting pressured from above. You know FW isn't always a patient man, however much he protests otherwise.'

Calvin thought he sounded unusually nervous. 'Believe me, Guy, I haven't invested this much time myself to . . .' he paused to find the right words, '. . . come up empty-handed. As one of the family I'll be at the funeral Friday, and I'll call you after the weekend, but don't cramp me. This is a delicate process, and I need their trust if I'm to help you.'

'Help us, Calvin. Don't forget what's at stake for you.' The phone line clicked off.

Alex found Courtney Denham in Amel's office, scrutinising some test results. 'I can come back later.' He swung on his heel.

'Don't worry, man, I'm done. You'll be pleased to hear that Lucy King's operation went really well. The tissue match might not have been quite as close for her as the first organ we found, but the heart itself was light years better. She's a fighter, that girl.'

Alex was genuinely fond of Courtney. He was Trinidadian, and his accent – which had never quite left him – was mellifluous and always full of humour, which was especially welcome today. He was also an impressive cardiologist.

He walked towards Alex and grasped his hand. 'Sorry to hear the news, Alex. Will was a special human being. Wicked sense of humour. I was an admirer.'

Alex couldn't manage a 'thank you'; but he felt it, and confirmed the pressure in the hand. Courtney left the room.

'You shouldn't even be here today, Alex. I asked your secretary to tell you that. We can manage without you for a while.'

'It's easier, Amel; I'd rather be here, and be useful. Besides, Lucy has no family in the UK, and I think she depends on us more than usual. That back-up from relatives is such a vital part of post-operative care, and she's completely without it. I understand her flatmate is like a sister, but it's not the same thing. I'm happy to do my bit.'

Others, being alert to heightened sensitivities, might have avoided the subject; but Amel judged Alex's needs differently. 'It was some kind of accident, I gather. Do you have any idea how it happened?'

Alex felt oddly relieved by the question. He couldn't seem to go into this with his father, who was reeling from the loss of his wife and son in less than a year. He hadn't wanted to answer Alex's questions about police reports, and other possible drivers.

'Supposedly Will crashed into a bridge over high-running water, in the midst of thick fog. They suggest he was probably tired and not paying attention.' He spoke without emotion, then gazed up at Amel. 'But I find that nearly impossible to believe. Will was too experienced on a bike. If he was tired – too tired to get it right – he'd have pulled over. He lived dangerously, I admit; but he knew the line between daring and madness.'

'The fog wouldn't have blurred the two?'

'He knew the river; he knew every lane, better than anyone. I just can't believe his misjudgement would be that serious. How do you get right across Italy, France, Greece, unscathed, and then make a tragic mistake a mile from home?'

Amel looked at his friend and colleague earnestly. 'Alex, are you actually thinking there could be more to it?' He would have backed the young doctor, to anyone, against any charge of a fanciful imagination. A conspiracy theory would never be a child of Alex's brain.

'I do wonder if another driver could have crowded him. A neighbour was first on the scene, gave him basic first aid and got the emergency services. She told my father and the police that she thought she might have heard another vehicle – an engine. She couldn't be sure. And I don't want to upset my family. But I do think it's possible that someone bumped him, then panicked and didn't stop.'

Amel saw his friend and young colleague coping with all

of this very well on the outside, just as he had when his mother had died earlier in the year; but he was sensitive to an unfamiliar note of strain in Alex's voice. He knew better than to expect him to admit to it, however. 'Leave it to the police, Alex.' Amel came over to him and laid a hand on his shoulder. 'Let yourself mourn your brother. I'm sorry I didn't know him – everyone here who knew him speaks well of him, and they're all in shock. But I will come to the funeral for you, if you will allow me?'

Alex, who always thought Amel the busiest human on the planet, was moved. It took him a moment to phrase his thanks. 'That's kind, Amel. It would be good to have you there, if you can get away. It's Friday.' Alex looked at his hands. 'I hardly seem to have time to think what Will would have wanted for it.'

'Funerals are for the living, Alex, not for the dead. It's what you and your father and friends need from it that's important. Try to satisfy that – the need formally to say goodbye.' Amel understood that Alex had no faith to speak of – actually was a non-believer. They had talked honestly about it before. 'Did Will share your religious views? Or lack of them, perhaps I should ask?'

'I think Will would have been happier with a testament found in Shakespeare than any from the Bible. But he had some strange corners to his spirituality. Practically the last message he left me was about our mother's Bible; and there was a postcard from Chartres, and a copy of the Song of Solomon, in French, inside his jacket. So, I don't know really.'

'Shakespeare sounds good to me. Let others make their

own contributions. But you know, I like Hamlet's advice to Horatio, that there might be "more things in heaven and earth".'

Alex offered a quiet laugh. He knew Amel was a great scientist, and yet a believer too. Long talks had revealed him to be a complex man, and Alex respected Amel's views – though they were not his own. He had suggested that Allah watched with humour as they all tried to gain clues to the immense secrets of his universe – that he watched their progress like an indulgent father – Darwin, the lot. For Amel, God and Science were not opponents. Science just gave them some of the tools to find their own godlike powers. And they had a long way to go, Amel said.

Alex looked up at his kind, wise face. He would be happy to have him there on Friday. It would help, somehow.

9

Crabtree Lane ran down to the river, and at weekends it was a little haven of peace that, spiritually, moved it miles from its relative centrality in the capital. On this chilly October night there was just a hint of mist settling on the water's edge. Alex parked his car outside a period cottage, which had been witness to the amorous excursions of Charles II, when he brought one mistress or another up the Thames more than three hundred years earlier. With a little help from their parents to get the deposit, he and Anna had bought the house opposite eight years before, when Anna was pregnant with Max. It was handy for work and close to the water, which he loved, but it also had a country feel that his wife had been enchanted by. Mother and son had remained, and at least occasionally Alex wished that all three – Anna, Max, and the house with the two pretty trees – were still his to come home to. It wasn't that he hadn't appreciated them before. But his life as a doctor in organ donation and research demanded dedication and uncounted hours, which he gave; and he hadn't noticed his home life steadily eroding without the attention due to a young wife and baby son. She was never especially vindictive about it, never even held him personally to blame for what she knew he couldn't change; but one day they had woken up to find their relationship had passed them by. There was not too much hostility, or fighting about custody or maintenance, but a residual sadness that two intelligent people couldn't avoid the pitfalls of a career that would come second to nothing.

Max was a tall child for his age, with hazel-green eyes that were similar to his father's. He pounced on the door when Alex rang the bell to collect him for the weekend.

'I've got to show you something amazing!' He started to drag his father up the stairs before he could get his coat off in the hall. 'I've been playing with the new Sims you brought me back. You won't believe what they're doing, Daddy.'

Anna appeared before her son could quite get away with the new arrival. Her blond hair was clipped up neatly at the back, and she was simply but elegantly dressed in a long cream shirt belted over matching trousers. It looked like she might be on her way out, but Alex was pleased when she didn't sound at all hurried.

'Are you finished for the day, Al? Can I pour you a quick glass of wine?' She looked with concern at her former husband, for whom she had a lot of time and respect as a person and as a good father to Max. He looked harrowed, like someone who hadn't had a full night's sleep for the whole of the last month – which was likely. But whatever demons Alex chased, he did so alone, telling no one what was in his head or his heart. Keeping his own counsel was his habit – and, in her mind, still his worst personal failing.

'That sounds good, Anna, thanks. Today started a lifetime ago.' He took a step towards the kitchen with her. 'Dad rang and told me he'd had an unofficial chat with the coroner – although the full inquest won't be for another couple of months. I've been at work since six this morning, and I've got to sort out the last of Will's things in my flat tonight. I keep tripping over them, and some of it ought to go to charity. Plus we got the bike back today from the insurers. Very little wrong with it, but I can't decide what to do with it now. I guess I'll get it back down to the country and then think about selling it. Typical of Will, isn't it, to move in, and never properly move out again. I've been completely unsettled with him half in and half out of my life since May.'

She noted that his voice seemed steady, and passed him a glass. 'Do you need any help with that? It's going to be a difficult job.' Her words came with an inflection that was more an enquiry whether Alex wanted to talk, than whether he would accept her offer. Max was still tugging at his father's arm, not at all willing to let go of him – which Anna understood very well; but she also sensed a possible moment that would be gone in an instant if she couldn't get their son to give them some space.

'Max, let Daddy have ten minutes to talk to me, then we'll both come up and see your game.' He was hard to dissuade, until she mentioned that the Sims' house might burn down – or the husband lose his lift to work – if it wasn't properly set on pause.

Max left them both at speed, and Alex followed Anna up

the step to the sitting room. It had recently been redecorated – her once favourite country style giving way to a clean, modern feel, which added an airy lightness. White lilies in a plain glass vase, one white scented candle, which gave the room an air of sanctity, an Ingres-style drawing on the wall. The fire was lit, and he sank into a chair not far from it. He began by asking about their son, whether Max had said a lot to her about his uncle, how he seemed to be coping.

'Very much like you.' Anna's answer was voiced in a mixture of irony and sadness. 'He doesn't say much unless he's asked directly.'

Alex heard the criticism, and managed half a smile. 'I'll talk to him.'

'It sounds like a lot of practicalities are still dragging on?'

'The whole thing is just a nightmare.' This was strong stuff from Alex. 'You know there was a robbery when Dad was at the hospital – extraordinary timing.' Anna nodded. 'The police think it was kids, because they took a little loose cash, some CDs, nothing of any real value, like Mum's jewellery.'

Anna had been horrified when she'd heard this at the funeral; that someone could be so callous. But she quickly realised that whoever was responsible had just seen an opportunity with an empty house, and not given the circumstances or grief of its occupants at the time the slightest thought. How could they? 'It never rains . . .' she started to say.

'But there are two or three things we've now realised *are* missing. A couple of Mum's old books that were in the house; including her family Bible – which had been given to her by her grandmother, and was with them all for generations. Valuable, I gather, and absolutely impossible to replace. Dotted throughout with marginalia, and births and deaths recorded for generations.' Anna was shaking her head in disbelief. 'And a very tiny portrait, which we always meant to get valued. Hardly more than a miniature really. A lady in late sixteenth-century dress, very much in Hilliard's style – though not one of his, we think; and no one has ever suggested who it might be. But it's gone now. And I know Mum was really attached to it.'

'Yes, I think I can remember it with its midnight-blue background – on Diana's desk. So they did know what they were taking – knew what had some serious value after all?'

'It looks that way. Even the police are revising their theory now. Besides, no one in the village can believe it would be locals. They all feel that sort of thing doesn't happen in Longparish.' Alex smiled, but with no mirth.

'What do you think the coroner's final verdict will be, Al?' She had to check her own voice now; she hadn't come to terms with Will's death at all. Four weeks had passed, and she still expected him to ring at any minute. How could someone so alive be gone? He was one of the worst casualties of her failed marriage to Alex – the brother she'd never had herself. Kind and funny with her, indulgent with Max, he was always the first to answer an SOS call if Alex wasn't free. She'd miss him dreadfully. Could anyone but God even begin to guess what Alex and Henry must be going through?

'It will probably be accidental death – resulting from a cranial aneurysm. Unless they conclude that the haemorrhage was triggered by a previous head injury Will was aware of. That would change it to misadventure. But they're not looking at anything more unusual. Dents on the helmet confirm that he wasn't even travelling fast. Just the unhappy coincidence of fog and tiredness, they suggest. And if you believe that, you'll believe the world is still flat.'

Anna couldn't answer him. She agreed. She could see Will wrecking his back, breaking a leg, gashing himself with his tools, burning himself because he was always talking while he cooked. Never could she imagine he would miss a bend or crash into a bridge on that bike of his. He loved it, and rode it with style. She'd giggled like a teenager when he'd first come to show it to her and Max. 'I've never had a bike that's so easy to do wheelies on – it feels like the front wheel is on a loop, and you can reel it up and down like a yo-yo just by twitching the throttle: watch me!' He'd ripped down Crabtree Lane, got the revs up, and launched himself towards them, the wheel leaping up to the squeals of delight of her son and his uncle and the consternation of the neighbours. No, she thought, Will wouldn't crash the bike. He cared for it far too much.

'Daddy, *please* come and see the Sims.' Max, impatient on the stairs again, made the word 'please' last an age. 'I've made the whole family look like us. You've got to look at them all. Your Sim even forgot to shave properly – just like you have today. It's weird.'

It was true, and it made Anna laugh. Alex had had such a succession of early calls, and been so pushed for time generally, he'd grown a little five o'clock shadow – very unusual for him, though Anna was noticing it looked rather sexy and relaxed like the Alex of old. Will always teased him about his neatness, and would have enjoyed the joke.

'He's put our whole family back together again, good as new, with that computer game you gave him. You can design each character to look like anyone you want. It's his way of coping – with everything.' Anna looked at Alex sadly, well aware that the little boy had already absorbed enough shocks in his young life, with their marriage break-up and his grandmother's death, to begin to process the news about his uncle properly. 'He's apparently pleaded with someone called the "Grim Reaper" to bring Will back to life – which isn't usually successful, he tells me, but somehow our Max managed to persuade him.'

Alex shook his head in a mixture of humour and disbelief. He privately thought this sounded perverse, but understood the wish well enough. 'Let's go, Max – show me how it works. Are you going to bring the disks back to Chelsea tonight?'

As Alex stood to put his wine on the mantel over the fireplace, he physically jumped and almost dropped the glass. A postcard had caught his eye. 'The Chartres labyrinth?' He looked at Anna for an explanation.

'Will. He sent it to Max. It was so strange, Alex – it arrived on the Saturday morning after the funeral. It was like a voice from another world. It's postmarked Friday, nineteenth September. Just the day before the accident.' She lifted it off the shelf and handed it to him to read. There was an intersecting group of five squares on the back, like a puzzle.

> *We never know where our path will lead. I'll bring you back here in the spring or at midsummer, and we'll walk this together. It's the best game of hopscotch ever. See you soon, love to Mum – Will x*

'He sent one to me, with just the same pattern on it, but it was from Lucca in Tuscany.' He looked at Anna, thinking. 'Could I borrow this for a few days? I'd like to make a copy.'

Anna's eyes widened with outright amazement. Was Alex being sentimental? Or was it just for him to try to recapture his brother's last days? Both seemed so unlikely. Pleased to do anything, she put it into his hands. 'Will you copy it? Max won't want to lose it.' Alex put the card inside his suit jacket, and climbed the stairs to his son.

They were just bundling out the door with the overnight bag and computer software when Alex's mobile went. Anna placed a hand on Max's head, and resisted the temptation to sigh: she was waiting for the word that the weekend was off, that the hospital wanted Dr Stafford back immediately. Fridays and Saturdays were the busiest time for organ transplantation – which had destroyed their best-laid plans a dozen times.

'Alex Stafford.'

'Alex, it's Siân.' Her voice was high-strung.

'Everything all right?'

She cut short his reply. 'Alex, it's my birthday today.' She stopped for a moment, and Alex started to apologise for forgetting and wished her a happy day in a pleasant voice. She continued quickly: 'No, Alex, listen to me. I've just received some absolutely beautiful roses.' She broke off again, wondering what to say. Alex waited, not knowing what he should say, until she added: 'The card says . . . They're from Will, Alex. The damn things are from Will.'

10

Drizzling weather had given way, at the end of September, to a fortnight of stark October sunshine that suited the new clarity in Lucy's world. She had been warned about the probable depression that would follow her operation; none had occurred. She had understood that she might feel – apart from overall soreness – a lethargy that permeated her physical energies; but this had eluded her. Even the hair growth that commonly developed as a by-product of her drugs hadn't yet become a problem. She was walking around a little within three days, and was home in ten to the Edwardian mansion flat in Battersea she shared with her best friend, the lithe and long-limbed Grace.

They were both young television producers, and worked long hours in strange places. Grace's job was in light entertainment, which suited her permanently cheerful personality – though she was a bigger talent than this suggested, with a top honours degree in history from Durham, wasted for the present. But she was a vital part of Lucy's life, had known her almost since her arrival in London, aged twenty-one, when she had set sail for the wide world from her cocooned existence in Sydney's beach suburbs, fresh from university. Lucy's degree was in sociology, but her work as a producer/director of documentaries had taken her into the realms of anthropology and even the natural world. When a project had sent her first to the backwaters of Peru then on to Colombia, a strange illness had followed her home, and it was the canny Grace who took serious notice and hounded her friend to get it checked.

Initially she had simply felt tired – nothing new, as her work had been arduous physically, high altitudes had affected her, and she was sleep-deprived with long flights and early starts for weeks. She had begun the contract under par, recovering from a long bout of bronchitis – a weakness inherited from her mother that was inclined to disrupt her life during damp winters. When she set off in January she was still a little weak, but not enough to turn down an offer of work that really excited her. Days after her return in March, Lucy noticed a bad swelling over her eye; and then the fever came. Grace, rarely a person to panic, had pushed her into a cab and taken her immediately to the Hospital for Tropical Diseases. She was alive to the possible connection with Lucy's recent location work, and was insistent she see someone quickly. A swift barrage of blood tests ascertained – without any time lost – what her diarrhoea, vomiting, total loss of appetite and dramatic weight loss had already suggested: she had picked up Chagas' Disease. The telltale parasite, transmitted by a small bug, was easy to detect.

She was extraordinarily lucky, they said, though she didn't quite feel this herself. Only a small number of cases were acute enough to react so soon in this way; sometimes there were so few symptoms that diagnosis wasn't possible for years – meaning you would never be entirely free of the disease and it would grow more sinister with time. But fortunately for her, they could start her on the medication immediately, which normally meant a high chance of successful treatment.

Here, however, Lucy's luck ran out. Although she'd responded in reasonable time to the medication that effectively beat the Chagas', the vile disease had taken its toll and left her heart ravaged. It was apparent to everyone who knew her; and her gamine beauty had faded beyond recognition so that she was now a ghost of her former self. She was transferred to the Brompton for its cardiological expertise in early May, but the temporal world seemed lost to her in the days that heard the sentence pronounced: she would almost certainly need a new heart.

What seemed clear was that they might not be able to find her one. She wasn't especially pessimistic about it, but a lifelong habit of reining in her hopes made her, she would have said, a realist. She had never given up on life; she was too pragmatic, and had been a survivor from birth. Her childhood had been emotionally suppressed. She was raised by a well-meaning father who suffered from a strict code of behaviour dictated by his Sicilian-born mother, one that never forgave past hurts. He'd been deeply scarred when his wife had left without explanation. There was another man involved, Lucy knew; her mother had flown to Europe in pursuit of happiness. Husband and daughter were the casualties of this drama, and the crushed man had been unable to express any emotions, or let himself love or trust another being again. The daughter's clear resemblance to her beautiful mother had made the pain unbearable, and he had become a dutiful parent without ever being an affectionate one. The world – and especially Lucy's fiery grandmother – had judged the former Mrs King harshly. But Lucy defended a tiny space in her heart to try to understand some of what she had done one day.

Coming to London had been an attempt to put one foot nearer her mother, though she had no idea where to look for her. Europe was not specific enough; and while she guessed it might be somewhere in Italy, she had no address, no clue really. Her father would answer no questions, and probably knew nothing anyway. So she put the problem away until later, and lived as an orphan. She quite liked it – nothing to explain, no one else to please – but she was aware that she was living in half a world, exercising her cerebral faculties, though not her emotions.

Yet here, in this last hour of light on a chilly October Friday, with a new heart and a new sense of life, she was walking the mile and a half to Chelsea for her weekly check-up with her cardiologist, full of both hope and happiness, not at all tired. It was impossible to explain how she felt to others. She had never seen anything like the world she now inhabited. Her visions and responses to it – even her wild, vivid dreams – were excited and passionate. Trees, losing their leaves, seemed more beautiful to her than they had been in her own sickly springtime, when they were in blossom. Dog walkers had once irritated her, as she watched them turn a blind eye to their four-legged charges fouling the parks, but now they smiled and made real eye contact as they passed her; and school children, walking in a file to their buses, seemed full of vitality and laughter instead of smart remarks and clandestine cigarettes. She shared their energy – and she felt surprisingly well.

When Lucy entered the building, the receptionist smiled at her with recognition: 'Hello there, nice to see you.'

'Nice to be visiting and not practically living either here or at Harefield.' Lucy returned the smile with sincerity.

She took her time on the stairs, but wasn't at all breathless when she went into Mr Denham's rooms. They exchanged pleasantries while he listened to her heart and took her blood pressure; then he waved her into a chair with a satisfied grin.

'The last biopsy is just what we want, Lucy. No signs of rejection whatsoever. The drugs are obviously doing their work, and everything else is looking pretty good. It's still early days, but your incisions are starting to heal – you must be eating your B-rich foods, fish and so on. Your immunologist seems to have the balance of your medication just right. I can see how you look, but how do you feel?'

The exercise had given Lucy a little glow, and she was almost flirtatious in her reply. 'As good as I must be looking then. Better than fine. I'm far less dependent on Grace now. No problems with the drugs – no need for any electrolysis yet! – nothing. It's autumn and I haven't even had a sore throat.'

Courtney laughed heartily. 'Very good. I wish you'd go

and lecture some of my other patients about their attitude. Are you sleeping well?'

She nodded.

'No depression to speak of, no feeling of a loss of adrenalin?' Courtney looked mildly surprised.

Lucy shook her head firmly. 'No. Food is fine, and I'm cooking again. I have my separate bread board, which amuses Grace but she respects the reasons. Kitchen is dowsed in anti-bacterial everything. Dietician says she's happy with me. I get on the exercise bike for a few extra minutes every day. I can do quite a bit of walking now – I walked here today across the river – it's so much more interesting than hours on the treadmill. Although, I'm glad I didn't have to get into Harefield.'

She looked to see if he would give her a cautionary glare; but in common with many surgeons who spent hours on their feet, Mr Denham was physically ultra-fit himself; she knew of his reputation for being the best runner representing the hospital in the London Marathon, and that he played tennis on a rota with the medical staff. He obviously approved of her own new dedication to getting stronger, so she continued: 'Sleep is no problem at all – I can still feel my heart beating fast, even when I'm resting.'

'Mm-hm. You remember we talked about this? Your new heart hasn't yet got the nerve connections that would ordinarily help it to reflect changes in your activity, so it will beat significantly faster than the old one. It simply doesn't respond so promptly to any increase or decrease in physical stress. That reconnection will take quite some time to come back.'

'I remember you and Mr Azziz explained that – it's not worrying me. In fact I think it disguises how I'm feeling to other people, which can be useful.'

'Yes, you'll make a good poker player for a while. Just remember you can't feel chest pain in the normal way yet either, which is why we all have to keep such a close eye on you. But this is excellent, really. Is nothing concerning you then, Lucy?'

'No . . .' Lucy's answer was slightly qualified. Courtney Denham waited. 'Physically I feel almost unnaturally well, just so much better than before the transplant.'

'But emotionally?' he prompted her. He didn't know too much about her personal life, though he didn't think she had a serious boyfriend. Maybe there was some other problem at home. Or if she were seeing someone, the strain of aftercare would be a bit of a burden to anybody unprepared or unwilling. You had to be scrupulous with your cleanliness while your immune system was so heavily suppressed – and so did anyone in your love life. Intimacy was often frustrating even for long-time couples, and almost impossible unless your partner was unselfish.

A thought suddenly occurred to him. 'Are you thinking of travelling to Australia, Lucy, to see your family?' He looked at her for a moment, her emotions not in the least transparent. But it was entirely probable that she might want to go to them after such a knife-edge experience. It was a talking point to each of her doctors that her family hadn't come to see her here, in the UK. 'Our general rule about travel is that it's not really recommended to go abroad for the first few months after your transplant. We'll monitor you very closely, of course, and if you continue with this kind of progress, and you're keen to see your parents, I'm sure we would approve that some time after the New Year.'

She took her time, and looked at him intently, wondering what he would make of what she was about to say. 'No, I don't have any wish to go away, Mr Denham. It's more that the world I am in now, right here, is suddenly a totally different one.' She paused, aware she had his complete attention. 'My dreams are wild, really vivid. My taste in food has changed a bit. And . . . my orientation feels different.'

'Dreams, tastes – yes, I can see that. You've been through a lot. Taste might be your head dictating what you should be eating? The drugs normally make you feel hungrier, especially the prednisolone. You should talk to Dr Stafford about it.' Lucy wasn't a bit convinced by this, but let it go for the moment. 'I'm not sure I know what you mean by your orientation.'

'Mr Denham, I've always been right-handed. But now, I automatically pick up a pen with my left hand. And a soup spoon. And I feel like my left is stronger.'

'I haven't heard of this before. But it doesn't really worry me. Your heart is a pump, and we haven't interfered with your brain, which is what determines which hand you use. Possibly it's a response to the drip, a tentative feeling in your right hand, even a soreness after the operation – although that would normally occur on the left side, strangely enough. Have you had more blood drawn from the right arm? Anyway, let's see if it lasts – not that it's important at all.' He made a note on her chart. 'Anything else?'

'The food. I've been a vegetarian for around ten years. Now I want to eat some meat again.'

'Well, I approve. It's your instinct for strength, Lucy; and possibly the medication too. But try to limit how much red meat you eat, for the sake of your new heart. Fish and chicken will score high points with your dietician, though. Let's check that out later too.' He made a second note.

'And the dreams. I've been having really intense dreams, strange images, and even dislocated sounds . . .' She knew she couldn't make him fully understand.

'Lucy, your life was close to the edge. First the Chagas', then the harsh treatments, with strong drugs. Ultimately a transplant – a long, demanding operation. And then post-surgery. I would expect your mind to take some strange twists for a while.' He looked at her and saw she was not reassured by this. 'But let's see about getting you to a psychologist, and you can go into this in depth. These drugs can have some very unpleasant side effects. I'm sure you've been told all about the emotional highs and lows that come with some of the medicines. I'll set an appointment up and get someone to call you from the hospital within a day or two, but I'll mention it to Dr Stafford too – he's the expert in this department. He might want to suggest a new balance of medication.' He looked at her with kindness, but she felt as though she was being dismissed as an irrational female. She stopped trying to explain and smiled her thanks, bringing the appointment to an end.

He's made some notes about it, she thought: but not nearly as many as I have. If I do see a psychologist, I've got a lot of very strange things to say.

*

Alex and Max pulled up outside the flat he'd bought in Royal Avenue just over two years ago, when his divorce from Anna was finalised. It was ideally close to one of his bases. Set on the east side of the small gravel-covered square and cordoned off from traffic at the Kings Road end, it was a quiet retreat. Comprised of the bottom two floors of an early Victorian house – one of which he had only recently managed to acquire with money left him by his mother – it included a bijou garden with access from both the basement and the ground floors.

Max took his father's hand as they crossed the road together, to find a figure already waiting for them on the steps in the pink London twilight.

'You did say tonight?' Simon looked a bit apologetic about the intrusion. He high-fived Max, whom he knew quite well from days out with his uncle.

'Sorry, Simon, yes, absolutely. I was expecting you. Something rather strange held me up. Come inside.' Alex turned the key to the main door, then another to his own private internal entrance, and turned to his son. 'You can put your stuff away properly now, Max. I think it's all clear down there again.' He hadn't wanted Max to stay in his own room until Will's things were finally out of the space. He knew it would upset him, so the last few stays had seen Alex surrender most of his own bed to the boy. Now it was his plan to enlist Simon's aid and finish the job tonight, getting the last of the boxes out of his small hallway. He knew that, as Will's closest friend, he was pleased to have been asked to help, and to take a few things discreetly from among Will's possessions. 'Then I'll cook us all some dinner.'

'You've never learned to cook quite as well as Uncle Will, Daddy.' Max looked up sadly at his father, who didn't take offence.

'You mean, I don't give in so often to cooking you sausage and chips like Uncle Will would!' He smiled ruefully at his son.

Max nodded, and hitched the rucksack on to his shoulder to take to his room. He noticed his uncle's almost new laptop in the corner beside the coffee table. 'Uncle Will's Power-Book is still here. Do you think I could use it to run my Sims? The graphics are so much better on Mac than on a PC.'

'I think that would be all right. Although I'm not sure it will run on the Mac system, will it? But try, by all means.' He leaned towards his son, and said with an attempt at firmness: 'Now, please put your things away.'

While Max trudged down the stairs to his room on the street side of the basement, Alex shed his tie and unbuttoned his collar, then started cutting up some chicken pieces. He filled Simon in on the bizarre phone call from his brother's ex-girlfriend. It had taken some persuasion on all of their parts, but the florist – who had been about to leave for the day – had finally revealed the order number, which had subsequently been traced. They learned that Will had ordered the flowers in Chartres, on nineteenth September, at thirteen fifty GMT, so a little before three p.m. in France. What inspired him to do it then – for a date a month hence – was hard to know. Will was simply never that organised.

'It's not that Will couldn't be romantic, you know, Alex. It's entirely in keeping with his spontaneous nature.' Simon, in a clearly subdued voice, was trying to persuade himself that it wasn't extraordinary.

'It's not exactly spontaneous, though, to send flowers for a month down the line. And they'd absolutely broken up, Simon. Will told me it was irrevocable. His physical attraction to Siân was like an addictive drug, I know, but he explained there was no heart there any more, and there never had been that much intellectual meeting ground. I think Siân's a smart girl, actually, but her mind isn't trained in the same way as his, and their interests were simply different.'

Simon was in a strange mood, nodding at Alex. It tallied with what Will had told him too, over a few beers too many. 'He said to me that she spent three times as much money as he did, never read any books, didn't even want to go for a walk with him. But, maybe he had started missing her, thinking of reconciliation?'

'Of course, that's what she's thinking; and it's thrown her into a spin. But I'm certain it's not so. He always said Siân was like a beautiful, spoiled child. Used to getting her own way, used to the magnetic effect she had on men, and completely incapable of thinking deeply about anything that didn't concern herself. Which might be a bit harsh; but her lack of awareness for the rest of life drove him to despair sometimes, and their values were seemingly worlds apart. She loved pretty things, wanted a wardrobe of Chanel and Prada – which you could hardly blame her for, as it was part of her job – whereas he always said he'd like to work for an international aid agency for a year or so.'

An onion hissed as Alex tossed it into the pan. 'When she pressured him for marriage after Mum died, Will realised he'd let things drift for just too long – that he really couldn't marry Siân, could never be what he felt she needed; and that that was unfair to her, frankly. He had to fight the physical magnetism, which I guess was hard, because she knew what power she had over him – and how to use it.' Alex couldn't help being even-handed about them. 'And I think that worked both ways. Poor Siân – it's such a thing to survive. Was it her fault to have loved someone for three years who hadn't quite worked out himself where he was heading? And let's be fair: Will liked his creature comforts too.' He glanced at an almost empty bottle of expensive cognac that Will had opened, and had been steadily working his way through. Alex understood that, although his brother knew the break was the right thing to do in every way, it had hurt them both – not just Siân.

Simon had been shuffling lightly through a huge collection of books Alex had put aside in a box for him, and was just finishing taping it up. He carried them through to the hall where some other bits and belongings were grouped, and returned to help Max, who had just plugged the gleaming white Apple into a power socket. He smiled to himself about what Alex was saying. Yes, Will liked a few expensive toys as well. Not just a bike, but the Ducati. Not any old laptop, but the most state of the art iBook. Even his upright piano at the flat he'd shared with Siân was a Bechstein. He knew nothing except quality – would rather have nothing than something makeshift. His heart was in the right place, and his head was level, but he liked a few pretty things too.

'What was on the card?' he swung back to Alex. 'With the roses.'

Alex passed Simon and Max each a drink of a different colour. He took a piece of paper from his jacket. '"Swift-footed, thorn-pricked, blood-red, love-stained, heart-rent: now pure-white. *Bonne anniversaire. Toujours*, William." Siân was inconsolable.' He looked over at his son and his brother's friend, united in a task to boot the Apple. 'They were white roses. Did I say that?'

Simon shook his head. 'Bloody Will and his anagrammatic mind. But you're right. White roses are chaste love, not passion. Big difference. And it was for her birthday, so he was trying to tell her perhaps that he didn't hate her and would always love her in his way.'

'He still loved Siân.' Max looked up from the screen in front of him, and said this in an absolutely matter-of-fact way.

His father smiled at him. 'Yes, in a new way, I think. But there is a mystery,' he told them both. 'What was going on in Will's lost hours, between visiting the Cathedral, and getting on that ferry? His mind was engaged in something. And in his second-to-last message on my mobile he said he had something extraordinary to tell me. I've been wondering about that.'

Max had been trying to get the computer to talk to him, but he and Simon were unable to log in. The password prompt had flashed: *The only woman I can handle* . . . 'What was Uncle Will's password, Daddy? Who was the only woman he could handle? It's not "Siân"; and not Grandma either. We've tried both of those.'

Alex shrugged casually. 'What did he call the bike?' he suggested.

'Claudia.' Max and Simon returned in unison, and tried that.

'*Touché*, Alex.' Simon couldn't believe it was that easy, and he suddenly found himself looking at Will's familiar wallpaper of a favourite Joshua Reynolds painting, of Cleopatra dissolving a pearl in a glass of wine. It made him feel strangely close to him again right now, and he looked at Alex with a flash of inspiration. 'Whatever he was thinking, he might well have sent it to his own email address. He was definitely sending ideas and documents back from Rome – he told me that.'

'Simon, that's so simple and clever. Can you log on to his server?' Max looked disappointed about the delay. 'Let's quickly check the mail box, Max, then have our supper, and straight afterwards you can get back to your game. It'll be ready in about ten minutes anyway.'

'And I think your dad's right that the PC game won't boot on this, Max.' Simon tried to console him. 'It's a completely different system.'

Max looked slightly sulky as he sidled over to his father's desk-top in the other half of the large ground-floor reception room, which had the open-plan kitchen in the middle. He loaded his software and began playing there. Alex smiled resignedly, knowing the child's wish to use the Apple was about proximity to Will, and nothing to do with the graphics. He walked to his son and kissed the top of his head; then he picked up his glass to go and join Simon at Will's iBook. He realised Simon's insight was exactly right –

that all of Will's photos, thoughts, everything would be there. His Apple had been part of his working life – he'd enhanced his pictures on it before sending them off, edited them, stored everything. He wondered why he hadn't thought to look at it before.

'Ffff . . . frig!' Simon changed his first choice of word, remembering Max. "Claudia" doesn't open the email.' He looked deflated. 'And before you ask, I've tried the other obvious things. Your house name in the country. His first girlfriend.' Alex inflected surprise at him. 'Short of exhausting the *Oxford Dictionary*, I can't think what else to try. Anyway, Will was a bit dyslexic, wasn't he? His spelling was creative but erratic.'

Alex nodded. They might never know what he used, without a prompt.

He walked back to the hob and took the pasta off, tossing it with the chicken. 'Come and eat, Max.'

'Wait, Daddy. I've got to get them some more money, and then I can put it on pause.'

'What do you mean, more money?'

'It's a cheat.' He grinned broadly at his father. 'You can do this cool thing and the characters get more money to play with.' Alex walked over to see, and to extricate his son while the food was still hot. 'You just go, "Rosebud" and then type in some symbols, and the more times you do it, the more money they get. It's a gamer's trick. Uncle Will showed me how.'

Alex crossed the space back to Simon, who'd heard it too. '*Citizen Kane*. It's the name on the sled, isn't it, at the end? Will's seminal film.' But Simon was right up with him, typing it in. He was suddenly connected.

The pasta was cooling, but Alex's eyes were riveted by an email in the outbox addressed to him, awaiting editing and yet to be sent – which explained why it had never come to him. Simon's eyes consulted him, and he opened the file as Alex nodded permission. It was Simon who read aloud the first few words: '"In the Tree of Life, it is Kether which represents the Source. This is the Sun behind the Sun, the Ultimate Light, the reservoir of consciousness for all initiated alchemists. This Source can be tapped into, whenever there are Light Meetings – which are beyond both time and space. They take place in the imagination of the true 'Adept', under the protection of the Rose. At these Light Meetings all Adepts can connect with not only the Source, but all other members of their fellowship throughout the world, not excepting the past masters and early alchemists. Every red-rose king must join with his white-rose queen, to effect change not only in themselves but in those gathered nearest to them. And it is in this way that the underground river of wisdom flows without a break, from ancient times".'

The words simply broke off, but they had a poetic impact on both the men. The pasta was forgotten as the one looked to the other for enlightenment; but Alex knew no more than Simon. Perched lightly above his brother's close friend, he was shaking his head to signify that he hadn't the least idea what Will was thinking of. And then suddenly, breaking into the hush, Simon noticed a flashing icon at the bottom of the screen.

'Alex, someone's trying to hack into us. It's as if they've been waiting for us to go on-line . . .' His voice trailed off, and he and Alex stared at the alert together. The screen was dissolving through several colours, and the anti-Spyware had produced a map showing hackers were attacking from somewhere right here in the UK. The screen went into a loop, with a green wheel revolving in the centre, then settling into a square.

S A T O R
A R E P O
T E N E T
O P E R A
R O T A S

11

Lucy's stress levels were rising; not good for her heart. But what help was there for it? She had to be at Cadogan Pier at five o'clock. It was already four-thirty, and she was still at home with her hair unfinished, shoes undecided.

'Get it together, girl,' she told herself firmly. 'This time it's a proper date with Alex Stafford. Why should that worry you?'

It had been eleven days ago, first thing on a Monday morning: the phone call that followed the appointment with Mr Denham. He had quite casually invited her out for an express lunch, ostensibly to have an informal chat about her problems settling with the medication, but beyond a few minutes spent on steroids and mood swings, they hadn't talked shop at all. In many ways this lunch had been her first venture back into the real world. It was the 'please call me Alex' lunch; and she felt it crossed the line, surely, between work and a touch of play? She thought it a success. He'd sat, smiled, listened attentively to her, revealed nothing about himself. But it was a sociable starting point.

She'd thought he had felt a little interest in her, possibly, from the very beginning; but it was hard to be certain. Alex was the kind of doctor who scored excellence in his bedside manner, but he was impossible to read personally. She noticed that, if anything, he said less to her than to others – seemed a fraction shyer, or perhaps hesitant, which she read as mild attraction. But then, this might be precisely because she had no obvious boyfriend who came to visit, nor family – just Grace and a string of joking colleagues, half of them gay. Perhaps he wanted to show that he was *not* being over-friendly – a warning not to misinterpret his excellent care of her as his patient, and to define the limits of their professional relationship. That made most sense, in fact. Until she considered those flowers he'd brought her after her operation. So the barometer swung the other way, and she considered afresh whether she'd imagined more in his looks than there was to find.

Then the impasse broke with the invitation, at half-past nine on Monday, 20 October: 'Lucy, Courtney Denham asked me to have a word with you about your medicine, which gives me the perfect excuse to ask you if you'd like a bite of lunch? I don't have a lot of time, I'm afraid, but we could find some place away from the hospital where we can rely on the kitchen's standards of hygiene? I know a place close by that's perfect.' His manner was so absurdly easy, and she had surprised herself how quickly she'd accepted, how pleased she was to be asked. Lucy so rarely risked getting too involved with anyone: she was the girl of countless friends across the globe, and several male admirers – but the lover of not a one of them. Affairs were kept as flings, emotions always held at bay. As soon as anything looked serious, she'd run a mile. But then, he was her doctor, so she satisfied herself quickly that involvement was impossible and a lunch date solidly safe.

So the quick bite was taken in the lovely garden at Dan's Restaurant in Sydney Street, five minutes from the Brompton, on a perfect October, sunshine day: two simple courses with mineral water. And, she recalled, the sound of her own voice bubbling through some satirical vignettes about her life and her experiences in South America, which seemed to keep him entertained. Highly unusual for her to open up, but she'd been witty, she knew.

He'd politely dropped her back to her own front door, conversation flowing gently all the way. Then: nothing. Days passed. She kept an ear for the phone, but it was irritatingly silent. She recognised he had to observe a professional distance between them: he was still one of her physicians. He had less to do for her now, other than monitor her antibiotics and watch for rejection, but it was still a professional bond, with parameters, and it came with a reality check. It made sense to forget him.

But she couldn't. She consulted Grace. Thinking back, she revised her dismissive description of a working lunch and told her friend they had enjoyed a lively conversation for an hour, and a lot of relaxed laughter; though Alex had told her nothing personal about himself, she admitted. Grace cautioned her: this didn't bode well to her. Usually the woman listened while the man strutted his stuff. And yes, it was different, Lucy agreed, but she had an inkling that was just what made this man attractive. She was intrigued, and it didn't help that he was physically so appealing, tantalisingly divorced with a young son. Far too much trouble, she decided. As soon as she could return to work, she'd forget him in a day, she contented herself.

And then suddenly there was Alex, after nine days of silence, inviting her quite openly into a situation that involved his colleagues. It was the hospitals' Halloween Party. Apart from a get-together for the staff of both sister hospitals, it was also a fund raiser. He had cautioned her not to expect the Chelsea Arts Ball. Only staff, students and friends would get a ticket, but it did raise money for the hospitals, and if she could bring her best sense of humour – a must, apparently – it was a performance he had to attend, and he would enjoy it much more if she could join him.

'I promise to look after you properly,' he'd said. 'These kind of do's can get a little exuberant when the crowd becomes overrefreshed, as Amel reminded me when I mentioned I'd like to invite you.'

Concerned not to overtax the fledgeling's health, he'd assured her it was for a couple of hours only – a pleasure boat going up the Thames, the duration limited by tide, and time of hire. He'd apologised that she'd have to meet him there as he would be running straight from work at Harefield that day; but he would see her home after a quiet supper – if she wasn't too tired. 'Oh . . . it's a themed party – did I say that? "The Spirits of the Dead from the Past". You'll need some kind of costume, if you can manage it.'

Lucy had put down the phone almost wordlessly –

couldn't find a single throwaway line. In two days? Nor would he reveal what he was wearing, and she was anxious not to clash unintentionally with him. So with Grace's help, she had settled on Ariadne – she with the threads, and the thing for a clever prince. Grace mischievously thought it was appropriate. She suggested a classical costume could be draped to disguise the worst of her scars, but still show off her friend's best physical attributes – her beautiful dark Greco-Roman hair and face, long neck and petite, feminine body.

'Isn't that the whole idea?' Grace had pointed out drily.

Now, in something of a panic dictated by the clock, she adjusted her final pins and pearled clips: two tendrils of black hair curled either side of her face, the rest pulled up in a winding plait over her head, emphasising her lovely neck and shoulders. The divided cream silk of the classical costume, which she had thrown together with considerable artistry in record time, hinted discreetly at her breasts. She was a talented seamstress. The silk jersey flowed over her reflection, giving a liquid elegance to the apparition, and Grace pronounced it magical. In spite of the need for haste, Lucy had sewn parts of herself into the dress, finishing it with baroque pearls. This was not only for Alex, but for something she could hardly express. Yet now that the 'proper date' was on her, she felt strangely inert, regarding her own face in the mirror.

'Wear the Jimmy Choos, Lucy,' Grace woke her abruptly from the spell. 'Since your doctor is a little over six feet tall, they'll lend you the height you need, you'll look like a movie star, and you can still *walk* in them.' Her friend took control, and reassured Lucy's nervous visage that she looked quite beautiful: 'But get a leg on, or there is no slipper on earth that can save Cinderella from utterly missing the whole occasion.'

Lucy glanced at her watch with horror, grabbed her wrap and bag, and almost sprinted down the stairs out into Prince of Wales Drive. She thought of her racing heart and slowed down just a touch – thinking she'd give the doctors an immediate crisis instead of a night off. She hoped a taxi would somehow just appear or she'd be chronically late.

Her wishes were horses, and a taxi – white to match her outfit – made a neat U-turn on Chelsea Embankment and dropped her at the pier head. She hesitated on the pavement. At the gate stood the Grim Reaper. The costume was alarmingly vivid in detail; it looked almost as if its wearer had also come straight from work – calling the dead in another world. She felt a curious sense of dread.

Lucy jumped as a rich voice suddenly spoke behind her: 'Who is this goddess?' She turned to find a classic Venetian *Carnevale* figure – with an exquisite mask of gold leaf rising to a crown, wrought from lacquered music paper, borne on a stick. She was genuinely surprised when it dropped to reveal a smiling Alex. He looked breathtaking, almost Byronic, which she thought utterly out of character. His hair had grown a shade longer and very slightly curlier, and he was sporting a hint of stubble. She liked it: it really suited him, and it was a new person for her to become acquainted with, a new facet of his character. Was this the immaculate Alex off duty; or was it only affected to enhance his role for the evening?

He had been concentrating on the vision of Lucy, while she made these mental adjustments to his changed physiognomy. He took his time; then, without comment besides a deep, appreciative smile, he closed his hand over hers, and led her towards the Grim Reaper.

'Tickets for the boat ride to Hades, quickly please, Dr Stafford . . . and Goddess. We're about to sail, and half of them on board are ripped already.' The cloaked figure glanced at the tickets. 'You'll find a band in the saloon on the right, and drinks in the bar to the left, or under the canopy, outside on the forward deck, up the stairs through the bar. Enjoy your evening.'

Lucy was amused by Death's chirpy informativeness, but as they stepped off the gangway on to the boat, two masked figures dressed as spirits sprang at them, blocking their progress.

'A thousand pardons, good souls, but you must pay the ferryman for this voyage. To the realms of the dead.' The man held out a hand.

Alex pulled a ten-pound note from his pocket and proffered it to the spirit. His female companion took the note, holding it between her long white fingers. She rubbed the fingers of the other hand over it, blew magically, and it disappeared. She bowed with a grand gesture.

'Perhaps a Troilus for this Cressida, good doctor?' she begged.

Alex reached into his pocket again, and this time took out a five-pound note. 'More an Elizabeth Fry for your Charles Darwin.' He grinned as they moved forward.

'True, sir, but while we beggars do have to move with the

times, there's something lost in the translation, don't you agree?' Alex laughed. 'It is for a good cause, as you know. So I thank you, good sir.'

'Left to drink, right to dance?' Alex offered Lucy the choice as they hovered in the passageway between the halls.

'Let's take a peek.'

She pulled open the main door. The wall of noise escaped for a moment, and the room looked like a reproduction of Dante's *Inferno*. Through a haze of artificial smoke, costumed figures of every age and description gyrated. Arms and legs waved in a kind of frieze. Real skeletons stood on either side of the door. The participants seemed to be waving body parts over their heads as the whole vision throbbed to some primordial beat. Lucy had a distinct impression that the props were not from any theatrical hire place, but she couldn't hear enough of her own voice to ask Alex. She'd heard about the students' jokes and the housemen's macabre humour on these occasions: she'd leave it there.

Alex – with mock horror – firmly closed the door to the dance hall, sealing in most of the noise. 'Left to drinks!' They nodded agreement, turned to the other door and entered the bar.

The room was packed with costumed characters, with a bar set up at one end. Its attendants were a wild-haired Dr Frankenstein and a collection of his followers. The back of the bar was set out like the inside of an anatomy lab. There were rows of bell jars, mixed with chemical retorts, coloured flasks, and other apparatus that exhibited specimens of brains, livers, kidneys, hands, feet, all preserved in formalin.

'Damien Hirst would be right at home here,' Lucy remarked as they crushed forwards.

'Too close to the bone, do you think?' Alex was confident Lucy's ironic humour could go the distance; but it was certainly not for the faint-hearted.

'Hello, Dr Stafford.' Frankenstein spoke. 'Maybe you and your guest would be happier upstairs? I just saw the honourable Azziz go up, talking to an administrator, ten minutes ago. Take the stair over there.' He gesticulated with his right elbow as he opened two beer bottles with one hand, then dextrously poured all four bottles that he was holding in both hands into four glasses. 'Six pounds, please.' He addressed Queen Elizabeth with flaming red hair, as she dug in her purse.

'Bloody uncomfortable, this corset, i'n it,' the queen complained to Alex in a strong South London accent, as she paid and swept the glasses from the bar in both of her hands, ploughing back through the crowd.

'I wouldn't know,' Dr Frankenstein commented to no one in particular; but he made eye contact with Alex, whose face crumpled into laughter. Frankenstein rendered up a half-bottle of champagne for the two of them and some fresh orange juice, and waved them up. As he had no free hand, Lucy hooked hers securely behind Alex's upper arm and they pushed across the bar floor, up to the fresh evening air.

The boat was already progressing up the river in the dusk as they emerged at the top into what appeared to be, at first glance, a gathering of the medical aristocracy of London and their friends, circa 1750. The effect on Lucy was almost surreal. After a moment she recognised some of the characters before her from endless trips to one hospital or the other. There were about fifty people standing or sitting. Three fresh-complexioned nurses, in long flowing dresses, giggled at Dr Stafford. The Three Graces, Lucy mused. Then they took in Lucy's appearance behind him, and turned away, resigned, mingling with a group of young housemen. The registrars made small talk with the younger female doctors, and the wives watched one or two of the housemen. The senior staff gravitated towards the administrative heads and board members. The whole scene had a kind of unnatural naturalness about it; a costumed period quadrille.

Odd. No Jane Cook. Lucy could see she was missing. She whispered something to Alex. 'Minding the shop,' he explained. 'Otherwise she'd be here. She's loyal to the hospital first and last, but she'll be sorry not to be able to fraternise with Amel off duty. He's her hero.'

'Mine too. We all need them, you know.'

Outdoor heaters warmed an area of tables and chairs, which was covered with an awning and surrounded with clear plastic screens keeping the heat in while affording a panoramic view of the passing river. The macabre decorations in their most obscene forms seemed to have failed to climb the stairs. Amel, absurdly dressed as Scott of the Antarctic, was standing at the edge of the deck deep in conversation with two women – a tall, willowy, dark one, and a curvaceous but equally eye-catching blonde. Alex and Lucy edged their way across, and Amel greeted them warmly.

'The Great Alexander. Strange you didn't wear something Macedonian. I am so glad you have come amongst us. And your radiant companion, Lucy. How lovely you are. I am not at all surprised, but entirely enchanted.' He took her delicate hand in both of his, looked at her properly, and she felt the sincerity of his compliment. 'Please, say hello. These beautiful ladies are also eminent doctors – Zarina Anwar and Angelica LeRoy, leading surgeons both – though we don't often let them out of Harefield! They assisted Mr Denham and me in your transplant. Ladies, six weeks on and in a form more collected than you first met with, may I now present Lucy King, television documentary maker.'

Lucy's eyes widened in awe at the two women before her – the one dark, cool and refined, with immaculate nails; the other blonde, smiling and vivacious.

'Lucy, you seem surprised? Good as I may be, I could never concentrate alone for so long – it was almost eight hours with you – so I allow my alter egos to take over at certain specified moments and do some little things that they do better than I. Angelica executes the neatest little sutures.'

Angelica, who looked like a slightly older, blonde version of Scarlett O'Hara, held out her hand. She noticed Lucy was admiring her lavish outfit. 'Do you like the dress? I must say, I just love this period. This kind of thing reminds me so much of home.'

'Home?'

'Why, yes, you know, Mardi Gras. New Orleans is my family home.' Lucy was enchanted by the honeyed voice that made the place of her birth into one elongated syllable. 'I have just arrived on a year's exchange to have the opportunity to work with Mr Azziz. One of the great artists in this field. He seems to bring something more, something "other" to his work, which made me want to come see. Don't you think so, Mr Stafford? Oops! Sorry, Dr Stafford?'

Eavesdropping on their conversation from a neighbouring group was the Chief Administrator – clearly butter in Angelica's hands – who now came gallantly to her rescue. 'Don't worry, Angelica. Only the Royal College of Surgeons can understand the mysteries of the "Misters" as opposed to the "Doctors". I still get it wrong.'

Alex laughed and nodded his agreement. He couldn't explain it to his friends, who thought it must be proper to address him as 'Mister' by now, never mind to a baffled American colleague. 'Please, just "Alex", Angelica. But to answer your question, yes, I really do think Allah is pleased when Amel puts on his surgical gown and goes into battle in the theatre.'

Lucy couldn't gauge Alex's tone, but Amel smiled broadly at him. 'Mock me not, young Stafford. I try not to forget that you are one of the People of the Book – though there are those who forget this decree for respect in the world today. Of course, I haven't decided whether to believe that you are really an unbeliever yet, so I will reserve this position and accord you respect – which I do, willingly. You have earned it, in any case. In every way.'

He then turned with the whole force of his attention to Lucy again. 'My dear Lucy, how lovely it really is for us to see you here as one of us tonight, and looking so healthy. Let me take your shawl. You won't need it just yet: it's as warm as a summer evening, with the heaters on. At least for now.'

'Thank you.'

Lucy understood intuitively that Amel was trying to help

her dissolve the divide between patient and doctor; but she responded in a somewhat subdued manner; she shed her wrap and gave it to her surgeon, who draped it on a chair. Alex had quickly been drawn into a conversation with the six-foot-tall Zarina, as though they had picked up on something serious from earlier in the day, but he tugged Lucy gently towards them to try to include her. She appreciated the gesture, and listened and smiled for some time, putting in answers to questions she was prompted with; she felt surprisingly shy, though, and apart from the group. She observed the subtle interplay of relationships that passed between all of these people, and felt out of her depth. Their lives existed in a kind of rarefied bubble, she thought, which displayed the entire panoply of human behaviour. Perhaps not that different from her TV world, but with a different cast. Would she ever get back to work? The thought trailed across her mind, while she was at sea with a new social dynamic here. Well, at least she was still on the planet, thanks to this gathering.

'Lucy.' She heard her name. 'Lucy, do you know the river?' It was Courtney Denham, with his melodic Trinidadian accent. He was standing close by with his wife, listening to the exchanges, observing her insecurity. He looked arresting as Othello.

'Hello.' She was relieved for his attention, and slipped away from Alex for a moment. 'No, not very well.' She wasn't sure what to call him off duty. She still saw him professionally on a weekly basis. 'But I should. I've lived here long enough. Isn't this where the Oxford and Cambridge Boat Race takes place?'

'Not bad for a colonial. Yes, from the bridge we passed under a while ago at Hammersmith, past the Eyot at Chiswick up there. Catherine, my wife.' He broke off and introduced his Desdemona, who was a full-figured and sexy woman as tall as her husband. She smiled back with energy at Lucy.

'Courtney has mentioned you to me, Lucy.'

'We live just behind those trees, off Castelnau, in Barnes,' her doctor continued. 'Then we will come on to Mortlake shortly.'

They all three chattered without formality. If Lucy was concerned that she might have crossed the professional line with them, she found she needn't have worried. She followed Courtney's finger picking out the landscape for some time, until his commentary was interrupted when the boat lurched unexpectedly. Everyone steadied themselves, and a champagne bucket and glasses collapsed on to the deck. The boat swung sharply towards the shoreline, the prow dipping as the engines were thrust into reverse for a second. The klaxon sounded three warning blasts, which made Lucy jump and the entire assembly turn to see the cause of the disturbance as they regained their balance. The sight from the upper deck caused a blanket of silence to descend over the revellers. A barge appeared from under the bows of their boat. It was one of the most beautiful vessels Lucy had seen, perfect in every detail, sleek, in red and gold. It elicited sighs and expressions of wonder from the Three Graces.

Even in amber-streaked light, Lucy could see its occupants with unusual clarity. Two rows of trumpeters lined the rails of the boat below them; the oarsmen pulled hard to bring the barge clear of the wake made by the hired boat, as it took evasive action. A gold-trimmed canopy sheltered a small gathering of people dressed as noblemen. One, resplendent above the others, stood out from the cluster; and beside him was a man in a dark robe with a chain of office.

A film scene, her professional eye told her; but the detail was fantastic. The cost must have been almost beyond the reach of even an expensive Hollywood production. What was this barge doing here on the Thames at Halloween? Perhaps the Italian ambassador was having a Venetian Carnival of his own. Or young celebrities? No one she recognised. There it was, on the river, watched by maybe two hundred people, blissfully unaware of the mayhem it was causing by cutting a swathe through the waters under the other craft. Mind you, most of the hospital staff were fast becoming so inebriated they wouldn't remember what day of the week it was in the morning. All these hangovers in a good cause – she could hear Alex jesting about it, and giggled: then she shuddered suddenly. What *was* she looking at?

The dance lounge doors now opened below, as some of the dancers rushed to see what was happening from the upper decks. The noise levels escalated a hundredfold, at least in Lucy's mind. Cutting clearly above everything else was the clarion blast of trumpets. A trumpet fanfare. She could hear it clearly across the modest distance between the two boats.

'What a Halloween outing,' remarked a camp South African voice to her right.

'It can't be that, it looks too slick. So cinematic,' responded his partner.

'An opera, darling. There's no Cecil B. alongside. Wish that was me on there. Those divine costumes. And just dwell on that gorgeous vision with the cloak over his shoulder. Risqué as Lord Byron. Bet he goes off with a bang!'

'Well, they've upstaged us,' was the rejoinder.

'Let's get some canapés. Ooh, isn't your dress gorgeous, sweetie.' The first voice drooled at Lucy, as they flounced off.

Lucy hadn't taken in their remarks, nor noticed that Alex had moved just behind her. Her mind and her entire being were focused on the group on the barge. They, in their turn, stared back – right at her, she thought – their eyes and faces riveted on Lucy and the boat. A dark, velvet-robed man held Lucy's gaze magnetically. They were like parted friends. For an eternity of seconds they locked together, unable to free themselves.

He was heavily accented when he spoke, as the magnificent barge came almost abreast of the gunwales of her boat. She could smell an exotic mix: roses, and limes, as well as cats and drains and dinners. Bizarre. She heard the words toll from him like a rounded bell: '*Sator Arepo Tenet Opera Rotas*.'

He pronounced them in her mind as clearly as if he was standing beside her. The two vessels swung past each other and on at speed, sweeping through the uneven water levels that momentarily brought the Scylla to the Thames. There was a sucking, eddying current between the two boats; then they were parted by the moving tide. The barge straightened and headed for what Lucy perceived in a descending darkness to be a set of steps on the foreshore, with a garden, and a lane just visible between some houses leading towards a church further inland.

Lucy's heart thumped, actually *thudded*; her immediate world sounded hollow, as when your head dips under water, with a resounding echo filling in the space. The people on her boat appeared in limbo, though she could feel the heat of Alex's physical presence somewhere close to her. She could see clearly to the shoreline. A large bearded man, dressed like a robed academic, followed by others, came running through the garden, and the occupants of the barge began to spill on to the steps. The clarion call came again, but now it clanged instead of ringing out sweetly, like a cracked church bell. What an astonishing retinue – an amazing party. They were all in perfect period costume, the trumpeters in their bright red still sounding a fanfare; and the robed professorial man bowed before the princely being who had been on the barge. The foreign man – a monk, perhaps, though more grandly attired – with whom she had locked eyes, disembarked, as did several finely clad noblemen, and a number of other people of seemingly less importance. They turned back towards the river for a second, saluting her discreetly, before moving across the grass in the disappearing light.

On her boat the hush gradually lifted; conversation leaked out in every quarter as to what all had witnessed. 'Lavish costume party,' one voice offered. 'Stunning! Someone's really gone to a lot of trouble to get it right,' said another. Someone else sounded unnerved with the comment: 'Sinister, if you ask me. Like spies watching us all.' The noise flowed and then ebbed again, as the dancers returned inside, opening and then closing the doors behind them.

The boat had travelled to the end of its upstream journey, turned, and headed back down river. Lucy was speechless, and Catherine Denham tilted her head pensively to one side. They exchanged sympathetic looks, but no words.

'Seems like they came right from Hampton Court Palace,' Angelica said to a preoccupied-looking Zarina. The speaker was like a delighted child who'd witnessed a special privilege. 'Through the crack in time that's supposed to link the worlds of the living and the dead.'

'Twickenham Studios, without question,' Zarina insisted.

'It was from Oxford, actually,' Lucy confided only to herself.

Alex and Amel had broken right away from their clique, and stood either side of Lucy as she perched, glued to the rail, staring across the darkened water, studying the river's edge for signs of the red-gold barge and the stairs on to which its passengers had alighted.

Alex looked through everything, everyone, repeating the strange words he'd seen with Simon, just a fortnight earlier: '*Sator Arepo* . . .' He placed a gentle hand that radiated heat on to Lucy's back, then quickly reached for her wrap and tucked it around her shoulders, sensing her shivering. '"The moving finger writes",' he suggested quietly, and Amel nodded contemplatively.

No one spoke further. As the boat traversed Mortlake Reach, they were all engaged in their own thoughts. There was the spire of St Mary's, Mortlake, set behind a row of cottages, though under the deeper shroud of darkness they couldn't pick out the houses they had seen a short time ago. Warehouses stood; a pub; a pretty Georgian building.

But the great barge, the stairs, and the people, had been swallowed by the night.

15 JUNE 1583, MORTLAKE

The Queen's royal barge is swinging across the rising tide of the Thames and heading towards the steps at Mortlake Reach. Shouts and cries can be heard from the occupants of the barge, as it wallows momentarily in the ripe currents created by the other, strange vessel. An autumn wind, it seems, has disturbed their June day. The river is always awash with traffic; but ordinary mortals should be steering clear of the Queen's own craft.

Signor Bruno silences them: 'She is no mortal. She has been through the realms of the dead. A goddess. An angel of light. Lucina – the light giver.' His thick Italian accent pronounces the English words with marked clarity. He signals to someone hurrying to greet them.

A tall man, slender and handsome, with a fair face and a tapering beard, appears in a pale artist's robe with wide hanging sleeves at the water's edge. He is followed by his wife and servants and a tangle of children, who are scurrying across the garden and down between the houses and out-buildings towards the embankment steps. He has been hoping that the royal barge would stop on its return journey from Oxford to London. The fanfare of the royal trumpeters announces the arrival of his Royal Highness, Lord Albert Laski, Palatine of Sieradz, with his charismatic friend and pupil, the courtier Sir Philip Sidney, and their other companions. His hopes are realised.

John Dee has been alert to the great debates that have been taking place at Oxford over the past few days. Rumours of them have been swirling down the river with the current. Now, Dr Dee is curious to meet the infamous Italian monk, Giordano Bruno, who has thrown the University into turmoil by propounding a series of scientific and philosophical theses that Dee believes are beyond the area of understanding – and therefore acceptability – of the conservative university fathers whom Bruno has called 'pedants'. 'A juggler', they have called Bruno in their turn; but sterner charges of heresy and blasphemy are also being levelled against the man. He has ideas about the immortality of the soul and the doctrine of reincarnation, as well as talk of other solar systems and the suns – many suns – being self-luminous, the planets merely a reflection of that light. Copernicus' theory is heliocentric – the sun at the centre of all; Bruno talks of a theocentric universe – God at the centre of all. Dee has been taken with his ideas: that we should look for God in Nature, in the light of the Sun, in the beauty of all that springs from the earth. 'We ourselves,' he has said recently to friends, 'and the things we call our own, come, vanish, and return again.' It is a powerful and compelling idea – a little strange, perhaps? And yet, from what Dee can gather, Bruno's work is also closely within the area of his own study, which he wants to explore further.

'Great Prince, you are come to do me honour, for which God be praised.' Dee's bow is deep and elegant before the velvet-clad man. 'Lords and gentlemen, you are welcome to my cottage and my house of books.' He addresses now particularly the arresting young courtier, who bows gracefully in his turn, then clasps his own hands very warmly to those of his host and long-time tutor in a less formal greeting. The two men turn briefly to look out across the Thames.

Dr Dee now studies the small, dark man from Naples. Unconcerned with social courtesies, however, and much preoccupied with the river itself, the Italian asks Dee simply: 'You have just seen? The dark beauty?'

The old man is nodding slowly, deep in thought, following the expanse of the river, where the torch-lit boat, which has only just preceded the arrival of his friends, is already receding from sight. A haunting vessel, he decides. He turns back to his guest, grasping his hand. 'Signor Bruno. 'Tis strange, this vision. Yet devils may tempt, through spirits seeming light.'

Signor Bruno is unperturbed. 'Though she is dark, she is the truest fair. The cabbalistic tree teaches us through Kether that the source of Light guides our intentions and activities. Did you not hear her? She is the breeze that breathes upon Apollo's lute. When love shall speak, so shall the gods together; and they make heaven attend their harmony. *Sator Arepo Tenet Opera Rotas.*'

'God holds the wheel of creation in his hands.' Dee completes the words in English. 'And what an exceptional, complex, marvellous world it is.'

They turn together and walk in concert with their party across the lawns towards the house.

'And she is celestial,' Bruno whispers, turning back one time to search for the vanishing apparition.

12

When they returned to the pier, Alex enfolded Lucy – now enveloped in his gilt-edged rococo jacket – in a protective arm, and then ushered her quickly to his car. He was disgusted with himself for risking her apparently too soon after the operation. She hadn't shown the least sign of any illness since going home from the hospital, was a model patient in every sense recovering in copybook fashion; but she had gone unnervingly quiet, and something had plainly exhausted her tonight. He was more anxious that perhaps she had taken a chill, as she felt cold to the touch – which would be catastrophic if he wasn't on to it quickly. So the doctor immediately took possession of the man as he chauffeured her along the streets towards the Brompton Hospital. He reached across from the wheel and quickly crushed, then chafed, her cold hand in a gesture that was concern, examination and affection. It would have been romantic, she thought, had he not seemed quite so alarmed.

As they came through a side entrance to the hospital, she took comfort in the fact that he walked her into the lift and ignored the possibility of a wheelchair. He settled her smoothly into a private room and attached her to the cardiograph. Then Alex seemed to regain a perfect sense of calm as he spoke quiet commands of instruction around him. A pair of bemused junior doctors were surprised to see him shed his accustomed immunologist's role and resume that of a knowing specialist registrar. He would relinquish care of her to no one else.

'Am I really at Death's door?' Lucy was secretly aghast at the drama she was causing, and tried to dismiss the fuss. 'I thought he'd released me into your custody tonight – at the pier.' Striving for a little levity, she wasn't as worried as he was, clearly, but her instincts watched the hopes of any chance for closeness between them fade away, just as the good humour had from his face when he'd become aware how cold she felt, and how drained of colour.

'I'm undoubtedly overplaying the tragedic elements of the comedy,' he tried to laugh, aware of her embarrassment. 'But you'll have to indulge my cautious nature this one time.'

'I'll try to be flattered.' Lucy attempted to tease, but Alex was single-minded, concentrating solely on the task at hand, oblivious to her ironic tones which would have passed for flirtation to an observer.

Amel – trailed by peals of laughter from the skeleton staff at his appearance – soon followed them in, despite Alex's pleas for him not to disturb the rest of his evening. 'Are we going to lure you back from your beloved immunology, Alex?' Amel was amused to see that he was checking Lucy's blood pressure and assuming full responsibility for her. 'I think you're overreacting, but I will just come and ascertain that an informed assessment and my instincts are not at odds. My dinner reservation will keep for half an hour.'

Lucy looked apologetic: this was just what she didn't want. But as the monitor clicked with the read-out, Amel made contented noises. He agreed with Alex, looking at his patient, that she was a little ghostly and unnaturally cold. 'However, nothing to worry about, I am sure of it. Don't even mention an angiogram. The heart is very strong, beating beautifully. The nerves are not even beginning to take, of course, but the heart itself is sound. Nevertheless, your face is pale, Lucy, and I can see in your eyes that something has given you a fright tonight. So I think my colleague here is right.' He threw an amused glance over his shoulder at Alex. 'We should probably keep you in for observations just for one night. A formality on my behalf, Dr Stafford,' he added, with a smile dedicated to the patient.

Alex was grateful to have Amel take charge personally; but when he left them for a moment to call Grace and explain her flatmate wouldn't be home tonight, she communicated her disappointment to her surgeon with the look of a child whose hopes had been crushed on her birthday.

'It is his way of telling you how important you are.' He tried to offer her some consolation, more aware than she, perhaps, of the growing strength of her feelings. 'I think he is erring on the side of caution, and that you simply took a slight chill on the boat. A warm bath and an early night might have done instead; but it never hurts to do things in the proper way. It's only six or seven weeks since your surgery.'

Lucy nodded with resignation. 'It's typical of me to make an awkward exit. You could say it's a habit I've cultivated all my life.' She looked at him despondently.

Amel leaned forwards and peeked over the rim of his glasses at her. 'You needn't be in such a hurry, though. Get used to the idea that you have time on your side now. In fact, on the positive side, your pulse and blood pressure are fine, and I think you're far too well to be in here. I am very pleased with your progress, and we have a biopsy and echo due very shortly, and a mini MOT around Christmas-time, so this is an excellent sign. This little episode has nothing to do with rejection, in my opinion. And no one knows that better than Alex. He has a sharp instinct for these things.'

The owner of the sharp instinct returned, and Amel thought it appropriate to remind them both that he had a dinner reservation and two delightful companions to rejoin. 'I'm happy with the ECG, but an echo isn't necessary, Alex. Perhaps just an antibiotic, and we can let her out in the morning. She'll need some better food by then.' He smiled at them whimsically. 'Interesting evening, don't you agree?' He started to leave, and then to Alex he directed the words: '"And having writ, moves on."'

Alex didn't need the caution, having elected not to speak further of the strange incident on the water, although the words he had heard resonated with him. It had taken him at once to the extraordinary safety device Will had loaded on to his notebook – the mysterious Sator Square. There seemed to be echoes and reverberations in everything happening around him now, and he wondered about Will's email – the mention of an unbroken river of thought – in the light of their own journey down the Thames tonight. Neither Amel nor Lucy, he recognised, had believed there was an entirely rational explanation for what they'd seen.

He watched Amel go thoughtfully, then turned to Lucy. The celestial goddess's place had been usurped by a fragile creature in a hospital gown, and he played wardrobe mistress with the wonderful silk creation and a padded hanger he'd brought back with him specifically for the purpose. She looked exhausted; yet there was a radiant clarity in her face. As wise as Athena, maybe, he thought; but as vulnerable as any Florence Dombey or Catherine Morland, too; flung into a wider world without familial protection. This was certainly not a moment to desert her.

'I have some patient notes I need to finish. Would you be comfortable if I just sat here and got on with it?' He gestured at the chair beside her bed. 'I'd be happier keeping half an eye on you myself.' Lucy ventured a curious smile at him. 'It's not that I don't trust the housemen – some of whom will have been awake for thirty hours or more. But you'll assuage my own sense of negligence.'

Lucy's face relaxed for the first time in an hour. She nodded, not trusting her voice. Alex read what he believed her expression said, and returned her smile. 'But you must try and sleep, Lucy; don't let me prevent you from doing that.' So she immediately closed her eyes like an obedient child and drifted fast into a sleep – so fast it came upon her – initially peopled by richly dressed men on a great barge, melting thereafter into an icy dreamscape.

A scantily dressed man kneeled opposite another who was seated, this second man dressed all in thick, splendid red robes trimmed with brocade. The man on the ground was not at all prepossessing, Lucy saw; he was rather small and dark, wearing a coarse, woollen gown that might once have been a monk's habit. She felt he was about to receive some kind of judgement from his adversary. But the kneeling man was perversely distracted, not paying enough attention to his judge. He was squinting in pale wintry light through the narrow slits of the windowed chamber they were in, out on to a bridge. 'The Ponte Sant'Angelo, Lucina,' she heard him say to her; and he looked deeply into her eyes as he had before – earlier, on this very night. She tried to smile some solace at him. It was her robed man from the barge, the monk. 'This bridge is where Beatrice Cenci, just twenty-five years in this world, was beheaded for murdering her father,' he was telling Lucy quietly, 'after he repeatedly raped her. Her older brother was drawn and quartered here, too – just one year ago. His Holiness wished to make an example of them to other unruly families.'

Lucy had no idea how to react to him, and then she watched him turn his head away from her, and from the window, back to the man in red. Then he spoke again, as clearly as he had spoken to her earlier tonight: 'The Church is flawed, Your Grace. It has lost touch with the pure teachings of the Apostles, who converted people with preaching and the example of a good life. But now, anyone who does not wish to be a Catholic must endure pain and punishment. Force, and not love, is used to convince doubters of the "truth".'

And then he turned quietly away from the man whose power held his earthly fate, and looked again at the bright spirit of Lucy, as though he were a man possessed, talking, he might have said, to angels: 'The soul of man, Lucina, be very sure, is the only god there is. And how shall we honour it?'

And now the man – he must have been a cardinal, Lucy thought – was saying something Lucy could hardly hear to the man on the floor; something about him locking himself into his own prison, his own fate, and throwing away the key. His voice then rose to a volume Lucy could hear clearly as he addressed the man's gaolers. 'Hand him over to the city authorities to do what they must; but see he is given a merciful death inasmuch as it is possible, without the shedding of blood.'

Lucy saw that he had been forced to kneel for some time; but now the monk rose to his modest but full height. 'It is with far greater fear that you pronounce, than I receive, this sentence.' His voice was utterly calm, without anger or fear. The words silenced everyone present.

She watched these actions play out in front of her, devoid of any physical strength or bodily control of her own. She was paralysed by the sound of boots on stones, saw the frosty breath of the figures in her mystery play, felt cold herself, thought her limbs were heavy and far away. She moved in her bed and felt the wires that were attached to her chest through her half-sleeping state, saw the shadow of an angel sitting near her with his head bowed; and then she closed her heavy lids again and slept on.

When she woke it was a sunshine morning, her body felt

as light as a feather, and her heart was thrumming musically according to her own impressions. The chair was vacant but for her own familiar overnight bag, which must have come courtesy of Grace; but on the table next to her she found a tiny bouquet of miniature pink roses and a note written in pen and ink, in a bold italic hand:

> *For sleeping Ariadne, when she wakes. I have my son today, but tomorrow I am free. Are you brave enough to join me with some friends for lunch in Mortlake?*

It was signed 'Alessandro', his alter ego from the previous evening. The doctor had exited again; and perhaps the man would reappear. And yes: she would be very interested to see Mortlake again, in the daylight.

'Shall I put them in water for you?' a cheerful voice in a nurse's uniform asked her.

Lucy smiled serenely. 'No. Thanks. I'm not staying, and they're coming home with me.'

13

Three discarded outfits lay on the bed. Siân hoped to exude a confidence today that she was totally lacking. A stylist by profession, she found it second nature to orchestrate a carefully chosen wardrobe that belied any trouble and looked nonchalant, as though she'd thrown something together in minutes that could grace the cover of *Vogue*. What was wrong today? She couldn't carry off this feat of effortless polish.

At Calvin's request, a walk across Barnes Common to Mortlake was planned first. Flat shoes, she thought, or boots? Then lunch at an old pub on the river, so she had to be practical as well as feminine. It was hardly The Ivy. Plus it was a chilly day for early November. There was her new boyfriend to keep one step ahead of. And there was her ex-lover's best friend meeting for a second time this relatively 'new' man of hers, which she felt anxious about.

But worse than all of these, she feared the censure of Alex, the pressing worry that he might think ill of her for replacing his exceptional brother with a cousin he'd met only once to date. And that was at his brother's funeral when everyone was in shock, too numb to think. She thought Alex had been cool with Calvin. Well, he would be. Or maybe Alex had just been somewhere else in his head, that day? Though somehow he'd given the eulogy to a packed country church without a quiver in his voice – a rich, strong cadence that had made even the downcast Simon, seated next to her, look up appreciatively and listen with something close to a smile, as Alex had delivered a speech of warmth and delicate humour. It still made her weep when she thought of the words he'd closed with, about our being only what dreams are made on, and our lives being 'rounded with a sleep'. Will had sometimes said these words to her, from *The Tempest*, as though he'd had an inkling of his own fate. Her throat caught now; but she staunchly held off her tears. That would be *too* much today.

The entry-phone buzzed, and Calvin's voice was on the intercom, on his way up. She'd have to settle it now, and try to relax. She threw on a pink hacking jacket with multicoloured buttons on the cuff, and pinned a silk rose to her lapel. She looked quirky, and stylish too, and it would have to do. 'Will left me,' she whispered to herself, 'so they can hardly hold it against me that there's someone else in my life now. Alex has always been too kind to make me suffer for it.' But she felt an anxiety, an edginess, that she couldn't fathom.

Alex rescued Lucy from her Sunday solitude promptly at eleven a.m., noting that the ill spirits of Friday night seemed to have fled. Her dark hair was pulled back into a high ponytail, knotted with a scarf, and she looked somehow chastely sensual, but certainly lovely. He held her hand softly down to his car. Their talk had a light rhythm as he filled her in on the rendezvous, aware that meeting his friends might seem a bit daunting. He explained the proposal had come from a cousin he'd never properly met, who wanted to see him before he went back to the States in a few weeks. With Alex's busy schedule, it was now or never. He thought he'd omit the intricacies of this cousin's present love life. He hadn't considered how he felt about it himself, though he had no conscious objections he could identify.

Simon waved as Alex parked behind his distinctive four-wheel drive in Woodlands Road. He whistled appreciatively to himself as he took in the apparition that was Lucy, ushered on Alex's arm, walking towards him. The men shook hands firmly, Alex making the introductions. Whoa! thought Simon. Why are doctors always blessed with such good fortune?

'Have we met?' Lucy asked him immediately. She was very comfortable with his open, intelligent face.

'I'd definitely remember.' Simon's gallantry couldn't always be relied upon; like Will, he had a powerful critical eye and satirical wit, which stubbornly refused to bend a knee to social mores. However, the lady was disarmingly lovely, and he added with honesty: 'But I'm delighted to do so now.'

Lucy smiled naturally at him, and stepped comfortably between him and Alex.

'Siân and Calvin will be somewhere near the duck pond.'

Alex's tone was placid, but Simon wondered how he was feeling inside.

'I'm very curious,' Simon replied. 'I hardly spoke to him at the funeral.'

Lucy was hushed. She had heard from Amel about this dreadful recent death in Alex's family, and she knew the ghosts couldn't possibly be laid to rest yet; but he had said nothing at all to her about it, and she didn't know him well enough to broach the subject herself, to say that she'd heard of the loss and was desperately sorry. So she would wait for an evening when, perhaps in the right mood, a glass of good wine might invite him to talk to her. She was longing for him to do so. Such an evening, and such a confidence, would mark a change.

The men chatted as they walked across the Common, until they spotted a couple moving towards them from the pond. As they came close enough for Lucy to see their faces, she tensed. Introductions were made between them. Alex was all courtesy, and gave the girl a warm hug. Simon put on a good performance with the boyfriend and similarly gave the girl an affectionate kiss. Neither seemed to warm to the man; and Lucy also felt herself apart from him, and only him. He was good looking, after a fashion; squeaky-clean blond hair, smartly dressed, with a chocolate jacket and chinos, and a button-down collar. But she felt a wariness towards him – which was unfortunate, she realised, as he was apparently Alex's cousin.

But the exotic girl with him – a year or two older than herself, she calculated – transfixed Lucy. She was a Rosetti painting come alive, with strawberry-blonde curls, model-girl height, and some magnetic quality she couldn't define. Lucy was instantly drawn to her. She looked the type who was always outgoing, yet she also projected some vulnerability. Lucy recognised torment in her, and wondered why.

And in her turn, Siân looked searchingly at Lucy, and decided in a second she liked what she saw. Other women often made her nervous – she was far happier with men. But this fascinating classical face – so different from her own, with its huge warm eyes – reassured her, communicated some essence of sympathy; and she was glad she had come, pleased for Alex if this was something special unfolding in his life. He'd almost been an island – by his own choosing – since the end of his marriage to Anna. Today he seemed relaxed and happy, stylishly dressed in a light pink shirt and duck-egg sweater over jeans. Siân smiled approvingly.

Lucy was so caught up in her impressions that she hadn't followed the conversation. Calvin was explaining the family relationship, she realised. Their grandmothers were sisters, but one had gone to America and the relationship between all parties had lapsed into sporadic correspondence.

'I do remember my mother writing to a cousin – in Nantucket, I thought.' Alex had never said anything about his family, so this interested Lucy, wrenching her back to what they were discussing.

'Yes, that's totally correct. Grandma met my grandfather when he was in Paris, I believe, and she was learning painting or improving her French, I think. It was love at first sight, by most accounts, and she followed him back to the States. Nantucket was home to his large family; and my mother and her paternal cousins are still there.'

'How do you come to be in the Midwest?' Alex thought Siân had said Kansas was home for him.

'My college – it's where I'm studying.'

Simon had been taking in the details of his expensive shoes and Hamptons style. He figured him for a business graduate. 'Studying?'

'Theology.' Calvin flashed a smile, and Simon tried not to hold the row of perfect teeth against him.

Alex stifled a laugh as he looked down at the path. A cousin of mine and Will's connected with the Church, he thought. That's different. A similar thought must have amused Simon. 'Very nice.' Calvin detected no irony.

Alex brought them towards White Hart Lane, and asked the others to walk on to The Ship while he took Lucy by car. He wouldn't repeat the mistake of Friday night and wear her out; but she protested.

'Please don't worry about me. You know I'm dedicated to my treadmill, and I walk from Battersea to the hospital whenever the weather is fine enough. The exercise is good for me.' With a mixture of sweetness and firmness she challenged the doctor to disagree.

'In moderation.' Alex refused to be overruled, so she gave in to his protectiveness and he jogged back for the car.

'Have you been ill, Lucy?' The concern in Siân's voice was genuine.

'A heart operation a couple of months ago. But I've got to get back on my feet some time. I definitely don't want to be wrapped in cotton wool.'

'I'd enjoy it if I were you.' She threaded her arm through

Lucy's. 'Alex will love to take care of you; and he's excellent at it.'

The car spirited her away while the others walked briskly down the lane towards the river; and when they met up again ten minutes later, Alex and Lucy were settled comfortably at a round table by the window, overlooking the water. He was talking her through the reverse image of their view from the boat the other night.

'Great place!' Calvin enthusiastically pulled out a chair for Siân.

'We used to come here and expect war to break out between the brothers every March,' she told him. 'Will was at UCL, but he supported Oxford in the Boat Race just to irritate Alex, who did his degree at Cambridge. You never rose to it, Alex, although Will had been pretty noisy about Oxford winning these last two races.'

'You definitely need to book on Boat Race day.' Alex's emotions were caught in crosscurrents, but he managed some laughter. 'But the view of the Thames is a good tonic even in winter.' He poured them each a glass of wine from the bottle he had waiting, neglecting only his own, which contained mineral water.

'Oh, Alex, are you working later?' Siân had a long acquaintance with his teetotal lunches; but he rarely complained about them.

'On call, but it comes to the same.'

'I imagine that's why doctors binge drink – is that right, Alex?' Calvin flashed an earnest look at them all, but Alex only raised an eyebrow.

A blackboard menu arrived, and there was some

discussion between Alex and Lucy about the safest choice for her: nothing that might be reheated, avoid salad bar. She settled on char-grilled chicken, and once the food was ordered, Alex turned to his new cousin with interest.

'Why did you want to come here? What's the attraction of Mortlake Church?'

Calvin brought his hands together in front of him and looked squarely at Alex. He paused, with a dramatic effect that almost made his cousin laugh. 'Do you know very much about Doctor John Dee?'

'The Astrologer to Queen Elizabeth? Not much at all. I seem to remember he made a translation of Euclid – or wrote a Preface to it? He was the first to teach Euclid across Europe, since classical times. The original of Prospero, I think. An odd mix of science and magic. Am I right?'

'You are. But you know that we're related to him? Did your mother tell you about it?'

'No, not at all. It's through him we're connected?'

Simon leaned in to give the conversation his undivided attention. He watched the American intently.

'Through our female line. It must be entirely through the female line.' Calvin's reply to Alex seemed unexpectedly intense.

'Which means it could be traced through our mitochondrial DNA.' Alex met Calvin's eyes with a hint of humour, but his cousin in turn looked at Alex without paying much attention to his last comment. He appeared instead to be weighing something in his mind. He didn't want to make a mistake and rush this.

'I believe your brother may have inherited something

from your mother when she died. It would have come down from Dee, or actually, from Dee's daughter, Katherine. I'm amazed you don't know, Alex.'

Lucy noticed Simon's hands tightened a fraction. He was working to conceal some agitation. 'Sorry, Calvin, what period exactly was it?' she asked. 'Queen Elizabeth's?'

'Yes. His life extended right through her long reign. He died in the earlier years of James' kingship, but James had no time for him. His best years were with good Queen Bess. He's buried right here, at St Mary's, which is why I thought it appropriate. I'd like to look at the church after.'

Alex's green eyes were contemplative, but betrayed no thought or emotion. He shifted his gaze to Siân as she spoke energetically.

'That key, then, that Will had – when Diana died. Is that what you mean?'

'Possibly. Probably. I might know if I saw it.' He turned his gaze on Alex again, attempting what the latter thought was a casual look, but not quite succeeding. 'I don't guess you know what would have happened to it?'

Alex, though usually such a private human being, reacted to the question in a moment, which concealed the deliberation of his answer. He drew something easily from his shirt pocket, which dangled on a chain in front of them. Three pairs of eyes were transfixed by the object.

'I have it.' His voice was mild.

Siân looked at it like a fleeting ghost, and Will's hands were there with her, turning it over reverently; but she was almost more touched that Alex – normally such a level man – had it with him, a piece of Will, an inextricable link;

a revelation, to see Alex with such an object. She wanted to cry.

Calvin was trying not to let his hands betray him. He wanted to reach for it; but before he could speak, Lucy, who had been only an observer for most of the conversation, stretched a hand towards it, then cradled it in her own palm.

'Alex, it's beautiful. Can I hold it?'

He smiled with some surprise at her fascination; it was a fairly simple silver key, old perhaps, but with only the modest decoration of a tiny engraving and a small pearl. Yet he passed it to her freely. She closed her hand over it respectfully, and her eyelids closed as well. Sunlight played on her long, dark lashes, and she was a part of that light.

In the moment that was suspended Calvin was trying to find a way to ask for it too; but Alex was moved by something intangible on Lucy's face. 'Would you like to hold on to it? Keep it for a time?' Saying anything seemed a travesty. He felt his words broke across an evanescent moment, but he had to voice them. Without shattering the spell, she answered him silently, with a look Alex had never seen before, but hoped to see again. It communicated a powerful 'yes', and other emotions Alex couldn't translate.

Simon was the only one at the table whose eyes hadn't jumped from their sockets when Alex produced the little key. He had been watching Calvin, whom he now saw struggling with something. He decided to ask a very practical question.

'Does anyone know what it opens?'

'The most precious jewel in the family.' Calvin's answer was fervent. 'But we don't know what that is.' He looked at

Alex for a second before returning to the key in Lucy's grasp. 'You know it's supposed to be unlucky, if the key doesn't pass from mother to daughter?'

'I didn't.' Alex's voice was no-nonsense. Charms and curses weren't any part of his vocabulary. 'Will was given it, and whatever my mother may have told him, it's a secret between them now.' He looked at his cousin with a flicker of amusement. 'You seem to know much more than we do.'

'My mother told me that it must pass from mother to daughter – or we think perhaps a niece if there is no daughter. Otherwise, something bad could happen. It's supposed to break the chain in some way.'

Lucy's expression was a mute challenge to Calvin, but she articulated nothing.

'Well, it hardly seems to matter if we can't find the desk, or the door, or the box, that it unlocks.' Siân felt the need to diffuse whatever was going on here. She resolutely wanted the key to stay in Alex's care. Will had lost far too much sleep over it in the months since Diana's death, and she associated it sadly with his deep well of pain at her loss, and even perhaps their own break-up as he'd become so obsessed with it. Let it remain with Alex: he wouldn't let it haunt him, as it had Will.

Lunch arrived and broke the tension, and Calvin found that, despite his best efforts, there was no opening to return to the subject of key or curse. But he had little appetite for his food, and was glad when they could rearrange themselves for the walk to the church.

Strolling down the street, he couldn't quite let it go, and he turned directly to Alex. 'There should be some kind of document that goes with the key. It was still intact in my grandmother's recollection of it. It tells something about the location of whatever the key unlocks, I think.'

'I'm not aware of anything, but I'll check among Will's papers. Some of his effects are still with the coroner.' Alex affected a lack of interest, and for the first time, hid something of what he knew.

As he opened the heavy door of St Mary's, Alex asked, 'What of Dr Dee, then? What should we remember him for?'

Before he answered, Calvin took in the little church, which looked sunny inside and yet felt heavy. He saw out of the corner of his eye that Lucy had immediately picked up on this atmosphere. Her hand was pressed to her chest, and he wanted to talk to her, yet not to appear rude to Alex.

'He was the first to use the term "British Empire" – and to help the Queen's ships discover it, using his maps. He had a vast library, one of the great libraries of Europe. His collection ran to more than three thousand volumes and rare manuscripts, when your university at Cambridge had about three hundred books! Some people believe that when it was ransacked and dispersed it was a loss comparable to the burning of the library in Alexandria.' Calvin had focused back on Alex.

'Yes. Some of the volumes are in the Royal College of Physicians – I remember, now you say that. Clearly the inspiration for Prospero's books . . .' Alex was drifting somewhere Calvin didn't follow, but he picked up his narrative.

'He was also the very first James Bond, so to speak – one of Walsingham's rather special clique of spies, which had included Sir Philip Sidney – his own son-in-law – and

Sidney was tutored by Dee. "007" was Dr Dee's personal cipher – it signified that he was the Queen's "eyes" alongside the spiritual power of the number seven, which was the holy number, of course, and had some further personal significance for Dee. But what's even more interesting, he and a man named Kelley,' Calvin cleared his throat, 'performed alchemy. And they could also talk to the angels. Astonishing secrets were said to have been given to them.' He looked right at Alex. 'If you believe all that.'

'Possibly you do!' Simon had been hovering and had overheard this account from the American.

His retort encouraged a smile in Alex's face again, bringing him out of the curious mood he had entered a moment before. He had been lost in the lovely vision of Lucy, who was looking searchingly at the high altar, and the chancel, as though she'd misplaced something, with all the hushed reverence of a small child. Such a delightful day, Alex was grinning, his thoughts his own. So many diverse and unexpected entertainments.

All Souls' Day 1609, St Mary's Church, Mortlake

'How good it is, to step into this quietude.' Finding refuge from the unusually cold November day, Katherine Dee's words are only a whisper as she closes the heavy church door and slips quietly into the building. Still only in her twenties, she is a kind-hearted but rather steady girl, wise beyond her years, glad to escape the giddy noise of the revels and the dancing of the feast-day fair on the green outside. Just for a moment she breathes in, closing her eyes, catching her breath: there is a faint smell of incense, and also of the late autumn flowers that decorate the church in celebration of All Souls' Day. Under the great Elizabeth, the two festivals have merged into one, All Saints' and All Souls'; but the people are still enacting the traditions of their grandparents, bringing small cakes and food gifts for the souls of the dearly departed, still offering up prayers for the faithful. This she too will do.

She thrills at the unpeopled space: busy with the activities, the food and the music that fills the High Street, everyone has gone from here now, the service over long since. She walks quickly to the chancel steps, and kneels to lay a posy of herbs and flowers she has gathered from the last offerings in the garden of the cottage, just across the way from the church. The rosemary is still growing strongly, and a few pinks have survived – as has a late-blooming damask rose; in her late mother's favourite shade of rich cream fading to blush pink, it has miraculously defied this morning's early frost brought on by last night's cold new moon.

Enjoying the serenity, she sits here in peace at her father's feet, studies the bright new brass, recently fixed to his grave. Paid for by subscription at the wishes of her father's good friends, it has taken months to arrive and grace the heavy tomb slab. Her father would be pleased, she decides: there is a glow of light about it, a sense of alchemy that transmutes the colourless stone beneath it into something golden and brilliant.

'Indeed, I think it looks fine, Miss Kate.'

The voice makes her jump suddenly; it is the curate, and

he approaches her. She is nodding at him, reassured by his familiar face. He looks closely at the flowers.

'The pinks are for a private love,' she tells him. 'Oft times I made from them the spicy sops in wine, to ease his health towards the end.'

The curate looks sadly at the girl, who has dedicated all these last years of her life to the great but impoverished man. He wonders how she fills her days now, her chance of marriage surely past. 'The rosemary is for remembrance, Kate?'

She nods, and takes her time, considering whether to say more. Then: 'The rose, though, was his favourite – his perfect companion. It is a code, showing the aim of all humanity, to attain divine wisdom.' She looks the young man directly in the eye, wondering whether he will contradict her from his own – a slightly different – theology. But he is quiet, and she continues. 'The only path to that wisdom is through love, and knowledge; the blooming rose translates the whole meaning of the universe – indeed, the whole meaning of the universe can be explained to us through just such a rose as this one. To understand the mystery of the rose is to comprehend the essence of the universe. Through its simple perfection, we may become more perfect.'

She is looking at him now, yet talking beyond him, through the space and the time. 'To realise the possibilities of the rose, mankind must develop the capacity for love to the point of loving all peoples, all creatures, all that is different and foreign to us. We must enlarge our capacity for knowledge and understanding through the loving intelligence of the heart.'

She smiles at the man, who feels as though a spell were thrown upon him, though it is a happy enchantment. And setting the flowers at her father's feet, she bows quietly to him, and is gone.

14

Simon's brain had synthesised a host of ideas across the afternoon, and he pursued Alex and Lucy to the car as soon as he could free himself from the other pair. His was an eclectic mind that could select details from a variety of sources and see their connection – a trait he had shared with Will, which explained one aspect of their friendship. These impressions worked on him now, and at the risk of frustrating Cupid he needed to consult Alex about them.

He suggested they find a quiet corner for a coffee, but Alex was concerned to get Lucy home and warm. She'd started to look a little drained about half an hour ago, and he wanted nothing to eclipse the special qualities of the day. Prompted by a tenderness that was not altogether welcome, or even visible to the lady herself, he suggested Simon meet him shortly at Chelsea, after he had dropped her at her flat across the river.

'I'm on call at the Brompton, so it's best I'm not too far away.'

Lucy tended to be undemanding because of her conditioning since childhood that no one would consider her wishes. But she was just now strangely stubborn and wouldn't be spoken for, taking a decisive part in her direction with Alex for the first time. Her health may have flung them together originally, but it was suddenly intrusive.

'Alex, I've had a gentle day and I'm not tired. I'd love to join you both for coffee.' She looked up at him with expressive eyes, so that Alex's objections melted.

'Only if you promise to let me light a fire and put you in a chair beside it.'

Thus she found herself comfortably settled with a pot of tea and Alex's – or more probably his son's – cat, Minty, on her lap, in a sunny high-ceilinged sitting room overlooking the trees in the square. She was taking in his taste, the details of the original grey marble fireplace, the fact that the room was just untidy enough to make it feel easy to relax; and she was very content. Alex was busy in an unbustling way in the kitchen, and she turned now to address both men and share some thoughts that had been gathering in her own mind for an hour or so, about their afternoon.

'Strange, at the church, didn't you think? Not to have any remaining sign of Dee, no hint of his grave anywhere? And nothing of the house left standing, except for a bit of old garden wall. It's as though all his earthly life was a dream, and only his spiritual self remains. The church has changed enormously since the early seventeenth century.' She said this with a note of sadness, but also insistence.

'Such stuff as dreams are made on?' Alex laughed. 'But I liked the rather mythic account in the guide book, that someone years later remembered him having raised a storm for Sir Everard Digby! A fitting piece of magic for the original Prospero!'

Simon was going to say something flippant to Lucy about the heavy-handed restoration of the Victorians in churches up and down the country, but he stopped short and changed direction. He had been watching her with growing interest, and suddenly flashed a look of recognition as Alex rejoined them and set a coffee pot down.

'Do you know, Lucy, I think you were right. I do know your face – it's distinctive.' She looked at him mischievously and understood it was a compliment. 'All through lunch I've been trying to work it out. Now I'm sure I saw you at the pub – the Phene Arms – a few weeks ago. I believe I gave you a thorough vetting . . .' He laughed self-consciously.

Lucy nodded slowly, and it registered: the man who winked at her on the rainy day of her hot-footed return. 'Yes! Not in it – but I was passing on my way back to the Brompton. You've a good memory.' She'd thought he was cute then, and his face must have subconsciously remained with her.

'The odd thing is, I was on my way to lunch with Siân that day. I should have dragged you off the street to join us – a perfect stranger! But seriously, you two really clicked.'

Alex spoke. 'That was nice. She's a lost soul at the moment – and not always at her best with other women. But I thought she enjoyed herself today – for the most part.'

'She's been through some pain, though.' Lucy looked from Alex to Simon and back, and didn't want to pry. 'She was your brother's girlfriend . . . ?' It was only half a question. She'd put unspoken facts together around the lunch table.

'More than three years they were together. But they parted in May. Not that they would have, if it had been up to Siân.' Alex was more pensive than his words suggested.

'She seemed to be making a fresh start – or trying to.' Simon looked at Alex, and changed his tone to one of grim humour. 'There's nothing like an early death in tragic circumstances to elevate you to quasi-divine status. A typical James Dean gesture from Will! Poor girl will never get over him now.'

'But he'd want her to,' Lucy offered.

'Yes, he would.' Alex smiled sadly at her, and closed the discussion. 'Simon, what were you thinking about this new man of hers?'

'My mother used to say, if you can't find something nice to say about someone, don't say anything.' Simon threw his head back and laughed. 'So, that would consign me to stony silence, I'm afraid.'

'There is something about him,' Lucy said to both faces. 'But is it because you just don't like him for Siân?'

Simon reacted quickly: 'I don't trust him. Period. Did you see his eyes when you gave that key to Lucy? He wanted it – plain as the nose on his face.'

'It's a bit *Treasure Island*, isn't it?' Alex was incredulous. 'I was surprised how much it fascinated Will; but I think that had something to do with his relationship with our mother, and his interest in her family and his place within it. He always felt that he was very like her. I think his curiosity was some sort of quest towards his identity. Calvin could surely only want it if he thought it unlocked the Queen's jewels. Which is very unlikely.'

'But the information about Dee is illuminating.' Simon looked for any mute commands from Alex, but none came. 'I don't know anything about him, but I was able to get that document of Will's checked – the original that came with the key. Did he tell you?' Alex shook his head. 'My cousin does radio carbon dating at Oxford. There's a margin of error, of course, but he gave it a leeway from about 1550 to 1650.'

'Which places it closely enough in Dee's time.' Alex stood up and crossed the room to a box file on a bookshelf. He returned with it and drew out a heavy folded leaf of ageing vellum in front of them both. 'This is the original – Will left it here with me for safe-keeping and took a copy on the road with him. That's among his things, too. Calvin was asking me about it in the church.'

Lucy had listened attentively, but now spoke with surprising strength. 'Alex, this has nothing to do with me, so perhaps I shouldn't say anything. But like Simon, I didn't feel at ease with Calvin. He has a way of not looking at you openly – or rather, shifting his eyes away again quickly, as though he can't meet your gaze. I agree with you, Simon. He wanted to take the key. And silly as it sounds, I had to stop myself from giving in to his intensity and just handing it over to him. My own impression is that it must unlock something he's particularly curious about, and perhaps he even knows what that is.'

'"The most precious jewel" . . .' Simon reminded them with amused mockery.

Alex laughed. 'Any precious jewel would have been plundered long ago. The house in the country belonged to my mother's family; and there are some old books and a few pretty things. But they weren't rich. I'm sure anything of value would have been redeemed before now.'

'Could I look at this?' Lucy put the cat softly from her lap and leaned towards the vellum, which Alex passed to her with care. A card dropped from the pleat inside and fell to the floor. Lucy picked it up without looking at it properly and placed it on the table, keeping her attention on the vellum. She knitted her brows. 'So this is sixteenth century?' A thought crossed her mind that she should possibly handle it with gloves.

'Or early seventeenth.' Simon came and crouched beside her to look at it again. 'It hardly looks like a conventional treasure map.'

'But this is only part of it.' Lucy spoke with authority, which surprised them both. 'Whatever the key unlocks contains another piece.'

They stared at her. 'And how does Cassandra know this?' Alex couldn't help a dry inflection.

'I'm not sure. But I feel I'm right.' Lucy's voice contained no mystical tones nor any petulance; but it was firm. 'This is the "key piece", if you like, so if there *is* another page, this one is dominant.'

Alex listened carefully to what she said but made no comment.

'Will emailed some notes about it among the other ideas from Rome.' Simon sat down on the floor, drew his knees up, and rested his chin on his arms. 'I've started going through them, since we got into his iBook a couple of weeks ago. Most of it is a dyslexic tangle – that convoluted stuff about alchemists and light we read, which I printed off here. But he did seem to be focused on the Inquisition – mainly because of the carbon dating, and these first words here, about the Field of Flowers, and the flames. He'd worked out that the Campo de' Fiori was the site of religious burnings during the relevant period, apparently. He'd made a list of names, and some facts about them. A man called Bruno seems to have been their most colourful victim – perhaps he chattered with angels too, so to speak.' Simon looked at each of them, and added: 'And if this Dr Dee was talking to angels, the Inquisition would have been interested in knowing the details of that as well.'

'Just like Calvin.' Alex laughed, without much humour. 'Perhaps he's the modern Inquisition.'

His pager went off, and he walked to the phone in the kitchen, but Simon's words followed him.

'That's not funny. Could Calvin have had any interest in hacking Will's computer?'

Simon looked at them both, realising they were all aware of a tacit sense of unease about him. 'I'm sorry, I shouldn't have said that perhaps; but that *Sator Arepo* stuff is just the kind of thing he'd be into.'

Here Lucy interrupted. '*Sator* stuff? Simon, do you mean the word square?' She was still playing with the words in her mind, from two evenings before.

'"The Lord holds the whole Creation in his hands." There are other suggestions as to how to translate it exactly, but yes. It's either a magic eye that wards off evil, or some kind of private handshake between early Christians. Will knew it was probably paranoia, but he texted me that he thought he was being watched while he was abroad; and we found the so-called Sator Square on his computer, presumably put there to stop anyone reading his mail. I've found in his notes that he was becoming quite frantic about this. But what's worrying me is, did Siân talk a little too much to her new man about her old one?'

Alex's troubled gaze stayed with Simon, and he was dwelling on the words when he spoke to the phone. 'Jill, it's Alex Stafford. Does Jane want me at Harefield, or do you need me there?' He glanced up while he was waiting on the line. 'Well, we know for certain someone was trying to read his emails . . . The problem's at your end? I'll be as quick as I can.' He put the phone down. 'Maybe we should look into this, Simon. I wouldn't put it past Calvin to be at least curious about Will's moves. I have the feeling he's not being entirely level with us. If Lucy's right that he's focused on the key, and he wants to examine it, then he could reasonably have discovered the password and account numbers – if he's had the freedom of Siân's flat. Have you got any time to check up on Dee?'

Lucy had been listening with her concentration partly divided between Alex's words with Simon and the face she'd started to notice looking back at her from the card on the coffee table, which had fallen from the parchment.

'I have time,' she now spoke up. 'Let me do something useful with my brain, Alex. I'm still on leave from work, but it's my convalescence, not my dotage. Research is *my* job, too.'

Alex was aware of a growing fascination to know her more, and smiled. 'OK, thank you. But I must take you home now. I'm sorry to break the flow. Simon, I'll call you in a day or two? I've got to rush. We have a sick ten year old en route from Ormond Street.'

'Let me take Lucy home then. You get on. If that's all right with you, Lucy?'

She glanced restlessly at the card and then replied more politely to Simon, 'Yes, of course, thanks.'

Alex crossed the room back to her and stooped to give her a gentle squeeze. 'I'll call you in a day or two too.' He looked from her to the postcard on the table of the beautiful face that had magnetically been claiming Lucy's eyes. He stood to go: 'Guido Reni's portrait of Beatrice Cenci. Will sent it from Rome. He read a lot of Shelley.'

The name burst from Lucy's recent, vivid dream, and she could only stare. With instructions to them both to pull the door hard when they left, the doctor was gone.

After twenty minutes of silence behind the wheel of her car, Siân now shut her front door with a flash of temper. 'Did you have to go on about that key? I don't want it anywhere around.' She swung on Calvin with surprising emotion. 'I feel like it took Will away from me some of the time.'

'Yes, I think it did.'

She looked at him open-mouthed. 'What on earth can you mean?'

Calvin was suddenly hesitant. 'What did *you* mean?'

'I meant that he was so preoccupied with it, he hardly seemed to notice me at times. It became a bit of an obsession.'

'Siân, I am very serious about this . . .' he closed his eyes for a moment and then mouthed the single word distinctly, '. . . *curse*. My mother told me flatly that the key must pass between the women of the family. It should never have been given to Will. She said it would cause mischief.'

'You don't really believe that? That Will's accident was because of some curse.' Siân had lived too long around a family of non-superstitious minds to give this idea a moment's credence.

'I do.' Calvin was stoical. 'I'm deadly serious. The whole accident was too strange. Sudden fog. The river. You said he was a really good biker. And to die from a cranial aneurysm – my understanding is that's often like an ancient wound coming back from the past to kill you. It usually happens if you've had a head injury before, and something needles it again, to set off the time bomb.' His blue-grey eyes were half-hostile to her. 'It should never have happened. And I might just as seriously suggest that you two probably broke up because of that key.'

Siân's jaw dropped. She was angry, upset, and completely astonished. She wasn't at all swayed by his argument. Will was sporty and physical. He'd had a dozen falls or blows in the course of his life. She understood about the clot: this was no curse. But she was worried by the fact that this strangely altered man with her genuinely believed in it. She searched his face to try to understand him. He was religious – she knew that – but it had never seemed to her that he was irrational. Only that he had a strict belief system that was different from hers, made him prefer to live somewhere else and just stay the night sometimes. And now to suggest that she and Will had parted because of some ill luck attached to an inanimate object? It was ridiculous.

Calvin had been examining his fingers for a few moments, as if deciding whether to say more, and then he committed himself. 'This girl Lucy certainly shouldn't have it. It's dangerous. It's very unlucky. Someone who knows what they're doing should be in control of it. It should return with me to my mom.' He closed the conversation without further explanation, and left, slamming the door heavily.

15

The Christmas decorations on the ward did nothing to lift Lucy's spirits. The last few weeks had been hellish, and she sat awaiting her biopsy with a sense of dread. Though not strictly a painful procedure, the feeling of pending discomfort was exacerbated by a mood of heavy gloom that had overtaken her ever since the headaches had started and the nightmares settled in. The sense that she was rebuilding her life with a future to look forward to was now almost terminated in her mind.

It was so difficult to understand. Her post-transplant period had initially gone well: her progress was exemplary. Beyond slightly shaky hands and appetite cravings and an odd feeling that her mind was sometimes not wholly her own, the drugs hadn't caused her any especially unpleasant side effects, and she was managing her health and her psychological wellbeing better than anyone had anticipated. Then in early November, she got a cold, which sent Alex and Courtney Denham into overdrive. She knew infections were serious, and she'd been fastidious about hygiene, diet and her lifestyle. It was just a cold, but her temperature soared out of control, and Alex – regardless of Amel's insistence that he had done nothing at all that was even close to negligent – blamed himself for the evening on the boat, the excursion to Mortlake, even the possibility that she'd somehow come into contact with the cat litter at his flat. Unable to account for anything else that might have sent her from the glowing recuperation period after her transplant to this current downward spiral, he watched her now like a first-time mother with a newborn. He was completely professional, never actually communicating alarm to her; but his actions told her he was her clinician again, and their journey as two attracted people was on hold. Long sessions talking to Mr Azziz, Mr Denham and a new consultant based at the Brompton indicated that Alex was seriously worried. He disappeared to the lab, ran tests personally, changed her medication, and fretted.

These worries were then compounded from another front when his son broke an arm badly in two places from a fall at a skating rink. It required an operation, and Alex all but vanished in his free hours. Lucy understood, but it was a blow; and within the confines of their present relationship, she couldn't talk to him and find out how he was. They had no private time, between the on-lookers at the hospital and the curfew that descended by the end of his working day with his return to his little boy. It was an absurd paradox: he was more involved with monitoring her immune system and the possibility of her new heart being rejected than anyone, but it returned them to an entirely professional relationship when their personal bond wasn't quite established. She thought the opportunity for closeness might be gone altogether. Her humour fought back against her fate, but the strain finally got to her, hitting her nervous system. Having ignored dwelling on it too much before, she now became aware, after the fact, of all the horrors she'd been through, the brushes with death the year had contained. And someone she was just learning to trust enough to possibly start caring for seemed to be withdrawing from her.

She succumbed to a series of terrible headaches, depression and bad dreams peopled with hostile faces. She would awake in panic, feeling as though she were being watched by someone she wished to hide from. So she was admitted again for a further series of tests.

Now it was 22 December, a grey Monday, and it looked as though she was staring at Christmas in hospital. At least, on the plus side, she might see Alex. He'd been away in late November at the other hospital with his research students, and was up in Cambridge last week. She joked with Grace that she'd forgotten what he looked like and wondered who was feeding his cat – but she lacked the levity she affected, feeling like a little girl abandoned. She was back to square one. He was her very kind – but presently very absent – consultant, Dr Stafford. The man, Alex, was elsewhere, perhaps at his ex-wife's house with their son. But at least she still had the key as a talisman, and she clung to it fiercely.

'It definitely isn't that bad.' Simon had descended on the monotony of her hospital room with Grace and a pile of books for her, and he immediately registered her crestfallen face.

She smiled ruefully at him: this was the one pleasure of the last few weeks. Simon had delivered her to her door as promised after coffee at Alex's, and sparks literally flew between him and her flatmate. Grace had been dazzled by him. His irreverence and lazy charm made an instant impression on her. And Grace – who'd inherited high cheekbones and sexy curves from her part-African mother and an easy, clever banter from her Jewish father – prompted the very best performance from him. He'd found an excuse to come back soon with books for Lucy to research Dr Dee, and Grace seized her opportunity. In a matter of weeks they had embarked on a whirlwind romance, and while Lucy was delighted for her friend – who'd had a string of broken promises in love for at least a year – it made her own lack of progress with Alex the pang more sharp. But she rallied herself for them now.

'A little light reading' was her comment on the groaning load of out-sized paperbacks in his arms.

'Grace told me to keep you busy. She says you're in danger of becoming maudlin. The Dee biography looks entertaining, but the maths and this Hermetic rubbish look like treacle to get through. Could you possibly want it? Will ordered it all from Amazon, got it sent to Alex's, so we thought you should have it too.'

Simon was trying to prick her interest about anything that might take her mind off her present stalemate, but her quiet, pale face reminded him of the studied calm of a young novitiate, nothing that was natural in his eye. Almost as an afterthought he added, 'Dee was originally supposed to have died on this very day, as a matter of curious fact. But scholars seem to have decided more recently that it was probably on a date in late March – a reprieve of several months. You'll have to read the biography to decide why this change of heart. And rather creepily, legend has it that his heart is buried somewhere under the high altar at Mortlake Church. I'm sure you'll be riveted to learn this last salacious detail.'

For some odd reason Lucy's face responded by deeper degrees of expression to all of this unfolding information – and Simon's interesting choice of words. She smiled a little cryptically, pleased to have something challenging to think about. She'd had difficulty reading with the acute headaches that had seemed almost other-worldly. They were only now coming under control with a change of drugs, so she hadn't got far with the research, but it made her feel closer to Alex – which was where she was inclined to be.

'Don't overdo it though, Luce,' Grace added gently. 'Getting better is the priority. Alex said so specifically. You know my parents are still hoping you'll be able to join us at home in Shropshire for Christmas.'

Lucy appreciated Grace's effort, and was grateful, although it wasn't the festive season she'd secretly hoped for. 'Thanks, honey. I'm sure I'll feel better when I know about the biopsy.'

'Your doctors will all have to agree to release you before you make any firm plans for travel, Miss King.'

Lucy blushed with pleasure at the voice; its owner had slipped in behind Simon without her noticing.

'And do I have any hope at all of influencing you, Dr Stafford?' In front of friends it was easier to be flirtatious.

'Every time!' In a fragment of a second he had lightened her mood. 'I hope you're not tiring my patient, you two. I've come to give her a bit of a pain in the neck, I'm afraid.'

Lucy laughed and gestured an explanation to Grace of the needle she had to have in that very spot. Her friend kissed her on the forehead and grabbed Simon conspiratorially to leave her alone with Alex. 'I'll call later and see how it went. Let me know when she's ready to escape, Alex.'

'You just leave her with me, Grace.' He gave her a wry smile, and they were gone.

Alex closed the distance between them and sat down casually on her bed, which seemed wonderfully informal to her. 'Are you feeling better at all?' He sounded fractionally hesitant, as though unsure of his reception.

'Yes, actually. It's very good to see you.' Her tone was searching too. She knew they'd be disturbed at any second. 'How's your son? I was hoping he might come in with you, and I could meet him.'

Alex shook his head. 'This is not the place for that. He's not too keen on hospitals just now! But the plaster's coming off on Christmas Eve. It certainly hasn't slowed him down – he still wants to go skiing.' Alex read uncertainty in her face. 'Are you dreaming sweetly again now?'

'I think so. That character with the black cape and the scythe doesn't have such a prominent role for now.' She retreated to irony. 'Simon's given me some homework here. These books were among the ones Will ordered. I'll tell you if I find anything interesting.' She thought this might reveal the cast of her mind.

'No need to rush, Lucy. We'll have time soon to talk about

it. I think for now we should concentrate on getting you out of here and back home.'

Someone with fewer insecurities would have heard the reassurance, but Lucy was not that cheerful soul today. An orderly arrived with a trolley, and Alex playfully took it over and waved him away. 'Right now, the Three Fates are waiting to put a wire in your neck.' He bent closer to her and whispered, 'And I've asked them to have a care for its fineness.'

Those words made her tentative smile more relaxed: and with Alex in control she wound down through the corridors towards her cardiologist, technician and radiographer, and felt safe again.

As Calvin passed through the reception area towards the breakfast room, there was a fragrance of lilies that almost stole your breath and made the wonderful old hotel seem even more luxuriant. He approached the restaurant carrying his pale camel overcoat, fidgeting slightly with one of the large buttons. He saw the reflection of the professor's head in the glass and thrust a hand into his pocket, then as quickly out again.

'Professor Walters is already at the table, Mr Petersen. May I take your coat, sir?'

The maitre d' at Claridge's gave Calvin's coat to an attendant and then showed him to a table in the corner of the breakfast room. It was occupied by an expensively dressed man of about fifty-five, with a pinstripe shirt and navy woollen jacket, and a cream silk cravat in place of a tie. Calvin could see his cufflinks catching the light from a distance away; and now, as they approached, Professor Fitzalan Walters set aside his copy of the *New York Times*, and rose from his chair. He extended one freckled hand to Calvin's, and placed his other hand on his guest's arm. As his chair was pushed in by a waiter, Calvin was struck again by how considerable a presence he had for such a relatively small man.

'What a pleasure that we could meet while I'm in London, Calvin.' Fitzalan had a deep voice, with the slight southern American accent that spoke of old money and commanded attention. 'Are you going back home for Christmas?'

'I'm leaving the day after tomorrow.'

The professor was an important and a busy man, one of the senior heads of the School of Theology at The College. Established in Kansas in 1870 with a sister college in Indiana, it had fared well over the years and listed among its alumni a number of senators, judges and well-known figures from all walks of life. In fact, a good degree from The College seemed a passport to a good job in law or politics or Washington. Walters proudly described it to the uninitiated as a neo-conservative fundamentalist institution. It seemed there was nothing – and no one – that Professor Fitzalan Walters didn't know. A decade ago he had written a seminal book around the subject of the Second Coming of Christ. It suited Calvin's moral beliefs and broader interests to look for a lecturing position that would pay enough to feed him while he got his masters and then, he hoped, his doctorate; and when an advertisement for a post at The College seemed to offer what he was looking for, he applied. Professor

Walters – FW as he liked to be called by his friends – had shown a keen interest in Calvin at their first interview. They had talked at length about his ancestor Dr John Dee, whom he already knew to be a forebear. It was certainly Calvin's job to ingratiate himself, but actually he was flattered: some people thought Dee a crackpot, but FW accorded him respect and was curious. Many people believed that Dee had indeed, as promised by the angel conversations, been given details about the Apocalypse and the Second Coming. What might have been contained in his writings, they had conjectured, and what had become of a great many of these? It was known that Dee's house had been robbed, and his library looted while he was abroad in Bohemia in the 1580s. Walters seemed to know many details about Dee's life and work, many more even than Calvin.

They had talked productively, and FW awarded him the teaching job he needed, then further helped him acquire a post-graduate bursary so that he could complete his dissertation with a research trip. Calvin came from a good family with some property and a few shares, but ready cash was always tight, so he was grateful for the patronage. Later in their association, as Calvin got to know Professor Walters better, he found some of his ideas on Intelligent Design, the Rapture and Creationism a little extreme, and he was certainly alarmed when Walters expressed publicly that the horrors of 9/11 could be laid as much at the feet of the pagans, the feminists and the gays as at any Islamic terrorists – although he never expressed such concerns to his patron. He had been taken into FW's confidence on a number of matters, and he liked to be there. But their association had recently blossomed afresh when Calvin had mentioned, in passing, the death of an English cousin, and a key with a fascinating history, which had narrowly missed descent to Calvin's mother. It should have followed the female line, he explained, but had gone to a male cousin in England, breaking a pattern of centuries. He believed it might be linked with books and papers that his illustrious ancestor would have thought were too sensitive to release into the doctrinally riven world of the early seventeenth century, and FW expressed surprise that Calvin hadn't told him of its existence before this.

As the waiter put Calvin's napkin on his lap, he thought how deeply he was becoming involved with this man. Walters seemed to be in a jovial mood as he invited Calvin to order. He had already chosen an old-fashioned English breakfast himself. 'Love these link sausages – can't get anything like them back home,' he commented. Calvin wondered what was on his mind. It was unlike FW not to get straight to the point.

'Got any further with your English cousins and Dr Dee?' Walters, between bites, never took his eye off Calvin, judging his every reaction.

'Can I take your order, sir?' The waiter was poised, and Calvin about to speak up for the eggs Benedict. Walters cut him off before he could mouth the first vowel.

'He'll have English breakfast, fried eggs sunny side up, link sausages, and hot buttered toast. Make sure it's hot buttered.' Walters ignored the waiter's close proximity and added to Calvin without lowering his voice: 'These Brits don't understand about hot buttered toast.'

'Oh, we Brits do, sir.' The waiter smiled quietly. 'It's when the toast is buttered straight out of the toaster so that the butter melts into the bread, making it limp and soggy. Anything else, sir? Coffee, decaffeinated, or regular?'

Calvin nodded his thanks before Walters said crisply to the waiter: 'That will be all. Thank you.'

The waiter moved out of earshot, and Calvin replied, 'Yes, as a matter of fact, I had lunch with my cousin and his friends a short while ago. I've been . . .' he searched for an appropriate word '. . . *seeing* the other brother's ex-girlfriend. He was killed tragically. I'm not sure if my supervisor told you? An accident – a few months ago.' Calvin's words were deliberately couched to sound tentative, but his cool grey-blue eyes were fixed on his breakfast companion. He wanted to gauge his reaction to this particular news item. He wondered if someone from the faculty might have known, and been responsible for the break-in to the family home at such an opportune time.

Seeing her brains out, thought Walters; but he looked gravely at his companion. He scanned Calvin's face, and nodded. 'Yes, Guy did tell me. I heard all about it. Most unfortunate. You can't ask him any questions.'

The breakfast arrived, and Calvin continued, 'No. But his former girlfriend was upset about their break, and told me a lot about the family. She needed an ear.' He was waiting to reveal something he knew would interest his mentor, who was listening more than politely. He didn't hurry, and finished an egg before continuing. 'Interesting . . . at lunch, I learned the brother now has the key. I've seen it. He's not sure about the paperwork that goes with it. It's very odd. I tried to tell Siân – the girlfriend – about the problems of not following the heritage. If it's not passed down the female blood line. The family knew nothing of the Dee connection. The father thought it was a lot of superstition, or something to be ashamed of. It worries me that they've disregarded the dictum.' Calvin talked freely, realising FW was listening to every word. 'I have to say I was almost expecting a disaster. My mother was clear that it would break the chain. I believe it had something to do with his death – just the kind of bad luck she would have anticipated.' He was still fishing slightly, but caught no response. 'They wouldn't understand. They don't seem to respect these powerful ideas. If God curses something, it is cursed; if an angel does so, the effect is the same.' He looked up at his audience. 'Things have been more strained between Siân and myself now. But I'm still seeing her.'

I bet you are, Walters thought. Having seen her himself, he was vitally aware of her charms.

'Calvin.' He leaned in quietly. 'We have discussed this. We could be looking at one of the great historical finds in our time. We'd both like The College to be part of this. Academic glory for you. A book in it, certainly. From a career point of view, it could be the making of you. And from a religious perspective, of course, it would be fascinating. I expect it could verify the whole theory of the Rapture, which we have been working towards for years. Dee certainly would have known about it. I would think you could just . . . state your claim . . .'

His voice trailed off suggestively, without any hint of urgency; but Calvin knew it was his chance to be something of a hero to The College. Many people – not least those at The College – would give a good deal to take control of what was in the legacy from Dee. Any man would feel the importance it accorded him, and for Calvin it came with an additional awareness of his value to FW, who was a politically and socially influential man. He recognised right now the directive he had been given to get the key back from Alex – or Lucy, if she was still holding on to it – by any means. FW wouldn't wait for ever.

The waiter discreetly put the bill on the table and Professor Walters signed without looking, tucking a large bill for a tip into the leather holder. They stood to go, and the maitre d' appeared with Calvin's coat. Walters pushed another American note into his hand and took Calvin by the arm.

'Have you got a minute?' It wasn't a question. 'Let's go up to my suite. There's something that might interest you, and a couple of people you should meet. It will help you to understand how crucial this might be.'

As they crossed the elegant Art Deco lobby, a man rose from a chair and stepped into the lift in front of them. Walters and Calvin followed him in and turned to face the door.

'Did you achieve everything, Mephistopheles?' Walters spoke without looking at him.

'Yes, Professor Walters. It was informative.' The stranger handed Walters a small leather document case.

'This is Angelo, Calvin, though I have other names for him. At times he can be a bit of a bad angel. He works for me in Europe.' Professor Walters' tone was oblique.

Calvin turned and stared into the unfamiliar face.

Everything about him was unremarkable, except that he had the yellow eyes of a cat. Calvin couldn't place the accent.

'Nice to meet you,' Calvin said without meaning it, noticing the stranger was immaculately dressed in a fine dark suit and cashmere overcoat. The man nodded politely to Calvin, which for some reason made him feel a shade uneasy. He wondered what FW meant by a 'bad angel'.

'I showed your people into the lounge in the suite,' the man was saying, 'and gave them coffee, as you requested, sir.'

'Thank you.'

The lift door opened and the party stepped into the hall. 'The Davies Suite is on the left,' Walters directed them.

Angelo opened the door and stepped back, and Walters entered in front of Calvin. Over his shoulder Calvin could see the beautiful main room in yellow and white with its polished wood floor. Two men stood in front of the window back-lit by the morning sun. Walters strode across the space and embraced each of them with a formal hug.

'This is the young man I've been telling you about, Calvin Petersen. He is my personal protégé and the man whom I hope will lead us to the answers we've been searching for, for years.' FW sounded unusually solemn.

'Calvin, my colleagues.' He gestured with his arm, offering no names, though Calvin was vaguely aware he knew one or both of the faces from the broad arena of politics, or perhaps from appearances on religious television.

FW lifted the briefcase on to the table and snapped it open. Out of it he took what looked like a parchment and an exquisite portrait miniature. 'Well, my bad angel?' Walters asked quietly.

Angelo stepped forward with his hands clasped. 'Sir, I explained to the V&A that this was a recent – bequest – to our College. They confirmed that the portrait is late sixteenth century, and just possibly a genuine Hilliard, but it doesn't appear to be catalogued so it may only be a copy of a lost original. They cannot as yet identify the subject. The papers – ' he turned some documents over – 'are of interest to the Fitzwilliam Museum in Cambridge. They are what they called fine copies of some original text, possibly now lost, which they said they could not without further study confirm; but they may be from Dr Dee's papers – except for this one sheet, which looks to be some kind of extract from a play-script. They took a copy and will have a hand-writing expert examine them – if we wish. They seemed quite excited about this one – though they are cautious in case it's a forgery.' He looked up at the eager faces and continued: 'The small books in Latin are still with an antiquarian bookseller for examination, but the Bible is very old, and valuable. I have someone working on the marked passages – which are revelatory, it appears.'

Walters nodded once to the complete report, and handed the miniature to Calvin. 'It goes without saying that this is all strictly *sub rosa*, Calvin. A beautiful lady, isn't she?' he said. 'Do you think she could be an ancestral member of your family?'

Calvin's eyes narrowed involuntarily as he looked at the face, grappling with the implications of the question. What had this to do with him? But it took only seconds for him to connect it to the theft from the Staffords' house in the country – knowing it occurred while Will was in critical condition in hospital. He opened his mouth to speak to Professor Walters, then changed his mind and tried to conceal a thought. How far *would* these people go? He was distracted by discomforting ideas that were quickly showing his instincts to be right about their willingness to do whatever it would take to get their prize; until he quite suddenly focused on the lovely woman who looked right through him from the blue background, in her richly embroidered bodice. His eyes widened.

'I'm not sure,' he said slowly. 'But I believe I had lunch with her a few weeks ago. It may even be –' he was so struck by the image that he found himself thinking aloud, but the words couldn't be called back – 'that she is currently the key-holder.'

16

The doorbell rang again. The porter was either away from his desk or he had allowed a man to come up right to her threshold. 'Taxi, love. Ordered for the name of King?' Lucy looked at the man mystified. 'I have this note to give you, and then I've got to hang on for ten minutes.' He winked at her, gave her a sealed envelope and turned. 'I'm out front when you're ready.'

Grace was running late for work with all the interruptions this morning. 'What is it now? If it goes on like this, I'll never get out the door . . .' She laughed and peered over her friend's shoulder at the hand-written words on the card:

> *3rd Feb. Mademoiselle. Bring a warm coat, sensible shoes – and your passport! Dépêche-toi . . . Alexandre*

'I'll put these in water for you.' She took over the luxurious box from the porter's previous intrusion. 'Get yourself together, Lucy. You're obviously off somewhere disgustingly romantic. Like Paris?' Grace started singing a Piaf song, and swooped on a vase.

'I don't get it, Grace. He leaves a card and an expensive bottle of my favourite Bulgarian Thé Rose perfume for Christmas, before I go to Shropshire; then he's unavailable in January. The longest phone call has been just ten minutes, and that's a poor substitute for seeing him. I could destroy a garden of daisies trying to work out how he feels. I could find it irritating you know: I do find it irritating! He's interested; he's not interested . . .'

Grace dismissed her attempt. 'Lucy, the man is *interested.* He took all the trouble to identify your perfume – then the greater problem of tracing where to buy it. And now, look at this!' She swept an arm across the two dozen long-stemmed reds that she was quickly arranging. 'As well as the taxi! I'm sorry, but you can't blame a guy for his workload. He was teaching, wasn't he? Simon says he had barely a day off for the whole of last month. He must have done something particular to arrange a free day today. And how romantic: he's obviously taking you somewhere very special.'

But Lucy's strong new heart was suffering an attack of nerves. Risking her feelings for Alex Stafford was complex. The possible breach of professionalism, the uncertainty about his private life, imparted heavy warnings. She looked at Grace, who was stifling a grin, and suddenly cottoned on to something. 'What do you know about this?' She flashed the note in her flatmate's direction.

'I haven't got time to tell you. You'll be late.'

'Did he set this up with you?'

Grace grinned without replying, and Lucy chased her into the kitchen.

'There has to be some reason why neither you nor any of my closest friends were free to have lunch with me today. Were you so sure I'd get a better offer?'

'Well – ' she noticed the roses were thornless as she started arranging them for Lucy and softened – 'I do know that he had to call on every favour to get a clear day in the week for your birthday. But I didn't tell him at Christmas what perfume you wear, and I don't know what he's planning for you today.' She looked at her friend. 'And only a simpleton could doubt he's interested, Lucy. He works twenty-four seven, right? Plus he's finishing a PhD. Not masses of free time there. Besides, I think he's extremely cautious of your health – which is sensible after the last fiasco. He wants to get you well – not woo you to your death. But somehow he still manages to find the time to call you every other day. And isn't it sweet, really? Reassuringly old-fashioned in a world where everyone's in such a rush, and affairs are over before they've begun. He's not like other men. Of course, if you're having second thoughts yourself, I'll keep the roses.'

Lucy shot her a look of agony. 'Two or three phone calls in a week is *not* every other day! And he doesn't really *say* anything.'

'Which is just the point! Now go on. Shoo!' Grace laughed back at her wholeheartedly. 'Put on something pretty – but warm! Cab's waiting.'

Alex opened the door of her taxi on the Chiswick side of the Thames at Kew Bridge, which had a light dusting of snow, and paid the driver. 'Happy Birthday, you!' He pulled her coat tighter around her.

'Not Paris then,' she teased him. 'I was expecting to be met at Waterloo Station.'

'Ah, you were hoping for lunch at Boffinger, were you?' He laughed and took her hand more tightly than usual, guiding her to his parked car. 'I'm sorry to ask you to meet me here. I had to drive from the North Circular. I was caught at the other hospital till the early hours and had some errands to run first thing.' Lucy waited, and when he opened the door the scent took her breath away. The black soft top of Alex's Audi had concealed its contents; the surprisingly roomy back seat was filled with fragrant bunches of jonquils, hyacinths, violets, and other spring flowers. She couldn't speak, and he was pleased.

'For the Return of the Maiden,' he said. She looked quizzical. 'Your birthday is a special date – well, the day after one. This is the first breath of spring – according to the Pagans. It's when Persephone and her myriad namesakes come back from the Underworld.'

'And so I have.' Lucy hugged him. 'And where are you taking me? I thought I needed a passport.'

'And so you do.' He mimicked her tone. He checked his wing mirrors, and as they moved off, he explained. 'I thought I'd take you to the country for lunch: to the village I grew up in, where my family home is. It's picture postcard stuff!' he laughed. 'And you know L. P. Hartley says the past is a foreign country? Well, it's my past.'

She laughed with pleasure. 'I couldn't think of anywhere I'd rather you take me, Alex. It's perfect. Thank you.'

She settled into the generous beige leather of the passenger seat and absorbed the delicious scent of the flowers, the physical proximity to Alex. She hadn't expected this today: had steeled herself to have a non-event for her birthday. Now, cocooned in warmth that belied the outside temperature – reading just one degree on the panel – she let the driver concentrate on the traffic out of town and opened the conversation on her own terms.

'I've been thoroughly fascinated about your illustrious ancestor, Alex. I'm only halfway through the books Simon brought me, but they're full of surprises.'

'I imagined they'd be very dry bones – especially if Calvin is so rapt with it all?'

'Not at all! I know you're an Enlightenment man, Alex, but we should try to understand your forebear through the lens of his own time, if we can, to appreciate the considerable impact he made on Elizabethan England. He was a true Renaissance man, with a thorough knowledge of astronomy and history, an authority on navigation and, by all accounts, an outstanding lecturer. If Drake and Gilbert found their way to the New World, it was because Dee helped them. I'm not sure if I can do justice to him, really.'

'Well, I know absolutely nothing, and we have an hour at least to get to Hampshire in this weather! Give me a taste of the man.' He was in particularly playful spirits today, and Lucy relaxed thoroughly to enjoy them.

'The first thing I should explain about John Dee, Alex, is that a lot of what we know – or if you like, how we see him – comes from Meric Casaubon, a seventeenth-century scholar who was determined to destroy any positives in his reputation. Casaubon is the reason we still can't quite look at Dee without preconceptions. He thought Dee was deluded, and that his practices were "dark", as he put it. He published the most salacious details of Dee's life. Not that he had a lot to go on there, but he did manage to dig up some oddities.'

Alex grinned. 'Not an even-handed biographer then?'

Lucy shook her head. 'Far from it. But what might be *most* of interest to us is that Casaubon was privy to an extraordinary stash of Dee's personal documents, which he happened on in the strangest manner.'

He looked at her, intrigued. 'Go on.'

'In the early seventeenth century it was Sir Robert Cotton – think Cottonian Manuscripts in the British Library – who was for some unexplained reason inspired to go and dig in the grounds of Dee's house in Mortlake. And he got lucky . . .'

Alex just looked at Lucy. 'So the possibility of our key, and some other find related to it, is entirely in keeping.' Her eyes affirmed this. 'Why bury everything? Was he really writing such dangerous ideas?'

'Cotton discovered a cache of papers which were damp-ridden, but still legible, and from among these came all the transcripts of Dee and Kelley's communications with angels, which Cotton's son later passed on to Casaubon.'

'With angels.' Alex's voice was in its familiar ironic register, and it made Lucy giggle. She repositioned her body in the seat, turning more towards him.

'You're on a promise – to grant him the perspective of his own time and remember that many of his sixteenth-century contemporaries cherished similar beliefs and ideas!'

Her voice was full of good humour and entreaty, and Alex was delighted at her passion for the subject. He listened appreciatively while she narrated with skill her understanding of the atmosphere of the time. The Elizabethan world had an eclectic mix of inhabitants: politicians, theologians, poets and playwrights, explorers and glamorous old sea-dogs like Raleigh and Drake. But the population also included an extraordinary array of spirits – fairies, demons, witches, ghosts, sprites – both good and ill: and conjurors to talk to them. It was totally within the fabric of their world for Spenser's great epic poem to be about a fairy queen, and for Hamlet's troubles to be set in motion by the ghost. This fascinating blend of the physical and the ethereal worlds owed as much to a philosophy of occult thought at the most intellectual level, as it did to a tradition of superstitions and folkloric influences. It drew on a legacy of magic and cabala, inherited from the great Neo-Platonists of the Italian renaissance. The aim was to comprehend the deepest spheres of hidden knowledge, blurring scientific and spiritual thoughts.

'The face of this movement in Britain was John Dee.'

Alex had been absorbed, admiring her professional control of the flow of so much complicated information; but when she came to Dee – the man he knew as the lecturer on Euclid – he was puzzled. 'It's hard to digest this – a man who's famous as a mathematician of some genius, obviously, but who is also infamous as a conjuror. I wonder how he was able to reconcile for himself these scientific and occult interests.'

'Hold on to the fact that at that time, even mathematics

was regarded as a subject very close to the "black arts". Calculating was an uncomfortably close relative of conjuration and the casting of astrological charts.'

Alex laughed at this, as it reminded him privately of Will's distaste for maths – the devil's subject, he'd always called it to Alex while he'd finished his younger brother's maths prep for him. 'And yet Dee always maintained a sober claim to be a devout Christian, from what Calvin told us – and even a supporter of the Tudor religious Reformation?'

'Yes, I agree that's odd from today's perspective. But Dee was influenced by the cross-currents of extraordinary ideas from fifteenth-century Europe. It was at that time that documents and books were pouring into Italy from Constantinople and Spain, where the Jews were cast out by Ferdinand and Isabella. One of the most important of these ideas was brought with the teachings contained in the cabala. The other was the discovery of a group of documents about Hermes Trismegistus, which became known as the *Corpus Hermetica*.' Lucy looked at Alex: this was the hub of her information, and she wanted to be sure he was paying attention while dealing with the icy road and the now heavier snow flurries, which tested the dexterity of the windscreen wipers. She paused to consider that the maiden had chosen terrible weather for her re-emergence.

'Don't stop.' Alex glanced at her, fascinated. 'I'm enjoying your voice.'

She smiled, relishing the role reversal that cast her as the authority. 'The Renaissance philosophers Pico della Mirandola and Marsilio Ficino worked for the Medici, and it was Lorenzo's grandfather, Cosimo, who asked them to put everything else to one side and concentrate on the Hermes' texts that had just come into his possession. These texts they translated – the writings of Hermes – sent ripples of mysticism across Europe. Hermes was a mythical Egyptian sage – not the messenger to the Greek gods. He was a sort of Greco-Egyptian hybrid who embodied the qualities both of the Greek Hermes and the Egyptian god and scribe, Thoth. He was called the Egyptian Moses by Renaissance scholars.'

Alex turned the heating up a fraction as the air temperature was dropping outside. 'It sounds as though he probably wasn't a real person at all?'

'More a kind of god imbued with hero-like human qualities. The books and documents that have become known as the *Corpus Hermetica* – Latin and Greek texts about him, and writings theoretically *by* him – arose around this mythic figure, but the Florentines read them all and assumed he was a real sage and priest. For them he was a fount of ancient, sacred wisdom contemporaneous with Moses, and believed to have influenced Plato, although it's more likely that the Hermetic texts were based on some of Plato's teachings, among others. But the thing to remember is that the texts were real enough, and fascinating, and they believed Hermes' wisdom to be very ancient. Many scholars now think they are in fact texts from about a century after the time of Christ, but that they preserve much older oral traditions about pre-Christian Egyptian religious ideas. And to liberal thinkers who were looking for religious truths which might transcend the religious factions they were living through, they were a new vision! These texts allowed them to escape the life-and-death struggles about faith – whether to remain true to Rome or join Luther and Calvin, and whether to vilify Muslims and Jews. The ideas expressed in the Hermetic texts took them to the very essence of God's being. And they were right in many ways to give them such respect, because we do know now how much the Egyptian religious view of the world influenced Moses.'

Alex laid a hand on Lucy's lap, asking her to pause. The heady scent of the flowers in the close confines of the warm car, combined with the powerful ideas she was communicating, made him suddenly light-headed.

'Wait, Lucy. Have I got this right? When we speak of Hermeticism, it's the literature that grew up around this supposedly human Hermes, who was invested with the divine attributes of the Greek god of the same name?' She nodded, and Alex asked: 'And the significance of Hermes was . . . ?'

'That he seemed to be speaking to them of a pure religious truth, unbranded, if you will. Ficino called the Hermetic documents "a light of divine illumination". By contemplating these teachings he felt one could rise above the mind's deceptions, and understand the Divine Mind. This was compelling stuff at a time when differing doctrinal issues pulled people in so many directions. Through this course of study you could apprehend the mind of God *directly* – or so they thought. Hermes even seemed to have anticipated the coming of Christ – but from a vantage point of Egyptian wisdom. There was a strong tinge of magic and occultism which was imported with his Egyptianised teachings – and a respect for women, too, from the worship of Isis. Hermes was so respected that his image was set into the altar at Siena's cathedral.'

Alex, listening to Lucy's words, considered how this school of thought might have interested his mother, with her ecumenical approach to spirituality and her gentle feminism. 'OK,' he nodded pensively. 'The Hermetic texts were widely believed to rival Genesis, as far as their origin and spiritual authority were concerned?'

Lucy nodded emphatically. 'Correct. Especially for thinkers like Giordano Bruno and Ficino.'

In the scant traffic and eerie silence of the snowy conditions, which were close to causing a white-out even on the A road, a lone deer suddenly sprang across their path not far from them, into a copse. They both smiled, bewitched, but Alex held his thoughts.

'And what about the cabala?'

'Right, this was Pico's interest. The teachings of the cabala came to Italy with the expulsion of the Jews from Spain, both in a verbal tradition and in written texts. Pico understood it as an ancient tradition of mystical wisdom connected with the Hebrew language which descended from Moses: Hebrew was the language of God for them, remember. Cabala assigned a number value to each of the ancient letters – it's called Gematria – and preserved a secret knowledge of the magic believed to be embodied in the Hebrew language itself. Every letter has a corresponding number value. Even the actual words in Hebrew were thought to contain divine power.'

She broke off for a second to get his reassurances that he was following all this, but she needn't have. Their eyes met just for a moment, though Alex was mindful of the road. 'The idea was that the language itself contained deeper information than had been widely disseminated – that it had a hidden subtext. A sort of message to the elite. I'm with you.'

'Good. YAHWEH is the tetragrammaton of God, the four Hebrew letters YHWH, which traditionally make up his name. Some say it's not pronounceable, because it has no vowels, but Jehovah is a variant – as is Jove, in fact.'

Alex broke in. 'Amel tells me, you know, that the word Yahweh owes its parentage to an Egyptian word which means "the moon's power rises". It referred to Yah, an Egyptian moon god, and also to a Babylonian moon goddess of the same name.'

Lucy rolled her eyes with humour. 'Alex, that's very interesting, but please don't sidetrack me. We're coming to the essence of the excitement about cabalistic doctrine.' He smiled and nodded at her. 'Now,' she resumed, 'for the Christians, an appealing aspect of the cabala was the way in which the tradition of cabala seemed to confirm the truth of Jesus as the son of God. In this way: when you have the name IESU for Jesus, or better still Jeshua – like Joshua – which is its variant, you are, so they thought, adding in the substantial medial letter "S" to the consonant only name of Yahweh. They saw this letter "S" making the unutterable name utterable; YHWH is otherwise entirely without vowels. For the Christian cabalists, the name made audible was the same as the Word made Flesh.'

Alex laughed aloud, glancing at Lucy as they turned off the dual carriageway towards the little village of Longparish.

'Well, even taking the etymology of "Yahweh" out of it, it's a strange argument. And I can just hear how much more irreverently my brother would have put that.' She laughed. 'Did they buy it?'

'Depending on how deftly you manipulated the Hebrew alphabet, and stretched the consonants to allow for elided vowels – yes! It seemed convincing to the adepts of the time. But part of the agenda was to convert Muslims and Jews to the idea of the Trinity – to Christianity.'

Alex nodded pensively. '*Plus ça change!* But, haven't we come a long way from John Dee?'

'It must seem so. You need to understand this rather complex web of thought to see what excited Dee's fine mind. Christian cabala gave its blessing to communion with the angels, via their holy names in Hebrew, which had a magical power to bring the magus, or conjuror, directly to God without doctrinal restrictions—'

Alex added: 'In ancient times, names carried power. If you knew the real name of an entity, and spoke it, you had power over it.'

'And this, effectively, was what they believed Moses himself had had access to, as a special magus or initiate. And Hermes Trismegistus too. The journey of the initiated person was from the physical world – earth – through the ether or air – demi-paradise – to the celestial world – true heaven, or nirvana, if you like. But the angels protected the magic and the journey from bad spirits. So Dee could be both an ardent scientific enquirer, and a conjuror of angels. For him, the concepts of Neo-Platonism – which had been the spirit of the Renaissance and seriously upset Lorenzo de'

Medici's implacable foe, poor old Savonarola – were high-minded ideas. He followed a Venetian friar, named Giorgi, who wrote a book on the teachings of Hermes and the cabala called *De Harmonia Mundi*, which was a philosophy of universal harmony.'

Alex laid a hand on her arm: 'But surely any hopes of achieving some gentle unity in the practice of religious faith simply weren't materialising in Dee's time?'

Lucy laughed quietly. 'No, that's certainly true. The man Simon mentioned, Giordano Bruno, put it beautifully. He said that the methods used by the Church to bully people back to them were not those of the Apostles, who had preached with love. Anyone not wishing to be a Catholic in the sixteenth and seventeenth centuries faced torture at the hands of the Inquisitors – or, conversely, in any number of northern European countries, burning at the stake if you wished to remain Catholic. The Reformation and the Catholic reaction fuelled disunity. What a pessimistic prospect for the more liberal intellectuals of the time. Bypassing the Church – in all its forms – by talking to God's angels directly seemed to offer hope. But then, magic and communion with the angels? It was seen as wildly heretical.'

Alex had been taking the car through a series of turns on snow-covered lanes, and it was a moment before he spoke. 'So, Dee was a man of the late Renaissance, exploring occult philosophy in scientific directions, through alchemy and astrology, mathematics and geometry – all of which could bring you closer to the workings of God. Amel still feels some truth in this.'

'And, Alex, crucially, the *Hermetica* justified their study of astrology, because it showed them how the Egyptians had laid out their buildings to reflect the constellations. Many scholars today recognise that this was the impetus which led them to understand that the sun, and not the earth, was the centre of the solar system. It moved them out of medieval thinking.'

He was contemplative on this point, and took some time to answer. 'But, Lucy, you think Dee was really attracted to the reforming aspects of this occult philosophy?'

'No doubt. He helped to build up Queen Elizabeth as a Neo-platonic heroine. Dee directly influenced the writings of people like Spenser and Philip Sidney. He also challenged Spain's colonial power through his belief in the British right to commit to their own exploration. The term British Empire was coined by Dee – was part of his worldview.'

'Calvin mentioned that – but surely that weighs heavily against him!' Alex suggested.

'Yes, now it would, but not when you place him in his own time and environment. His concept of Britannia was a deliberate challenge to the Spanish/Catholic control of the globe. That Americans speak English rather than Spanish owes something to Dee.' Alex was lost in thought, and Lucy looked at him, laughing self-consciously. 'I've exhausted you.'

'You've woven a spell on me.' And this was the truth. He slowed the car right down now as they entered the village. 'Look at the snow on the thatch.'

Lucy hadn't noticed, but now she took in the aesthetics of

the place, with a long breath: an unspoilt English country village, airbrushed white by the weather. Houses bowed with the weight of years; roofs sagged under tiles baked in the sun of previous centuries; windows leaned on beams that ran downhill. The river plashed along the front of the gardens, and under old bridges. She was captivated.

'Thank you for this. What a relief from the city. Can we walk a little?'

It was about half-past eleven when Alex parked at The Plough, his mother's preferred pub. He swathed her in his own scarf and gloves and buttoned her coat to the top. Together they moved along the lane, walking close to share their body heat. A watery sun struggled with no more power than candlelight on the roofs and paths. But Lucy was a world of feelings away from the cold. She let the quiet, the patches of colour on the doors and in the waking flower-beds, the mere survival of the village itself with its shop and church and post office and playing fields, enter her soul. The weather snuffed out most signs of life, but one or two people coming out of doors or cars nodded at Alex. This was his space. His childhood lay all about him.

They passed the cricket ground, and he pointed out the clubhouse with its thatched roof looking weary of the cold weather. 'A second home in the summer months. First kisses under those trees, early hangovers after lost matches. Even bigger ones if we won. My mother used to come and help with the teas.'

His commentary seemed to Lucy to dally behind other, unspoken thoughts. But she said nothing to push him, absorbing instead these details of his life like hungry grassland scenting the rain. It gave her a sensation she'd never experienced – the vicarious pleasure of seeing the world through someone else's eyes, someone becoming beloved. She realised how the absence of such memories in her own childhood had made it harder to know herself. Alex – sure of his identity – was able to touch people closely, with gentleness and strength, unafraid of the dark. Whatever happened around him, he was still himself. She found resilience by keeping her affections leashed, but one storm of serious emotion would threaten her with obliteration, she thought, sweeping away her only creed. It suddenly struck her that it was no surprise her heart had been her Achilles heel.

They now turned the other way, Alex pausing briefly to collect some white, double jonquils from the boot of his car, and they came to the church. He swung the gate open for her. She played tourist; he showed her the thirteenth-century features of the building, the oldest stained glass, the fine wooden roof. They emerged from the unlit space into the garden, where some sunlight now softly illuminated the sparse snowfall; and in silence they walked to the newest part of the graveyard. Lucy knew what would follow, but she doubted whether she could be of any help. Alex was upright and pensive, though, and didn't ask for words or consolations. He crouched over the pair of graves, one much too fresh to venture to discuss the pain and the other hardly less so. He soundlessly placed the flowers, and whatever words he offered were unspoken. Soon he stood again, hooked her arm, and they left. All possible words had frozen on Lucy's lips: she literally couldn't speak. Perhaps she'd let him down or missed a moment, but she was reassured by the calm strength in his body as their feet marked the path back and crossed the road to the pub.

Returning from a dream they ordered lunch – and their mood changed. Everyone who came to drink or eat said something to Alex, and over their unhurried courses he asked questions of those occupying and vacating the barstools and tables – about holidays, relatives, building work. He knew their stories. It was a community he was a part of, and she liked it. It rescued her from a lack of faith in others, a belief that everyone was caught up in their isolated pockets of interest, and she was chirping and light-humoured.

'So man can still be a social animal?'

'Oh, I hope so. I'd want to give up if I thought we couldn't appreciate others' diversity.' He looked at her more seriously than his tone might have suggested. 'Now, if you have the strength for it,' he asked when the decaffeinated coffee and shared pudding was cleared, 'I'd like to show you my home. Just for you to see it, really.'

He was surprisingly tentative. Was he concerned the suggestion might be unwelcome? She couldn't tell. Did he want time alone with her there? Or was he worried about what would be expected if he created that space? Lucy sensed a pivotal moment in their relationship and was racked with uncertainty.

Then he explained: 'I've had no pleasure going there – not for months now. It's a family home. And my family aren't at home any more – except my poor father.' When he looked up at her, his face clean-shaven and his hair perfectly trimmed, he looked younger than she'd ever seen him. His usual calm authority was absent. 'I think I'd be happy if you came there with me. Dad will be at work in Winchester, but I'll leave him a note.'

Lucy took control and said freely: 'Yes, please, Alex: you must take me.' The awkwardness passed.

Thick clumps of snowdrops laced the border along the path, and winter jasmine over the porch struggled against the elements. Lucy's first impression was of the garden: someone had taken a lot of trouble over it. The house was large rather than grand – possibly of Tudor origin, she thought; and the thatch was herringboned with little details that would reveal the identity of the thatcher to the cognoscenti.

It was warm inside as they entered, and she was immediately in thrall. A fireplace large enough to sit in; a baby grand piano in front of French windows that looked out into the garden; an air of peace. 'My mother would have had flowers everywhere – even in winter.' Alex was apologetic for its present lack of cosiness, though this was softened by a comfortable old settle with a chintz cover and creamy throws and other soft furnishings. The feeling of a strong female anima was tangible in the room above the more masculine items of a pair of soft leather slippers and the folded newspapers.

Alex leaned against a table. 'Shall I make you some tea? I think you prefer it to coffee.'

'Please.' She started looking around. 'Is it all right if I explore . . . ?'

'That's why we came.' He walked through to the kitchen

and put a kettle on the Rayburn, then noticed a package on the oak worktop. While Lucy peeked in a study-cum-library and a dining room, Alex fumbled with some cardboard packing and bubble wrap. He took in the contents, then picked up the telephone on the wall and dialled a number.

'Dad, you're not in court. I'm at the house. I brought a friend down for her birthday, for lunch in the pub. Is everything all right? I've just seen the package from the police. What's the story?'

Lucy heard Alex's voice sounding agitated, and perched on the arm of a generous chair while he talked.

'And that's it? They don't know any more? Nothing else returned?'

Lucy listened as he closed the conversation: the weather was bad, they'd be setting off soon, but he'd see him again with Max at the weekend. He put the phone down and looked at Lucy. 'Come and see this.'

With immense care and almost a hint of ceremony, he put a tiny picture in her hands. She was surprised by its weight – more substantial than she'd anticipated. She searched the face of a woman with dark hair, beautiful brown almond eyes, a richly needleworked bodice depicting stags and tiny trees on a blue background, the whole object only a few inches long and wide. Lucy couldn't look away. A grandfather clock chimed the half-hour, and perhaps another minute passed before she consulted Alex.

'Who is this?' There was no volume in her voice.

'Some distant ancestress of my mother, we think – we're not entirely sure. It was stolen from the house a few months ago, and it's just come back through Interpol – my father's not completely *au fait* with how they found it. We'd more or less given her up.' He looked at her with a half-amused, half-serious expression. 'Does she remind you of anyone?'

Lucy looked straight back at him. 'Of course.' She sat down with the portrait while Alex made the tea. No one could miss the similarity. It was her own face.

She was aware of a powerful headache growing on her, and feeling dizzy, but she wouldn't tell him. Since her operation she'd had these sensations before. She told Grace she thought it was because she'd come close to death and was now acutely sensitive to the pain of others. Grace joked that it was a near-death experience. No, she wasn't turning into Joan of Arc, or St Teresa, and she wouldn't be mentioning it to her present companion either. But it was real enough, and holding on to the painting tipped the scales. He gave her tea; she felt nauseous. She would have liked to lie down, but refused to let another outing with Alex become disrupted by her poor health. He talked to her, but she couldn't concentrate on what he was saying.

She looked once more at the lady's face, the details of the picture. She left the settle next to him holding it distractedly. She made a few strides across the room and sat at the piano without asking if he minded, caressing a few keys absently with one hand. Some densely coloured chords escaped. Alex was asking if she could play. She said something meaningless about having completed grade eight, but her words sounded thin and she stared back at him blankly. She was going to be sick. He was beside her in a second.

'It's just the journey, Alex; I'm tired. Don't panic. I think I've just relaxed properly for the first time in weeks.' She wasn't going to let the day go, and she fought the gut-wrenching discomfort. 'I've been happy every moment of the day, and I'm so pleased you brought me here.' She looked at his troubled eyes, which were busy searching hers in a semi-professional way, she realised. It made her uncomfortable that she could conceal nothing from him; so she glanced away and down again to her left hand, occupying herself with the details of the lady's dress, and she tried to decide what kind of tree she thought was embroidered there. The tree of wisdom.

'This is a mulberry, isn't it . . . ?' She touched the key around her neck. 'Alex, whatever this opens, it's here. It's under a mulberry tree. Here in your garden.' And with the effort of expressing this, she put her head in her hands and bent over double. He collected her up gently. She was a weightless figure in his arms, and he took the stairs two at a time, laid her on a bed, slipped off her shoes and covered her with a heavy throw. She was aware of him stroking her temple for a few moments, holding her wrist with his other hand, checking his watch without apparent distress; and she spiralled into sleep.

When she woke it was much darker, lights were on, and she found her way back downstairs. A well-dressed older man was reading a paper by a lamp, the fire lit; and he looked up at her kindly.

'What a terrible house guest I am. I'm so sorry. I'm Lucy.'

He was on his feet quickly. 'You poor lass; please don't apologise. Are you feeling any better? Let me call Alex.' He directed her into a chair and opened the back door to bring his son inside. When Alex reappeared he felt her hands and checked her pupils carefully.

'You gave me a fright.' But there was relief in his voice. 'We'll put it down to too much rich food, shall we?'

She nodded gratefully. She wanted to pretend that her strange reaction had never happened, and would have kissed him had his father not been there. Alex understood all this and let the matter drop; then he smiled at her mischievously.

'Did you see what I put beside the bed upstairs?' She shook her head, and he left for a moment. When he returned, he placed a lightly moulded wooden casket on the side-table next to her. 'I believe you have the key!'

She sat looking at it for a quarter of an hour: a plain oak box, somewhat soiled, not at all large, spotted with mildew in places, finished with metal fastenings that she took, despite their tarnish, to be silver. It looked anything but precious, and she felt a little deflated inside, as though it were an anticlimax – a plain object, clearly containing no jewels, she thought. Was it right that it should be her role to unlock it? Alex had brought her tea and some toast, and sat watching her now, amused but equally intrigued; while Henry managed to strike a balance between polite disinterest and gentle curiosity, tending the fire and drawing the curtains but keeping half an eye on the tentative Lucy. Neither of them hurried her, and the grandfather clock ticked deafeningly in the quiet atmosphere.

Now, she took the key from around her neck and placed it in front of the tiny silver-wrought lock. She looked earnestly at Alex and his father and asked, 'Is this for me to do?'

Alex smiled, left the settle, and came to kneel beside her. He closed his hand over hers to still the tremble. 'Go on.'

His tone encouraged her; and she fitted the key into the mechanism, and turned. She half expected it would be rusted and stubborn, even that it would fail. Instead, it yielded cleanly. Lucy put on some gloves Alex gave her, and both men watched while she drew back the lid and released an aroma of centuries, of mustiness and old scent, into the room. Henry stood and came over.

Lucy peered in, hesitated, and then reverently withdrew a straw-coloured leather wrap, which was secured lazily with a cord thong. She gently unbound it, and found herself holding some folded sheets of vellum, sealed with a red sigil. There was a sparse dusting of white powder on the surface – was it salt, or perhaps alum or lime? Alex was asking – but the condition of the papers was sound. Henry came and went wordlessly, returning with a small sharp knife; so she now slipped the blade through the wax. 'It's orris root,' she told them, very familiar with the delicate scent of dried iris that underscored pot-pourri and helped to preserve the dried flowers.

And in a moment they were looking at a cache of beautifully calligraphed riddles, keeping company with a small golden coin that had slipped from within their midst.

17

'You can come with me; or you can stay. But whichever you choose, I'm going.' Despite frustrations and confusions Lucy had never quarrelled with Alex: but she was close now. She was very emotional about this decision. It had taken her weeks to get permission, and everything was in place. She was back at work part time and had to juggle her own schedule now. She had booked a room to stay from Friday to Sunday, and was ready intellectually for the experience. More than that, something drove her to the necessity of going. It had to be now.

Alex was distraught. He'd worked a month straight every hour he wasn't with students or at the hospital to get his thesis in – which in itself had been a mountain to climb – but what had driven him was the desire to free up some time in the future as a by-product. Lucy had mentioned a fortnight before that she was going to Chartres for the spring equinox. She was particular as to the time, and had arranged with the Cathedral to walk the labyrinth before the season officially started, after closing hours. He knew she'd gone to a lot of trouble and used her television credentials to help make it happen. Will's postcards had intrigued her. She wanted to see whatever it was that Alex's brother had seen at first hand. She wanted to dance the ancient Rite of Spring at the proper moment.

While he was surprised it meant so much to her, Alex was in fact quite curious himself and concerned about her going alone. So he told her simply at lunch a few days prior: 'I'd like to come with you.' Delight and relief flooded her senses. She hadn't expected this.

They'd grown closer since her birthday, considering the usual frustrations of time. 'It's not advisable,' she had sighed to Grace, 'to start feeling anything for a man who is divorced, with a son I still haven't met, a full-time job and a research degree to complete.' Secretly, though, she had a deeper worry, questioning for weeks whether Alex's failure to get intimately involved with her had anything to do with the uncertainty of her health. She knew he'd lost his mother and brother in less than a year. He didn't talk about it, and never let his mask slip, but she understood without explanation that the pain was still raw. Could she blame him for holding back on starting a full relationship that might end at any time? Heart transplants were achieving better and better results for survival beyond the first crucial year, but there were certainly no guarantees. But now she'd hoped she might be able to put her doubts to rest. She would find out what there was between them and settle the uncertainties, and she'd been able to think of hardly anything else for weeks now.

For his own part, Alex had managed to clear the whole of Friday as well as the weekend. He was looking forward to walking the maze with her in the evening and then finally being allowed to spend some time alone with her, when suddenly their progress was blocked in an unprecedented form. It was impossible to digest. If she'd been listening, the distress in his voice would have told her half of what she needed to know; but Lucy felt absurdly thwarted. She felt fate was against them, and convinced herself that it was not to be. It was a lesson not to give away your heart. Moved only by her own sense of rejection – the ebb and flow of unexpected pleasure followed by intense disappointment – she was deaf to the emotions Alex's tone communicated. All she processed was the unwelcome news that his ex-wife had asked him to have Max for the weekend because of a family crisis on her side – something to do with a mother in hospital.

'It's fine, Alex,' Lucy told him – and it was transparent to him that it wasn't. She said she accepted that he had duties. But she would go alone. She hadn't asked him to come in the first place. She was just polite enough to force out 'good night', and then she hung up in tears. She'd completely forgotten how that felt.

Alex put the phone down and snapped the pencil in his hands. He'd never let Anna down in a genuine emergency. And he'd never let Max down. There was no Will to help him out. Was there another solution or must he let Lucy down? She couldn't change the date, and he couldn't change the problem. Impasse.

*

Early on Friday, Grace and Simon drove her to Waterloo, and Simon lifted her bag out of his Land Rover. 'Are you sure you don't want company? We could always ring in sick.'

Lucy gave Simon a big hug. 'You're wonderful. No, I think I want to do this alone. I need some time alone, actually. I find I have a lot to think about.'

'Do you know what it is you're looking for?'

'I've no idea. If I find out I'll send you a postcard!' She managed a laugh.

'Make sure it's one of an angel!' Simon added with a wry smile.

The two of them had sat on the floor at Alex's London flat on the previous two Sunday afternoons, with gloved hands, surrounded by the texts of the astonishing documents Lucy had unwrapped in the silver-wrought chest at Longparish. A strange birthday present, Alex had called it: eighteen leaves of ancient vellum, which had kept them from their dinner on the snowing night of her birthday; each one of those sheets crisscrossed with riddles and clues to some other, equally obscure find. The first of them was the one Will had a copy of – some kind of original of the text that had come to him, bequeathed with the key. There was now, as she had thought before, a quire of them, inscribed front and back. The whole legacy had been buried under the giant mulberry in Alex's family garden, exactly as she had said, with only a golden Elizabethan 'angel' – a coin of considerable value – buried with them as a bedfellow. Henry had suggested it was Dee's way of paying the ferryman – an angel that assured the box's survival down the passage of centuries. It had been there, clearly, for four hundred years – the coin having been dated from its mint mark of '0' to around 1600. All of the paperwork was still legible, fairly uncorrupted, spotted with only the smallest amount of mildew – not even particularly deep in the ground, Alex had retold them as they sat mesmerised by the lines of verse and the intersecting patterns on the reverse. No one had known anything about them being there, it seemed. Alex told them both, with a healthy dose of scepticism, that the tree was alleged to have been a cutting from the great mulberry of Shakespeare's – which itself had been a gift from King James when he was obsessed with seeding the silk industry. He'd imported the wrong genus of mulberry, and *Morus nigra*, the black tree, refused to support the silk worms. But the ancient tree was wonderful, and Alex remembered coming back into the house with stained hands and mouth throughout his childhood as the first flush of berries every season enticed two little boys to gorge themselves. He could still taste them. Why it was the mulberry – why Lucy had made the leap of understanding – was a riddle itself. All she had been able to say, from that day to this, was that the portrait had told her.

She blocked the thoughts of Alex and his space now as she kissed her friend.

'Look after yourself, babe.' Simon handed Lucy through the barrier and put an arm around Grace's waist. She stepped on to Eurostar and sank into her seat in sadness. This was no longer the trip she'd been anticipating for the last few days, and she wished the phone hadn't rung last night. But it was a trip she was determined to make, and she hung on to the compelling feeling that she would satisfy some unspecified desire and deal with the problem of Dr Alexander Stafford later. The Three Fates were in league against her and she must, sensibly, resign her hopes with him. But some other very different destiny was out there for her; and she would find it.

Alex picked Max up from Crabtree Lane early that morning to give a distracted Anna a head-start north to her family where her mother, he learned more fully, was about to undergo exploratory surgery. He sounded upbeat for her sake and gave her some good advice and a few reassurances. He decided to take Max out for breakfast as a treat, then dropped him at school; but when he drove back home with the groceries, weariness crept over him. This was his first day off for weeks, and he was at a loss how to fill it. He'd mark some of his students' papers. He'd go for a walk along the river. He'd read for a while. All he wanted to do was call Lucy. To say what? She wasn't happy with him. Her rational brain understood his dilemma. Her emotional being was undermined. He'd let things cool down a little, he decided. Then he picked up his phone and dialled her mobile number.

'Yes?' Her voice unreadable. She must have seen his number ID.

'Lucy.'

'Alex?'

Since she was steeling herself to cope with disappointment her voice was crisp. He couldn't phrase anything. He wanted to remind her to take her medication with attention to French time, to eat something regularly, to stay warm – which was really an excuse to communicate how strongly he wished he were with her. But she'd resent him overcosseting her – a poor substitute for his presence. He felt wrong-footed, and said simply, 'Good luck tonight.' She said nothing; and he spoke again in no more than a whisper. '"Tread softly . . ."' He had no idea if she knew Yeats' poem, but it was all he could say to her.

He replaced the receiver, and picked up the postcard of the Chartres labyrinth Will had sent to Max, which he'd hung on to. 'Well,' he whispered, 'you'd never get yourself into a problem quite like this one, would you? What to do?' He put the postcard on his dining table and took out the baffling bundle of documents that had come to light after Lucy's bizarre revelation. He had a day off. Perhaps it was time for him to take a proper look at them.

It was six thirty p.m. The verger met her under the arch of the transept.

She'd never been to Chartres, never been so affected by a religious space. She'd spent the last hour of the day letting the light of the stained glass tickle her face, her eyes fixed on the rose windows. She'd sat and just looked up. It was awe-inspiring, and she couldn't quite take it in. She thought about the way the light worked: it was a high space, and the light drew your eyes up to it. In England, cathedrals were longer and lower, and she'd heard Alex say that was perfect for the lingering light of English twilight. French sunshine was more brilliant perhaps, and the power of the light to penetrate the gloom was exceptional, forcing your head up all the time. She'd lit a candle for her mother, wherever she was; one for her father; and two others, for two people she'd never met. She had tried to leave her thoughts of Alex and his family out of today, but she found she couldn't. She was affected by what he said on the phone – albeit in the briefest words. She wished he were here. A man had been watching her – an unpleasant reality of being a young woman travelling alone. She'd forgotten how irritating it was – in fact, how disturbing it could be – and she wished she had Alex's arm to hold. Now, in any case, she was here with the verger and just three other people who were sharing this private tour. They would each walk the sacred path, he told her. The seating had been moved, and candles were lit along the great looping coils. The setting was transcendent.

A guide with the verger began explaining in English. 'In the twelfth century certain cathedrals were decreed pilgrimage cathedrals to relieve the numbers of people making journeys to the unstable Holy Land at the time of the Crusades. Many of these had labyrinths added, which became known as "the Road to Jerusalem". Originally they were walked at Easter, just as the classical labyrinths had been a dance of spring to celebrate returning vegetation. The experience of walking, however, was meditative, calming, focusing. Many people find it brings them nearer to heaven, ready to comprehend the will of God. For the minutes that you walk it, you are outside of time: your concerns are inward and spiritual, rather than material and temporal.'

The stream of information bubbled along, but Lucy's thoughts spiralled wildly. The candles made a liquid pool, bent backwards and forwards, cast shadows through the long nave. She wanted the others to go first: she had to walk last, without anyone watching her. Her mind skipped, and she gave herself up to the extraordinary play of light and shadow. She wanted to be outside of time.

And then it was her turn – more than half an hour had raced away, and her feet were heading into the labyrinth with a will of their own.

It was six in the evening. Max settled to watch some television after he'd eaten an unusually early dinner, and Alex stretched out near him on the sofa with a glass of Bordeaux. He had sorted the papers carefully into sections and picked up the first sheet again. He thought of Lucy in Chartres with Will's working copy of this same text; it made him feel close to her, and ache to be there. *Our two souls, therefore* . . . He felt that Donne understood something precisely relevant for them. Lucy and he were divided in space, but not in thought at the moment. He would describe their two souls as one for now – they were outside of time. It must be seven in France, he thought. He took up Will's postcard of the labyrinth and looked at it, then he read some more of the text of the old document. *I am what I am, and what I am is what I am . . . I have a will to be what I am*. Alex played with the words, all weighted monosyllables, over and again. He sat up after a minute and wrote on a notepad: *Will, I am*. William.

He turned over Will's postcard, looking at the message he'd written to Max, and he started working on the geometrical pattern Will had drawn. Max asked a question, and Alex said 'yes' without really computing what he'd said. He sat up again and stared at the card: and then the text. *Bottom left is a square. Bottom right is a square.* He traced the patterns

Will had made. He had quite literally figured this, then: the five intersecting squares were a visual representation of the words. It reminded Alex of the mathematical squares they studied at Cambridge: magic number squares. Usually the whole sequence added up to a number, but the interior sections of the square added up to a common number too.

I am halfway through the orbit. He swallowed some wine. There was a magic square on one of the pages of vellum. What was half the number of the whole? he wondered.

\+ ELOHIM + ELOHI +

	4	14	15	1	
ADONAI	9	7	6	12	ZEBAOTH
	5	11	10	8	
	16	2	3	13	

\+ ROGYEL + JOSPHIEL +

They told Lucy to tread carefully among the lighted candles. Lucy nodded and tiptoed into the first snaking coil of the path. “‘Tread softly . . .’” she heard Alex's voice, and she thought of what Yeats said about treading on dreams. On my dreams too, she realised, and the words of the poem echoed in her mind. Then her mind skipped again, and this time Alex's voice was in her ear as though he were narrating

Will's document aloud for her: 'Our two souls, therefore . . .' She finished the line from the source, in Donne's poem, without a pause, '. . . which are one, Though I must go, endure not yet A breach, but an expansion . . .' Then she heard Alex's voice again in her brain: 'I am what I am, and what I am is what I am. I have a Will to be what I am.' The words swam in her head, and her feet traced back, and then forth, and then around; the flickering candles made her light-headed and aware she'd missed eating any lunch. She felt as though heaven indeed beckoned. She loved the sensation of having to be so careful with your steps, but so free with your soul.

She opened her eyes very suddenly to break the spell of the voice within. She thought she saw a man move out of the centre of the labyrinth, when she'd believed she was alone. She shivered: someone had walked on her grave. She swung back to see him again, and caught only the movement of the flames, the lights. And then Alex's gentle, rich voice was back in her head, comforting and calming. 'The truth is so; And this the cranny is, right and sinister, Through which the fearful lovers are to whisper.' She smiled. It was uncanny. She should be distilling her spiritual thoughts. The words – every single word from Will's sheet – brought Alex back to her. They were fearful lovers; she could hear him whisper, and they appeared to have only a crack in time, like a cranny, to catch each other. With a missed step, one could fall irretrievably behind.

She faced the Great Rose Window now; and she could smell her own perfume drifting back into her face. It was another draught, and it made the flames bend back and forth. She felt the movement again of someone in the labyrinth, but it was a trick of the light, and it made her tremble slightly. She heard Alex's voice soothing her, calming her down, helping her breaths to slow. Somehow he was there with her. He must be thinking about her, she decided. 'The heart is a square too.' She stepped into the very centre of the labyrinth, where there had once been a representation of Theseus, the guide had said. She felt something brush against her going the other way, and she held her skirt close to herself, suddenly worried by the candles. Then she relaxed. Again came a breeze, which wafted back at her the scent Alex had given her for Christmas, and she felt a physical warmth beside her, heard his voice right in her ear, as though he was standing immediately beside her. 'And I am halfway through the orbit.' It was Alex's voice, definitely.

Or was it? Her eyes had been lazy, half closed; and she opened them again. She sucked in a breath. Alex's face rippled in the haze of light and rose-scented heat from the hundred candle flames. His face was not perfectly shaved – was actually quite stubbly. His hair was longer and even a little bit curlier than she had seen it that night on the boat – not nearly as pristine as he had been on her birthday. She realised it was only in her mind's eye; but it appeared palpable. 'Look no further than the day, My alpha and my omega.' The voice again. Kind, reassuring, rich, musical. 'Make of these two halves a whole.'

Alex did his sums, and saw at once that the Tablet of Jupiter, which was drawn on one small sheet of vellum, made the exact squares that satisfied Will's sketch. *Halfway through* – this sheet was the midpoint, now he was sure.

He'd assumed it was the first piece of the puzzle. He took up his pencil again. *My alpha and my omega.* Someone whose beginning was also their end – the same day, or place? Alex had a flash of inspiration, and he reached a book from the shelf. He checked a date. Then he stood up and took the Bible out of the collection of items that had only recently come back from the coroner's from among Will's personal effects. It was a modern version of the King James – the Old King's Book, perhaps? A song of equal number. He glanced at the Song of Solomon, of which he now remembered Will had a copy in French among his things from France; but this wasn't strictly numbered, per se; had Will made the same leap and the same mistake? So he tried the numbered songs of Psalms in lieu.

A dreamy sensation now enveloped Lucy. She was floating in a field of flowers and flames; she heard the voice she immediately understood she loved best; and her heart beat with a wildness and pleasure she'd never felt. She was aware that the thudding and thrumming was dangerously like a heart attack, because she was letting herself go; but she was not afraid, as she was not alone. 'Equal number of paces forward from the start . . .' she recalled from Will's text. She realised she was halfway round the year, virtually to the day, from the date she'd had her life-saving operation; from the autumn to the spring equinox. It was halfway round the vital path of the first crucial year. And she was turning from the centre of the labyrinth now, ready to walk outwards, an equal number of paces to the end of it. '*Our two souls are one.*' Alex's voice was beside her, inside her, again; and then, '*I am what I am, and what I am is what you will see.'* She knew what the words on the copied sheet said, even if not in strict order. Our two hearts are one, she thought; and her eyes widened. Oh dear God! My alpha and my omega. My beginning and end.

Alex started with Psalm 23, 'The Lord is my Shepherd'. It didn't yield any cryptic clues or messages, he thought, nothing unusual. So he doubled the number, treating the number twenty-three as a half, and making of it a whole. It brought him to Psalm 46; and he counted the same number of words – or paces – forward. He wrote down the word this brought him to on the back of Will's postcard from Chartres. Then he counted the same number of words backwards, and wrote down this second word beside the first. Alex's breathing hushed and background noise seemed stilled. He'd created an intriguing new compound word of iconic significance. It produced something utterly extraordinary when he married it to the name he'd written right at the start, William.

He tossed the pencil on to the table and mouthed the whole thing, then laughed. Max looked up at him, puzzled. He had to show this to Lucy: she was in this with him. In the labyrinth.

Lucy reached the last step of the last looping coil of the path before she emerged from the intensity of candlelight and flame. She was barely aware of anyone else's presence. She had understood the vital words on this document that accompanied the key. Someone's omega had been her alpha.

What I am is what you will see. She had seen. She knew the name. She had to tell Alex.

She kissed the verger, put some money in the guide's hand, and ran with light dancing steps from the great cathedral, out on to the North Porch. She switched on her mobile and dialled the number, hardly pausing for breath.

'Hello?' Slight excitement in his voice. The synchronicity didn't surprise him.

She wanted to tell him immediately how she felt, that she was sorry for being stubborn when he'd rung earlier; but someone was walking quite close to her, and she felt self-conscious, so she began differently. 'I've got to tell you something. Well, perhaps, actually, I want to ask you something. Maybe I should come back tomorrow.' Her thoughts were in a whirl: how much to say, how to express thoughts that scorched her brain like a thousand candles.

'I want to see you too.' Alex was steady but his voice was resonating. 'I don't want you to spoil your weekend, but I've come to a realisation and I've got to show you something absolutely extraordinary. I've solved the riddle in the text that you have with you.'

'Yes, so have I! Look, Alex.' She said his name again, and he waited patiently for her to talk. It was difficult. She was trying to find words to ask a strange and complicated question and confide complex emotions, but there were people around. Yet she was bursting inside, and she had to share it – with him alone. 'Alex? Are you there?'

'Look, if you do want to stay another day, would you perhaps come back sooner on Sunday? I'm taking Max back to Anna's by three – possibly even earlier. Sunday afternoon would be a perfect time. I could cook.' Idiot, he thought to himself; if I were Will I'd just tell her I wanted her, and get her back here now. He'd push everything else to one side and get to the point. If Max was there, then Max was there. Life's like that sometimes.

'Lucy?'

She'd gone silent, her gaze suddenly caught by a man who'd been standing almost behind her, listening. He was now looking straight at her, moving towards her. She was very uncomfortable. It was the same immaculately dressed man who'd leered at her in the church earlier in the day.

'Alex!' Her voice was panicked. He heard the phone drop, muffled voices, Lucy's small cry like a child, and then all sounds retreated from the source of his hearing. He heard a clock chime the half-hour. Then nothing.

18

His hand was clamped so firmly on her mouth that she was, for a moment, labouring for breath. Such a speed. Lucy was unused to moving this quickly now, always trying to pace her exercise for the sake of her heart. Her arms were constricted, crushed tightly in his other free arm, but she caught her right hand against her chest and tried to steady herself. She thought that if she had ever had a guardian angel of any description, this would be a good time to meet her. Or him, indeed.

He smelled of limes. The strange truth was that the scent was not unpleasant to her; but the circumstances of smelling it were abhorrent. She forced her mind to try not to collapse, and worked even harder to place it at some remove from the pain she felt stinging her body. It was not her heart but her legs, arms, shoulders rebelling from his pincer grip. He seemed to make the angry wounds and scars from her surgery burn again in her flesh. Kicking was useless, she realised, since she was in certain respects still physically under par. Any odd contortion of her body bit into her deeply. She was trying to think but the pain prevented her.

They came to the mouth of an underground car park, and she was snatched almost off her feet. He started running with her, and she found herself winding down the many levels into a plummeting spiral. Down and down they went, and she felt her legs go, her head faint, her stomach churning with a nausea that reminded her at once of her Chagas'. Back into the underworld, she thought, literally. Another man was propped against a car in semi-darkness, and she thought briefly of crying for help until she realised cruelly he was there waiting for them both. She was bundled a little awkwardly into the back seat of a smart, dark blue car, with beautiful tan leather upholstery. Her assailant slid in beside her and shoved her head down on the back seat. The other man hastened them away. Two of them! She felt sick, weak, and frightened. Her mind raced at the sordid possibilities. She realised absurdly how lucky she'd been never to have experienced any serious sexual threat before – considering how often she'd had to travel alone to strange places. To survive any kind of sexual attack, you ought to stay as calm and collected as possible, she conjectured. Use your brain, Lucy: you've always been told you have a good one. How you behave might dictate whether you live or die. The chilling thought suddenly possessed her mind that the labyrinth might well prove her omega, if she got things wrong now. So she went limp and breathed slowly, making a prayer of the sound of Alex's voice. She hung on to the ecstasy she'd felt in the labyrinth, the oneness with him, the senses in her heart.

*

'Siân, I'm in trouble. Can you help?' His voice had an urgency at odds with the man she knew.

'Just say how, Alex.'

At an express pace he explained about Lucy in Chartres: he'd called the French authorities, reported her last moves and warned them she'd had transplant surgery.

They'd moved quickly enough to locate her mobile phone near the cathedral and called him straight back to inform him. Someone had rifled through her things in the hotel room, they said. He was frantic, not knowing her whereabouts, and if possible even more alarmed about her missing her medication and her health generally. Taking her immunosuppressants on time wasn't negotiable. He must get a flight now. Could she stay with Max?

'I'd be happy to, Alex.'

'Is it a terrible time to ask?'

'Not at all. We were on our way out to dinner. Unimportant after what you've just told me. Give me twenty minutes and I'll be with you.'

'Siân.' Alex hesitated. 'It's a liberty to ask this when you're dropping everything to help; but, would you come alone – without Calvin? It's just . . . Max . . .' Alex looked at his son who had come to stand right beside him, offering all the tacit support he could give even without an adult understanding of the situation. Alex was perfectly sincere about not wanting his son to deal with Will's successor yet; but something also repelled him about the idea of this strange cousin of a matter of months being in his flat, privy to his personal life.

'Not a problem, Alex. I understand. Give me time to get

a few things in a bag. If I need more tomorrow I'll bring Max here.'

She rang off, and was at his door before he'd finished his call to Anna to explain what was happening. He reassured her that everything concerning Max was under control. Anna knew her former husband to be a calm man who would refuse any provocation to panic; she saw this must be unusually important to him and that he was clearly very worried. Max trusted Siân, and Anna approved – though she'd get back when she could.

Alex was pocketing his passport and a few other things as he let Siân in, only to find Calvin with her after all. He looked at her uncomprehending while she greeted Max with an affectionate hug.

'Calvin's not staying, Alex; he's just dropped me off. But he has something important to say that I think you need to know.' She swung around and challenged her boyfriend with intensity.

Alex was wary. 'I'm a little pressed for time, Calvin. Is it relevant?'

'Very. Let me drive you to the airport, Alex. We'll talk on the way.' His voice tonight was not his usual mix of ingratiating charm and confidence, but had tones of apology and hesitancy. 'And you ought to bring these papers that relate to Dee – which I know you've found . . .'

Alex wanted to laugh: but the situation was painfully serious, and he couldn't believe what he was hearing. This was a family treasure hunt, wasn't it? A personal family mystery, or at most, an intriguing set of riddles for future generations to tease themselves on. But Calvin's words implied that the stakes were actually much higher – that this mystery may even have a sinister edge. Now, when Alex spoke, his voice was lethally quiet, and Siân realised she had never heard it sound quite like this before.

'What,' he asked, emphasising each syllable with weight, so that even his son looked up at him with concern, 'does this have to do with you?'

'Possibly I spoke too freely in the wrong quarters; perhaps I just have some associates with a questionable set of priorities; but certainly someone is now very keen to get their hands on a particular inheritance of yours.'

'Calvin, anything you know, *I* want to know. Everything you can tell me, you *will* tell me. Never in my life have I wanted to hurt a man. If anything happens to Lucy, that will change.' Alex met Calvin's gaze with such justified anger that the latter was forced to look way. Alex now glanced at the floor where Max had been sitting a little earlier, and saw for the first time that his son had made a kind of jigsaw out of the reverse sides of some of the leftover sheets he himself had not been engaged with. He'd never paid much attention to this pattern on them. He smiled, then winked at his son – who seemed relieved to have his more familiar father back with him again. Alex then scooped together the bundle of parchments, put them in their protective dossier bag again, and as quickly into a briefcase, grabbed his medical kit, and put his overcoat on one-handed.

'Be very good for Siân. I love you.' He kissed the boy and hugged him vigorously. 'You're a very clever boy.' He turned with almost as much feeling to Siân and embraced her.

'Thank you.' He mouthed the words. Then the two men wcrc gonc.

Among some silhouetted trees in the most inappropriately beautiful space in the hills above the Chartres plain, the car stopped. Lucy was pulled roughly from the vehicle by the driver – feeling nauseous, though not actually hurt, she admitted to herself, determined to hang on to the positives. But she was numb with cold. She'd dragged on her light spring trench coat as she'd left the cathedral, but it was no match for the chill evening air; the temperature was dropping while the weak March sun disappeared. She noticed a building in the last light; quite beautiful. It was a partially ruined farmhouse, she could see, but she wasn't interested in the architectural features. Strange how you could experience such terror in the midst of beauty. She was bundled through the door by both men, and found herself in a damp room with a wan fire, where yet another man was sitting reading at a table some distance from it. He seemed, she thought, almost unconcerned with the intrusion.

Oh God, what is happening? she wondered, incredulous, and her spirits sank completely. This didn't seem like an attack on a single woman now. Fear gripped her firmly; she had no notion at all how to approach this – or what in fact she was approaching.

'I trust you haven't been hurt, Miss King?' The sole custodian of the old farmhouse looked up from his book. 'Heart surgery is a serious matter. It changes you.'

That threw her into disarray: who could know such things? Lucy looked over at an almost attractive man, perhaps forty years of age and a little overweight, with greying curly hair, who appeared to be of about medium stature. He was seated at a plain farmhouse table with a partly played chess game in front of him. She wouldn't – or couldn't – speak, and forced herself into a mood of apparent calm, electing to leave questions about her arrival at this forlorn location unasked. Her eyes darted around the room, and returned to his face. He was amused, perhaps – or even quietly impressed – by her controlled silence. He soon broke the stalemate.

'Thank you, gentlemen. Mephistopheles, if you could step outside and make a call to our senior colleague, I think he'd like to hear from us. And now,' he half spoke to Lucy, 'we wait.' He sounded completely uninterested and picked up his book again, while the physical bulk of the unattractively named man who'd stolen her in Chartres disappeared through the front door. She thought grimly, and without humour, that she was indeed in some kind of hellish place.

After an hour Lucy still hadn't opened her mouth, but she began to feel she might not be in immediate danger. She moved her head about to search for a meaning in the murkiness. She was feeling more chilled, the fire inadequate in the draughty area; but she let them know nothing about her. The driver – a tall man with grey eyes – was now addressed by the seated man in fluent French; he moved into a very unrenovated kitchen area, out of Lucy's clear line of sight, and then came over to her with some water. She resisted a fatuous show of scorn and took it, still without a word, but wouldn't drink.

A mobile rang. The man at the table picked up without haste.

'Um-hm?' He listened for a very long time before he spoke again. 'Put him on the phone.'

Lucy noticed now for the first time that he was an American with a mild Southern accent – but not at all warm, like Dr Angelica's.

'We have the girl.' His tone was light and playful, and he reminded Lucy of a cat toying with an injured bird it has a distaste of actually eating. 'I believe we have the means to the lock.' He gestured at the man who had taken Lucy from the porch of the cathedral, who moved silently from a chair in the darkest part of the room. He came towards her and pulled at a chain around her neck – the slim gold chain Alex had given her for her birthday a few weeks earlier. The little key came free with it, and her skin felt pinched and bruised on her neck. She felt defiled, and stared at the yellow eyes of the well-named devil before her.

'Yes, we certainly do.' The cat's charming southern voice continued. 'Now then, good Doctor, I believe I have something you want. And you have something I want. There is no need for anyone else to be concerned in this – and no one else *shall* be as long as you follow instructions to the letter. But please believe me, if I find the *gendarmerie* curious at my door, or sense the slightest duplicity on your part, I'm apt to be irritable. The rather desirable exchange I am contemplating will be off. I hope that's quite clear?' Lucy observed that every word was succinct, and that he pronounced '*gendarmerie*' with an excellent French accent.

He got out of his chair and walked slowly across the room

towards the fire, and as he did so Lucy caught the quiet drift of Alex's voice from the ear-piece. This gave her heart: it sounded just as steady as usual. '. . . understand these papers which seem to excite your interest have very little fascination for me. I marvel at grown men becoming so enthralled by them. Do you really think . . .'

Her host turned away again to deny her the security of knowing what was happening. She watched his face, finding him somehow pathetic in his attempts to do verbal battle with Alex. He picked up a chess piece that had fallen over and played with it. He finally returned to her and sat close enough for her to hear Alex's voice clearly again. She realised he wanted her emotional reaction to it.

'. . . is recovering from surgery and requires very gentle handling. I will move heaven and earth to make sure that some very uncomfortable questions are put to you. And although Mr Petersen advises me that you're a man to whom nothing sticks, I promise you'll find me unrelenting. So let's drop the verbal chess games, make our arrangements and adhere to them. My flight for De Gaulle leaves in fifteen minutes and gets down at eleven p.m. How do you suggest . . . ?'

Lucy turned her own head away. She understood they wanted Alex to bring them the papers he'd dug up, but she had no idea how they knew, or why they were so important, or what on earth 'Mr Petersen' had to do with it. She refused to look again at the man who kept her hostage, and tried indeed to block out the last words he spoke on the phone:

'It is such a pleasure negotiating with an intelligent human being. It saves so much wasted time and pain. And

I've missed the opera tonight for this; although in fact, some very high-calibre people will assure you that I *am* there, even now collecting my glass of champagne in the interval. Don't you love the opera, Dr Stafford? *Lucia di Lammermoor?*'

Alex balked at the final command concerning the collection of Lucy, but he knew he'd played it out almost to his last card and would have to accept this stipulation. He flipped his mobile phone shut and fell in behind the last passenger boarding his flight. He was weighing up the quiet menace of the unspoken threat he'd just heard so very clearly.

Adrenalin had kept him focused for the last gruelling hour, but he clicked his seat belt home and allowed himself the privacy to evaluate in his mind what had been rushed upon him. After volunteering unsuccessfully to accompany him to France, Calvin had done his best during the car journey to acquaint Alex with these three men: not merely their obsessive interest in the papers of Dr John Dee but, more alarmingly in the light of Lucy's abduction, he had hinted at the nature of the company they kept, the connections they had right at the top in government in three continents. The one Alex had just spoken to was the man Calvin called Guy – 'the American in Paris'; he chose to live mostly in France because of some ancestral pride about being descended from a Templar, and he had all kinds of men in his pocket. The way Calvin pronounced his name, Alex could only think of clarified butter – which helped, for some reason. Slippery perhaps, he thought, but not solid.

In volley after volley of shocks that broke on Alex,

Calvin had spoken of other men connected with his college who seemed unduly fascinated with their ancestor and his supposed role as confidant to the angels. Alex noticed that they all had epithets instead of real names, and their chain of influence extended, according to Calvin, into lofty political offices. They never had to do their own dirty work, his cousin had told him, and Alex felt sure Calvin's tone had disclosed real anxiety about them. His summation had been precise: they were impossible to cross, and they didn't want treasure. He assured Alex that it was propaganda they wanted, and it would be put to a powerful political use. They would be heavily protected by many men of stature who were interested in their findings; but, he believed, they would almost certainly stop short of serious harm as long as they got exactly what they wanted. For the moment at least, it would be best to try to do things their way.

Alex's emotions about Calvin were in turmoil, vacillating between fury, incredulity and even pity. Listening to him speak at length, he'd once or twice wondered just how honestly Calvin was levelling with him, and whether he might have some altogether different agenda; but he'd sat and listened, to *what* he'd said, what he didn't say, and *how* he'd said it – preferring to venture fewer questions and expose less of his own mind. He wanted the liberty to reflect on all of this, and to look into it under his own aegis. But the one thing he knew was that he'd heard more than enough from Calvin in thirty-five minutes to make him ill. A truth was brought home to Alex that he'd considered many times, but never in so personal a way: there were people in the world who had just enough religion to hate, but not enough religion to love. In something very near despair, he realised he would do well to recover Lucy in one piece at any cost, and then to get out.

19

He spent the flight lost in thought over the implications of these people's obsession with Dee and the so-called angel books; could this be connected to his brother's fatal accident? The coroner's verdict had come down a month ago, corroborating accidental death; but Alex now had fresh suspicions. He'd have to save those ideas for another day, however; they opened up too many wounds now, and his immediate concern had to be to reach Lucy. This man Guy, the Templar relation, was disarmingly mild-mannered on the phone, but his methods would surely be unstable if put to the test, and he took Calvin's assurances as to their ultimate reservations to perpetrate real harm with a pinch of salt. He felt Lucy's life hung in the balance, and if he didn't get to her quickly, she would have a second – and potentially greater – disaster to deal with in the form of missed medication. The police had discovered her small purse along with the phone where she was taken. She would have none of her anti-rejection drugs with her, and Alex had to reach her with his own supply.

The plane landed ten minutes late, but his mind was unwearied and clear as he jogged to the rental desk to pick up a car they had arranged for him – pre-paid in cash, which indicated they had quite some network. He hated being so exposed in a car they could trace, but he hadn't much choice. In twenty minutes he had a small Citroën and was leaving the airport precincts in greasy rain for a house in Arbonne le Forêt. He'd have to ignore the elements if he was to make it in under an hour, by the appointed time of half-past midnight. Being late was not an option for them or for Lucy. She should have taken her drugs by nine o'clock French time. To be a few hours late could be life-threatening.

The journey towards Fontainebleau and on to Arbonnc was surprisingly swift in the deteriorating conditions. Nothing was on the road and Alex, who knew the route to Fontainebleau itself quite well, followed the additional directions without trouble. He turned into the village, swung along a lane, and started looking for house names on the walls. He came on the right house easily, as it was illuminated in an otherwise sleepy place. He knocked. A housekeeper came to the door.

'*Je suis desolé . . .*'

'*Oui, Monsieur. Il attend. Entrez, s'il vous plaît.*' She was nervous, and Alex realised something had been foisted on her unwillingly. She asked him to sit in a large room with great stone walls that had probably once been a simple farmhouse, but renovation had made it more baronial. There were photos of a very pretty young blonde woman on the wall, with amazing cheekbones. Alex looked at them in confusion.

'No clues for you here, Dr Stafford. The house belongs to a German actress who was once a lover of mine, but we haven't been on good terms for years.' A dark-haired man of tanned complexion in a cream polo-neck and dark cord trousers came down a showy staircase from what must have been a converted attic or barn. This was not the voice on the phone. 'She has no idea I'm here; and her pregnant daughter is in London . . . I'm not sure either of them would be happy to see me, so it would be politic to mind your manners.' A slight accent; unknown origin, now disguised behind English learned in an American school, Alex decided. He was reminded in looks – though not in manner – of a brilliant asthma and allergy specialist Alex knew, who was Israeli.

'I'm not interested. I have some documents for you. Then I'd like to conclude our business.' Alex kept his words brief and his voice level to project a control he didn't truly feel, but the act was convincing. The contents of the dossier bag from his briefcase were scrutinised, page by page, almost word by word, in gloved hands. Time spilled dangerously on, and Alex became nervous about Lucy's drugs. He indicated that the papers were old and vulnerable; they ought not to be subjected to unnecessary handling.

What did *he* think was in them, his interlocutor wondered. He was surprised at Alex's professed lack of interest or knowledge. Alex stated firmly that he had no idea, and thought the whole preoccupation with them a storm in a teacup; but he never revealed the word he'd written on

Will's postcard earlier that evening, and he kept his peace until he was allowed to leave.

Shortly after one a.m., he was behind the wheel of the Citroën and driving west. The rain-affected road back to Chartres would take the better part of an hour, even though much of it was motorway. His mobile rang, and the buttery voice of the Templar knight resumed.

'Highly impressive performance, Dr Stafford. And we're gentlemen. So: *la porte d'hiver*. Two o'clock precisely. *Je vous souhaite une bonne nuit. Au revoir.*'

Moments after the cathedral clock chimed twice, Alex found Lucy alone, huddled and trembling in the doorway of the north porch. This made him angry. He slid out of his heavy overcoat and flung it around her, then became aware glancing over his shoulder of a dark car with headlights dimmed, pulling away at speed. He returned to Lucy's face, rapidly assessing her mental condition, then her physical state. Her battery was low, but she smiled at him.

'They won't get me back. I didn't eat a bite they offered me. Not even a sip of water.'

Alex took a second to register that she was talking as the goddess returning from the Underworld, then he managed a quiet laugh of relief and disbelief. He held on to her for a moment before he could move, ostensibly to infuse his own body heat into her; but she felt him shivering almost imperceptibly. His real anxiety of the last hours was oddly transparent to her. She felt stronger for once than Alex, showing no fragility when she reciprocated his embrace and tilted her face up to his.

'I'm all right, Alex. I knew you'd get me out of it.' Then she asked: 'But, what do those papers contain?'

He couldn't answer.

'The hotel's very close by.'

'We're not going there.' Giving her a bottle of water from one deep coat pocket and some capsules from the other, Alex scooped her into the car and stopped briefly outside the Grand Monarque Hotel, refusing to release her hand even while he settled the bill with the night porter and collected her passport and belongings. He paused for the briefest moment to thank the police, pick up her purse and phone, and tell them she was unhurt but in shock. His first concern now was with her health and they would answer any questions later in the day after some rest. His French was fluent and his manner refused challenge, and they were quickly off. In the car he held her hand through the thirty-minute trip, releasing it only to change gear. It was approaching three o'clock when they turned up the drive to the house near L'Aigle, and despite the hour Alex put the car in the garage and properly secured the door. They sprinted through icy rain, and he produced a key from a pot of over-wintering geraniums.

He turned on some lights, left the windows shuttered, pointed out a bathroom to her, then bounded upstairs and fiddled with some switches. He was back before Lucy had found a chair.

Her face was tired but shining. 'This space.' White wicker furniture freshly upholstered, a small orangerie off the large sitting room, watercolours on the walls, a piano, a cello leaning against the stool, photos everywhere. She felt like a lost child who'd come home. She settled in an antique carver at the table beside a dresser brightened with china.

Alex adjusted the oil-fired stove and flicked a kettle, then rummaged in a freezer down a tiny passageway, returning with a brown sandwich loaf. He was not yet ready to relax and enjoy her impressions.

'I'm not sure how long this has been here, but it will revive with toasting. I don't think we can trust the butter . . . but you have to eat something.' He hadn't yet been still when he passed her a swallow of hot tea and a slice of toast drizzled with honey from meticulously clean hands; then he disappeared upstairs for a few moments again. Lucy's blood returned with the warmth of the drink and the house, but she was aware of a woozy fatigue creeping over her when he reappeared and propped himself on a corner of the kitchen table. He smiled at her huge tired eyes, which were dark-circled underneath.

'OK, you. I've got a small fire going upstairs; and the water should be just hot enough for a very quick shower.'

She stood up and put her fingers lightly over his lips to still them. 'It's not a shower that I need, Alex . . . nor a doctor.' Her thumb traced the line of his smile and he kissed it, aware of the delicious sweetness from the honey. Green eyes searched brown to determine their mood: then in a second his hand was behind her head and their mouths came softly together.

As long as they'd waited they refused now to hurry. Alex lost himself in her honeyed breath and kissed her languorously before he gently reached down and lifted her small frame up on to his. Her legs wrapped around him easily. Her eyes never strayed from his, and he carried her lightly up the steps. The room was already mildly scented with pine and wood smoke, and he rocked her back, sitting her softly on a thick woollen throw on the bed. They undressed each other without haste, conscious of savouring the moments. He kissed her cheeks and lashes and then leaned down with her on to the soft wool, caressing the contour of her waist and tiny belly. His hands moved reverently upwards; and he followed the cruel scar that curved around her left breast, almost from her rib to her collarbone, with sensitive fingers.

Lucy strangled a breath and wanted to cry. 'It's so ugly.'

'No, it's beautiful,' he countered. 'It saved you,' and he traced the stark wound slowly with kisses until his lips and warm breath brushed her throat, and then found her mouth again.

This time their hunger was raw and their passion urgent. Lucy's senses were screaming for his body heat, the delay now an agony, the pleasure close to pain. 'Alex!' She wrenched free long enough for the sound to escape with such longing that he swept his hand firmly from her breast to her hip; then hearing his name again he lifted her slightly and pulled himself inside her. Their breath escaped in a rush together.

His hand pressed into the small of her back; her legs wound around him involuntarily; and she felt the depth of him in her sensual body so intensely that her mind unravelled like yarn, her breaths butterfly light. He still hadn't broken from her kiss; now his fingers looked for a path between their locked bodies, moving downwards from her belly button, but she stopped him. 'No, Alex. Too much.' He opened his eyes to understand, looking right into her; and it laid her soul bare. Without warning the tightening coils in Lucy's body sprang free. Her whole physical being was racked by almost aching sensations her mind couldn't hold back. She had never felt so exposed, but so imperatively open. Her senses had returned from a long-imposed exile. Somehow – she couldn't say how – she had let herself trust him, craved this oneness with him, and the physical effect was mesmeric. He absorbed all of her pleasure, the exquisite and unrepeatable first chords of intimacy between them; and only then gave himself up to her rhythm.

Time was irrelevant. Lucy had no idea how long it was before he finally locked his arms around her, and they admitted to satiety. She drifted to sleep hearing Alex's heartbeat and the wind.

20

She was aware of a tapping sound, then felt the space beside her. Her lids rose indolently, and she saw his shadow teasing up the embers, adding logs to the fire, releasing a fresh smell of pine. The shutters weren't latched and wind rattled the glass.

'It's early – not yet seven. And the weather's filthy.' His voice was soft and husky, and he retraced his steps to her. 'But my lady is fair. A good reason not to move.' He slipped in next to her warmth and cradled her. His fingers had an aroma of smoked almonds, and she kissed the tips – a prelude to other explorations with her lips.

He laughed. 'Are you always this demanding? After two hours' sleep?'

'It's time I was more demanding . . . I've never felt this good after two hours' sleep.' She leaned up on an elbow to confront him, noted his emerald eyes glittering back at her playfully. '"Nay, come, I prithee. Would'st thou be ruled by me?"' She hovered to take a dominant position.

'"Madam, I will."'

It was past ten o'clock when Alex kissed her awake and laid a single finger across her lips to hush her. 'I'm going to check in with Siân, then I want to run out for some milk and something to eat – there's not much here.'

'Should I come?'

'I'll be quick. Do you feel safe?' She nodded drowsily. 'Then just stay put. Or run a bath. The water will be steaming now, and there's a tempest at the door.'

After a late breakfast, they let the weather seal them in. They talked as they never had, without interruptions. First, about the house, the paths and walks through the woods, the orchard, the history of the building, the family photos inhabiting it. Lucy drank in the smells of wood smoke and blossom that warded off the damp, asked about family holidays and memories shared within the walls. Alex spoke a little about Will, and more about his mother. Lucy said something of hers. Both were thoughtful, each was attentive. They were relaxed, no one needed them, Max was being spoiled, Siân was relishing her maternal role – 'Stay where you are,' she had told Alex, 'and just take care of Lucy.' So they discussed their ordeal in more depth, their impressions of the protagonists involved; and he told her about Calvin's strange place in the scheme of things.

'Somehow they knew you'd been given the key – information they can only have had from Calvin. Which is, I think, what made you a target.'

Alex's words told her he was still ruminating on everything he'd learned. She listened without adding much, but contemplated Siân's relationship with Calvin in a new and troubled light. Later they phoned the *gendarmerie*, sensitive to the warning not to bring the police in and attract more trouble. While Alex didn't want to give in to this tepidly, he thought it wise to be pragmatic, so they gave noncommittal statements, and stayed close to each other.

In the early hours Alex had noticed the venison in the freezer mentioned in his mother's card to Will; and it was sufficiently defrosted for him to start preparing a slow casserole at about five. When he had opened a bottle of fine wine and poured some on to the meat and a little into a glass for each of them, he reminded Lucy that she'd wanted to ask him a question when she'd phoned, breathless from the labyrinth.

For the first time she tensed, and Alex sensed a dilemma, knowing not to push her. The question had usefully preoccupied all her conscious energies while she was confined with Calvin's friends. Turning the ideas over one way and then another had focused her mind and loaned her a stubborn resilience; but she knew that any words she chose now would unleash strong winds she couldn't control, and she wondered how she and Alex might be buffeted by them once the question was put. She had never wanted to ask anything more desperately, but never felt less able to do so. She began at a tangent.

'When did you first notice me?' She wasn't being coy, and looked at him seriously. He understood the question had complex undertones. 'I think I want to ask, when did you become interested in me? Can you remember? Was it after my transplant?'

His fingers smelled of crushed bay leaves when he touched her face; and she tried to select further words to explain her thoughts. 'If I only had to ask, "How strong are you?" I wouldn't have to deliberate so long. But I'm also thinking, "How strong are we?" and I can't answer that yet.'

'It wasn't your liminal state of being that attracted me, if that's what you're worrying. I've never seen you as a victim needing protection. To the contrary: it was your independence and self-composure I loved. The first time I saw you . . . was that about May? I heard you laughing and thought: what a fascinating woman. You were young, and beautiful, and staring at the real possibility of death, yet you kept your grace and humour. I wouldn't have had your courage. You hung on to hope, and you never felt sorry for yourself for a moment.'

The corners of her mouth twitched upwards as he said this. She remembered the precise hour too. Alex was someone who seemed to drink up all the light in a room, and his physical presence had a powerful luminosity for her at a dark time. 'So you quite liked the old me?'

Alex ran his hand through her hair and nodded. He wanted to find her soul in her eyes. 'What's troubling you?'

His kindness – the way he looked right into her like this – often made Lucy feel vulnerable, almost uncomfortably naked. She stood and crossed the kitchen to look away and regain some physical autonomy. Then, when she could face him again, she said simply: 'I think I have your brother's heart.'

It was perhaps thirty seconds, but it seemed to Lucy as if whole minutes froze.

'Say something, Alex.' She had physically put space between them and was uncertain how to bridge the gap verbally. When she examined his face, searching out his thoughts, they were a mystery. She tried another tack. 'I thought, perhaps, you'd know who my donor was?'

Tenderness answered her, rather than shock. He saw she was grappling with something enormous. He shook his head quietly: 'I wasn't there. It's at best only a detail for the co-ordinator's knowledge – although sometimes some aspects of the donor's life, or cause of death, might be relevant to the whole team.' He seemed calm. 'But remember, at that moment I wasn't a part of that team. Why would you think it was Will's?'

'Well, the date matches.' She broke off and saw Alex nodding, thinking, and she continued, 'But it's much more. When I think back over the last few months, I don't understand why I didn't realise sooner. Will was obviously going to have been an organ donor with you for a brother.'

Alex was looking at her with scepticism, and she rounded on him defensively. 'Just listen a moment. I'm no longer vegetarian, have such unfathomable dreams.'

'Medication.' He said this without meaning to be condescending. 'You've got such a powerful cocktail of drugs in you for the first six months to a year. They're beasts, Lucy.'

'OK, yes, Courtney said as much, so I went with that. But every time I met someone from your circle of friends, I knew them. Siân, for instance; and Simon. They were so familiar to me.' Alex looked dubiously at her, and she managed half a laugh, aware that it seemed crazy. 'I know I sound loopy,

Alex, really; but I'm not losing my mind. I assure you, there are just too many things. I knew your house in Hampshire; and I felt like I'd come home here, as soon as we walked in.'

'Lucy, you were relieved to find a safe haven . . . Nothing mattered to me except creating that for you as soon as we got here.'

'Yes.' She smiled appreciatively. 'But think how that headache seized on me, Alex, that day in Longparish. The sensation of nausea and pain and chill. I honestly thought I was going to die. I'm sure it was seeing Will's place, the churchyard – everything.' He was going to interrupt, but she kept on. 'And I've wanted to call you "Sandy" half a dozen times, which was far too intimate when we were just getting to know each other; but I think that's what Will must have called you?' She challenged him softly.

Alex laughed with surprise. It was true – his pet name to Will alone since their childhood; but while he didn't want to prejudge her, this was strange territory for him. 'Have I let that slip? Or did Siân?'

'No, Alex, no one's told me. And I think he called you that because of your . . .'

They finished the words together: '. . . sandy hair.'

He looked at her, thinking, trying so hard not to be closed to this for her sake: but it was odd.

'I want to ask you a silly thing. Was Will left-handed?'

Alex's eyes shot up. 'And you've been more left-handed since transplant surgery. Lucy, these things are interesting: really.' He responded sympathetically to her stressed expression. 'But it doesn't add up to a case. Your anti-rejection drugs could account for a lot of this.'

'So they could, I quite agree. Would you put it on the line? Are you able to find out?'

Lucy saw clouds in Alex's eyes. They were still strong, but there was something else in them, another emotion. Questions, ideas, mute debates. Another man would do her less justice; but Alex might be the one person who would try to see the world through her eyes. He stood up and found his mobile, dialled a number, and crossed to Lucy while it was ringing. 'They may not tell me. I haven't mentioned, I passed your case over to James Lovell early this week. I thought it might be time – Hi, Jane, it's Alex Stafford.'

Lucy had only a moment to embrace the implications of Alex resigning professional care of her; then she listened while he commiserated that Jane was working on yet another Saturday, joked with her that he didn't want to be called in, it was his weekend off, anyway he wasn't in London, he'd bring her back some Calvados. She thought he was more conversational than usual. Then his free hand swallowed Lucy's and he asked the question: could she check her files, let him know from which region Lucy's heart had been harvested? 'Jane it's important, or I wouldn't ask.' Time was suspended. She watched Alex for the answer. He was nodding. 'Yes, I see. Jane, can you look at any more details? Are you able to tell me anything about the actual hospital?' And then he stopped shilly-shallying. 'Or, Jane, could you just simply tell me – the donor?'

Lucy heard the silence: the chirping through the receiver had ceased. Alex looked at her obliquely. 'Can you say . . . I won't ask more than this. Might the name mean anything to me?' Lucy heard the bounce in Jane's voice – her usually infectious Irish energy – go suddenly flat. Lucy realised that, in the wake of Will's death, many more people would have heard his name spoken in connection with Alex, and if it hadn't meant anything to Jane at the time, it would in hindsight. Alex crushed her fingers. 'That's fine. Don't worry. That's a huge help. Thank you. Jane, get home to your family.'

Alex rang off. He looked into Lucy's velvet eyes, the brown now a steel grey; and he folded her in his arms without words. She returned his hug with compassion, and when he loosened his arms after a while he said only: 'How did you really know?'

She made a swift decision. Alex was a reasonable man. He was immensely tolerant of whatever others thought, whatever prayers they needed, whatever faiths they held; but he was firmly grounded in this world with his five senses. Now, however, she took both of his hands and looked at him with placid strength on her own part. She felt she had seen the land of the dead; she would tell it like it was, even at the risk of ridicule.

'I saw Will last night. In the light. In the labyrinth.'

She picked up their glasses and led Alex into the sitting room to the wood-burning stove. She explained about the script, Will's page. She had played with the name and got: Will, I am. She had heard the words about being two souls, now one. At first she read it as her growing feelings for Alex – which was right. But she felt it included a second layer of meaning. Someone's omega – their end – had been her alpha – her beginning. And then, she told him, she really had *seen* Will's face. She'd thought it was Alex's – the face she'd most wanted to see. But it was distorted in the candlelight: a slightly squarer chin, broader shape, a shade less refined, much darker hair, fuller curls, but otherwise strongly reminiscent of Alex's own handsome face. 'It was the face of this lovely boy, grown to a man.' She identified Will in a photo of the brothers as children, about ten and twelve, on the mantel over the fire. She could appreciate more of the similarities than the differences between them.

And then, she explained further, she'd heard the voice. *Heard* it. Alex must have been talking to her in his mind. 'Yes,' he showed surprise, 'I was.' And Lucy knew. But she also believed that this had a second significance too. Will's voice was also there, so like his brother's, slightly more melodic perhaps, a little lighter and less calming. And she'd felt something tangible brush past her. Will was there, walking the labyrinth a second time, with her. He could believe her, or disbelieve. It didn't matter. She knew it to be true.

It was some time before he spoke. He was thinking of the South American doctor who'd given him the Márquez book, inviting him to consider the space between reality and spirituality.

He sipped some wine and spoke to her. 'Research has been done on this – is being done. Cellular memory, they call it. Some doctors firmly place it in the realms of myth. Some are outraged that anyone even considers the possibility. Others propose that cells have a mind of their own, in a way, and that moving living tissue from one body to another doesn't terminate the memory from that "mind". It's possible that the chains of amino acids which send messages between the brain and other parts of the body are also generated in the heart. I've never taken a position on this subject before. I know there are some famous test cases, particularly in America; some really extraordinary stories where it would be unfair not to keep an open mind. But nothing unequivocal has been proved. If the brain isn't our only centre of knowing, and the heart does – as some suggest – have its own intrinsic nervous system, then perhaps it may be possible.' He looked up at her and saw she was listening intently to him, trying to understand for herself. 'Courtney would dismiss it outright, but I'll talk to Amel. He'll have an opinion – one worth hearing.' He held the wine in the firelight for a moment. 'But it's strange, because not everyone experiences this. If they did, it would offer more consistency.'

Lucy looked at him sadly, her fears not yet silenced. 'Alex, whether you can digest the impressions I've told you about or not, what of the issue itself? Of me actually having Will's heart. Can you still think of it as just a pump? Is it a problem for you?'

Alex had been leaning back on his hands on the floor by the fire. He quickly rocked forwards to touch her, stroking her cheekbone with his thumb. 'Lucy, Will had gone. I checked all the data myself – I was there at the very end. Which you'll now understand was why I couldn't be with you.'

She placed her firm hand on his back.

'Whatever Will was taking with him, it wasn't a living heart. If my brother's death was in any way a means to your life, then I'll thank him every day I breathe.' He cupped her face in his hands and poured assurances into her eyes. 'Is it a problem for you?'

'It's you who's kissed my soul awake, Alex. It had been hiding in near-darkness all of my life, until you made me trust you. But I believe Will's had a part to play too. For the first time my instincts have been to *listen* to my heart. He must have been a passionate person, and the great legacy of his heart wasn't going to be happy in a cool place. If that's just psychological, well, I'll take that. For me it's more than a pump. I think I can feel his –' she searched for some language to explain strange impressions – '*joyance*, at the end. He wasn't hankering after anything, Alex; he isn't haunting me. I feel him standing in clean air, somewhere high up. I feel his humour, right to the final moments. I was unafraid of death before; but he's made me more unafraid of life.'

'Of the things you've said, the idea of Will's irreverent wit to the last is the most persuasive.' Alex laughed at this; it appealed. 'We often argued about one thing especially heatedly. Will placed himself with the Romantic poets, when it came to the idea of Newton. Keats – and Lamb, I think – argued that Sir Isaac had destroyed the poetry of the rainbow by reducing it to a prism; and Will joined in their chorus, partly to test me. I've championed Newton's vision all my life, and I still would now, but tonight you've made me reconsider it. Perhaps the heart isn't only an organ. And maybe we need to hold on to a little bit of the goddess in the rainbow. See it as more than the sum of the parts.'

Alex now loosened the ties of Lucy's soft cashmere ballet cardigan and placed his long fingers between her breasts with tender sensuality. He kissed her. 'It's wonderful to have you here with me.' And if 'you' addressed more than one person, Lucy was equal to it.

The image caught in his side mirror of a man passing close to his car in expensive designer jeans and a more expensive light corduroy jacket put Simon on the alert. He waited just a few more seconds, then swung out of the driver's seat and door-stopped a totally unprepared Calvin. Leaping up a short staircase he raised an arm ready to take a swing, but Calvin countered too quickly and held the surprisingly well-developed arm of his attacker at length.

'We can have this out right here if you like, but would it be better if you came inside?'

Simon was caught a little off guard. 'I never had a brother, Calvin – there's only my mother. Will Stafford was everything to me: and I have an uncomfortable conviction that you know something about his accident you haven't mentioned yet.'

The two men stared at one another, the tension visible to a woman hurrying by along the pavement with a bakery bag and an averted glance, trying to mind her own business. Each man was tight-coiled, focused on what should follow; until Calvin finally offered his unexpected guest some 'meagre hospitality. My rooms are rather small. But you'd better come inside.' He released his grip on Simon's arm, unlocked the door, and the latter pushed his way in rather forcefully behind.

No experience of student digs bore any comparison in Simon's mind with Calvin's space. Looking around the living and study area, he carefully noted the exaggerated degree of cleanliness, the neat row of a small number of books, the immaculately placed shoes, the coat in a dry-cleaner's dust cover. Everything was expensive, though it was sparsely furnished. Alex was organised and orderly; but his cousin seemed to border on obsessive-compulsive behaviour. A stranger successor to Will in Siân's life, Simon thought to himself, couldn't be imagined.

Calvin folded himself up primly on a sofa, his body language tautly controlled. He took a moment before inviting Simon into an Art Deco-style chair, brightly upholstered, directly opposite him; but his visitor preferred to remain standing.

'Straight answer, Calvin: because you're unfortunately involved with people I care deeply about.' Simon's voice was full of thinly disguised emotion, and he was cross with himself for that. 'I want to know about the key, the Dee papers, and the people you're in bed with. I'm disinclined to believe anything I've heard from you until now, so cut the crap and tell me the truth. You might gag Alex, who always wants to believe the best in anyone, but I'm not so forgiving, and my two best contacts at Scotland Yard would love a good tip-off.'

Calvin took his time replying. Eventually he confronted Simon in a flat, quiet voice. 'Things have . . . spiralled. What they want is not what I want.' He stood, crossed the small space to open a desk drawer, and withdrew a pair of well-thumbed paperbacks, which he handed over to his visitor. He sat again, determined to master his own time and environment. 'The people I study with believe what's in the Bible – and have distorted it just sufficiently to write that literature. You can laugh at them, Simon –' he reacted to the other man's wry humour and dismissive incredulity – 'but please don't underestimate them. They are sure that Christ is coming, and they're convinced that day is very near for them. Dee's ideas are of interest to them. Those books are part of a series, and their author is one of the most successful in American history. Their theology is not my theology. Their politics are not my politics.'

Simon looked down at the stark covers of the books without understanding Calvin. He saw four horses galloping on a cover, and a view down the barrel of a gun, but he couldn't take it in. He was aware, though, that Calvin was in a strange mood when he continued speaking.

'I do believe in the person of Jesus, Simon, and preaching, and the lessons of scripture. But that faith should impact on our culture and our political agenda – that it should be used as a moral argument to promote war? I don't go along with that. The head of my college is a charismatic man, but he is using his religion as a gun in the world. I distance myself from that totally.'

Simon stayed and listened to the things Calvin offered him for a little short of an hour, and left clutching the oddly named and disturbingly covered volumes from Calvin's personal library. It was just about credible. Calvin might, he thought, have shared their theology but not their politics. But the journalist's instinct in him niggled, and he had a deep suspicion that Calvin was concerned with buttering his own bread, and that he had revealed, in fact, very little of what was really going on. He came away no wiser as to what the cherished Dee papers might have offered Calvin's

Christian evangelists – and not at all sure of what personal and unconfessed allure they had for Calvin himself.

But he was going to find out.

21

'Did you pick this rose for me yesterday, and bring it up?' Lucy, clutching a warm towel to her, rose from the bath and examined the delicately fading bloom more closely. It was scented and colourful, but now she looked more closely, she saw it was perhaps slightly rain-damaged. 'You should have done it today, the twenty-first – for the spring equinox.'

Alex appeared beside her from the adjoining room, the bathroom serving each of the brothers' bedrooms from either side. 'No, I thought you must have. I was amazed you'd found one so early in the season.' Alex shook his head. 'You make me wish I'd thought of it – though I doubt there's anything in flower yet. Who's been here? Perhaps someone borrowed the house.' He stepped closer and studied the flower properly. 'Actually, it's faded, isn't it? Beautifully preserved. As though it were touched by frost on the bush.'

'It has a wonderful myrrh fragrance, though. Can it have been picked long ago?'

She returned to the bedroom without waiting for his answer, and found the shutters thrown back, and a window open. Alex had brought a breakfast tray up with a teapot and brioche. 'Are you drinking my brew now?' She laughed at him. 'You're spoiling me. I've got to go back to the real world tomorrow and put in rather a long day.'

Alex wondered a little what that 'real world' might consist of now, but answered Lucy with a deliberate lightness: 'Like the rest of us then. We'll need a flight around four. I've got to return the car first, and pay the excess. We should have an early lunch.'

'I wish we never had to leave here.' Lucy easily sensed Alex's train of unspoken thought. 'It feels safe: as though it's got its arms around me. And the linen smells of lavender . . .'

She had been deeply affected by coming to this, Alex's mother's house, and felt she'd found something she never realised was lost to her. Despite the tensions they had been through, the place itself worked like a love philtre on them, and made her feel relaxed, and whole, and healed, in Alex's presence. She dropped her towel and walked to the window, forgetting the compulsion to cover her scarred body for the first time in months. With the victory of sunshine over the rain there was a double rainbow.

'Look, Alex.'

He joined her, putting his arms around her from behind and leaning into the windowsill. 'Poetry, and science.' His eyes smiled at her. 'You must see the garden before lunch.'

'Let me cook for you today,' she offered; and Alex didn't protest.

The grass was soaked, and a few small branches littered

the orchard, but there was little damage from the storm. Lucy looked at a hundred rose bushes coming into bud, tiny shoots alive everywhere, but no proper blooms yet. She fingered the spiral in the fountain which was set at the heart of the beds, and Alex explained it was his mother's handiwork. The water was overflowing, freezing; but she scooped some out and looked at the depiction of Venus in the centre. On a stone wall forming a windbreak behind the flowers Lucy noticed a sundial – an ancient arm of iron pointing its finger back at Venus. There was enough sunshine to check its accuracy; and she looked at her watch like a little girl proving a mystery. She screwed up her nose when it wasn't right, and Alex laughed.

'It's been calibrated as a moon-dial. My mother was called Diana, like the goddess of the moon; and she loved moonlight. For a while she used the sundial in the other part of the garden, and we used to have to make adjustments – I recall forty-eight minutes of correction for every day either side of the full moon, when midday was accurate to midnight. But thereafter you had to do a lot of maths. So this has the corrections set into the brass.'

'How magical. What a wonderful mother you had.'

Alex nodded. The sadness Lucy discerned on his face was less about the loss of his, more about his empathy for the absence of hers during her life. But he deferred mentioning it to her for another day. 'Shall we walk in the orchard?'

As she stepped away from the moon-dial's domain, she trod on a loose tile set in the ground, with a large star on it. Alex heard the click. 'All this needs repair. If I can get down here for another long weekend in good weather I'll try to give it a tidy up. I'll bring Max to help. Would you put on gardening gloves too?'

'You know the answer.' She appreciated the inclusion with his son, took his hand, and walked towards the grove of trees. When the grass became long, wet and tangled, he piggy-backed her. She thought about her drugs, wondered if she was hallucinating. But Alex was there, smelling of the vetiver top note of Acqua di Parma and the earthiness of wood smoke; and she kissed his neck.

He telephoned Max – who was dragging Siân to all of his favourite pleasure spots – while Lucy cut shallots and lemons and arranged the St Peter's fish from yesterday's market in a dish. The kitchen was lovely to work in – good light and space, properly equipped, a huge variety of herbs. She put the fish into the oven and set the steamer whirring with some rice, then picked up her water glass and strolled back into the sitting room, walking straight to the piano. Alex had explained it was effectively Will's; and she wanted to touch it. It was years since she'd played, though she'd once been quite good, but she needed to know if she could pick it up again. She glanced at the music on top and gulped.

'Will you try it then?' Alex rejoined her.

'This is a bit out of my league. The Waldstein, Schubert Impromptu . . . all this impossible Chopin. Not one simple nocturne in sight. Was he this good?' Alex nodded his head decisively, and she shook hers: 'I'll have to practise then.' She moved the cello, and glanced suddenly at Alex. 'This was yours. Property of the god Apollo.' She laughed, but it wasn't put as a question.

'I've given up now. No time. We played trios together – and I was the weakest. But my mother was a first-rate fiddler. When she got too ill to play, I stopped altogether. Will would always play for her. He'd spend whole days there when it rained. I don't suppose she was ill, the last time we all played here.' His words lost volume and clarity. 'Please, make some music. It's sad for it to be silent. It's a lovely instrument.'

'Don't expect too much.'

She said this self-consciously, but she desperately wanted to play. She looked at Alex long enough to form a thought, then sat; and her hands sure enough found their way without embarrassment. Alex listened: she played Debussy. Not an especially difficult piece, well within her range; but she performed with great feeling. What affected him was her choice. It was short; and he nodded approvingly when she'd finished.

'"La fille aux cheveux de lin",' his voice trailed. "The Girl with the Flaxen Hair". Will used to call it "The Girl with Horse's Thighs".' Lucy laughed. 'I forgot how pretty it is. Can I hear it again?'

She was happy to comply; and the years eroded. It was his wedding day; he was marrying Anna, whose hair Will had said was like 'wind in the cornfields'. He'd played this piece for them in the church of Anna's Yorkshire village, told Alex to hold very tight to her if he really loved her. Alex found himself wondering what Will might be telling him now, through Lucy – not to repeat the mistake and lose hold of her? Her hair was dark silk and she couldn't have been physically less similar to Anna, but he felt the thinness of a veil he'd never have imagined even a day ago, and it surprised him. He walked over to her, and kissed her hair. 'Thank you.'

Lucy was scraping plates and Alex tying up fish bones in the rubbish when his mobile rang. He was regretting switching it on today, but he couldn't get back to the hospital, so he gave her a sanguine look and answered it. 'Alex Stafford.'

'This is half. We've been right through it, and half of the pages are missing.' It was the voice of Alex's verbal fencing partner on Friday night, with its slightly assumed Kentucky-sounding lilt.

'I have no idea what you mean. That's everything I have. Perhaps you'd like to check in the books you undoubtedly relieved us of.'

'Then you haven't found it all. The ultimate sheet here is clear: "halfway through the orbit". This is half the documentation. I imagine the rest is the writing we're really looking for. Now think for me, Dr Stafford: a lot depends on it. Where would the rest be?'

'What is it you're hoping to find? The hem of an angel's robe?'

'Mockery sits too lightly with you, Dr Stafford. Consider the equation I've just put to you. You know me already for a man who'll go after what he wants. I'll call you this time tomorrow. Have an answer.' He rang off.

Lucy searched his expression, had heard some snatches of the voice, knew at once what it implied. '*Did* you give them everything?'

Alex nodded. 'All the originals. I still have the set of

photocopies I made for you to work from to preserve their age. I left nothing out for them – that I know of.'

'How nervous should we be of these people, Alex?'

'I wish I knew.' He hesitated. 'You've had excellent instincts about all this so far. Do you get the feeling there's more?'

She took off her rubber gloves and leaned against the sink. 'You still haven't told me about the answer you arrived at from Will's first sheet. You told me you'd cracked it too – I would guess rather differently from my own take on it?'

Alex took her hand and led her to the bookshelves in the hall. 'Can you find a Bible?' They both hunted, and she came up with a slightly worn cover that was inscribed inside for Alex's Christening, 'Palm Sunday, 1970', from his god-parents. 'Yes, good – it's a King James.' She followed him to the sofa and Alex talked her through it.

'Like you, I got the first part as: "Will, I am". I assumed it meant that it was for Will. Then I started thinking about someone whose alpha and omega were the same day; and I thought straight away of Shakespeare – the period was right, and the given name. So I checked, and I was right to remember he was probably born on April twenty-third, and he died that day too; so it seemed a chance. I thought of the "song of equal number in the Old King's Book" and decided it might be Psalms, after the Song of Solomon yielded nothing. So I tried the famous Psalm twenty-three, and looked at it, and played with the counting in it: nothing. But look what happens if you double the number twenty-three, to make of the two halves – or "birth day" and "death day" – a whole number.

'Forty-six?' Lucy flicked through to find Psalm 46, and they looked at each other as a folded piece of palm, wrought into the shape of a cross, came free from the fold of the page. 'They make these on Palm Sunday. Has it been here since your christening?'

Alex shook his head in disbelief. 'Curious . . . marking that place. Count the same number of paces forward from the start: and tell me what you get.'

Lucy's nail counted forty-six words from the start, and she looked at him half smiling: '"Shake"? You're not going to tell me that if I count the same number from the end . . . ?'

'Omit the exit word, do you remember? It's "Selah" in this copy; but it's "Amen" in the one at my flat that Will had packed in his rucksack.'

Lucy followed instructions, trembling as her finger hovered over the forty-sixth word: 'spear'. 'Alex, you're a genius. But is this for real?'

'Do we agree, the whole message yields "William Shakespeare" – who was, incidentally, forty-six years old when the King James was printed?'

'"Is't not strange, and ten times strange?" Is it a deliberate code?'

'My feeling is that Shakespeare is implicated in the documents – how, I can't imagine. But it doesn't help with this question of "more", does it?'

Lucy sat glassy-eyed for a moment. 'Did Will get this far?'

'Maybe you know?' Alex was teasing her, but without malice. 'I would love to discover what he did with his hours after he visited the cathedral and walked the labyrinth. Messages he left me suggest he had things to say; and when

I went through his effects, the card from Chartres was there – the one my mother left him about the venison – along with a brasserie lunch receipt, and he had his hair cut; he'd sketched a stag, or a deer, on a small sheet of artist's paper; and you know he ordered Siân some flowers a little before three. But the ferry didn't leave until very much later. What was in his head in the intervening hours?'

Lucy looked at him. 'I wish I could tell you, Alex. I'm not Will. I just have a rather resonant piece of him with me. But if my instincts are anything, I'd say a few things seem particular. These flowers he ordered Siân – did you say before they were roses?'

'White ones. For her birthday – which was still a month off.'

Lucy nodded. 'I smelled roses in the labyrinth – probably the perfume you gave me wafting back in the warm air; but maybe that's a phenomenon of the labyrinth too – or maybe not. Could that rose upstairs be six months old? Would it fade so perfectly? Might it have been here when Will was?'

Alex shrugged. 'Possibly he picked it, you mean?'

'That was the autumn equinox. So, there's an equinox rose, the venison. And the stag. That's interesting, don't you think? Isn't the hart a device of Diana the moon goddess?' She wasn't waiting for his answer. 'And there was a hart on the bodice of the woman in your miniature – the painting. I'd say Will might have come back here. Is it on the way to the ferry?'

'Ish. What are you thinking?'

'Was your mother signposting him?' She looked at him seriously, suddenly struck with an idea. 'What was the wording of her legacy to him – with the key?'

'Something like: "For Will when you're someone you're not now . . ."' And Alex followed her thoughts. 'I suppose that's you now, Lucy. If you think like a poet instead of a scientist. Perhaps the key really was meant for you.'

'They took the gold copy you had made for my birthday.'

'No matter. When we get home, you must have the original silver one again.'

'We're part of this riddle, Alex. You and I are supposed to solve it. Didn't Alexander cut the Gordian knot, or something?'

He laughed. 'Oddly enough, our family insignia is a knot: for the Staffords. I think my parents were having a quiet joke when they named me Alexander. It's been part of the Stafford heraldry since at least the fifteenth century. But that's not my mother's side of the family.'

'Yet the Staffords seem to be included in the mystery somehow. A Stafford was the ambassador to France at some point during the reign of Queen Elizabeth. He was the contact with the Hermeticist Giordano Bruno, who was burned at the stake in no less a place than the Campo de' Fiori – the "Field of Flowers" – which is what that very first document Will was given must be referring to, and I think Will realised it. I read about it while researching Dee, and I think Simon mentioned it too. The connection with the Stafford name struck me. I'll check my notes. I'm wondering if he was a relative.'

Then she looked at him with a flash of insight. 'The knot garden. The roses. The moon globe. Diana's realm. Let's take a look.'

Lucy's finger looped along the spiral Diana had created in

her fountain. Made of mirrored glass, it picked its shiny path through a pattern of blues and ruby reds all mosaiced from broken china plates so carefully colour matched that Lucy realised they'd been purposely broken. The fountain was shallow, edged with shells; and Lucy was reminded of the Lady of Shalott working in reflections to weave her embroidery, as the silver shards reflected the sky and the landscape all around it. She traced the route to Venus in the centre, and thought of Alex's gentle fingers curving along her scar around her breast, circling her heart. The motion itself was sensual, mesmerising, a gesture of mystery.

She turned to him to say something, but he was lost in thought, looking at the altered sun dial, and she hesitated. He read her empathy, and invited her into his mind.

'The sun doesn't preside here. Its vitality is essential for the roses; but even at midsummer, when the smell is overpowering, my mother would bring me out long after the shade had deepened to prove that the scent was strongest, most alluring, in the evening. All the flowers are night-scented. Under the moon's light the white roses are luminous, almost palpably so. The moon-dial makes it midday at midnight. The fountain reflects down the stars: a fragment of heaven on earth. The spirit of this garden is female. My mother created this space to express another view of the world, and subvert the norm. The sun is consort, and a vital partner, but not the sovereign lord. It wasn't enough for us to understand it cerebrally: she needed us to witness it.' He turned to Lucy. 'Maybe because hers was a house of men.'

'She seems to have held her own.'

'Yes. But it was something she cared about. From prehistory, before the male role in procreation was understood properly, women were the bearers of the secrets of life and death – because they could bring forth life without any properly explained male contribution. They were understood to have an innate knowledge of the mysteries of the gods, to be the initiates of divine wisdom. Then there was a shift towards a more male, Apollonian, rational view of the world, downplaying mystery and the dreamy, lunar, female aspects of religion. The sun god, Apollo, brought clarity and an appreciation of what was knowable rather than inexplicable. Dionysus was the god of ecstatic visions and the rite of the moon.'

'You and Will,' Lucy suggested.

Alex laughed. 'In some ways. But Mum hoped that a marriage of clarity with mystery was not incompatible, and that the best understanding of the world would come from it. Possibly she thought that she and my father – in some respects – embodied this.'

Alex said no more, but Lucy understood it all, and she walked over and took his hand. 'If I could choose a mother, yours would be my choice,' she said with feeling; and Alex was touched. She looked up at the talon from the clock pointing back at Venus's watery haven, noticed it was showing a time, by chance, of between three o'clock and four, when it should have been at least an hour earlier.

Alex followed her gaze. 'Much more than forty-eight minutes out now.'

Lucy thought about Alex's mother in the light of this garden. 'Did you know that Botticelli painted the *Primavera*, and the panel of *Venus and Mars*, to draw down the magic of an exact aspect from the planets, to breathe the harmony of the heavens into the onlooker? Your mother must have known that the individual human being, as microcosm of the universe, was believed to express the whole of creation and the whole of the divine.'

Alex heard her; but Lucy's attention had moved to the shadow from the clock. It was the spring equinox – within a day – when the balance of male and female, sun and moon, day and night, was equal. A celestial marriage. She was thinking what a perfect moment that was for them both here at the house – 'a consummation devoutly to be wished'. It could be about this inaccurate time – around four o'clock – just before dawn, the last hour of the moon's light, before the first breath of sunrise at the equinoxes. 'Alex, look where the shadow happens to fall.'

The true time was only a shade after two, but the finger of shadow touched the star tile which Alex had said earlier needed repair. He leaned down and re-examined it; and this time its looseness attracted him. Lucy took her hair down and gave him her heavy clip to prise the edge. The tile came away from its lodging place with little effort, and they found a space underneath it, a deep hollow, with no object below it.

'Something was here, unquestionably.' Alex looked at Lucy in bafflement. Here was territory he had no map for. It suggested that for years his mother had created this secret place with a deeper agenda he'd known nothing of. Some object had nestled under the star, to a depth of roughly an old-fashioned English foot. It was enough to hide an upright box, or a bottle.

'Someone got here first,' he suggested.

Lucy reached across Alex's right hand, his fingers still grasping the top of the tile. She closed her fingers over his and inverted it, the underside now face up. They locked eyes, and smiled.

'Will.'

On the reverse of the tile was a second star – squared and petal-shaped – painted carefully, dotted with numbers, with some words below. It had been fired to preserve it.

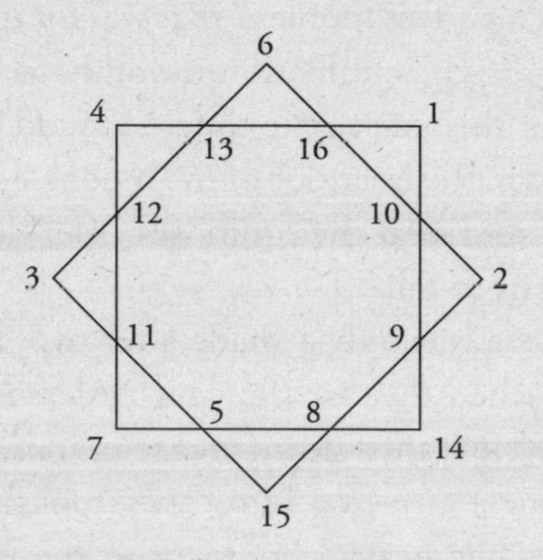

Under the star were the Italian words: *E quindi uscimmo a riveder le stelle*. And in the very heart of the space, a key was taped. The spare to Will's Ducati.

22

Simon scanned the reflections coming towards him in his rear-view mirror, but his mind was still on Calvin. He was absorbed by the oddities he had seen in Calvin's rooms – the entire absence of anything personal, and the strange scarcity of academic books on his shelves. Hardly the lair of a dedicated post-grad student, he thought. And that disingenuous response about the books he worked with being too old and valuable to remove from the library. Did that add up? What was he up to? Simon kept hearing the echoing words of Iago: 'I am not what I am.' How apt, he thought; and then he noticed three bobbing heads hurrying towards him, and started the engine.

Lucy had been locked in her own thoughts, cocooned in Alex's physical proximity, and had spent the hour's flight from Orly adrift from the world. Despite the intrusive, discordant phone call followed by the strange find in the knot garden, she couldn't rivet her mind on danger or urgency at all until she saw Grace's strained face at Arrivals.

Now, noting Simon's furtive expression as she slid into the back seat of his battered four-wheel drive, she shivered. Alex jumped in behind her while Grace got in next to Simon, who was pulling away before the doors were fully closed.

'I owe you one, Simon. I hope I didn't sound too conspiratorial on the phone.'

'Not nearly conspiratorial enough, Alex.' Simon laughed uneasily. 'Your place, or the girls' flat?'

Alex registered Simon's remark with a wish that he could be amused by it – but he evaded a direct verbal response to Simon's expressed unease and answered instead the question of their destination. 'Actually, I wondered if I could buy us all dinner at The Cricketers in Longparish? Unless you have plans?'

'Great pub. Wasn't it Will's favourite for real ale? It's a long while since I was there. Why tonight?' Simon was driving with an eye on the rear-vision mirror.

'Lucy's been unearthing more interesting archaeology: this time in the house in France.'

She stretched the seat belt and leaned forward, showing them a quick glimpse of the Ducati key, still taped to the tile as they'd found it. 'This was left to germinate in the rose garden.'

'Odd place to keep the spare,' Simon grinned at her in the mirror. 'Ducati's in the garage at your father's?' Alex nodded, and Simon looked at Grace. 'Dinner at The Cricketers, then.'

He accelerated, still with one eye in the rear mirror: 'You've got things to tell us, but I'll give you a modern history lesson first. I've unearthed some things myself over the last forty-eight hours. I tried to reach you at your flat, Alex, and Siân told me what had happened.' Grace turned and squeezed Lucy's hand sympathetically. 'So I paid Calvin a little visit.'

Simon's eyes darted from mirror to road and back; now he pointed the car on to the slip road that would take them towards the motorway, but as they approached the roundabout after the tunnel he swung up the ramp and back towards the perimeter road, cutting in on a car taking the same route. His passengers looked puzzled. The perimeter road ran for a few miles inside the airport precincts, and the other car continued behind them. Further on it closed up behind them, then held back again.

Lucy frowned as they approached the roundabout at the interchange for the M25 and the cargo terminals: the other car gathered speed again, flashed its lights, swung alongside very close to them. A passenger rolled down the window. Simon braked hard, turning the off-road vehicle on to the pavement. The passenger shouted an obscenity out of the window, then the car swerved across them, and disappeared out of sight.

All were silent, aware of what Simon was doing. He bounced the car back on the road and continued towards the M25. 'Was that necessary?' Alex's voice was quiet and, accepting that his romantic weekend was very much at an end, he started to experience that same sinking feeling that had come over him while talking to Calvin two nights before.

'I may have provoked a case of road rage, and nothing more sinister,' Simon suggested. But his nervous state was a surprise to Lucy. 'So Alex, M3 and A303, isn't it?'

'Against the Sunday traffic it won't take long, Simon. We'll be there by six. Could I use your phone to ring my father and tell him we're on our way?'

'If they're talking to you on yours, don't use it at all.' Simon passed Alex his mobile, and when the call was complete, he took a deep breath. He had a long story he knew Alex and Lucy would have difficulty with. It was irrational, and yet so simple it frightened even him.

In the steadiest tones he could command, that nevertheless couldn't disguise his anger, he communicated what he had extracted in the heated confrontation with Calvin the day before. In his years as a journalist he had run up against all kinds of people. In his view his job was to observe others and let the public draw their own conclusions about what he presented. Get the facts right, then the truth was what you made it. What he saw confronting Lucy and Alex was a group of people who believed in the rightness of their position so staunchly that they felt they were above the law.

'Dictators, presidents, religious leaders – I've met them. You know, Alex, that whenever Will was available we went together; I was the wordsmith, his pictures told the story. At day's end we often sat at a bar in some international hotel, some faraway capital city, asking each other how the hell these guys got away with it. Sometimes we were so outraged by the rubbish they'd tell us, it would leave us lost for words. Our conclusions varied, but mostly we raised a glass to freedom, democracy and the Western way of life – "Long may it live."' He was unusually emotional.

'I really got to know Will when we worked closely for a

time in Africa. It was initially a follow-up to the landmines interest that Princess Diana generated. We decided to travel on for a month together and ended up in Maputo, at the Polana Hotel, in post-civil-war Mozambique – the classic colonial setting in the midst of abject poverty. Children playing and laughing on dirt streets with only a Coke can for a toy. It got to Will. On the second day we witnessed a bomb blast which took out a bus – all the passengers were small children and their mothers – all that destruction the result of some obscure agenda. Neither of us could comprehend it – the lengths others will go to, to assert their will, their vision of the world. A five-year-old girl bled to death in my arms, and Will couldn't click the frame. He knew the world should see it – but said it would feel like rape.

'More recently we didn't have to travel to the Third World for horror. We were together in Washington, open-mouthed at the devastation, the plume of smoke that smouldered over the Pentagon for days; that terrible stench of burning, the air thick with fatty ash. A climate of fear followed, understandably, allowing extreme religious elements of all persuasions to use the situation for their own purposes. The taking-down of Saddam, suicide bombers and religious fanatics of every type, everyone has their own take on it . . .' Simon was afraid he wouldn't be coherent enough to make his friends comprehend the danger that he now believed they could be in.

'Alex, what started Will on this epic quest after your mother's death was, I think, a need to explore something complex in himself – his restlessness, his inability to settle or, more particularly, to acquiesce to injustices everywhere.

What he ran into could have cost him his life. Talking to Calvin, I'm not convinced the plummet into the river was accidental.'

'I'd always thought that; and these new details make me certain there was something sinister involved – just as you feel. But let's not make accusations we can't prove yet. And please don't – in fact, none of us must – mention this idea to my father. It's hard enough for me to digest – and death is part of my everyday landscape. And,' Alex added after a moment's consideration, 'I think it might be better not to tell him about my reasons for following Lucy to France – at this point. I'll talk to him when I think the time is appropriate – but he's been through too much in the last year or so, and I frankly don't want to worry him more than I have to. But, Simon,' he continued after a long breath, 'what I don't understand is, what on God's earth do they want? And, come to that, who are "they"?'

'I'm not sure that what they think they want is on "God's earth". Alex, what you and Lucy have found is a document which they believe is the key that opens the door to salvation. They are convinced that, with the help of whatever it is these papers will lead them to – some kind of Ark of the Covenant – they will be able to talk to the angels to establish the moment and the precise details of the coming of The Rapture – or that the conversation has already been recorded by Dee's own hand some four hundred years ago. According to Calvin, there is a theory that Dee buried it because it was too hot to handle. He buried a lot of things, apparently. They got you to hand over the pages you had by abducting Lucy; now they've discovered they have only part of the puzzle. They want the next instalment, whatever it is, even if you don't know where to look. And they won't wait.'

Lucy had sat silently, considering the implications of what Alex had asked, as well as what Simon was saying, but now her mind fixed fully on Simon's words. 'Sorry, Simon, I'm lost. What are you talking about? And who? "Rapture"?'

Grace understood Lucy's confusion. She was fully aware that Simon's mind – normally well able to absorb information and communicate it smoothly – was out of control with anxiety. She had noticed he was changing lanes at high speed, and driving erratically.

'You and I have been talking about this since you saw Calvin, but why don't you just rewind and tell them what you've learned? And could you slow down a shade? He's a bit dislocated,' she explained to Alex and Lucy.

'Quite right, Gracie. Sorry. The people who are interested in you and your ancestor, Alex, are theological fundamentalists – although it's a bad word to use, as it embraces too much. For our purposes, let's understand that Calvin's friends are only a handful among many for whom religious authority is absolute and admits no criticism. They expect that specific demands and dictates derived from scripture should be not only publicly recognised, but legally enforced. They're obsessed with combating the erosion of religion and its proper role in our society, as they see it. They are Christian, of course, not Muslim; and their rather unforgiving and unchristian morality permeates all thought, all aspects of their outlook on the world. They teach Creationism, vilify Darwin, insist that all religious truth is revealed and unified. They are interested above all in the Apocalypse, so their interpretation of history reassesses all defining moments as an aspect of the cosmic struggle. Jesus is neither the Lamb of God nor the Prince of Peace for them; he is a blood-thirsty Messiah looking for revenge.'

Grace suddenly interrupted him. 'It is entirely male-led, by the way.'

'Yes, I have to say that's true,' Simon agreed before resuming. 'Now, these theological fundamentalists of Calvin's are quite certain that the Second Coming of Christ is on the verge of taking place. This is a basic Christian tenet, that there will be a Second Coming; but be scared – because they want to nudge it along, no matter how many busloads of mothers and children bleed to death to facilitate their vision.'

He drew breath to make sure his audience were following. No one blinked, though Lucy felt stunned and a little night blind with the headlights flying at them from the London-bound traffic on the opposite side of the motorway. She squeezed Alex's hand unconsciously.

Simon continued: 'So here is the crux. First, at the Coming, this group believes those who are the faithful will be literally lifted off the earth into eternal heaven. Lucy, this is what they call The Rapture.'

'Lifted off the earth? Just like that?' Lucy wondered if this was an aspect of Simon's ironic humour.

'Like the lady in *One Hundred Years of Solitude*,' Alex said, 'too beautiful to be placed in a grave, so she is just wrapped in the sheet she is hanging out and lifted up to heaven.'

'Ah! Nothing as literary as Márquez, I'm afraid, nor as spiritually uplifting! Although oddly, the idea has gained currency through a series of Christian science fiction books that have popularised the whole mad notion – and sold in bucketloads. But for millions of Americans it's not fiction. So yes, Alex,' Simon continued, 'I suppose it bears some comparison. Except that in this scenario, only the select few will be enraptured. It's an elitist club with no conscience. The rest of us poor souls – and this includes most of the balanced and humanitarian Christian population, plus, say six hundred million Chinese, three hundred million Asians, I don't know how many Muslims, Sikhs, Jews, and certainly all cynics, like me, and men of science like you, Alex, will be left behind, as the saying goes, here on earth, to fight it out or clean up the mess. While Calvin's mad academics drink champagne with St Peter, we secular humanists will face the Battle of Armageddon and be expected to perish in a bloodbath. Or so they hope.'

Alex wanted to laugh aloud, but knew his friend was deadly serious. 'Simon, I long ago learned to understand that people who have faith are sometimes willing to die for what they believe. That is their right. But faith is *faith* – it derives from a willingness to *be faithful*. It is nothing we can *know*. And not only is it not knowable, it is very often not in the least plausible. In today's developed world of educated people, there can't be any group who could inflict their blind faith and implausible ideas on others to this extent, and actually get enough government backing to send us all to war over it! Not in the West, at least. You're being too pessimistic.'

'Don't try to rationalise their arguments, Alex. It has nothing whatever to do with logic. It's all about a fear of being excluded. And they are working feverishly to turn back the clock and repeal the Enlightenment. Like James I and his witchfinder general – what would Shakespeare say today to a Western leader who would use a climate like this – indeed, would promote it? A president of "fantastical dark corners" who's come out on record as being in favour of The Rapture? Here is the nub of it.

'To open the way for this Second Coming, a group called the Christian Zionists believe that the Jews must be allowed and indeed helped to rebuild the Temple in Jerusalem. This would require the removal of one of Islam's most holy and beautiful places, and it might upset a few people. But no matter: this group is committed to creating the gateway for the Second Coming. They are well connected. They see themselves as part of a cosmic struggle. They demonise their opposition. They are anti-modern – but not anti-modernist. They will use all technological advances to their advantage. They are ultra conservative about the role of women, and scientific research. They strongly resist those Enlightenment values for which we enshrine your heroes, Alex, Kant and Voltaire, and the very principles of the American Constitution – which is ironic, don't you think, given that this wonderfully idealised liberal-thinker's paradise is exactly where they've risen to power and has – arguably – allowed them a voice in the first place. And they have certainly seized the airwaves very effectively to get their message across. Remember, I'm not talking about someone in a cave in Afghanistan. These people are right-wing Christians who have a revenge fantasy which sees them winning out, in the most brutal way, over the rational, modern, scientific and at least ideologically egalitarian world. Their verbal war is waged through their literature and control of the media against the liberal thinkers and the gays, women they would deem overeducated, Muslims, Arabs, and especially the United Nations.

'Their obsession with rebuilding the Temple in Jerusalem is because it would pave the way for reclaiming the biblical lands of Judea and Samaria on the West Bank – and they insist this is part of God's unalterable covenant with the people of Israel, according to the Old Testament. Their Revelation prophecy assures them that a reconciled whole nation of Israel is a necessary precursor to the Second Coming of Christ. And, once they have their Temple,' he glimpsed Alex's staring eyes in his mirror, 'once this is achieved, then the Second Coming will, apparently, begin. When the last block of stone is in position – or maybe even once the first is set in place – The Rapture follows. Now, we all know that bringing democracy to the Middle East is a laudable goal, but in this case the agenda is not to enhance the lives of anyone living in any of these countries. Rather, it's to place these worthies in a position to effect the rebuilding of the Temple. They've been preparing for this ever since Israel was designated a self-governing country in 1948. The Temple is their prime inspiration.'

Alex looked at Simon's reflected eyes sceptically. 'You're trying to tell me that my new-found cousin and his mentor, the self-styled descendant of a Templar knight with his skin-deep courtly manners, genuinely believe this? And that they think the papers that were preserved by Dee four centuries ago will miraculously clinch their woolly thesis?'

Simon moved into the slow lane, getting ready to turn off from the fast-moving A-road on to the slip lane towards Alex's village. The reduced speed and road noise was a relief to all, who had felt an assault of their senses from the stark lights, the pace of the traffic and the fast flow of information.

But Simon was still in full stride and wanted to make Alex aware of the high stakes. 'That's what they are fighting for. They know the rules of propaganda. Moreover, they will use any tools of fear and intimidation – as you discovered first hand, Lucy. So if you thought the Inquisition was an unrepeatable and tragic piece of ancient history, think again. They are frighteningly well funded. In the current political climate they are finding powerful and gullible audiences. The intention is what it ever was: to convert the Jews to Christianity on the way through – my apologies to your Jewish father, Grace. It's a fresh Crusade they're looking for, and the magnitude of death they are anticipating will dwarf even the Holocaust. Their extended nation of old Israel runs all the way to the border of the Nile and the Euphrates, and the Mediterranean Sea – and even Jordan's wilderness. This would force a showdown with the Egyptians and the Syrians as much as the Iraqis and the Lebanese.' Simon turned right round to confront Lucy and Alex from the driver's seat, making Grace's stomach lurch. 'Can you imagine the scale of the conflict?

Red clouds streaked the early evening sky after what had been a day of blazing heat, and Professor Fitzalan Walters took his panama hat off to allow a cooler flow of air to his head. It had been a gruelling day, driving from Caesarea in scorching temperatures to visit the archaeological digs that showed layers of civilisation over thousands of years, right to the fortifications of King Solomon. He had been schmoozing his two guests with energy, aware that they brought both funds from the oil business and power from Congress: it was worth everything to get them fully on board. Now they had arrived at the site of Armageddon, and it made his heart jump. The elation couldn't really be translated – but he had a sufficient power of oration to give it his best try.

'Gentlemen, here we are at last at the awe-inspiring Megiddo, the site of more than twenty civilisations over ten thousand years, piled one atop the other. From the time of Alexander through the blessed Crusades, and even down to Napoleon, men have fought and wept over this land. Ours will be the last layer – for this is designated Armageddon, the place for the cataclysmic battle of the Revelation, the site of the future victory of our Lord.'

'Well, that's just why we should pay no mind at all to this silly talk on global warming, FW!' The taller of the two men, with a huge girth and intense grey eyes, laughed. His strong Texan drawl spoke of merriment and would have been charming in any other context.

FW nodded solemnly, took each man by the arm and led him up the last few feet of the winding hill of Megiddo, where he paused to reflect. He swept his hat across the space in front of them in a grand gesture. 'It is from here that Jesus will come on the clouds of glory, to call us home. This two-hundred-mile-long valley will be a metre deep in blood by the time He finishes His great work.' He squeezed their arms again from behind, wanting them to be a palpable part of his joy. 'Just envision this beautiful Valley of Jezreel awash with the blood of what my people have calculated must be more than two billion people! And we will be with Him!'

The spell he created lasted right through their descent, back to the parked armour-plated Mercedes and two waiting point-men below. The professor was in a rare place, and the mood was hardly broken when his cellphone rang in the dusty half-light. He waved his travelling companions into the cool of the car, and answered.

'It's Guy, FW.'

'A little later than expected, Guy. News?'

'We have a very interesting collection of papers, but judging from the notes in the family's Bible, this is not the whole set. They may be holding out on us; but I have a feeling they may not know about them – or where to get hold of them.'

'Yes. I see. And Calvin hasn't been able to add any illumination?'

Guy hesitated. 'No. Well, not as yet.'

'So, Guy, it's perfectly clear what you must do. Keep watching the house, keep close to the boy; and try not to let anything –' he considered for a moment – '*untoward* happen. I abhor unnecessary violence. Call me tomorrow.' He ended the conversation and climbed into the car, which had only waited for him to be off, raising a cloud of fine red dust as it trailed away.

The peace of the quiet lanes stood in sharp contrast to the

disturbed minds of the driver's three passengers; but eventually it was Lucy who spoke.

'It's true, Alex. Your ancestors – Dee and his circle – were involved in searching for illumination and tolerance outside the religious narrowness of their times. They started from a more unified premise of belief in God than we have now. You remember they believed that communication with the angels was a path to the truth, without doctrinal interference. They hoped the angels could tell them what God really wanted, in the same way that Moses had received the word of God directly.

'Bruno died at the stake in the Campo de' Fiori,' she went on, 'for suggesting that the earth not only moved around the sun, but that there were *several* solar systems, all revolving around their individual suns. He was far ahead of his time – even ahead of Galileo. But it didn't obscure his sense of God: he felt God was everywhere, in everything, in everyone. His most offensive heresy was to question Jesus' birth from a "virgin" mother – he knew the classical models for this idea, the many mortal, beautiful women whose exceptional sons were fathered by invisible, immortal gods. While he believed in the beauty of Christ's teachings as a man, he wanted us to open our eyes and ask questions – to see what was irrational. He also doubted that the bread was actually made into flesh at the Eucharist – a major part of my Catholic upbringing. Such moderate revisionist questions that it's hard now, centuries later, to see the outrage it provoked then.

'And it was similar for Dee,' she added. 'The effort to avoid doctrinal differences turned them to explore the mysteries of nature – in a religious spirit. It contributed to a climate in which science could advance. They all sought expressions of a religious life without hard-line adherence to a tissue of impossibilities. But, Simon, you're saying that the people who still read these metaphors as actualities – including those who took me in France – might really have enough influence on politics in the West today to be pushing the world back into the chaos and dogma Dee and his kind were trying to escape from four hundred years ago?'

'It's teetering, for sure – unless those who try to be tolerant of others' views are still allowed to speak and think independently, still allowed to ask rational questions, be intelligent sceptics – or even thinking believers. Unfortunately, Calvin's teammates see no holes in their theory – they believe it to the letter, which curtails any debate. It's the most negative, doom-and-gloom stuff. Calvin himself has, I think, reservations, but his right-wing associates believe unquestioningly that your Dr Dee talked freely to the angels. And if this little clique get their hands on how to do this, the alphabet he used, the instructions for opening the cellphone to heaven, they believe they can have a little chat and find out exactly what the deal is. Or what has already been revealed. And they'll push others out of the way as aggressively as is necessary to get the angels' contact number. Interesting, no?'

There was a stunned silence. As they drove past the beautiful, unassuming outline of Longparish's church, which had offered centuries of quiet devotion to the villagers, Lucy felt a stab of pain, and spoke fervently. 'No wonder God was so angry with Eve – for eating the fruit from the Tree of Knowledge. According to Genesis, knowledge bestowed

Godlike powers. It was Eve who was responsible for moving us away from naïvety, closer to the status of gods who can think and act through reason. Yet only by lapsing back into such ignorance could we believe all this Rapture nonsense. In your family, Alex, the women wouldn't be dissuaded from the pursuit of knowledge, or made to feel guilty for wanting to know more. They refused unquestioning obedience to a vengeful God. The mulberry, the tree of wisdom, is where they chose to hide Dee's documents. They preferred the classical model of Ariadne, as rescuer of man from the labyrinth, to that of Eve as the cause of the Fall and all man's unhappiness.'

Alex looked at her with quiet appreciation. He kissed her. 'What a lot you make me think about. "*Sapere aude*", Kant said. "Dare to Know". He was on Eve's side.'

The hour of fervent discussion had brought them to Will and Alex's family home. The outside light flicked on automatically as Simon pulled into the driveway, but no one moved. It was a minute before Simon turned to face Lucy. 'But do you dare to know where Will's key will lead? What Pandora's Box it may unlock?'

She didn't answer; but seconds later, the upright figure of Henry Stafford opened the front door, delighted to receive guests.

'Well, are you going to sit out there all night, or are you coming in for a drink?'

23

'Champagne, Dad?' Alex laughed. 'That's extravagant for a Sunday evening. What's wrong with your Laphroaig?' Alex took the icy bottle from the bucket, eased the cork into his hand, and poured some into each glass. Lucy alone, who since surgery had savoured just the occasional glass, waved him graciously away.

'It's Mother's Day today, Alex. I hoped we might drink to absent friends?' Henry raised his glass with the new arrivals. 'I don't want to leave you out, Simon. The cleaner was here on Friday; fresh linen on all the beds. The guest room is ready – if you'd like to enjoy a few drinks with dinner and drive back first thing tomorrow?'

'Henry, how kind. It would be churlish to refuse – if everyone else is happy with an early start?' Simon looked at the relaxing faces around him all nodding their agreement – a very different mood from that of the car journey. 'But, Grace, I wish you'd warned me to ring my mother. I'll get a terrible bollocking tomorrow.'

'I rang mine.' Grace was on safe ground. 'Here's to my mum, and yours, Simon. And,' she added quietly, 'especially to Mrs Stafford.'

'Lucy, should we drink to yours too? I suppose it's a different date in Australia?'

Henry's charm was so natural that Lucy found it easy to reply warmly, 'I'd be very happy to drink to Alex's mum, Henry. Alex, give me a little after all.' He gave her his glass and poured another for himself. 'To Diana, then,' Lucy said with real feeling; and they echoed her.

'Oddly enough, Dad, she's the person I want to talk to you about. As soon as I ring Elaine at the pub and book a table,' said Alex.

'*Fait accompli*, Alex. She's expecting us. We've got the table in the window for seven thirty. But we have an hour in hand before we stroll down, if that's agreeable?'

Since his visit with Lucy to the Normandy garden, Alex's world seemed to have shifted a few degrees. He'd always been in awe of his mother's gentle strength and the diversity of her interests and knowledge; always thought her artistic hobbies were an expression of some aspect of herself that had been submerged for the sake of her marriage. Today, she would have painted professionally, possibly; or sculpted; or been a designer. But she was in the comet tail of a generation and a middle-class convention that put family first, and she'd made the boys and her home her life's work, with her art embellishing the edges. But today had unearthed a secret – a side to his mother he hadn't known existed – and he was restless to understand more. His father, he knew, would be unprepared for this line of questioning coming from him rather than Will. Alex's life had been so full of certainties, so assured, and here was something less tangible, less straightforward, to grapple with.

'I haven't told you, Lucy and I made an impromptu trip to Normandy. It was lovely there – although it rained almost solidly.' He looked at his father attentively. 'Why did you buy the house in L'Aigle? Your choice, or Mum's wish?'

'How good that you were there, Alex.'

Simon had been about to refill Henry's glass and, looking up for his permission to do so, caught him smiling at Lucy and his son. Simon read it as a blessing, and it told him Henry had been much more concerned about Alex, with his locked silence about the family deaths and his failed marriage, than anyone would have guessed.

Henry addressed his son's question: 'It was her choice, very much so. Less her wish than her *will*, I would say. I was happy to go along with it – although the weather is so much warmer in Provence, of course. She said the Pays d'Auge was close enough to enjoy on a regular basis.' He looked quizzically at Alex. 'Why do you ask?'

'OK – in at the deep end. Lucy and I realised today that she'd created her knot garden for a purpose. She explained to me and to Will – when we were little – about the significance of it as her moon garden, and that it was dedicated to her patron saint-cum-goddess, Diana. And the knot she laid out for the roses was the Stafford knot – so the whole place was like an Elizabethan rebus for her name.' His father was nodding. 'But I think she meant it to be sacred, somehow – a reliquary. Am I making any sense?'

'Go on.' His father was quiet, reflective; and Grace and Simon sat motionless.

'I think there must have been something significant for her about the region itself – perhaps its proximity to Chartres. More by luck than intention, we discovered earlier today that the garden was a place of repose for . . . something. I'm not sure what. We found a loose tile with a space below it, large enough to put anything from a small statuette to another box perhaps – like the one Lucy scented out here under the mulberry.' Alex looked at Henry as evenly as possible, aware he would be surprised by his son's interest. 'Did you have any idea she'd planned something like this?'

'Alex,' Simon said, 'your mother designed a garden just to hold a secret object – until some unspecified later time – and you and Will never knew about this?' He swallowed his champagne quickly.

'I have no way of knowing when it was thought out, but it looks like there was an object, or some information, that she was storing. And I have to say I knew nothing about it – nor, I should think, did Will. But I'm certain for reasons I'll go into in a moment that he knew at the end, and that's part of what he wanted to talk to me about so urgently.' He turned to his father. 'Did you know of this?'

'She'd have kept it from me, Alex. I wasn't the most sympathetic soul in the world when it came to anything mystical, or people like John Dee, with his secrets, or indeed any other arcane information. But she was a fascinating mix herself. Not conventional in her religious ideas, but she was nevertheless respectful and interested in all faiths; she was what you would call "spiritual". She was patient with most people's ideas about God, and faith; she had her own unique take on it. And she was perfectly unworried by our . . . agnosticism. You're probably more of a true atheist than I.'

Henry didn't seem agitated by the questions, and he moved to retrieve a framed object from the passage leading from the sitting room up towards the staircase. 'You ask about the region. Do you remember this embroidery she did? A long time ago. There's a cushion like this in the house in Normandy too.'

He handed Alex what was in fact a tapestry, to which he'd paid no attention since childhood. Now he looked closer. 'It's connected with the sacred geometry of Chartres,' his father was saying, trying to recall its significance for his wife.

Alex studied the canvas. It was a winged female angel, woven in blues and white; and she was holding a branch of palm in one hand and a sheaf of wheat in the other. The background was filled in with many shades of blue – mainly a lapis colour, but in some areas, dark as midnight. Superimposed on her robes and features in gold-thread-like wool was a strange kite shape, with a tail leading off in the lower left of the frame. This kite was reproduced identically below the seraphic creature in the frame – a reciprocating version without the human details. He tilted it for Lucy's view, next to him on the settle.

'I think that's the constellation of Virgo,' she hesitated.

'Yes, Lucy,' Henry responded, 'I believe you're right. She started working on it just after Alex was born – that's your sign, Alex, isn't it?' He nodded, mystified, at his father. 'We bought the house before Will was on the way – you weren't a year old. We started looking in the early spring for somewhere to buy, stayed with your godparents near Rouen while we house-hunted. You know you were baptised at Chartres? Your mother was keen, and it was arranged by your godfather, who knew someone. Will's baptism was at Winchester.'

Lucy looked at Alex, who was shaking his head in surprise. 'I didn't know.'

Now she stared intently at the tapestry, noticing that the gold thread looped along between the individual white stars in the Virgo constellation – tiny crystalline shapes of pin-prick light resembling jewels – and then linked the whole shape to make the kite figure, repeated in the lower diagram. The upper picture was labelled with symbols at the stellar points, which Lucy couldn't read. Simon and Grace leaned over the settle to see.

'This top left symbol is the number 3, written in mirror image.' Grace scrutinised it without success.

Alex explained. 'It's Greek – nothing more cryptic than the Greek alphabet. This one,' he pointed to the reversed 3, 'is a Greek E, Epsilon, where the wing joins the arm. This one at the lowest part of the diamond shape is G – Gamma, the edge of the robe. And the top of the wing is Nu. They are three of the main stars in the constellation of Virgo. All these others are more minor – but still bright I think. Nu is top right of the constellation; Eta, in the middle of the kite shape; and then this one is Beta at the sharp point of the rhomboid, Delta just opposite, and Alpha – the brightest of the stars – on the kite's tail, marking the wheat.' He pointed to the clusters of other pin-pricks, which had a series of tiny symbols embroidered next to them. 'I believe the whole constellation of Virgo is named after the Greek letters, which is unique. But what's going on in the lower diagram? The shape of the constellation, without the figure drawn in?'

They all leaned closer to look. Lucy read aloud the names of various French towns in corresponding positions, embroidered beside the stars. 'Bayeux seems to correspond to the point on the map for Epsilon; Amiens is where Nu is; then Evreux fits neatly with Delta. What are these others again, Alex?'

'Well, Reims accords with Beta – one of the most important cathedrals in France, where the coronations took place. Do you think Laon fits Kappa?' He frowned a little. 'Paris matches Eta; and Chartres seems on target for Gamma. Very strange. But why did she care?'

Henry took spectacles from his nose and answered with a surprising liveliness. 'We made a tour of them together, when you were a baby, Alex, and she told me that these great French Gothic cathedrals are "Notre-Dames" cathedrals – each dedicated to Our Lady. She said that they encrypt the constellation of Virgo, the virgin, on the earth below – which I always thought was a little far-fetched, but it pleased her so much! Virgo is the only female constellation in the zodiac, and she's connected with Ceres, the corn goddess, and Isis in the Egyptian pantheon.'

'And, of course, subsequently, the Virgin Mary.' Lucy had been thinking about this in relation to what she had absorbed from the guide book for Chartres. 'These other cathedrals – Reims, Bayeux, and Amiens – all had labyrinths, though only Chartres has had its original intact since 1200.' She was fascinated, and thought of the palm cross in the bible at the house. 'It's interesting that the Virgo figure holds the palm leaf, and you were christened on Palm Sunday, Alex. What about this star – Alpha, you said – which is at the bottom of the tail? Could that be the house in L'Aigle?'

Alex looked at her. 'It's an interesting idea. "My alpha and my omega." Do you feel it's related to Will's central document?'

Lucy smiled at him. 'It could be, if whatever was in the garden is both the alpha star of Virgo, and the omega of the clues – beginning and end.'

Alex suddenly felt uncomfortable. 'Dad, you don't believe all this sacred geometry means anything, do you?'

Henry took a moment. 'What's important, Alex, is not whether there is actually any truth in it. There may be, who knows? But what's interesting is that the Gothic architects *believed* it. It does seem to have been constructed this way – whether you accept there's anything supernatural about it or not. The overlay of Christianity on the site of some presumably older female shrine would have excited your mother. She loved that woven feel – the way one deep myth was the background of another. The plurality of faiths, she called it. She would have found it heartening that they had embraced rather than eradicated the old core rituals. She felt it gave continuity to the shape of human belief – that it showed how there was one common thread behind such a variety of religions. Virgo's connection with the Virgin Mary would have delighted her.'

'There's something written on the back of the frame,' Grace alerted them.

Turning it over, Lucy read: '"She is both sister and bride."' She spoke with animation. 'And your mum obviously attached some significance to it, Alex. She made this tapestry, created that garden. Something was in her head. And Will must have started to decipher it too, don't you think?'

At this point Alex looked at the intrigued faces in the room and softly asked Lucy: 'Would you show my father what we found in the garden?'

She produced the tile, inverted it carefully to reveal the strange star-shaped pattern with its motto below, and the key taped teasingly in the centre. 'Whatever was there, Will found it first. This has to be connected with his bike, doesn't it?' Lucy asked him.

Henry looked closely at the object. '"And we came forth to look again at the stars,"' he said wistfully. 'Dante's *Inferno*. They're the same words as the inscription on the back of the miniature. I looked at it carefully after it came back from Interpol.'

Alex's brows knitted, but Henry's thoughts had turned to the motorbike, and he shook his head doubtfully as he rubbed his thumb over the key. 'You know, Alex, the Ducati was away being repaired for weeks, even though it wasn't much damaged. The police went over it thoroughly, so I can't imagine there's anything still in it. We went through the saddle bags, which only leaves the tank box. Anything else would have been returned to us by now.'

Unless someone got to it in between, his son thought. But he said: 'You're right. Still, shall we check it, just to be sure?'

*

Alex loosened the dust cover, and the racing bike shone primrose beneath.

'His tetchy beauty, he called it. It's in showroom condition.' Alex leaned against the bonnet of his father's car with his arms folded, looking at the seemingly benign super-bike. 'Half again the cost of my Audi. He bought it with money from Mum, before she died. No one could talk him out if it.'

'It *is* beautiful.' Grace looked with admiration. 'I think my brother would sink to his knees and pay homage to it.'

'It suited Will.' Simon ran a hand along the seat, and against the bodywork. 'He was never late to a shoot. And he told me it was easier to ride than his first Ducati. Of course, you can't be carrying any beer weight to ride one – real tail-in-the-breeze stuff. Only for a fit man, and bloody uncomfortable over any distance. Where's the key?'

Lucy hesitated for some reason, reluctant to pass it to Simon, then freed it from the tile and put it in his hand. In a moment he had swung into the saddle, twisted the accelerator, turned the ignition. It roared, started first time, and then stalled immediately in the hands of the novice. Everyone laughed nervously at the sudden noise.

Alex took back the key with a grin and unlocked the tank box: empty, as Henry had anticipated. Then he, too, ran his hand along the sides of the machine. There was no unusual feature, no compartment, nothing besides the fuel tank, and he knew that Will would never have risked its smooth function by putting anything in there. He shook his head and asked Henry: 'Was there anything in the saddle bag? Or the rucksack?'

'Nothing unusual, as I recall. Of course, I wasn't looking

for anything particular. We could go through the odd bits and pieces again. What did you hope to find?'

Lucy had been standing meditatively a few feet away; and now Alex noticed her expression. He wondered if she might have one of her sudden changes of mood, feel ill, or go quiet. Whatever was going on in her heart, she definitely felt a propinquity with Will, reacted to things connected with him – even though he was inclined to believe it was just psychological. But she seemed calm and in charge tonight, simply held out her hand for the key. He smiled with dry amusement and passed it to her.

She put her hand on the seat and bent over it, looking upwards from under the seat back. She groped underneath, then slid back a small sprung cover under the casing behind the seat with her right hand. With her left, she inserted the key into the neat space that had been revealed. Alex squatted to watch, and the back half of the seat-housing slid back just centimetres, exposing a small, carefully designed compartment, obviously custom-made to Will's order. She was now able to slide the cover – which blended into the bodywork – right away, and she reached inside.

Four silent faces watched as she took out four small leather bags, then something rolled in a fine black velvet cloth lashed with a leather bootlace. A shadow passed over Simon's face as Alex reached out for the last object, which Lucy gave him.

Grace looked at her friend, uncertain whether to be more mystified by the find, or the unusual manner of its discovery. Certainly Henry's 'Good heavens!' indicated that he too was at least surprised.

'Will's Leica,' Alex said, with a tone of magic in his voice. 'I wondered where it was. He kept it like this all the time, unless it was casually stuffed into his pocket when he was working. Almost impossible to buy them now. They change hands for a small fortune. This is the camera, and the bags must hold spare lenses – at least two of them.' Alex now sounded more like himself, but Amel would have detected something different in his voice – and both Lucy and Henry could too.

Simon tested the weight of a leather bag. 'I remember. I think your grandfather gave it to him – is that right? *Your* father, Henry. Will told me it was passed to him on his eighteenth birthday.'

Henry looked steady, but his face twitched. He explained: 'My father exchanged it for a truckload of food outside Frankfurt, very end of 'forty-four or early 'forty-five. I think he took it just to make the man feel easier about it – honestly never understood its value. The family were trying to cook a frozen horse apparently – children looked traumatised and hungry.'

Simon nodded. 'Will told me his grandfather gave virtually all the supplies his company had to some starving refugees. They were retreating from the Russians, so I understand; had travelled all the way from Dresden. And one of them gave him the camera, virtually forced it on him. For Will, no modern camera came close to matching the finesse of an original Leica.'

Alex was untying the wrapping with careful fingers, and now he unrolled the camera. All the mountings were of warm-toned nickel, the case vulcanite; it looked well-used and loved but in excellent shape. He glanced at the count: the roll was not used up.

Meanwhile, Lucy had taken the other leather bags and begun to investigate. As Alex had predicted, two beautiful original lenses were in two of the pouches; but in the third she found four film cassette tubs, which she shook. Simon found another two in his pouch, plus a small cassette which sounded empty when he shook it. Lucy relieved him of it, popped off the lid, and probed her finger inside.

'It's a bunch of exposure notes for processing, and there's a delivery slip, registered.' She scanned the paper. 'Sent special service, from the post office in Caen. Addressed to somebody called Brown on Thirty-Fourth Street in New York City.'

Alex leaned across to see the writing. 'Roland Brown – an independent, but associated with Magnum, Will's photographic agency. They syndicated most of Will's best stuff in the States. Roland was a good friend – kept an office in London too, I think. He was mad about Will's Leica II, because the old uncoated lens gave a completely different quality to the pictures. Loved it even more fiercely once digital pictures started to dominate.'

'Will loved it because its shutter was silent, and no one knew you were taking the pictures,' Lucy stated calmly.

Simon nodded, but Grace looked at her, startled. 'How on earth could you know that?'

Lucy smiled. 'You learn a lot of useless things working on documentaries in South America, Grace. Not the same education you get from Light Entertainment,' Lucy suggested.

Alex looked at her. They hadn't discussed keeping her secret – which would have a complex impact and be highly emotive for everyone; but he saw at once that they would never have to.

He took her hand appreciatively. 'We're late for dinner. Shall we bring these to the pub? Much too valuable to leave out here.' Henry turned off the garage light, they pulled coats on and started ambling down the lane in the cool air. 'It's only five minutes' walk,' Alex assured them; but he slipped an arm around Lucy once out of his father's hearing, and added for her alone: 'Just five minutes down the road at the end of a rainbow.' And they grinned at one another.

24

Dinner was partnered with a vibrant discussion about what it was to be 'Rapture ready', and Simon – having put his anger at their politics aside for the moment to enjoy the entertainment value of relating some of the more ridiculous aspects of their theology – was in noisy spirits. He held forth about the woman who'd designed a toilet for the Rapture-faithful: if you were caught in an embarrassing position when Jesus arrived, his portrait on the cistern would ensure the angels understood the politics of your religion. And there were those who were nightly expecting to be levitated from their dining rooms in the midst of the family meal – ready to be raised through the rafters and embraced in the clouds. Some especially vocal Rapturists professed that Catholics meant well but were misinformed; the Pope was an Antichrist because you cannot pray with other people and their gods.

'Since these other gods don't exist, God would be jealous and call it "spiritual adultery".' Simon held them entranced:

the mood at the table swung from incredulity to hilarity to a suspicion of poetic licence on the raconteur's part.

'It's all true, I promise.' He put his hands up to defend their attacks. 'I know it seems far-fetched, but the people who subscribe to these ideas don't read the fictional element of the propaganda with any critical function. I've decided to do a big piece on it for the paper. It will make a great exposé for the *Saturday Review*. Just watch this space.'

Henry was fascinated by this information, and drew a line between the absurdities Simon presented with such humorous relish, and the more dangerous aspects of the belief. He recognised the political possibilities. He mentioned a friend from his Oxford days who was now in the Deanery at Winchester – they still had lunch on a regular basis and remained close. He would ask him about these Christian Zionists, get another perspective. He also warned Alex not to be too naïve in his idealistic corner of medicine, where he preferred to believe that most people were committed to an altruistic, life-saving world.

'I know you chose your field, Alex, because you feel this kind of research opens the way to a better world, with fewer illnesses for children especially. You genuinely believe that stem cells are one of the best hopes for the future. But you've come back from your conferences on occasions and confided that not everyone shares that view, and that certain political lobbies are noisy and unrelenting in their protests. We've talked about the way they accuse you and your peers of playing God and use aggressive, inflammatory language to shut you down. These people want to confine your research for all sorts of narrow-minded reasons – not all of them purely moral – and these hardliners you've clashed with outside your conferences are very closely related to Simon's zealots. If this material of your ancestor's is bringing you to the notice of such people, Alex, please tread carefully. Your own outlook on life is exemplified by your choice of career, but it would be a mistake to ignore the warped passion of the kinds of fanatics Simon is speaking of. Theirs is such a narrow perspective – they see only their view and won't even debate anyone else's. They speak with bigotry, hatred – perhaps even fear. They can't allow liberals, and scientists, to be right. It undermines everything they base their worldview on. The words of their Bible mean exactly what they choose, and they don't appreciate anyone taking issue with them. Don't underestimate their mania.'

Henry was a mild man, and such an impassioned plea from him worried his son. The warning hung in the air, and Alex registered his father's tone. He would check on Max and Anna, who was due back by now, when they got back to the house – but play everything down so as not to alarm them. He and Lucy were surely in the front line, being, as they were, immediately involved in the legacy and discovery of the material.

Lucy had listened attentively without adding more than a comment; but she now suggested to Alex that, if Henry wasn't averse, she would like to get into Will's darkroom and process the current roll of film, to see if it might provide information about the object under the tile – or at least of Will's movements in France before the ferry crossing.

Alex had no idea if this was a skill she had possessed for years: it would be easier to assume so. But he was worrying that it had been a rather long and stressful day. 'It's getting late, Lucy. Let me bring you down one afternoon this week and you could deal with them then.'

Lucy was mindful of Henry's words, and didn't want to delay. 'I'd rather get on with it. Time is against us. In an hour I can knock up a contact sheet – if you're happy for me to do it, Henry?'

'I don't mind in the least. Do you know what to do, Lucy? I haven't the first idea how to process film myself – have you, Alex?'

'Lucy is a lady of surprising gifts.' Alex shot her an ironic smile. 'But would you call it a day by eleven? We'll have to be up early and off by seven-ish to make London comfortably. After three days off work, I need to get in and catch up.'

They planned the details of their departure while Alex waited for the bill; but Henry returned from the bar with a beneficent expression and suggested they leave. Alex's eyes narrowed humorously at him. 'What have you done?'

'Let me treat you. It's such a pleasure to have the company of four fine intellects for dinner. Don't argue, Alex. You've all saved me from cheese on toast at home. And hearing Simon's sceptical approach to the politics of life is like having a little piece of Will with us. I haven't laughed so much in months.'

This cheered Alex, and he and Lucy linked arms with Henry as they strolled back to the house in a far better frame of mind than they had shared during the drive down.

By ten fifteen Grace and Henry were deep in discussion about some contrasting interpretations regarding the Apocalypse. Alex – having satisfied himself that all was well at Anna's, and asked his neighbour to feed the cat – was now making a second round of coffee.

Simon was impatient to slip away and see how Lucy was progressing. He was surprised she knew about Will's darkroom. It was unusual these days for someone to prefer to do his own processing. He had witnessed the master many times, and while he couldn't remember the precise steps to replicate the expertise, he wanted to be there and watch Lucy, so he poured out a cup of the coffee and excused himself.

The dark room had been converted from the old buttery, as it had running water and a Belfast sink. He found the door locked, so he rapped sharply and then called to her.

'Simon?' He grunted affirmation. 'Just give me a moment. I've almost fixed the negatives, then I can open.'

Moments later, a white cotton-gloved hand eased the edge of the door and waved him in. His eyes adjusted to the satanic glow, and she offered him a stool to perch on while she completed the job with the processing tank. She emptied out the fixative chemicals and flushed it with water, carefully opened the tank again, removed the developed negatives, and hung the strips over the sink to partially dry.

'Where's the discussion got to?' She smiled authoritatively while she picked up a chamois and slipped it over the strands of film to remove the excess liquid.

'The Angel of the Apocalypse. Henry and Grace are at it! I didn't realise she was so sharp on her history.'

Lucy smiled proudly for the compliment to her friend. 'She's a very clever girl, that Grace. Has a soulful singing voice too. There's a lot you don't know about her yet.'

'They were talking about the Revelation of John written in the first century AD – an allegory foretelling the destruction of the wicked, the overthrow of Satan, and the establishment of Christ's kingdom on earth. The author, John – popularly believed to be John the Evangelist without a shred of evidence to corroborate that, mind you – was writing about the Christians under the Roman Empire. But every age has insisted on its own prophetic interpretation.' Although he talked with characteristic energy, he was completely focused on what Lucy was doing.

She smiled at Simon, and continued to cut the negatives into smaller strips and place them into the dryer. 'He's got all the best equipment. I'm not used to the luxury of a drying machine.' She finished and brought up the full light, ready to move to the dry area to deal with the contact sheets.

'You've done all the rolls?'

'All but one, with special instructions for processing.' Lucy looked thoughtful. 'I'll need to do it carefully, maybe because of the light it was shot in. But as for the rest, once you've loaded one, it's as easy to do them all. I'll settle for contacts tonight; but we'll see what we've got, then I can print what we choose.'

Simon was impressed, watching her place the negatives in strips into the contact sheet frames, moving comfortably around the equipment. She knew what she was about, all right.

'You're quite a girl, Lucy. Will would have liked you – I think Alex would have got full fraternal approval there. One of the remarkable aspects of Will's character was that he always found something special to say about a woman –

every woman. He'd always find her true feature of beauty – her *one* true feature if that was what she had – and celebrate it. It was a mark of his generosity, but I think he would have been overwhelmed with appreciative things to say about you.'

She was deeply touched by this, peeled off her gloves, and kissed his forehead. 'Thanks, Simon. That means a lot.' She switched the red light back on and took sheets of printing paper from the box, then placed them on the dry surface and put the contact frame on top of one. He watched her through the process of flashing full lights for a few seconds, placing the exposed sheet in a safe dark place, then repeating this for each sheet of contacts.

'How much longer will you be? Shall I fetch you a coffee?'

'About another fifteen minutes, I guess. No thanks – to the coffee: I have a pretty strict caffeine-free diet, I'm afraid.' Still on red light, she moved across to the wet area again, put on rubber gloves, and put the contact sheets in the developing tray, handling everything with tongs.

'No bloody coffee. No chocolate. No cream. No fats. No salt. No smoking. Watch the sugar. Not too much booze . . . That's class. I hope . . . some other pleasures are allowed, are they?'

Lucy had been watching the print start to appear and laughed out loud, blushing unseen in the strange light. She knew what he meant, but even though she was at ease in Simon's company, she was too private to discuss this with him. She removed the first contact and rinsed it, placing it in fixer again. 'You make me sound very dull. Other pleasures are fine . . . but don't even think that gives you a licence to be prurient.' She threw him a warning glance, but there was just the hint of a grin underneath it as she rinsed the contact again and hung it to dry.

'Mm, I'm delighted to hear that.' Simon hadn't meant to touch a nerve, but he was aware through Grace of the frustrations Lucy had experienced with Alex. He was sure Alex was just being professional and not rushing her after her surgery, but he'd noticed quietly that she seemed changed on her return from France, that she now exuded something very sexy. Good for you, sweetheart, he thought.

She swivelled around to face him with an expression of dry humour, and put the full light on again. 'Put those gloves on and help me get these out of the frames.' He heard the caution in her voice not to ask further.

She took some negatives out and labelled them while Simon struggled with some clips; then something caught her eye. She grasped the viewing glass and placed it over the sheet, nearer the light source. There was a knock, and Simon enquired if it was safe to open. She nodded, not taking her eyes off the contact sheet. Alex came in with lemongrass tea, anxious to know what was happening; he noticed Lucy's fixed stare on the pictures. Something about it alarmed him, and he walked straight over and put a protective hand on her back.

'What is it?'

'This. The car.' She looked from one man's face to the other, then back to the images. 'Here. I don't know where Will took these shots, but this is the car that picked me up in Chartres. The car I was abducted in.'

'Are you certain?' Alex locked on to her.

'Definitely.'

Some minutes later she was seated on the settle, watching the others scrutinise the last contact sheet to see if they recognised any features in it. Alex was beside her, intent on her, but she seemed calm – if pensive.

Simon suddenly whooped. 'This is it.' He had the viewing glass over the final sheet that Lucy had developed from the roll in the camera itself; only thirty-two of the forty frames were exposed. 'He's photographed some kind of texts – and it looks like there are . . .' he counted quickly, '. . . eighteen of them again. Just as before. Impossible to read the details from the contact sheet, but it looks like it's all handwritten. In different styles of writing too.'

Alex and Lucy lunged forward to the table to see, and Alex realised this was what they were looking for – what Guy Temple and his associates wanted so desperately. Whatever it was Will had found, he had photographed every sheet with a twenty-five-millimetre lens. 'This must have come from the rose garden,' Alex said firmly. 'I suspect the originals went in the packet to Roland. He obviously wanted to safeguard them there.'

'So,' Simon took control, 'we need to enlarge these, and see if we can trace the originals as well. Clearly he thought them either sensitive, or dangerous.' Simon was no less alarmed and aware than Alex and Lucy; and Grace and Henry each bore an expression of bafflement.

It was the latter, however, who quickly resumed his scrutiny of another group of shots that had caught his attention, and said at length: 'Alex, when you've finished with the glass, could I have it for a moment?'

His son, sensitive to his father's changed voice, passed him the optic glass, and Henry trained it on one of the frames. 'This might be Lucca Cathedral – very distinctive square it's in – beautiful. Your mother and I were there a few years ago. But it's this car parked here. It's exactly like another I've seen – quite distinctive in this country, but I would say even in Italy it would be a classic.' He looked at Alex matter-of-factly. 'And what I particularly notice is that it seems to be the same vehicle here – outside Chartres.' He pointed to those on the sheet that had caught Lucy's eye as well. 'Now that's odd, wouldn't you say?'

Lucy looked at him unblinking. 'Have you seen this car, Henry?' She didn't want to reveal more; but Henry had indeed picked out the dark blue car that she could still smell when she closed her eyes – the leather, and the fragrance of limes from the man beside her, a whiff of cigarettes clinging around the man at the wheel. She shivered involuntarily.

Henry removed his spectacles and searched his memory. After a moment, his face altered. 'Yes,' he said with conviction. 'It's the car that parked me in when I was at Winchester Hospital. I remember very well – it was around the midnight hour, no one else was in the visitors' car park, and this car had pulled right across my space, hemming me in. It took Melissa and me a full five minutes to get out. I had plenty of time to observe it, so as not to hit the darn thing. Very pretty car – left-hand drive, foreign plates. A Lancia – midnight blue, I think. I remember thinking that some poor tourist must have had their holiday ruined by a medical emergency.'

'It was at the hospital the night Will was in the ITU?' Alex felt a stab of panic, though he tried to conceal it from his father.

Henry nodded; Lucy looked at Alex; Simon at Lucy; and Grace at Henry. The incongruously musical ring of the carriage clock sounded twelve times from next door, in Diana's tiny study. The temperature in the room dropped. Everyone understood.

Siân was aware it must now be midnight, as the *News on the Hour* intruded on her agitated mood. She picked up the remote and silenced the television. Across the room the telephone answering machine still showed a single steady light, so she had to satisfy herself that she hadn't dozed off and missed a call. She walked across the large room to her compact kitchen, took a nearly empty bottle of wine from the fridge door, and poured its remaining contents into a glass. She returned to the sitting room, looking from her open window across the darkened square. Everything was still.

It was too late to try him again, wasn't it? She'd left things very tense, with a feeling of animosity between her and Calvin, but she'd have liked the comfort – now that forty-eight hours had elapsed – of talking with him. She walked again to the kitchen, pulled down the blind, and cut the lights. Retracing her steps one more time, she reached out for the phone receiver but then hesitated, glancing at her watch. It was barely five minutes after the hour. Yes, it was definitely too late to call – or her pride advised her that it was so. He surely wasn't out with anyone else? But she'd never give him the satisfaction of knowing she'd wondered.

She slid the switch of the floor lamp across, killing the light, and walked through to her bedroom. She'd prove to herself – and Calvin – that she could still get a good night's sleep.

Outside in the square, a pair of yellow eyes had watched as each light was successively extinguished, had seen her slim silhouette through the window retreating against a paler light source coming from the rear of the flat. A chubby hand pulled a mobile from the inside pocket of an immaculate navy silk suit jacket, and in darkness texted a message, observing the hour and the unexceptional event. Then, without a hint of fatigue, the eyes returned to their original post, and settled to watch the location fixedly again.

25

As he inserted the key into the door of his basement entrance, Alex noticed a delicate spider's web spanning the frame, its dewy threads glinting in the sunlight. It seemed he'd been away weeks rather than days. On the doormat he found the early post, but barely glanced at it as he passed through to the bedroom for a change of shirt and a tie. He consulted his watch: eight-fifteen; he'd be at the hospital by half-past.

He'd left Lucy sleeping in Will's bed, where she'd instinctively retreated while he was showing Grace and Simon to their room near midnight. He'd found her there, already dozing. It was an odd prospect – sleeping in the room that had been his brother's for thirty-two years; but he didn't want to leave her and go to his own bed. So he'd slipped silently beside her and enclosed her in his arms, his own thoughts pressing quietly into the spirit of the space. They were still in that same position when his watch buzzed their wake-up call. She turned and smiled to meet his kiss, then informed him that she wanted to stay for the day to do the developing. She'd cleared it with Henry, and he would drop her at the station when he returned from work. She would appear at her office the next day in lieu. Alex hadn't objected, kissed her, and left with Simon and Grace.

He bounded up the spiral steps to the kitchen when his mobile went.

'*Ti amo, Alessandro*.'

'You too. I'll call later today. Eat some breakfast.'

He smiled lopsidedly and rang off, gathering his briefcase from the island as an envelope caught his eye. Hand-delivered and wax-sealed. Siân had propped it there for his attention. He examined the writing, noted its weight. He took a deep breath, carefully broke the red bloodspot and peered in. It contained a blank piece of heavy paper and a metal object he now shook from it. His brow furrowed. It was Lucy's broken chain with the pearl-inset replica key he'd commissioned for her birthday. Had Calvin retrieved it? He hoped so, but somehow doubted it.

He pulled on his overcoat and pocketed the envelope, dialling a number as he headed for the door. He was crossing Kings Road as it redirected and Siân answered.

'Thanks for taking care of things here. You survived?' He played down any hint of anxiety in his voice.

'I enjoyed it. Max spent most of the weekend working on those papers you two were studying on Friday night. He's got them all across your desk, I'm afraid – I hope you don't mind. Listen, Alex, I can't chat. I'm at the wheel on my way to a commercial shoot. But tell me, is Lucy all right?'

'I think so. Siân, tell me quickly about the envelope in the kitchen?'

'Put through your door on Saturday. Max and I lunched at the Rainforest Café, and it was there when we came home. It had something in it, so I didn't leave it in the hall. Is there a problem?'

'Not sure. Any idea who left it?'

'Sorry, no. What is it, Alex?'

'Lucy's chain, and that key of Will's which I had copied for her. They tore it from her neck on Friday night in France. That's a statement – for it to arrive here next day.'

Siân felt the same threat. 'Should I talk to Calvin?'

'Yes – if you would. But I'm late for the hospital now. I'll have to phone you this evening. Listen, thanks for this weekend.'

'No problem, Alex. Love to Lucy.' Her voice wavered.

His secretary was waving at him as he walked in. He was wanted urgently by Dr Anwar who'd been assisting in theatre since the early hours. Jane Cook had left him a message; one of his students was looking for him; and Mr Azziz would be here from Harefield shortly: could he join him around eleven for coffee?

'Oh, and you've been asked to step in for Dr Franks and lecture tomorrow evening at Imperial about T-cells, if possible.'

He smiled. It wasn't nine o'clock yet. Welcome back, Alex, he thought.

'Don't panic, Emma. Say yes to everyone, and I'll find Zarina Anwar now.'

*

Sunshine flooded the breakfast table. It was so comforting, and the presence of Alex and his family so strong, that Lucy had trouble connecting her immediate circumstances with the realities of last night. No one had said as much, but everyone realised the Lancia's low-profile presence in Will's photos suggested he'd been followed for some time – and although they had no way of knowing whether he had realised that, it might explain why he'd sent the documents away. Henry's chilling description of the car blocking his exit at the hospital on that painful Sunday morning had prompted Alex to speak again of Melissa's story, about a possible car engine near the bridge at the time of the accident. And was it connected with the break-in that night? They'd all retired to bed with things to think about – including Lucy's extrication from the same vehicle near Chartres. But paradoxically, she had fallen into a blissful, undisturbed sleep broken only by the muted alarm and Alex's early morning kiss. Nothing broke into her peace; she'd come home.

A show of normality continued in the face of threatened danger. She recognised Alex's need to maintain a sense of calm control and not to escalate the tension. He had left cereal out for her; but Henry had made a point to give her his number in Winchester. 'I'm in court this morning, Lucy, but don't hesitate to let my secretary know if you need me. Otherwise, I'll see you after five. There's a train from Andover on the half-hour. I'll be sorry to see you go. Come back with Alex and Max for Easter.' He pressed her hand and gave her a set of keys; then he was gone.

In an hour she had the printing process underway,

selecting the negatives she wanted to enlarge. And by eleven o'clock her safe-light was displaying the first run of prints. She had to adjust the focus a few times for the documents: but Will had done a brilliant job and the quality was excellent. She held her breath as she read the first words in the tray by the coloured light. In a neat feminine hand – perhaps eighteenth century – she saw:

Lucy Locket lost her pocket . . .

And on the next:

Oh – But the king's daughter is in danger of dropping a stitch. Losing the thread. Letting it go to her head.

On yet another:

TAURUS 4 – THE RAINBOW'S POT OF GOLD.

And on one typed on a funny old typewriter:

The music died that day.

Why did she read herself into these texts? She was Lucy. She'd lost – not a pocket, but her key. And she was Mr King's needleworking daughter, telling herself many times not to drop a stitch as she patched her quilt in the hospital, thinking it emblematic of the thread of her life. But this was surely a coincidence. Wasn't it? And the rainbow? It was her running joke with Alex. But what about that last riddle? Too bizarre. That was definitely Lucy; but she'd run it past Alex and Simon – see if they had the first idea what she was on about. No one else would know the reference, would they? She'd say nothing: she'd show them, then put the question.

The batch finished, she decided to have some tea before doing the next sheets. It was getting towards noon; she could reach Alex, hear his voice.

The kettle on the Rayburn whistled, and Lucy poured water over the teabag. She took her mobile to the back door looking for a stronger signal away from the thick house walls, and tried the number again. This time it connected, and his direct line rang. Alex's secretary swooped on it, sounding like Cerberus. They'd spoken in the past about appointments, but she felt self-conscious now that her relationship with Alex had changed.

'No, I'm sorry. He doesn't seem to be anywhere in the building, Miss King. I've just been looking for him myself. He's having a busy day and running late all over the place. Can I give him a message?'

Lucy recoiled, feeling guilty at intruding on his 'busy day'. It wasn't important; she'd have a word with him later. The house phone rang, and she prevaricated about whether it was right to answer it.

'If it's an emergency, I could call Dr Lovell to the phone?'

Lucy tried to get off the line politely: it wasn't an emergency, she'd wait and catch Dr Stafford another time. She brought the call to an end, just as the house phone stopped ringing. She felt temporarily thrown, and considered calling Alex's mobile. He often had it on mute or even switched off at the hospital, as was policy if he was in clinic or somewhere close to the monitoring equipment; but at least she could leave him a personal message. Hearing his voice on answer mode would be some consolation. She tried to be positive.

'*Buongiorno, Alessandro*. Just tried on the off chance, but you weren't at your desk, and you have a first-rate defence secretary. We'll talk later? Intriguing images in the first batch of prints. Tell me how events go when that call comes at one o'clock. Don't forget the time change between here and France. Oh, the land line's going again. I'll pick it up – maybe it's you. *Ciao*.' She broke off quickly and ran to the phone in the kitchen. 'Hello?'

'You'll never guess what I've just found in Will's photo-files. I hadn't looked at them since I emailed them to my own computer from Alex's.'

'Hiya, Simon.' She covered her disappointment. 'Anything interesting?'

He'd discovered four frames, all taken on Will's Nikon digital camera in Sicily and Rome, that revealed the car. Three of them were quite indistinct, but one was very clear. He was going to talk to his contact in Scotland Yard and see if they could enhance it to read the plate. 'I think there's a good chance Jamie McPherson will come up with something. Don't worry, Lucy, he's very discreet – young, but a clever boy. Leave it with me. I've also found several photos of a beautiful girl who looks not at all unlike you, but with longer, very curly hair. Oh, and I have to call Roland Brown when New York wakes up later. How's things your end?'

Lucy shared a few details of what the enlarging had revealed, including her growing feeling that she herself was implicated in the word games in the documents. She heard her mobile go; but Simon was immersed in the investigative work and hard to interrupt. Should they meet up for dinner? He was keen to pursue the trail with the new clues. Lucy hurried him off, and picked up the mobile phone, only to find it was her message service.

'Lucylu, it's quarter to twelve – I've escaped to a quiet space to call you. No answer on the house phone, and your mobile has gone to message, so I guess you're still buried away in the red-light district. It's a zoo in here today: I've had clinic all morning, and I was asked to help out in theatre for a while, but I'll try you again over lunch. Tell me your train and I'll meet you at Waterloo. I'm off now to catch Amel for a quick word about you. Call my direct line when you surface. It may be safer.'

Damn. She slumped on the oak bench in frustration. How could she miss both calls? Well, she'd leave him to Amel and his lab-work, and phone after lunch. She picked up her tea and retreated to Will's lab, lost in thought about the riddling Lucy Locket.

'You look different.' Amel handed his guest a properly brewed coffee and invited him to share some falafel and vine leaves.

Alex smiled enigmatically. 'I feel different. I've been transported to an unfamiliar place this weekend. Which is not as cryptic as it sounds.' He looked at his mentor. 'Amel, do you have an opinion on cellular memory?'

'Cells in our body containing information about our tastes and personalities?' Amel twinkled at his favourite protégé. 'Interesting digression for you, Alexander. Has it anything to do with the question you put to Jane on Saturday?'

'She told you?'

'She's very worried how it will affect you. Said she thought it might "do your head in", in her words. I told her not to give it a second thought – that it wouldn't distress you at all. Was I wrong?'

'No. I'm not affected that way, except to feel that Lucy is . . . even closer to me now. But it's how she knew: *that* affects me.'

'Courtney would dismiss it. "Utter nonsense," he'd say. Not everyone would, though. As a concept, there are theories that might help us approach it. Lucy must have said something to provoke your interest?'

'Some of it stems from her medication in my view: new palate for food, vivid dreams. But one or two things are intriguing. Will was extremely musical; and Lucy's felt a compulsion, she said, to take up piano again after years of not playing. She told me she's had classical music inside her head since the operation. Which could be other psychological factors at work; but taken in tandem with other points, I'd consider it noteworthy. She also seems to recognise my brother's friends. Gets close to his way of thinking about some things – when it's unexpected. And oddly, she's become more left-handed since the transplant, which I can't ascribe to her medication.'

'Will was left-handed?'

'And slightly dyslexic with it. You'd think she'd favour her left side after surgery, if anything. And there are other things – I'm trying to think objectively. Anytime she reacts instinctively – rather than remembering a fact or an event – that instinct has some parallel with Will's.'

Amel, nodding, said, 'I remember speaking with a brilliant neurocardiologist at a conference in Holland some time ago. He was interested in the relationship between the brain and the heart via the nervous system. He felt the relationship between these two organs was dynamic, a mutual conversation. Each organ could conceivably influence the other's function. He agreed with the idea of the heart as a brain in itself, comprised of a network of neurons, transmitters, proteins and support cells that allow it to act somewhat independently of the cranium – perhaps even to *feel* and *sense*.'

Alex became more interested. 'So, information is translated into neurological impulses, travels from the heart to the brain along a number of pathways, and reaches the medulla in the brain stem. These impulses then regulate blood vessels and organs. But if they were to reach higher centres of the brain, they might affect our perceptions and other cognitive processes?'

'Exactly. The heart's own nervous system functioning independently of the brain is just what aids the transplant. Heart and brain would normally communicate via the nerve fibres in the spinal column; but when these nerve connections are severed and can't reconnect for some time, the heart's intrinsic nervous system allows it to function in the new body. If we agree it could have its own minor brain, it may well be able to retain some version of what we think of as memory.'

Amel looked at Alex, considering something further. 'We haven't said anything, Alex, about the possibility of Lucy's *spirit* adding something. We've talked about the scientific basis for a theory; but might we ponder the chance that her personality could be . . . additionally empathetic, to your brother's? She feels strongly for you, you were close to him. Is she more sensitive to the nuances in his heart in a subtle way, as though she's able to access some essence of him in a way we can't explain?'

'Like identical twins?'

'Perhaps, yes. It's nothing precisely *scientific* – unlike the arguments for cellular memory, which are being analysed in a proper empirical way. But it's fascinating, don't you think? Personally, I find the whole premise intriguing. I would be cautious in what I ascribe to it, careful about being emphatic one way or the other. We often make the mistake of linking two unrelated things for our own purposes. But we could be open to this research. Stronger conclusions will eventually spring from intelligent patients like Lucy, who are alive to the changes they're experiencing, and unlikely to embellish the details. Ask at your next conference, Alex. You'll find plenty of doctors and researchers who have some experience of this question. But, Alex,' Amel looked at him with concern, 'there's another important question here. Will it get in the way for you two?'

'I can't judge until I know more. I've no reason to doubt what she says she feels: in fact, I'm convinced she's not imagining it. Some of it is compelling. I'll make a note to bring it up at future conferences and learn what I can from the people you're talking about. If it's just the drugs at work, they're certainly having an entertaining effect.'

'Mm! But that's not what I meant. Is it a psychological hurdle to overcome? Your brother being Lucy's donor? I've put the price of a good lunch on it with Jane that it wouldn't be; but it must be a little strange. Part of Will is resting with Lucy – making her your quasi sister in one oblique sense. And the circumstances by which the heart came to her. She should have had a different heart a day or two earlier; she was first on the list, we'd already brought her in, and you know I don't like putting our patients through these stops and starts. But it was a second-tier organ, not quite good enough for such a young woman. The remarkable thing is that the tissue match with Will's heart was virtually perfect.' Amel's pager broke the mood between them, but he picked it up without hurrying his visitor. 'Of course, none of us was aware of the connection, Alex – you know that.'

'It's a miracle, Amel?' Alex grinned. 'Yes – it is astonishing, to have such a resonant piece of him so near me. But it's wonderful. I'm not spooked by it – you know we don't let these things affect us. But it's one thing for her to evince some of his sensitivities. I just hope she doesn't take on his opinions! Fortunately, she has a very distinctive personality of her own.' Now Alex's own pager echoed Amel's, and he got up to leave. 'And of course, she's much prettier than Will.' Alex glanced at the air call message, and was relieved when it was a routine hospital emergency.

'I'd noticed.' Amel laughed aloud as Alex opened the door. Nothing was amiss about Alex's state of mind. He'd won his lunch bet. 'It's the porcine valve, Alex. I need you to come back to theatre with me to work with the anaesthetist. We've got a difficult immune response to cope with.'

Alex raised the pager, indicating he'd already been called. They flew off together down the corridor, and it was some time before Alex noticed the clock in theatre showing it was fast approaching one o'clock. How prompt would they be? He hovered between duty in one place and concern about the other, then peeped at Amel over the mask. 'Can you do without me for ten minutes? There's something urgent I've got to do bang on one o'clock.'

Amel blinked 'yes'. 'Come back when you can.' And Alex quietly disappeared through the folding door.

It was four minutes before the hour by the corridor clock – one minute to, if Alex's watch was right as he dragged it from his pocket. He swiftly put his head around the partition of Emma's desk. 'Any calls?'

'Lucy King phoned, Jane Cook wants a word yesterday, and Dr Anwar said to say "thank you amazingly". And that very pretty student with long, long legs and a short, short skirt dropped off her paper just now – said it was "late".' She looked at the question forming on his lips. 'Nothing else. Jane's rung thrice.'

Alex was amused at Emma's clipped tone, but he dashed towards the door outside, glancing at his mobile. 'What time was Lucy?' he called back.

'Hours ago.' She shot a dry look after him. Well, he'd taken his damned time, but he'd obviously made a move now. 'Just before twelve.' She raised her voice, but he was gone.

Wanting privacy, he rushed into the garden where a group of specialist cardiac nurses were having their lunch-time cigarette. His phone showed a stronger signal and displayed two missed calls: and two messages. He took it off mute and paused for a full minute, watching the time on the display, until it was showing two minutes past the hour, and his watch, five past. He was sure his phone was accurate to Greenwich, and after deliberating for another heartbeat, he played back the voicemail, steeling himself for Guy's lilting Southern voice.

They were in reverse order, most recent first. Simon had sighted the car among the digital photos . . . Alex impatiently deleted it before it had played out. He'd call Simon tonight. Next, a brief, lovely message from Lucy, which made him smile. He'd call her shortly. That was it.

He stared at the handset. The phone time now made it four minutes past, his watch about seven after one. He stood still, thought of ringing Lucy, chose not to busy the line.

Three more minutes passed. He felt hot, angry that they were toying with him. They would call at two, and ignore the time adjustment. He started back to the building. Then it rang, and he inhaled silently.

'Yes? Alex Stafford—' but he didn't get his name out before he realised it was his voicemail again. A message left at three minutes past one, the robotic voice reported. A change of gravity made Alex's stomach lurch. 'Dr Stafford. This is the appointed time to talk. I don't appreciate being asked to wait. I'll find you later. If you have nothing for me, there's something I'll take.' He hung up.

The voice was so disembodied, Alex repeated the message

and noted the time code again. He'd clearly missed by just one or at most two minutes, which frustrated him. It must have happened while he was clearing Simon and Lucy. He ran his thumb around the keys, hunting for the missed call number, but nothing had registered. He dialled the last number service so he could phone them back, and this produced an equally obstructive result. The caller's number was withheld. The practised calm of the doctor came under pressure, and he recorded a new message saying he couldn't always pick up during working hours. He left his personal extension. Would that satisfy them?

He paused to ring Calvin: he would have a contact number. But Calvin's own number rang without answer. His thoughts ranged. He started back to alert Emma to mind his mobile for him while he returned to theatre, and to locate him the second they rang either of the numbers – which he had no doubt they would. But then a more unpleasant idea crystallised, and he broke into a flat-out run.

'Get my father on the phone. If he's in court, have his secretary bleep him to call me urgently.' Alex left Emma staring as he sprinted to the phone in his office. Lucy's mobile still went straight to message: she must be in the dark room. His voice was a studied calm that would have fooled anyone other than Amel or the woman he was calling. 'When you get this, please ring my office immediately. And, Lucy, don't open the door.' He dialled the house phone hoping she'd hear it. Nothing. His head drooped, then Emma caught his eye and shook her head at him through the glass. Her single finger raised appeared to explain Henry was unavailable for at least an hour. Without a word he stood, grabbed his coat off the door peg, then waited. He quickly swung back, threw it on the chair and scanned the address file on his mobile. He located a number and dialled it from his extension.

'Melissa, thank goodness. It's Alex Stafford. Could you do something for me?'

Printing up four of the rolls Lucy had found her doppel-gänger. A girl a shade younger than herself, she thought, with a great mane of curls billowing out over the sea in the wind. Yes, at a quick glance they were strangely similar – it made Lucy feel as though she were looking at a ghost. Another girlfriend of Will's? She felt she recognised the face from somewhere in her dreams – but perhaps this was fanciful.

The best discovery, however, came late. She hadn't noticed its significance until she blew the frame up another size. She thought at first it was simply the tile with the Ducati key that Will had left in the rose garden. And so it was: until she saw that the key was markedly different. With magnification, she realised that Will must have taped his spare into the centre of a tile that had already harboured a key in that spot. She enlarged it as much as possible without distorting the image: it was very like the silver key – of companion shape and size, she thought. But it was golden. And she could see an emblem engraved on it, and a ruby inlaid. Where the silver one had a spiral and a pearl at the stem, this had what looked like a stag – similar in every way to the one painted on the miniature portrait Alex had shown her. And now, thinking about it, she recalled Alex saying that Will had sketched one too.

A slapping sound came suddenly at the blacked-out window, and she heard a young woman's voice calling her name. She tidied her space and then hurried up the passage towards the rear kitchen door. Someone was frantically waving at her.

'Lucy? So sorry to worry you. I'm Melissa – I live in the village. Alex rang and asked me to flush you out of the dark room. Can you please call him urgently?'

Lucy beckoned her in but she was gone again in an instant. Flustered, Lucy used the house phone to call his private line and got straight through.

'You're all right?'

'Fine.' Lucy was mystified.

'I don't mean to alarm you, but I need you to stay out of sight and not open the door to anyone. When Dad gets my message he'll head straight home.'

'Alex, if I hadn't opened to anyone Melissa couldn't have asked me to phone. You're sounding like Simon. What's going on?'

'I don't know. Maybe nothing. I'd set my alarm to buzz just before one, to remind me to take the call; then I was called to an emergency in theatre, still nipped out in time, so I thought, but missed the call clearing my other messages. I should have waited, I know, but they were a fraction late themselves. I don't trust them. I'm sure it's me they're watching, but they may still think you have the original key, or something else to attract them. And they may know from Calvin that you dug up the documents there, at the house. Lucy, stay put till you see Dad's car, and make sure he sees you right onto the train. I've tried Calvin once, and will try again now, but I'll phone the house again in one hour – to reassure myself. God, and I've left Amel in theatre. Are you OK?'

She hardly answered before he was gone. She was left feeling slightly unnerved, and she checked the time. Nearly one thirty. She made tea, walked once around the house. Everything was blissful. It smelled of the fire, and flowers, and comfort. There was nothing to disturb her, and she hoped Alex was overreacting. So she shut herself back in Will's tranquil world and picked up where she'd left off.

Her eyes returned to the pictured tile. Will had switched the keys, then. The Ducati duplicate had been exchanged for the other. Was it now with Roland? Lucy raked through every picture again for clues, and the time slipped away. She'd made a second set of some of the prints when she noticed it was after four o'clock, and, feeling guilty and worried about Alex, she'd ring.

Lucy Locket lost her pocket . . . she thought, while she waited for the phone to answer. His number was being redirected . . . and *Kitty Fisher found it*. But where is Kitty Fisher?

Emma's voice was unexpectedly agitated. 'Hello, Lucy. He asked me to find him if you called, but he left the hospital urgently about ten minutes ago. Try his mobile, but I'm not sure he'll pick up. His little boy's been in some kind of accident.'

Lucy slipped from the taxi and rose up on tiptoes. The lights were on, the curtains open; she could make out the top of Alex's head through the raised ground-floor windows.

Climbing a few steps and leaning out over the basement areaway for a better view, she saw he was resting on the sofa with eyes closed, his head tilted uncomfortably. She considered ringing the bell, hesitated to wake him, then drew the keys that Henry had given her from her coat. She was through the main house door and the second private door, heard the soft strains of a Mozart symphony, quietly placed her bag in the hallway with the cat brushing her ankles – all before he realised he had company. Exhaustion showed when he smiled at her over his shoulder.

He spoke gently, without apparent alarm, which she decided was a good sign. 'I hoped you'd come.'

Her volume mirrored his. 'I rang, but your mobile was off – and then I thought I'd better not intrude.' She moved through to the sitting room, and was spell-stopped. Alex sat with his sleeping son stretched partly on the sofa, partly curled in his arms. Lucy's emotions were caught off guard, eddying between tenderness and distress. A small gash on the child's forehead was stitched, his nose grazed, but he was otherwise angelic and peaceful.

She whispered: 'Good God, Alex. Is it serious?'

'No. He's fine. I wrestled him away from Anna to watch over him, but more about my guilt than any real danger. He's worn out, but his pupils and pulse are normal and he never lost consciousness. I'm being pre-emptive.'

Lucy perched on the coffee table and gently brushed a lock of fair hair from Max's temple. 'He's so like you. Tell me what happened. You feel guilty?' She kept her voice low.

'He was aggressively shoved outside his school, Lucy. Running to Anna. She saw a broad-shouldered man rush past him, and didn't realise at first how hard he'd fallen. *Not* an accident. She assumes it was.'

After Alex's alert to her earlier she was assembling ideas fast, and didn't like them, but she tried to keep her voice even. 'Are you very sure it wasn't?'

'The missed call.' Alex looked at her levelly. 'A heavy man. You mentioned a heavy man, also. It's too much of a coincidence. I carried him straight to Courtney, and Anna wouldn't watch the stitches. That allowed Max to tell me the man had seemed to knock into him deliberately. He'd kept that from his mother. You know it's about the missed call, and as a warning it's a masterstroke. They know where I'm most vulnerable.'

Lucy looked at him sympathetically.

'I didn't properly consider Max or Anna,' he said, almost to himself. 'They have nothing to give these people – they're not directly involved in any of this. I was focused on you, since we seem to be in the front line with these documents. But it's not a mistake I'll repeat. I'll find a reason to convince Anna to take Max to her parents in Yorkshire for a few days – get them right out of the way till this packet of Will's turns up.' His expression showed self-disgust. 'And targeting Max – it's worked, Lucy. Whatever it is, whatever they want, if we can find it, I'll hand it over. It's just not worth this,' he said firmly, glancing down at Max. Lucy looked thoughtfully at the father and his small son, biting her bottom lip unconsciously.

Alex carried Max down to bed while she threw together a salad. When he returned and they held each other, it was the body language of mutual support rather than desire. Then, with little inflection, Alex asked: 'Dad gave you Will's keys?'

She nodded. 'Do you mind? I felt odd taking them, but he was insistent.'

'I suggested it. And I have one more for you.' He reached the envelope with its broken seal from his coat pocket, and placed it in her hand. He moved away a little to choose a new CD while she emptied out the contents, then looked across to see her staring with shock.

'When did this arrive?'

'Some time Saturday.' She responded with a gentle exhalation through pursed lips, and Alex raised his eyebrows. 'They want us to know they can reach us anywhere and at any time. Have you developed anything we can give them?'

Lucy was nodding, carrying food to the dining table while he got a bottle from the fridge, and some glasses. She told him about the second key on the tile in his brother's photograph, then posed a question that was troubling her. 'Is it your wish, then, that if we can find this other key, in addition to the first silver one, and the original documents, we should just hand everything over to them, and halt our own efforts to compete to find the answer?'

Alex deliberated. He knew her thoughts: that his mother had gone to considerable lengths to create a space as a repose for the key and second batch of documents; that undoubtedly, umpteen generations of the women in her family had preserved this secret 'treasure' until some moment when it should be revealed. But Will had died for it – or because of it. That was surely not part of the design.

'My mother wouldn't want all this. Will, Max, the threat I feel overshadowing my happiness with you now. You know my view, Lucy. I admit a strange curiosity about it all; what can have been so important to them? But no family heirloom, however precious, could be more valuable than the people I love. We must let it go. I'll make sure I find a way to cover that call tomorrow and get them the pictures you've developed – hopefully that will buy us time to unearth the rest. There's nothing else to be done. I want no more to do with them.'

'Alex . . . ?' Lucy was about to walk on uncomfortable terrain, and wanted to choose her words with care. She understood his reluctance, especially after today's events; but she had a case of her own to put, and somehow, it mattered desperately to her. 'This may be painful to contemplate – obviously, even for me to talk about. But without Will's death, I wouldn't be alive; and Will would not have become what he was not. This was emphatically more than a parlour game to them, if only *because* of what your mother did to save it all.'

Alex listened to her without anger, sensitive to a passion in her that was not Lucy's habit. He knew she had strong emotions, though they were so often suppressed; but like he himself, she concealed the depth of them from others with care.

She realised her words had moved him, and decided not to give him time to contradict her. 'Besides,' she added now, 'Bruno gave up his freedom, and even his life, for what he thought was important. Dante had a special place – a sort of ante-hell – for people who were too morally weak to speak out against injustice, or have any opinion, those who compromised over important issues. They were despicable to him – fence sitters and neutrals, who lived, he said, without occasion for either infamy or praise.'

Alex half smiled. 'Unworthy of heaven, but forbidden entry to hell lest they should make the damned feel superior?'

She smiled at him and nodded. 'No moral cowards in your lot, Alex. They'd rather stand up and be counted; and you're no different. And anyhow, can we just wish them away, these people of Calvin's?' She looked at him, but it was a question not really asking for an answer. 'What does he say about this latest development?' Her voice was bitter when she pronounced the last word.

'He's nowhere to be found tonight. Siân doesn't know where he is.'

Lucy frowned, before posing her question. 'Alex, shall I take your mobile tomorrow? I can answer the call whatever time it comes. I'm not living with medical emergencies all around me. Let me arrange the handover. I've met them. I'm truly not afraid.'

'No?' He tried to smile, and Lucy responded in kind to rally him. Her heroically calm Alex was a humanly wounded man tonight, because they'd struck at someone he loved. This was a shadow of Alex.

'Of bullies? No. I grew up with one. My grandmother was probably the reason my mother left. She's scarier than any Rapturist.' His response was near to laughter, and she smiled. 'The only thing I'm terrified of is depending on another person to make me happy – or surrendering myself to passion.'

He laced his fingers in her hair, borrowing a little of her strength. 'Still?'

She nodded slowly. It was only three nights since she'd walked the labyrinth alone in Chartres, while Alex was here with Max. A lifetime of pent-up emotion had started to burst free during their weekend, changing the climate for them both. A short time ago, nothing had meant anything; but now, suddenly, everything meant something. For months the magnetism between them had made it difficult to think of anything other than having Alex. Now, she'd have to conquer a lifetime's addiction to shutting out her strong feelings. But Alex read her fears and refused to let her slip backwards. He gave himself completely to her now and kissed her, changing the nature of the tension.

'Stay . . .' he said.

'I can't,' she said. She breathed hard, shook her head to persuade herself. 'It's inappropriate. You'll be checking your son every hour.'

He agreed.

'But, tomorrow?'

Alex nodded; then hesitated. 'I'm lecturing at six.' He was still bringing his own desire under control. 'Supper later?'

It was settled, and with enormous effort she stood to go. She pointed to a packet on the kitchen work-top. 'I've made two sets of prints. Have a glance at the new documents, if you feel inclined. More labyrinthine riddles.' She smiled ruefully, recognising he was so close to losing heart for the chase. Was he right to think of letting it go? It was certainly becoming dangerous.

'Before you go.' Alex stole her hand and walked her to the desk in his open-plan office overlooking the rear garden.

'Look what Max did with the set of copies, before I flew to France to find you.'

Lucy's eyes widened. The clever seven year old had brought another perspective to the puzzle. He'd pieced together the pattern on the reverse of the texts, linking the pictures in a way no one had thought to try. And now, it was clear half of the picture was missing. It resembled part of a face, in a kind of labyrinth.

'It looks as though, if we had the original new documents, there could be a path which would trace right through the coils, to the middle.' Alex showed her with his finger that part of the path Max's pencil had drawn in: it worked as a proper maze.

'We'd need the originals, as you say: Will has photographed only one side. But what a discovery from Max!' Lucy shook her head, astonished. 'Clever boy. Like his dad . . .' She was impressed, and proud of them both. 'I never considered the details of these pictures on the back. Look at the boat here. Doesn't it remind you . . . ?' She didn't have to finish the question. She saw that Alex had also recognised the barge they'd seen from the cruise boat. She almost caressed the trail that included part of a river. 'And this is someone walking in a labyrinth. It makes me shiver, Alex.'

He nodded absently; and she saw his mind whirling – assembling, so she believed, a collage of images. She reframed the question she'd asked earlier. 'We've got this far. Can we, in all honesty, just walk away from it? You and I found the papers after they'd spent hundreds of years in the earth. Will found the second group. I can't shake the conviction that they were meant for us; and for some reason to include even me.' She saw his hesitation. 'At least take a look at the enlarged prints. There are some fascinating conundrums to amuse your mathematical mind.' She started to go, but then turned to him, her face suddenly curious. 'Alex, on what day did the music die?'

He looked at her with amazement. 'The song?'

Her eyes blinked yes; and he thought aloud for her.

'And the event? The plane crash?'

She smiled at him again.

'February?'

'Mm,' she nodded, pleased. 'Enjoy your reading.' And she brushed his lips and slipped away before her resolve left her.

26

The morning sun lit a thin film of dust on the instrument. Siân opened the cover, breathed the wood. Last night she'd invited Will to haunt her, her need so strong that she was sure he'd come back and sit here. Coiled in an armchair, she'd watched and waited, listened for him after too much wine: not for the first time. But she was no Heathcliff and he no Cathy. As before, no sound came. She wished she could play the piano and reanimate the sounds he'd left there. She folded the cover down, stretched her arms over the wood and pressed her face against its scent, straining for a note in the silence. Where were the angels who were said to come in a crisis, when you called? Calvin told her about them when Will died, and she believed him, too; but she couldn't reach one now. Even the tears wouldn't flow.

What perverseness had made her resent his playing? She had thought he retreated into the piano to escape her. Now she realised that this was how Will thought, and voiced his emotions, when words couldn't express his reality. Returning from foreign assignments he'd sometimes played for days without speaking. She'd felt walled out – though their sexual relationship never suffered. Lost in shadow, producing bittersweet sounds, he'd sense her confusion and take her wordlessly to bed. She knew there was no one else, but she was excluded from this place Will went to. She was emotionally careless with him, pushing her insecurities too far until they forced a battleground. She wasn't able to translate the silences into a language she could understand.

Now his death appeared in a new light: had she played a part? From Alex's words last night on the phone, connections were emerging between Calvin's associates and the events concerning Max and Lucy. And while he hadn't said so, his questions told her Will's accident could also be related. She was horrified. She knew she wasn't a stupid woman, but she was critically unthinking – and there was nowhere to hide from this realisation. For the first time since Will's crash, she felt utterly alone, and the loss was greater now than at the start. Echoes of their past arguments distressed her.

The door buzzed like an angry wasp. She jumped. Calvin. But should she see him? She'd rather be cloistered with Will's ghost. Doubts about Calvin's loyalties now made her nervous. Had she talked too much? Did she mean anything to him – or was she a means to an end? Maybe she'd been indiscreet about Will's life and his family. The buzzer came again, more insistently. She looked down from the patch of sky in the window to Redcliffe Square below, and leaned out a shade. It was incongruously sunny and tranquil. A dark green Audi with the roof down was double-parked below. She quickly crossed the floor and pressed the door release, then opened hers and waited.

When he appeared at the top of the long stairway, one hot tear came, followed by a second. Alex gathered her in a hug and closed the door.

'The only person . . .' She mumbled indistinct words against his black linen suit, unwilling to look him in the face.

He tilted her chin. 'I knew you were in trouble. I had to drop Max off, so I thought I'd check.' He placed a thumb on each blotched cheekbone, looked in her eyes and frowned. 'What did you have for dinner last night – a bottle of Sancerre?' And what else besides, he wanted to ask.

Her mouth twitched. Alex had lived through her crises two or three times.

'Siân, listen. Max is fine – completely well this morning. He arrived at school with a magnificent battle wound to show off. I believe it was intended as a warning, not a serious strike. You're not to blame for this. It's not in your nature to suspect guile in anyone. I do need to reach Calvin, though. I hope he can shed some light. Still no word?'

'Nothing. I've tried the halls of residence. He's not answering his cellphone, and no one answers the main house phone either. Have they broken for Easter already?' She looked up to see Alex shake his head. 'I'm almost worried about him.'

'Well, perhaps we should be.' He'd considered this. If they thought Calvin was having second thoughts about their crusade, or about serving their ideologies, he might be in an uncomfortable position – depending on how much he knew about their intentions. But it was equally possible he was a consummate go-between, having talked Alex into parting with the valuable Dee papers under the guise of concern for Lucy, yet effectively delivering the haul they wanted in the simplest manner. Alex couldn't quite make up his mind about Calvin's sympathies. The second thoughts Simon suggested he might be having about his cohorts and their theories could be opportunist. He might still be a card-carrying member of the Rapturist party. None of this, however, did he impart to Siân. 'You last spoke to him on Saturday; and not a word since?'

She shook her head, curls springing from their combs. 'We've quarrelled before, and he'll go to ground for a day or so; but he's never done this. We've been seeing each other for eight or nine months now. I'd say it's out of character. But I seem not to know him. Perhaps he realises I'm in turmoil this time, and he's taken off.'

Alex looked at her pensively, unsure of her true feelings for Calvin. 'Listen, I'm badly parked and late for work; but I'm worried about you. If you need me to stay, I'll explain I have an emergency. Even I can make house calls occasionally.'

She met his eyes – clear green, unlike the hazel of his brother's – and couldn't help smiling. They had an inexhaustible strength that she'd called on more than once.

'Alex, I'll survive. You get to the hospital. I'll phone if I hear. But thanks for appearing. I needed you.'

'We'll speak later. I'm at Imperial tonight, and seeing Lucy for supper after; but call if you need me. Drink some water.

Alcohol's dehydrating and a terrible depressant, and I'm not sure what the wine chased down . . . ?' He suspected her of popping or snorting something – was looking surreptitiously for evidence on the coffee table – but she avoided the invitation to level with him, and he avoided the lecture. 'Cook something for breakfast, then go to bed. You forgot to do that last night.' He gave her a hug and started to go, then turned back. 'We'll take you for dinner tomorrow night. Are you free?'

'Of course – unless I hear from Calvin.'

'Either way. I'll bring Lucy and we'll go somewhere special. She'd love to see you, and I should talk to him. If you've not heard by then, we'll reassess. I'll ring before, but we'll come around seven.'

He insisted. An hour after Will arrived on his doorstep after the break-up last May, Alex had visited Siân. She could be unstable on her own, and he had found her in black despair, although he never shared this knowledge with Will. Today she looked even worse than on that night. He had a lot to juggle, but he'd have to keep an eye on her. She was feeling duped, and seemed worryingly near the edge.

'The licence holder has diplomatic status. That's all Jamie Mac can tell me. His own hands are tied. We can't positively connect it to a crime, so it's a no-go zone until it's clearly implicated in something. But it has Rome plates and diplomatic status in France – that much we know.' Simon's frustration boiled over. He was burrowing through the papers on Lucy's desk, examining the prints he'd made from

Will's digital camera, and he slapped them down next to him for her to inspect.

'And my abduction doesn't count?'

'You didn't press charges, and the existing records can't even be located for the moment. Very convenient.'

'I suppose we did rather give in to their dictates about keeping the police at arm's length. Alex was erring on the side of caution. They're genuinely untouchable then?'

'Bollocks! No one's that fireproof. I'll have to try another way, that's all.'

Lucy ditched the editing she was trying to finish. Her screensaver had long since covered the badly delayed script for her narration. It was useless to fight the distractions. She was lost in Alex's bay leaves and Diana's roses and the uncertain proximity of a man smelling of limes. She was at work in body but not in soul, she informed her unexpected visitor when he flew off the sofa in the production office reception at sight of her. He'd been too impatient to phone, had to speak to her now; and honestly, she welcomed the break.

'Who do you think really funds them, Simon?' She'd lowered her voice.

'The College? Your guess mirrors mine, I'd say. Their alumni have picked up a lot of appointments with the incumbent political order. I'm looking into that. And where the hell is Calvin in all this? He engineers more escapes than Houdini.'

Suddenly Lucy's mobile rang, and she jumped. Her senses were keened for the sound, but it was her own handset. She picked up with an embarrassed glance at Simon, but the 'Good morning' at the other end made her happy.

'Yes, it is. Is everyone blooming today?'

'Max is in fine fettle, but Siân's crumbling under the pressure. I'll have to monitor her. She'd upped or downed something other than wine last night, but I hadn't the heart to chew her out for it this morning. She feels responsible for some of this mess, and she shouldn't. Anything your end?'

'Poor Siân. No, Alex, monastic silence so far – apart from Simon, that is! He's invaded my desk, doing his best to derail my healthy diet and Protestant work ethic.'

'Oh, give in and have a pastry!' Simon roared this for Alex's benefit, but instead of the expected protest, he just laughed.

'I think I can trust you. I called because something obvious has just struck me. Those number squares – both of them. There's one in the first cache of documents, remember, and a new one which was under the tile. I'm sure you've realised, they're both magic "thirty-four" squares. The older one is known as the Tablet of Jupiter. I think it's used in Dee's angel magic – especially the words around it, all names for God or the angels that may have been relevant for a magic circle. I spent the night hours combing through Will's esoteric books while I sat up with Max. It seems Jupiter and Venus were the planetary influences seen as an antidote to too much Saturnian melancholy – and Saturn governed the scholarly mind for the study and practice of the magic. The Jupiter tablet calls down the presence of God, apparently. The Renaissance historian Frances Yates feels this may be why Dürer included it in his etching of Melancholia, which in her view depicts an adept working into the night on alchemy and angelology, neglecting all other material pleasures. The Tablet of Jupiter prevents the magus from becoming mired, and balances his mind – Jupiter is his protection.

'Now then, the star on the tile also adds to the number thirty-four. It seems that this was considered *the* power number by the ancients – related to God, and part of the Golden Proportion. It's a Fibonacci number. I was wondering how many connections to this number there might be in the puzzle texts.'

A transfixed Lucy hushed Simon with a finger. 'You think the number might be the key?'

'I do. Dante chose it specifically for the number of books that make up his *Inferno*; in fact, the words under the star tile are the very last words of the *Inferno*. Are you following me, Lucy? They're the closing words to Canto Thirty-Four. The number is said to symbolise the axis of the world, and the power of the Realisation of Man, making a god of man, if you like. So yes, I think it's possibly a key. Look at the riddle about the enamels and the painting of miniatures. There's a link there. And the one about "the little girl in the state of the twister", and the Madonna's robe. There's a bridge between it and the number. And if you can't find it,' Alex laughed teasingly, 'you can buy me dinner tonight for the answer – now that you're a working girl again. And by the way: the latter was typed on my grandmother's distinctive old Olivetti. I recognised it immediately.'

'Curious, said Alice.' Lucy decided to probe a little. 'It sounds like you've had a close look at the photos. Does this mean you haven't entirely consigned the chase?'

'Curious said *Dorothy*, in fact – on this occasion. I'm sure you noticed how many "king's daughters" are mentioned. It's piqued my interest, yes. I must run. Call me when you hear. Emma's on a pledge to bleep me.'

Lucy rifled through the bundle of pictures, pulling out the two Alex had nominated. She placed them in front of Simon. 'Focus on these. Alex says the number thirty-four is in there somewhere and that his grandmother wrote – or copied – this one herself. It's her typewriter, apparently. My pride will be mortified if we can't find the connection.'

Simon downed the last of his coffee, then bent his head to join her over the sheet.

'It's particularly this bit about the twister and the girl and the Madonna's robe. Is it something to do with the life of one of the saints?' Lucy searched in her Catholic upbringing for what she could remember about the lives of the earliest martyrs. 'Maybe there's a Rapture-relevant event that happened in AD 34 ?'

Simon read aloud: '"The history of the state is written on the flag – and all begins in the silk of the same hue as the Madonna's robe."'

'Well, a state sounds much more modern to me. A dozen possibilities exist, but the most obvious is surely the United States. What colour is the Madonna's robe?'

Lucy was animated. 'Oddly, they have the gown the Madonna is said to have worn when she gave birth to Christ at Chartres. I saw it – a particular treasure. It's white; but in art history Mary is usually depicted in a blue robe to represent heaven, of which she is queen. And her robe proper, or habit, might be red: so take your pick.'

'Clear as mud, Lucy. You've just offered me red, white and blue. Enough flags there for a summit meeting. How about this "twister" in the next bit? It's a tornado, right?'

They read in unison: '"The little girl in the path of the twister looked up at the gathering storm – a veritable tempest blew. Without its weather the story would never have taken off. The smell of the orange blossom is like a walk through a field of sunflowers – one of which has been plucked and placed centre stage. The brickwork matches, but the shoes do not."'

'Let's put a sunflower centre stage, then.' Lucy entered the word in a search engine on her computer, and Simon scanned the opening data.

'Begins blooming in July . . . Eleven species of sunflower found in . . . Kansas. That's interesting. It's the state flower, it says here. Awarded 1903.'

'The colour of a sunflower is yellow, which will make the brickwork yellow.' Lucy flew on at another angle, grabbing her mobile simultaneously, while Simon usurped her seat and added a new search. 'But the shoes are a different colour . . .' She drifted into a new vapour of thought, as the line connected.

'Amazing. You answered your own phone. No call yet. Listen: what year was your grandmother born?'

'Lucy! I can tell you my son's birthday, and yours, and my mother's. Not quite sure the rabbit can produce my grandmother from the hat, though.'

'Have a go.' She was in bubbly spirits and wouldn't be shaken off.

Alex calculated aloud. 'My mother was born in 1942.

First girl . . . boys before that . . . war got in the way . . . I think my grandmother was thirty-eight or thirty-nine then. I'd take a stab at around . . .'

'1903?'

'Sounds about right. A reason?'

'Wait until that dinner you promised me. Later.' She rang off. 'You heard, Simon. It's a yellow-brick road, isn't it? And the shoes were ruby slippers. Dorothy and *The Wizard of Oz.* But I've no idea about the Madonna's robe, or the number thirty-four. Alex's grandmother was older when she had his mum.'

'Aha.' Simon adjusted the angle of the screen to show her what he'd found. Kansas had a sunflower on the flag, which was set on a blue silk background – the colour of the Madonna's cloak. 'How many stars does it have, Lucy?'

'Am I supposed to count?' She laughed, followed his finger down the text, reading aloud: 'Thirty-four stars in the constellation.'

Simon picked up, 'It's the thirty-fourth state admitted to the Union, it seems. And, as you've quickly gleaned, the home of *The Wizard of Oz.*' He gave her the look of a smug cat that had ousted the dog from a favourite chair. 'Looks like Alex is paying tonight, sweetheart. Make him take you to Gordon Ramsay's.'

Now they refocused on the remaining text. '"The lady who explained about them defeated her sister in a sizzling final, but it was written by a man, and it's hard to know how much he understood. Was there no place like home, or was that just what the little girl was expected to sing, garlanded with flowers?"'

'Film, and book. Glinda was the Good Witch, I suppose the wicked one was her sister; and Dorothy got back to Auntie Em saying there was "no place like home". But the rest is a bit of a mystery, Simon.'

'Strange. I was thinking that part reminded me of the Williams sisters, in sizzling finals – and that their destiny was written by their father. But yours is more plausible, especially in the light of the rest, with Kansas.' He refused to give up, scrutinising the text while Lucy's mind wandered out of the window.

Glinda certainly had the good advice, but
of course, it was the Wizard's domain.
There is a parallel . . .

The Mariner tells
how the ship
sailed southward
with a good wind
and fair weather,
till it reached the
Line.

'This is a chunk of Coleridge, Lucy. From *The Ancient Mariner*.' Simon was seeking a connection, when a taut expression from his companion made him set the paper down again abruptly. 'Have you seen a ghost?'

'Simon, how could they have known? This must have been written years ago. It's Calvin: do you remember where he's been studying?'

Her face was ghastly, and they said with absolute synchronicity: 'Kansas!'

But the word was dwarfed by another sound: Alex's mobile.

Lucy breathed deeply, then picked up calmly. 'This is Lucy King.' Her voice was rock steady.

'Ah, what a nice surprise. You slipped below our radar for a day or two.' It was the voice of the man to whom she had been unwilling companion on Friday night, and she chalked up the information he'd just – perhaps unwisely – let slip.

'Very ill-advised of you to make an enemy of Dr Stafford. That was a crass gesture yesterday. I'd have had you down as a man of more subtlety.' Lucy had gauged the American Frenchman as a man of ego, and explored this ground with him now.

'My aide, whom you had the pleasure of meeting, can occasionally be clumsy executing orders. Which, however, you'd do well to bear in mind.'

'And I'd have seen you as a man in much tighter control of your team.' She shot Simon a look and saw he was impressed, which emboldened her. 'Now, let's make arrangements. Don't imagine you can do any of this without Dr Stafford. You know he's implicit in the whole design of this quest. He is sewn into the saga, and you can't surgically remove him. If you've been sharp enough to solve any of the riddles, you'll know it would be better for you to work with him, not to lose him completely.'

'A valid point, Miss King. But don't underestimate our reach. We have long arms.'

'Well, let's see if they're long enough to scratch your own back. Shall we decide how to proceed?'

Simon grinned. Her adversary had met his match.

He could taste salt in the sharp clear air. The vista stretching away from him had a band of tight daffodils coming into bloom at the bottom, a thin ribbon of sand above that and a broader swathe of varying blues at the top broken with minute dots of white. From the veranda overlooking the garden there was a long view out to sea, and it was here that Faith Petersen set the coffee pot down with a padded cover for insulation. It was impossible to miss the chance for lunch outdoors with her son on a day as fine as this one. She settled in the cane chair and pulled a quilt over her legs.

'Does this mean you can't get home in a couple of weeks for Easter?'

He concentrated for a second on the burst of colour as a spinnaker ballooned out in the distance. 'I'll promise to try; but I have obligations in London, and I'm not sure how they'll pan out. I'm still tied up with research.'

'I was hoping you'd bring this girl, Siân, home for us to meet. She sounds very sweet. It's been going on for some time now. Is it getting serious?' She was goading her son into a confidence that she knew better than to expect he'd make. He was in his early thirties, good looking, a desirable catch; yet he'd never shown the least inclination to settle down, and he kept himself completely to himself. One of her closest friends had even questioned his sexuality, which made her wonder about it herself. He'd never done anything that might clarify the case, but he was secretive.

'We'll see.' He changed the subject. 'Mother, did it ever occur to you that you should be the next holder of the key, after Diana Stafford died without a daughter? Did you discuss the possibility with her?'

Faith had known something was on his mind, and she'd waited patiently over lunch for him to get to the point. It was out of character for him to turn up unexpectedly like this, and she had sensed there was a purpose. 'It's funny, isn't it? It's a mystery – which makes us all want to know more. But in truth, Calvin, the key would never have been likely to come to us.' She looked at him with a curious expression. 'Have you actually seen this mythical little object? I've always wondered whether it was beautiful and precious?'

'It's decidedly ordinary, as far as I could tell. Though I haven't had a hold of it. But surely,' he resumed his line of questioning, 'you – or Grandma – are the nearest female kin, so it might with some justification have come to one of you?'

'No, no! Diana had brothers, and one of them has a daughter. She could have been the recipient. But there are other considerations, you know.'

'Yes, but if the key had to go through the female line, then the next girl would have been up from Diana, and sideways – otherwise it would have had to pass through one of the boys surely? And the other thing I don't understand concerns the country property in England, where Granny grew up. Why was it never shared among the siblings?'

'Are you feeling short-changed? You're hardly badly off. Your grandfather has left us all with a comfortable income from the cottages here on Nantucket Island.'

'Let's just say I'm intrigued. I told you they found the collection of Dee papers under a tree at the family house. I'd like to understand the legacy better. And this notion of a curse. Can you explain it for me?'

'Discussion about the key and the legatee has been a closed subject traditionally – except to those directly concerned. I suppose Diana didn't even tell her sons much – the uncertainty about who should have it would have muddled her. This much I know. The family legend says that the key, a written document, and the cottage – with one or two other things I can't recall – must pass as a whole to the first girl. It's the exact opposite of the English passion for male primogeniture. Once or twice it went to a granddaughter, I believe, in the instance that a mother predeceased her mother. But once the inheritance was given, it couldn't be ungiven – so it was usual practice to wait on it, more or less. Other siblings were given small cash sums in lieu, or the chance to be bought out of the property. But until recently, I don't think the Hampshire house was all that valuable. Property prices there have only jumped in modern times. I wonder how she planned to divide it between her boys. But I guess she knew she was at the end of the line, and something would happen.'

'What do you mean, "end of the line", and that it couldn't be ungiven?' Calvin gave her more coffee without taking his eyes from her.

'Mom always said that the key to the treasure was pledged, right from the start. There's an aural history that goes along with it: it must find its way into the right hands. If the wrong person tries to take it, grief will follow. It's been dedicated – like a curse, I guess. And once given, it mustn't be taken back. It must be willed upon very careful consideration.'

'You mean like the Ark of the Covenant? That was said to make people ill if they stole it.'

Faith laughed openly. 'Something like that – if you believe it. And I know it had so much time to run. So many generations – I'm not sure how many. But don't be out of joint, Calvin. It's a blessing only to the one person it's destined for: to everyone else it's a burden.'

Now she broke off and changed the subject. 'But tell me more importantly, how long have I got you? You haven't even told me what you're doing here. Have we got time to walk along the beach?'

'For sure. I'd like to stay tonight; but I've got an important meeting in Boston tomorrow, and then I'm booked on the late-night flight. I really wanted to be back Wednesday, but Thursday will have to do.'

Faith thought he looked strained and, as usual, had no idea of the real cast of his mind. But she said lightly: 'Too bad. Hardly time to get the boat down. You'll have to come back with your girlfriend, for Easter.'

27

Lucy was transfixed by the sunflowers on the desk. They gave her something to look at while she waited nervously; and she considered whether they indicated a private joke, if Alex had brought them in for Emma. When he appeared around the corner in response to his pager, she stifled a laugh at their mirrored appearance. His dark linen suit was relieved by a light grey shirt and grey silk tie. He stopped in his tracks, seeing it too: they were Whistler's *Symphony in Grey*.

'Hello! You're suited! I've never seen you like this.' He threw down some files next to the flowers, his lively eyes appraising his unexpected visitor. She exuded poise and control in an immaculate, gun-metal satin jacket and trousers, kitten heel boots. Her leisure wardrobe drew on a palette of watercolours, feminine and unstructured. But this crisp, professional Lucy was new and mysterious to him.

'Is there somewhere we can talk?' She accepted the compliment his eyes paid her, but felt awkward in front of

Alex's secretary. He waved her into his office with an unfamiliar boyishness, then perched respectably on his desk, the expanse of glass denying them proper privacy.

'You've heard from them.'

'It's all in place. Can you get this batch of prints to Calvin?' She offered him an envelope. 'He's to play courier, and they've given me one week to find the originals. I asked for more, but that was their limit. With luck, Roland will have the documents and whatever else Will sent on – the other key, I hope. I can make copies from those.'

That Lucy seemed to be taking all this on herself had not escaped Alex's notice, and he exhaled heavily. 'Calvin still hasn't surfaced. I'm somewhat loath to depend on him as the liaison. Did you say when he'd deliver?'

'I wasn't specific – but I suppose I gave the impression it would be fairly swiftly. Surely, Alex, they must know his movements? He was the suggested contact.'

'Presumably.' Alex wasn't entirely assuaged by this, but let it go. 'I should speak to Roland then.'

'Simon has it covered. They've apparently met a few times in New York.' Lucy tentatively took Alex's hand, shy of being seen by the passing world outside his office. She was unclear as to the ethical considerations of their relationship, although he was technically no longer her doctor. 'I can't make dinner tonight. I'm on a flight to JFK in a few hours.'

'Oh, Lucy . . .' Alex's eyes flashed sudden alarm at her. He started to voice a more coherent protest. 'I know theoretically you have clearance to travel now, but long haul isn't really advisable, unless it's for a holiday. Stressful trips should be avoided. I'll go.'

But she laid gentle fingers across his lips to hush him. 'It's much more stressful for me to be idle here. And with your schedule, there's no point asking you – not even to come with me, which would have been nice. You know that Courtney already gave me permission to travel to France – even home to see my father, if I wished to. It's six months since the operation, and my echoes and blood pressure are fine.'

'There's a madness spilling right to our door at the moment, Lucy. I'd rather you weren't too far from me while all this is so unresolved. And I'll be frantic about you travelling alone. You're still getting over major heart surgery.'

She shook her head gently. 'Sorry, that won't wash. I'm going to quote your own words back at you, from before Christmas. "We don't recommend you going abroad in the first few months after a transplant" – those few months are up, don't you think? "And when you're ready to go it's important to choose a country with high standards of hygiene and clean food." Now, Alex, I think the US qualifies, don't you?'

He looked tired, and frustrated, and a little in awe of her. She didn't offer him space for further objections: 'I must go, Alex. It's something I have to do. For Will. And for me. Trust me. I'll be quick and to the point, back Friday at the latest. I'm a big girl.'

He kissed her fingers, then clasped her hand to his chest. 'I'll be worried. You've got a major medical next week, and I hate letting you out of my sight, as things stand.'

'Then keep me in here.' She reciprocated the pressure of the hand that had kidnapped hers. 'Try not to worry.

Simon's coming, and he's protective of me too, like a brother. I think he's caught up in the drama now. We solved your sunflower mystery – the thirty-fourth state.'

'And sunflowers most often have thirty-four petals, like daisies, and even thirty-four spirals of seed heads. And they track the sun.' He kissed her now, oblivious to comment from onlookers. 'I'm not happy.' He tried to look stern, but part of her appeal was that she would never be subordinated to anyone else's will. If Courtney had refused permission, she'd undoubtedly still go.

Lucy grinned at him, as though she could read these thoughts and was not unpleased with her power. 'You'll get used to me.'

'To your impossibly strong will, you mean.' And they both laughed. 'You'll keep Simon close the whole time?' She nodded, mock-demurely. 'What time's your flight?'

'Ten thirty. We should be there two hours before. Simon's waiting in his car to take me home, so I can pack.' She took a step backwards, unsure how to say goodbye, then slipped his phone from her pocket. 'Oh, I almost forgot this. Could you or Henry fax Roland permission for us to collect Will's packet?'

Alex nodded, but wouldn't release her hand. His arms circled her waist and he took control. 'Tell Simon to get to you by half-seven, then I'll pick you both up in Battersea. I'll come straight from the lecture without the mandatory drink. We'll make it in time.'

She flopped into the comfortable seat out of breath, but her travelling companion was unwilling to settle.

'Simon, come on. We've almost held the plane up.' Lucy hated cutting things so fine. Although they'd arrived at the airport with time to spare, Simon had held back, buying newspapers and feigning interest in Duty Free. She guessed what he was doing, and it made her anxious all over again. 'If you carry on with this furtive behaviour I'll need another new heart.'

'Sorry.' He folded his jacket into the overhead bin and sat down at last, putting the document photos in the seat pocket in front. 'It looks fine. I'm starting to suspect my own shadow. But you don't mind the up-grade?' He'd darted out of the check-in queue without warning, and thrown down his considerable Air Miles to put them both in the front of the plane.

'As long as it hasn't cost Grace a week in the Greek Islands with you.' She looked at him, inviting explanation: but she understood it was a ploy to move them from one place to another at the last minute in case they were being watched, and he knew she knew. He shot her a wry look in return.

He had Will's iBook closed on his lap – a parting gift from Alex, along with tight hand-written instructions about Lucy's medication and the number of a colleague in New York to call, if Lucy so much as sneezed. 'I thought we'd use the time going over the clues with Alex's new slant on it? I'm in the mood now – especially after your verbal chess with the Rapturists.' He accepted the glass of champagne he was offered. 'We can't access reference books or the Net up here, but there might be some clues on this that we can have a crack at?'

'I was wondering if you knew what Will's pet name for Siân might be? And hers for him?'

'That's out of left field, isn't it?' Simon shot her an odd look. 'I'm not aware of any. Is it connected with the riddles?'

'Might be. Alex didn't know of one either, beyond her letting "Willie" slip out at Sunday lunches. He told me Will wasn't thrilled about that – it might have been appropriate in private, but not in front of his parents. But I'm sure there was a pet name they had for each other.'

'If you're right – and I remember "Willie", now you mention it, and the filthy look that followed it! – it would be something suggestive, with a clever twist, if I know Will. But let me know where you're going with this when you feel like sharing!'

Lucy smiled in a secretive way. 'In the meantime, you might give some thought as to why it could be important that a sunflower tracks the sun. Does anything track the moon? And what did they mean on the phone today about "weaving straw into gold"?' Lucy had been pondering this all afternoon.

'Hm. Here's your conundrum.' He opened the Apple. 'I want you to look at these notes of Will's – they're from the very last day in France, which he emailed back from some internet café in Chartres. Random thoughts, perhaps.' Simon booted the page, with only a short paragraph of text in the body of the email. It showed the date and time it was sent – Friday, 19 September, in the early afternoon.

Lucy read out softly: '"Be open to the presence of the rose. It is a complicated flower, full of symbology and paradoxical meanings. It indicates what is secret and silent, but also knows the human unconscious. The rose guides adepts, alchemists and society members, heart-to-heart."'

She felt powerfully affected by the words, as though she understood some of this through her own experience in the labyrinth. She couldn't put this into words for Simon, so she settled back for take-off. Grace had promised to fill Alex in on the history of Chartres. And he, silencing his own protests, had decided not to let their adversaries have it all their own way. He was dusting off his Latin and studying the texts from a mathematical perspective. Plus, she had a willing and genial accomplice here beside her. Will's troops, she thought. Within the allotted week we will have solved the whole mystery. She watched the screensaver on the Apple fade out to a painting: of a woman, dangling a pearl over a double-handed chalice. Who was she?

'Don't be anxious about her, Alex. You can't believe how determined she is – a woman with a renewed sense of purpose.' Grace stepped from the kitchen with a bottle of wine for him to open, then spooned some rice from a carton on to plates and put the curries on to a mat.

'Am I that transparent?' He laughed self-consciously. 'I know. She's come through everything we've asked of her. New York won't faze her. But she still has a fight on her hands. The least thing could carry her off – fever, a bad virus, even dirty food. She still has no immune system to speak of, Grace. The drugs shut down virtually everything. Eventually we hope to reduce them to the barest minimum, but until then we track every major temperature fluctuation. Infection, or rejection. Get it right and she's fine, get it wrong and we lose her.' He looked at his hostess, who seemed surprised to hear him think aloud. 'Of course, we have to balance this against the fact that she seems almost uncannily well. It's as if my head and my heart have a completely antithetical view of it.' He smiled enigmatically at Grace. 'I don't let things get to me; but worrying about her has become a habit now. A good habit.'

Grace smiled, pleased with the subtext. 'It's reassuring to know you're human. I have an image of you from Lucy as someone who can cope with everything without blinking – finding a cool path across volcanic ground.' She intended a compliment; but he looked at her, troubled.

'Does it seem so?' He hesitated for a moment, then smiled at her. 'I was catatonic when my marriage ended, Grace. I didn't see it coming. I should have. Poor Anna hardly saw me, and when she did I was always completely drained. She was working part-time at home editing books, with a toddler and no adult company, me on thirteen-hour-plus days. I was a senior house officer just before Max was born, doing emergency takes; and it was competitive finding a suitable specialist registrar post. Then, moving into immunology, there was more specialist training, and homework – five years of it, with the difficult pathology exams at the end. I know now that Anna felt deserted. Even now the hours are heavy, but they were non-negotiable then. I think she thought me selfish about medicine – obsessed; and I suppose I am. When she finally confronted me, I couldn't blame her. But it's taken a long time to even consider another close relationship.'

Grace rolled her eyes with a look of doubt, and he laughed.

'OK, I haven't been a hermit; but I've avoided anything serious, stayed busy. Something always needed doing – there was always someone in a worse crisis than mine. I volunteered weekend cover, when I didn't have Max. Transplant medicine is a philosophy course lived; your personal problems pale in the face of your patients' struggle for just another day, another week, hoping an organ will materialise. It feels self-centred to drown in your own emotional crises compared with such life and death realities, so you shelve them. Or try to. But I couldn't entirely fool Will.' He looked directly at Grace, who was listening quietly, without forcing him, and he answered her unput question: 'Yes, I miss him desperately. His existence subtly permeated my own.'

She put a gentle hand on his shoulder, understanding his delay with Lucy. Whatever ethical problems there may have been, he'd also been grieving – something they'd not given proper consideration to. 'Simon too. Sometimes a few beers will just set him off. Will seems to have had a big effect on people.'

Alex nodded. 'Give me a spoonful of that curry, and tell me about Chartres!'

She recognised that was as much as he was going to open up, so she moved on without a pause. 'There's more than Chartres, but let's start there. The night at your father's got me hooked as much as Lucy and Simon. I've spent hours researching the history of the cathedral – the one official guidebooks hardly touch. I thought your mum must have had her reasons. Now, a good historian always checks her sources, and hard evidence for early use of the site – before about AD 500 – is sketchy, so this is conjectural. But early literary sources tell us it was sacred to the Carnutes, a Gaulish tribe. A Druid grotto was dedicated to a pre-Christian virgin whom they believed would bear a son, which follows on directly from the cult of Isis and Ishtar. These were probably the same Druids Julius Caesar wrote about, with his famous mention of a "*Virgini Patriae*" in this region. This may be why the Christian story was adopted by the Gauls. A dolmen in the underground grotto pre-dated even the Druids.'

'What date?'

'About two thousand BC.' Grace crossed the room to find Lucy's guide to the cathedral, book-marked with slips of paper, and she opened it for Alex at a pictured statue of a Madonna and child. 'This existing statue of Mary with Jesus was based on another, destroyed in the sixteenth century. Some accounts suggest it was twelfth century, but the earlier object could just have been the one the Druids worshipped, a black Madonna – probably ebony. France has a rich cult in these.'

Alex looked carefully at the image. 'So, the Christian church was building on an existing, powerful female iconography?'

'Yes. We lack certain facts about the pre-Druid past, but we do know that Chartres' orientation curiously resembles Stonehenge, following the midsummer sunrise almost perfectly. This is different from the eastern orientation of all Christian churches: it's seemingly unique to Chartres. There are two different axes in the cathedral, just as at Stonehenge. The heel-stone and causeway post-holes there mark the longest day in the solar calendar, and the distance between that and the lunar calendar. It's a mathematical equation, called the Pythagorean comma—'

Alex interrupted her with energy: 'Yes, the slip between solar and lunar cycles. And, if the architecture incorporates the two axes of the skies, then the number thirty-four has to be significant at some key place in the building too. Because it's regarded as the "*axis mundi*" – the axis of the world.'

Grace looked at him sidelong. 'I don't know about that, Alex, but in Chartres the "comma" is clearly built in. The building tilts slightly – you can see it from the great west door, if you face east.' She turned to a view of the floor plan in the guidebook. 'You can't quite see it here, but the longer and shorter axis have been twisted, and there's a visible "wiggle" right across the transept. It's deliberate. Every other measure is precise.'

'A blend of masculine and feminine time?'

'Clever, isn't it? Both spires above the West Face have different styles and heights, which seems strange until you realise one carries a weathervane of the sun, and the other . . .'

'. . . of the moon,' Alex filled in. He put down his food. 'That must have excited my mother. She thought of herself as the moon. The building was designed to express a symbiosis of male and female energies.'

'That's an interesting way to put it. A marriage of the masculine and feminine pulses. It's been described as a "vibrato effect". And to underline the importance of the light, a tiny hole made in the aptly named window of St Apollinaire focuses a ray of sun on a nail in a paving stone, at noon on June the twenty-first!'

'Like Stonehenge!'

She nodded emphatically. 'But of course, there's no photo of it here – it's not even mentioned in an official guide like this one. It would emphasise the layers of worship across centuries and faiths – maybe like the labyrinth?'

Alex had torn off a piece of naan bread, but was too absorbed to eat. 'I had lunch with Amel today, Grace – Lucy's surgeon.' She nodded familiarity at the name. 'He's a Renaissance man – speaks seven languages, loves the arts – gives doctors a good name, a true ambassador for humanity. We talked about Chartres, and he told me about the Sufis. Are you familiar with them?'

'They're a mystical Muslim sect, I think?'

Alex nodded, and explained Amel's view that some of the Crusaders, who had remained behind after the successful First Crusade, had become fascinated by the architecture and ideas of Islam, and the spirituality of the Sufis. The Christians had been initiated into much wisdom and some arcane knowledge from the Jewish and Muslim population in Jerusalem whom they hadn't slaughtered, but in particular it was the beauties and ideas behind the Aksa Mosque, on the Haram el Sharif, that had left an indelible impression. This was the Temple Mount, from which Muhammad was said to have made his mystical ascent, the night journey into heaven. Contrasted with Constantine's lumbering Church of the Holy Sepulchre, it seemed effortlessly beautiful and spiritual. The Sufis taught them that the pointed arch raises the energy and spirit heavenward, whereas the Roman arch redirected the forces to earth.

'And the Sufis honoured Christ as one of the seven sages of Islam?'

Alex replenished the glasses. 'As do all good Muslims. But Amel explained they were strongly committed to a pluralism – which also interested Dee and Bruno. The Sufis recognised that every religion contained reflections and descent from one universal truth. They were tolerant, highly educated, at ease with the Torah as well as Christian teaching. A lot of coded architecture in great Gothic buildings – like Chartres, and St Denis in Paris – might be traced to the mystical teachings of the Sufis, through the Templars. They held the number nine sacred; and there were nine Templar knights. No more were added for nine years.'

'I've read about the arches. Let me check my notes.' Grace dipped in her work folder and showed Alex some pages with her own line drawings. 'The Druidic and Celtic associations are also linked with the number nine, the Triple Goddess. When the Cathedral was rebuilt after a fire late in the twelfth century, new doors were added to make nine, and nine arches – the mukhamma Islamic arches you're talking about. Hardly a coincidence.'

They studied the floor plan she'd reproduced, and Alex's finger bounced as he came to the data that the paved stones of the labyrinth were each thirty-four centimetres in length. 'A strange detail – though centimetres came in with Napoleon. But the number pattern suggests interfaith plurality,' he said. 'It's inspiring, don't you think?'

Grace's face betrayed deep thought. 'Not for all people, Alex. It might shake the absolutes of their religion. But, where does this bring us in relation to Doctor Dee and his friends? And why did it matter to your mother?'

Alex took out his wallet and carefully unfolded a small sheet of paper. 'I copied this last night from one of Will's reference books. I recognised it straight away from our old family Bible, where someone had drawn it – which always caught my attention as a boy. Now I know it's Dee's emblem, called the "Monas" or "one".'

Grace looked at it for some time, before Alex continued.

'He designed it. It combines the astrological symbols – and the signs we use for male and female – to form a cross, similar to the Egyptian ankh. He thought he'd gone too far in publishing it – because of its great power. Intriguingly, it places the symbol for the moon at the pinnacle, with the sun directly below.'

At this, Grace clapped her hands together mischievously and laughed aloud. 'Just as it should be! His boss was quite a lady, and all men were below her!'

Alex laughed with her. 'Yes, I agree, and I think that's important. Dee was designing something for all religious persuasions. And the recurring theme about a rose may connect with the rose windows in Chartres.

'And as Giordano Bruno spent a long time in Paris with the King, Henri IV, who promised the best hope at the time for religious tolerance, perhaps he visited Chartres and knew about this pure solstice light beam. It would have attracted him. It's all a labyrinth of speculation.'

'So let's check Bruno, the sun, and the rose before our Ariadne returns from New York. But in the meantime, a final clue for you. I consulted my father about the Hebrew letters that appear on each page of the oldest documents.'

'I noticed them, Grace, but they defeat me. Does he recognise anything in them?'

'I only faxed them to him today, though Lucy copied them for me weeks ago – but I wasn't into it then. He hasn't had much time, but just to give you something to ponder, he thinks every word has a cabalistic significance – like a magic word.'

'Like "abracadabra"?' Alex's humour didn't quite conceal his genuine interest.

Grace was relaxed and enjoying the wine and Alex's company. She laughed loudly. 'That's Arabic, silly. But he'll translate them and give us the meanings. He said something about "gematria".'

'That's clever, Grace. He's surely right. "Gematria" gives all the letters a numerical parallel: and I can imagine what some of the words will add up to. But, what will it all mean?'

28

It was close to half-past noon and their appointed lunch date as Simon and Lucy sprinted across 34th Street in mid-town Manhattan though the phalanxes of yellow cabs. They escaped into the door of Roland Brown's office building, glancing fleetingly at the boards to check which floor they wanted, then they swirled into the lift and were accelerated upwards. Lucy had been feeling tense and unusually emotional since she had checked in to her room last night, the time difference dissuading her from calling Alex; but she offered Simon a warm smile now. In an hour or so it would all be over, their mission hopefully accomplished, and despite their furtive looks along hotel corridors and across streets everywhere, there'd been no sign of anyone, or anything, to trouble them.

The elevator reached the top and slid open smoothly; and their faces fell. Before them stood a security man, and beyond him they could see black-and-yellow tapes announcing a 'crime scene', which was obscured by the heavy glass doors of Roland's seventeenth-floor office. It looked as if some removal men had been spirited away, leaving behind the chaos of an unfinished job. Files, books and other pieces of equipment were scattered about the area in disorganised piles.

A neat, well-groomed woman of about forty was in conversation with a uniformed policeman and a plain-clothed man not far from the lift door, and in the rear of the offices men in white overalls moved about like ghosts.

The trio closest to them turned towards Simon and Lucy as the elevator doors opened.

'Can I help you?' the woman asked a little sharply, stepping forwards. She directed her words to Lucy.

'Good morning. I'm Lucy King, and this is Simon Whelan. We've flown especially from London for an appointment with Mr Brown.' Lucy's words came in rather short phrases. It was obvious Mr Brown was not going to be 'at home'.

'Oh! Yes, he mentioned it. I'm sorry, I'm Pearl Garrett, one of Roland's partners.' They hardly paused to shake hands, before she resumed, 'He's been called away urgently to Boston, and I meant to leave a message at your hotel but, as you can see –' she broke off to invite their eyes over the mêlée in front of them – 'I've had my hands full since the police called me in at seven this morning. He'll call you, Lucy – that's what he wanted me to tell you. At around six tonight. He has the number, and suggests you meet at his apartment first thing in the morning. Which will be pleasanter than here.' Her voice inflected exasperation.

'Mrs Garrett. I'm sorry, but could we have you back with

us?' The plain-clothes man drew her attention to the gesturing from one of the men inside in a white jumpsuit.

'You'll have to excuse me. You can see we have a small problem. We keep a great many highly sensitive pictures in our files here, not all of which are backed up on disk. The older ones sometimes attract paranoia from interested parties in politics or entertainment. Dirty underwear closets, you could say. We still don't know what's missing.' She called the elevator for them again, smiling as the door opened almost immediately. 'You all have a nice day, now, and go play tourists. This city is like Disneyland for adults, don't you think?' And she turned away without waiting for a word of reply.

'Coincidence? Or should we worry?' Simon's voice completely lacked its habitual humour as the lift arrived at the ground level.

Lucy was unsure how to answer. A sea of faces came at her from the opposite direction; but even in the tide of humanity set free at lunch-time in this great city, and despite the events of the last twenty minutes, all she could think of was calling Alex. For an uneasy hour before the excursion to Roland's building, she'd had a sinking feeling he was under duress. She was wondering about Max's head injury. Privacy was elusive, and of course she was frustrated with the immediate situation – and also exhausted from a restless night in New York. But something else chafed, though she couldn't identify what it was.

Simon reached across through the throng of people, and put a friendly hand on her arm.

'Let's find ourselves a coffee and some lunch anyway?'

She nodded, grateful for a chance to stop. The frustrations of the morning threatened to overwhelm her, and she now owned up to her exhaustion. How bizarre – that a break-in the night before should leave police crawling through the building; never mind that Will's agent had cancelled their appointment. His partner had said only that he'd flown to Boston for the day. Wasn't that strange? After the great push to get there – the run from Lucy's office via the hospital, the lightning rush from Battersea to Heathrow, the oddly distressing wrench from Alex, a night without sleep, and now this cancelled appointment – Lucy felt flat and unwell.

They found the Tick Tock Diner, and while Lucy disappeared to the ladies', Simon ordered her an open sandwich and a full-strength coffee. Against her usual practice, she'd requested the caffeine to give her a jolt. Joining him at the booth, she peered into the bread at the filling, felt a wave of nausea, and realised she couldn't manage a bite. He read her alarm, put down the sweet potato fry on the end of his fork, and leaned over to squeeze her arm.

'I've ordered badly, haven't I? Should have taken the veggie burger?' Simon had tried following Alex's directive about low-salt, freshly prepared food, avoiding anything that might be reheated, and realised he'd made a poor choice. 'The look on your face says a good vet might recover that lamb's heartbeat!'

She managed a horrified laugh. 'I'm sorry – it's not the food. I don't know quite what's wrong. I want to be here with you, and see Roland. I'm even glad of the chance to reassert my independence – away from Alex. But I feel oddly torn, as though I've left part of myself behind. I'm not altogether comfortable with that.'

'Just chill, sweetheart. You're shattered – as am I. And not even a night of bingeing as an excuse. My mind was solving riddles through broken sleep. It was like a collision between Bilbo Baggins and Oedipus Rex! I was even trying to work out the numerology of certain words. I must be going mad.' He looked at her remarkable face, saw that it was blanched of all colour, and immediately recalled Alex's quiet dictum to make sure Lucy ate something regularly and took her pills on time. 'And if we admit to it, we're both thrown by this business with Roland. The circumstances seem odd, though we should keep it in perspective and wait until tomorrow before we panic. But, Lucy, for God's sake have some compassion and eat something for me, or your boyfriend's going to shoot me such a look of disdain when we get back. I'd rather Will's worst temper than Alex's controlled displeasure.'

Lucy picked at the salad on her plate and swallowed her immunosuppressants. 'I've been thinking, Simon. Alex is thirty-four, like the magic number in the Tablet of Jupiter. The clues about being "loyal" and "true" indicate the knot which is the Stafford insignia. When I consider the documents, I'm beginning to think they tell our story.'

'And we're having this conversation on Thirty-Fourth Street, which is spooky. What are you getting at, Luce?'

'You told me you were with Alex one night, at Will's computer, when that Sator Square we were looking at on the plane just appeared?' Simon nodded. 'There seems to be a pattern about the Venus and Adonis story in some of the sheets, don't you agree? The beautiful young man, pursued by Venus?'

'Go on.'

'Is that Will and Siân? She desperate to tie him, he runs off on a wild hunt – and here's the strange thing – literally is gored on the bridge, in the thigh, like Adonis. Alex told me the injury was brutal, though it's not what killed him. But it's odd, you'll allow? When Venus pursued her wounded lover, the white roses she trod on pricked her feet, and her blood turned them red in pure love. You remember Will's white roses. Though we've never determined why he sent them.'

Simon was intrigued by the connection of ideas. 'Strange leaps, Lucy. But Philip Sidney died of a wound to his thigh too – gave away his greaves to a soldier who needed them. And obviously more than his greaves, as it was a musket ball in his thigh which turned horribly gangrenous. It took him days to die.'

'You said that to show how unrelated things are; but he was a pupil of John Dee.' Lucy omitted to say how strongly Sidney resembled the man she'd seen that night on the barge on the Thames. She'd visited his several portraits at the Gallery – a man of many images, which testified to the cult status he acquired after his death; and the likeness was unmistakable. A nobleman, poet, critic, as arresting as Byron – indeed, the Byron of his age. But how could she begin to explain that strange Halloween experience to anyone who wasn't there? No sane person would give it credit, though, she thought. Alex and Amel might not judge it so. They'd seen something too. 'The words on one of the texts are

Sidney's, Simon,' she continued. 'The other odd thing is, my name means "light". Do you remember the lines about the "Lady of Light" starting her journey in the candle month? "Lucy" is a lady of light; and my February birthday is the month of Candlemas. I was born on February the third, and my father ominously used to say, "The music died on this day, Lucy." That reference is the one I showed you on the flight, in one of the texts.'

Simon thought this crushingly sad, and wondered what it revealed about her past. 'Yes, I remember now – the day of the plane crash, with Buddy Holly and Big Bopper and someone – in the fifties, I think?'

Lucy was nodding. She read the feeling in Simon's look, but didn't want to talk about it with him. She rushed on, 'We come to Alex. Some clues point to Alexander the Great, and the Stafford knot, and roses. And one I haven't discussed. One of the first texts, in the oldest batch, talks about the River Styx, going through the realms of the dead. That was my first real date with Alex, on Halloween. The cruise was called "The Spirits of the Dead from the Past"; and I dressed as Ariadne.'

'That's why you're interested in the pet names! We should analyse each text until we find out which place you've reached, in the story. Then we'll know how it resolves. And in the meantime, as we're on Thirty-Fourth Street, let's indeed go "play tourists" and look at the Empire State. It must be relevant.'

A few minutes after seven p.m., Alex swung the car around the corner into Redcliffe Square and glanced at Siân's apartment window. He relaxed a little when he saw her lights on, and made a circuit to find an empty space. Maybe she'd gone out for something. She hadn't answered his call a short time before, and he was worried she'd reneged on their arrangement. He climbed out, pressed the key and the lights flashed.

Walking around the square, he looked more closely at the bulk of St Luke's Church, its tall spire dominating the green. Since last night's conversation with Grace about the architecture of Chartres, he found himself more concentrated on the Gothic Revival shape – which looked forbiddingly grim, however, in the still wintry March light. The arrival of summer time after the upcoming weekend would bring a welcome psychological shift.

He noticed Siân's blue Fiat Uno parked in a residents' space just beyond the doorstep to her apartment building. She can't have gone far, he thought, remembering the emotional state she was in yesterday morning, and feeling some relief. He pushed the buzzer, but there was no response; he stepped back and looked up at the building again. That was her light, without doubt; so he returned up the steps and pushed the bell again. Nothing. He checked his watch: he was only a few minutes late. Was she in the bath? He dialled her number again from his mobile; the line was now busy. He pondered for a minute or two. She could easily reach the entry phone to let him in if she was talking – unless she was locked in conversation with Calvin and refusing to be distracted. Then he suddenly worried about whether she might have done something silly, and quickly pushed another bell. A voice on the intercom asked his name.

'Hi there. It's Dr Alex Stafford. I've come to see Siân, in flat five. The lights are on but she's not responding to her bell. Could you possibly let me in? She should be expecting me, and I'm worried she might not be feeling well.'

'Which flat did you say?' the voice tested.

'Siân Powell – in flat five. I'm Will Stafford's brother.'

'Oh yes – the doctor. The top-floor flat, isn't it?'

Alex shifted his weight, suddenly impatient, and listened for the door release. As he pushed, he saw the long badly lit corridor leading up the steep stairs that vanished into night. He moved quickly towards them. On the landing above the third floor, he paused for a hurried breath and realised he was tired. He'd left Grace rather late and hadn't slept one complete hour afterwards, hoping Lucy would call – fruitlessly, as it turned out – and an emergency had brought him in at six, meaning he'd just finished a twelve-hour day. Now he looked up towards Siân's front door, and from this angle it seemed to be ajar. Odd, he thought; and he continued upwards, before his eyes confirmed in poor light that the door was indeed unlocked. It was possible she'd gone up to the roof garden with a drink and left it open for him. He climbed the last two flights to the top of the building and pushed the communal light, which failed to come on. Trust Will to pick a place at the top of the world, with no lift.

In the gloom of the hall landing something looked out of place. He approached the door and could see the line of a long split in the frame, which showed the whiteness of newly cracked wood against the cream gloss paint of the door jamb. The security chain swung from the inside of the frame by its torn screws. What the hell had he stumbled upon? His senses were strained as he listened avidly. Not a sound. Gingerly, he pushed the door open to reveal the hallway of the flat and the living room beyond. Orderly chaos greeted his eyes; shelves were denuded of books and artefacts that had been placed in piles along the hall. Through the door leading to the living room he could see a continuation of the same disorder. Drawers had been turned out, books opened, some then placed upside down to one side. The lid of the piano was open. The flat had been professionally and systematically searched. Then he saw something move, three-quarters of the way down the hall, away from the light.

She huddled against the wall, her knees drawn up to her chest in a foetal position. She had her arms wrapped around her and she held something tightly to her heart. The phone receiver bounced gently up and down on its coiled cable next to her from the handset on the wall above. He picked a path between the debris and kneeled beside her. She turned her face to him, and he noticed a trickle of blood running from her nose. Even in poor light he could see that a large bruise was forming around the cut on the side of her high cheekbone. Her blue eyes stared at him.

'It's you,' she said in a small voice. 'I thought he'd come back.' She put her arms around his neck and hugged him, her tremble now giving way to a deep tremor.

'It's OK,' he said quietly. He pulled back a little and looked intently at her. No obvious head injury, pupils apparently normal, pulse a little too fast – this he assessed in seconds. 'What's happened, Siân?' He ruled out rape, given the condition of the flat. He reached for his mobile and started to dial; but she stopped him, shook her head, tried to pull herself up.

'I started to call the police, Alex, but he threw me against the wall and told me he'd be back if I rang anyone. I thought,' she said, matter-of-factly, 'that he was going to kill me. But he just hit me with the back of his hand.' She rubbed her nose and looked at the blood on her fingers, winced as she touched her cheek. 'He told me not to move and I wouldn't be hurt.' She started to rise again and this time made it to her feet.

There were a dozen questions Alex wanted to ask, starting with a description of who 'he' was, but his job had taught him to take things slowly and to calm her first. He suddenly realised the object she'd been clutching was the remnants of the leather jacket Will had been wearing on the day of his death. It was cut along its seams, for the emergency staff at the hospital to remove it efficiently. On the floor in front of Siân were the rest of Will's clothes from that day – the T-shirt, badly torn jeans, even the underclothes. He'd packed his full leathers away for the last phase of his journey home, had worn his lighter clothing including this favourite Ducati jacket, obviously chosen for comfort rather than protection. The plastic hospital bag that had held everything was upended in the bedroom opposite.

Siân traced Alex's thoughts, and looked at him guiltily. 'Henry handed me the bag from the hospital after it was returned from the coroner's. I only asked for the jacket: it was my last birthday present to him a year before the accident, and he loved it so much. It was a limited classic – do you remember? – and I had to order it specially from the

States.' Alex nodded once. 'I don't think Henry wanted to deal with any of it. I couldn't either, so I just stuffed it in the cupboard, forgot about it until he pulled everything out now.'

He listened to her explanation, and put his arm around her to support her into the living room. He propped her on the side of a deep chair while he cleared the books piled on the seat, then helped her into it. 'Lean right back for a second, Siân. I want to have a quick check for any real damage.' He pulled a pen-torch from his jacket and flashed her eyes until she flinched, happy with the reaction. Then he switched on her reading lamp, turned her face towards it, and examined the cartilage of her nose and the cut in her cheek. 'This needs a butterfly suture, but it shouldn't scar. He had a ring on.' She nodded. 'Which part of you hit the wall?'

Siân indicated her left shoulder and rubbed the upper arm area tenderly, her face contorting.

'Serious pain?'

'It hurts; but I don't think it's broken.'

Alex tested its strength, asking her to pull against his own hand, which she managed. 'No. Nor do I. Tell me about it?'

'I went out for wine. When I came back you'd rung. I heard the doorbell, thought you were just early, and I pushed the buzzer. When he knocked I didn't check the spyhole – the light's out in the hall. But the security chain was on. I turned the lock, then he threw his weight against the door. The chain just split away. He shoved past me, hit me, told me not to move. Then he did this . . .' She looked around at the mayhem, and started to cry for the first time.

'I thought if I called the police he'd come back, and hurt me seriously.'

Alex was gently moving her neck from side to side, and seemed satisfied that her spine was undamaged. She hadn't let go of the jacket. 'How long was he here, Siân? What did he look like? Heavily built?'

'I don't know, Alex. Twenty minutes? No, probably more. He was physically big, not particularly tall, wearing an expensive coat – MaxMara, I'd say; brown leather gloves – one of which he deliberately removed when he hit me, and then put on again. His shoes were expensive, matched his gloves.' Alex smiled quietly at the sartorial details Siân had absorbed with her professional eye. 'He asked me where my boyfriend was, threatened to hit me again when I didn't answer. He was searching for something I don't think he found. Did he mean Will?'

'I'd have thought Calvin.' Alex's mind was racing. He looked once around the flat, then picked up Siân's coat. 'I was supposed to get something to him today, but I couldn't find him anywhere. He still hasn't turned up?' She shook her head. 'Come on. I've a friend in Casualty up the road at Chelsea and Westminster. Let's get you seen to, then you're coming home with me. We'll clean up here tomorrow after it's been inspected; this has gone far enough.'

Lucy looked down, but the height didn't alarm her. The long, silky strands of her hair whipped back in the breeze, and the fresh air had brightened her olive complexion. She looked a thousand times better, and grinned at her companion. 'You knew it, didn't you? That this was the clue in the text about the "strange simian energy", and the movies, and the Art Deco foyer.'

'Not for sure until we got here. The *King Kong* riddle was easy, and the needle pointing upwards at the tip of the apple tree – the Big Apple, of course. But I wasn't sure about the ten thousand square feet of marble, until now. It's all about being on Thirty-Fourth Street. Why is this damned number so significant?'

Lucy realised her mobile was ringing, the sound almost dead in the wind. Too early for Alex, she thought. He was having dinner with Siân, and it was only nine o'clock in the UK.

'It's Sandy. Where have I caught you?' His voice seemed richer than ever amidst the American accents surrounding her. She cried with the pleasure of realisation – or the effects of the wind. What did that nickname tell her?

'On top of the Empire State Building on Thirty-Fourth Street. As you're always ahead of us, you'll know it's one of our mysteries.' She changed to a more serious tone. 'Alex, is everything all right? I've been worrying about you, but you're at dinner, and I didn't want to intrude. It's not Max, is it?'

Alex shook his head to himself, hardly surprised by her instincts any more. 'No, not Max, Lucy. It's Siân. She had an unwelcome visitor at the flat. I wasn't able to get the packet to our go-between – who was nowhere to be found. I've just tracked down his mother, and she said he's been in Nantucket for a day or so – though he's not with her now. He's on a flight tonight from Boston—'

'Boston?' she interrupted.

'It sounds very last minute, I think. I've no idea what he's playing at, but I won't say too much just now. Siân's here with me tonight. She's shaken and bruised, and her flat's not secure. I've slipped downstairs to run her a bath, but I need a word with Simon about his contact at New Scotland Yard.'

Lucy was too horrified to press him, and passed the phone across. Simon's immediate volley of expletives was unleashed so forcefully that everyone on the viewing platform turned to see what was wrong.

'The only reason we complied with their dictates to keep the police out of things was their promise to keep everyone else out of harm, as well – which they've now signally failed to do.' Alex almost sounded more tired than angry, Simon thought, but it was always difficult detecting just what was in his voice. 'They've broken the rules they set, so it's time we put things on our own terms.'

'Everyone is expedient in their politics, Alex. When you find Calvin, promise me you'll handcuff the bastard until I get back.'

Simon took his palm organiser from his jacket pocket, and a lot of detailed information was exchanged on both sides. Simon shook his head angrily. Lucy listened, an icy hand clutching the pit of her stomach, while numbers were given, notes taken, and Simon's opinions offered. From the responses at this end, though, Alex was clearly more unwilling to comment. Simon eventually gave the phone back to its owner.

She pushed her ear against it to block the wind. 'I love you too,' she was quite sure he said; but she hadn't spoken at all. Then, in a voice firmer than Simon's and surprisingly comforting, he closed the conversation with words that left her speechless. 'Work out the numerology of John Dee's name; it adds up to thirty-four. And Lucy, do you know your birthday is the thirty-fourth day of the year?'

29

Alex had picked up the morning newspaper, delivered to the front door, and drawing back the living-room curtain, he glanced at the date in the light: Thursday, 25 March. He was struck that Siân had never bothered to cancel Will's order for it, in all these nine long months. She hadn't really moved on, he thought.

He placed the paper on the dining table and turned to survey the room – the sheer chaos that was now Siân's flat. Not an item, it seemed, had escaped examination, even though all had been done with astounding economy of time. He could appreciate why Siân felt so personally defiled. He had raised the caretaker, who even now was repairing the woodwork around the front door, and for thirty pounds cash in hand he had further volunteered to find someone to tidy up and put everything back on the shelves – just as soon as Alex and the police had finished their work. Detective Inspector McPherson, Simon's contact, had sent some plain-clothes officers on ahead of him to meet Alex early, and they were already hard at work in the bedroom and along the hall, dusting for any trace of prints and searching for the least hint of DNA. Judging by their chat with one another, Alex didn't think it sounded hopeful.

He looked in broad morning light at the main living area, and there seemed to be a lot of mess – but in fact little, or no, real damage. It would all be put right in a matter of hours, and Siân could return home after lunch if she still insisted – though he'd prefer she remain at his flat today while he sorted things out. He had to be at work by eight, but he still had a lot of details to take care of before he'd even think of her coming back here alone. He glanced at his watch, wondering what was holding James McPherson up. But just then the voice of the caretaker alerted him from the front door that someone had indeed arrived at the top of the stairs, and Alex moved towards the door to introduce himself. What he saw, however, took him by surprise.

The tall, good-looking man who stood rooted to the floor in the doorway arch of the living room had a dropped jaw, his eyes were roaming wildly, and his usual lightly tanned complexion was blanched. Alex recognised in Calvin the genuine symptoms of shock. The face and expression were in no sense prepared for what was in front of him, and it affected him deeply. For Alex, this unprompted first reaction told him something he needed to know about the man, and he was quite certain that his cousin was not directly involved in the events of the previous night.

'Oh God. Where is she, Alex?' He placed a modest-sized weekend bag on the floor beside him and turned round briefly, incredulous, to see the two men dusting for prints at the other end of the hallway.

'She's safe.' Alex watched Calvin's colour partially return, though his eyes were still asking what had happened. Alex kept his voice steady, his tone noncommittal; unsure of Calvin's precise role, he was reluctant to exempt him from a possible charge of even *indirect* complicity. 'There was a break-in last night while Siân was here, and she was attacked and injured –' Calvin tried to speak, but Alex raised his hand – 'though not too seriously, I'm pleased to say. It was certainly someone you know. As you can see, he was looking for something, which we don't believe he found. He threatened her about going to the police, then struck her full in the face. She couldn't answer for the whereabouts of her boyfriend.'

'Oh, dear Lord,' Calvin said without volume. He sat on the arm of the sofa nearest the doorway, and Alex realised he was in fact unable to stand. 'Did they want me?'

Alex watched him closely, assembling ideas, but his voice was perhaps a shade gentler, though no less searching. 'I'm fairly certain it was a second set of documents Will found in France that they wanted. He sent them away, but not without making photograph copies. They set up with Lucy for you to be the go-between and collect them for your . . . entourage, but you disappeared without a word and neglected to let us know when you'd be back.'

'Yes. Be angry with me, Alex – it's right you should be. I've screwed up royally. But is Siân OK?' Calvin's shock was starting to give way to what seemed to be genuine rage at the prospect of anything happening to her.

'Yes, Calvin. She is.'

Alex quickly assessed Calvin's changing reaction and crossed the floor space between them. He recognised that Calvin needed some form of demonstrable support, and pulled up a single dining chair to sit close to him. In the tone of a reasoning man he reported the events of the last forty-eight hours, including the episode with Max. He chose his style well, preferring to speak as plainly as possible. The effect of underplaying such horror – especially about his own son – made Calvin appear quite sick, and he shook his head in utter disbelief, listening to Alex without a sound.

'Obviously, in light of what happened to Will, I took her back to my place,' Alex concluded, 'and she was still asleep in Max's room when I left.'

Calvin's eyes now met Alex's, and he nodded his head, thinking almost to himself. 'I'll have to find Guy – or Fitzalan Walters, who's the real power occupying the throne. Yes, Alex, I admit, I do have an interest in what's been happening; but not for myself. There are others who are deeply concerned . . .' He looked at Alex, whose expression was a surprising comfort to him – made him feel as though he weren't entirely alone. 'I'd like to be able to tell you.'

Alex smiled at him, and tilted his head slightly. 'But you can't. And yet, I think perhaps you just have.'

Calvin looked at the man beside him with an expression very near to relief.

'You're birdliming,' Alex said unequivocally. 'But, why Boston?'

'The people who paid for my European studies need to be kept . . . informed. About crucial developments.'

'So they can be controlled before they get out of hand?'

Calvin nodded, his eyes watching his hands nervously. He indicated – with a motion of his head back down the hall – that he was unable, or unwilling, to speak further with others so close at hand. 'But I'm honestly out of my depth, so I arranged to meet one of them in Boston. Alex,' Calvin whispered, 'that's all I can say, except you know I'm very fond of Siân and would never knowingly let anything happen to any one of you. I think Will's death might have been avoided if I had been a little quicker off the mark.'

Taut emotions hung between the two men, but Alex had reached an important decision. He was about to speak when he heard a Scottish voice intone his name.

'Dr Stafford?' The figure of a younger man occupied the threshold where Calvin had been quarter of an hour earlier. 'I am DI McPherson, or anti-terrorism James, if you like!' he said far less formally. His warmly humorous voice was a welcome relief for the swirling current of emotions that Alex and Calvin had unleashed in each other, and both men smiled at the newcomer, Alex extending his hand. 'We spoke on the phone last night, and I can see I've come to the right place. This will be Mr Calvin Petersen, whom you mentioned in our conversation.'

All three men were now on their feet, and James McPherson looked at the others directly. 'Let's talk quickly, as we all have other places we need to be shortly. And, Dr Stafford, you remember that I, in fact, am not here at all. No more are you, Mr Petersen. So, if you can find a mug in all this mess, any chance of a quick coffee?'

Alex laughed, and they both followed him into the small kitchen.

Lucy and Simon sat back a little uncomfortably as their taxi left the blossom trees and shopping precinct behind for a change of landscape. Simon regretted the extra pancake he'd taken for breakfast as the vehicle lurched and bumped, with impossibly soft suspension, all the way from their boutique mid-town hotel to the bottom of Jane Street, at the Hudson River end. They spilled out on to the corner of Jane and West Streets, at the fringe of Greenwich Village.

Lucy's expectations were surprised when the building they were looking for turned out to be a vast, unprepossessing brick warehouse that had once serviced the now disused docks along the Hudson. She pushed a buzzer apprehensively on a battered metal service door beside a corrugated iron trucking entrance. A disembodied voice said, 'Hi,' and when she gave her name, it resumed in the same breezy tone: 'Glad you could come! As you enter the building, walk to the elevator in the middle work area, then take the cage to the top floor. I'll send it down, and meet you at the top.'

She looked at Simon with wide eyes, and his own twinkled humorously back at her. After a 'click' he pushed the door, and in front of them, dimly lit by a dozen bare light bulbs suspended on bare wires, was an empty space as large as a football field. A strange smell of disused building and damp paper, blended with the tidal river, greeted them. As the voice had promised, an open plan cargo elevator shaft stood in the centre of the abandoned working area. Its twenties-style rusting iron frame disappeared into a hole in the floor, far above them, and the pair walked timidly across the empty space towards it as the cage hummed downwards from the ceiling.

'Do you think this thing is safe?' Lucy questioned Simon as it crashed on to the ground level and literally threw the iron gate wide. He made no reply, but stepped into its vast metal interior and pulled her gently in behind him, smiling quietly. 'You've been here before, you beast! You might have told me,' Lucy laughed.

'Wait until you see the pad,' Simon said, as he closed the door carefully. 'Views in three directions. The one across the river is unreal. Will and I went to some wild parties here on our way through, between assignments. Roland used to put us up, sometimes – when he felt like company. He's a very different kind of person.'

As the lift began its ascent, Simon answered Lucy's quizzical expression with a boyish grin and a few intriguing details. 'He comes from the Far West – Montana, I think – and let's say he's my idea of what a mountain man would be, if such people were real. He doesn't give a damn for appearances, used to be a serial marrier. Now he's more of a monk, but I know he still loves women. I've no idea how old he is; he's looked the same for ten years.'

Lucy thought Simon was constructing an impossible persona for anyone to fill: John Wayne, she joked to herself, with a strangely female anima. She simply smiled at the idea and listened to him talk about a man he clearly liked, with an eye for a photograph and a story.

'Whatever else he may be,' Simon continued across the noise of the creaking contraption, sputtering to the final stage of its destination, 'he knows everyone, so he's made a fortune for himself and the people he represents along the way. He bought this building for cash before anyone thought of lofts.'

The noise of the lift and Simon's commentary ended in unison, and a man with a broad, clear forehead and intelligent grey eyes opened the gate, immediately extending a hand towards Lucy. 'Roland Brown.' He shook her hand warmly. 'Really sorry about yesterday. I was caught in Boston.' He turned to Simon and gave him a big hug. 'Bad about Will. Come on in, and tell me what you know.'

Lucy was struck by his presence. He was six foot three at least, a big man with a shining ponytail; but he moved with the grace of a ballet dancer across the landing, through a reinforced door that led to the main living space. Lucy now understood what a New York loft apartment could be – a living room, as long as half a city block, with a line of windows on three sides looking out across the river to the west; uptown to the George Washington Bridge; and downtown to the stark space where the twin towers of the World Trade Centre once stood. She drank in the whole vision, noticed the sanded, broad plankwood floor, black and white Italian furniture, open-plan kitchen twice the size of Alex's. The remaining wall was lined with bookcases; and there were photographs – framed and unframed – everywhere, scattered over a dining table, the walls, the floor.

'Sorry I didn't clear up,' the easy voice was saying. Lucy liked its distinctive twang with the soft intonation. 'I didn't get back until late. The cleaner will be by on Friday. Simon, there's coffee in the percolator, cream in the fridge. Will you help yourself while I get the package? It's in the strong room at the back.' Roland turned to go, but was caught by the overwhelmed look on Lucy's face. 'This used to be the offices for the warehouse below. Do you want to come see?'

He led her through a door and down a short hall, at the end of which was an 1890s walk-in safe, with large brass handles and the maker's name, Steiner and Sons, inscribed in gold across the two doors. Lucy thought she'd entered another world as Roland pulled down on the handles and jerked the steel doors towards him. Inside was a small shelved room.

'Never lock it.' He looked her right in the eye, deciding something, she thought. 'The key was gone when I took over the building, but it's wonderful, isn't it?'

Lucy looked at him for a moment, and felt an overpowering emotion. He was a stranger, and she wanted to hug him. 'You really liked him, didn't you?'

'Will?' His nod said 'yes' in a very physical, emotional way.

'What was he like?' she asked, looking at him attentively. 'It's not something I can ask Alex, even now.'

Roland understood, and smiled at her. 'That's kind of hard to say. He was different from a lot of the people we work with. He'd get an idea in his head and off he'd go. No commission, just something he wanted to do. Then he'd make a hell of a stink when no one wanted to buy the piece.' He roared a laugh at Lucy. 'Then – maybe a year later – someone would ask Pearl, did we have anything on someone-or-other? Sure enough it would be what Will had done, way back when. Complete story in pictures, sometimes a few words too. People and details everyone suddenly wanted, but no one could get there in that moment. Ahead of the market, he was. Yes, I liked him.'

Roland had reached an outsized packet on one of the shelves, and now handed it to Lucy. 'I think – this is for you?' They exchanged a glance that seemed to Lucy to be full of meaning; yet beside her and Alex, and the people immediately connected with her transplant, not a soul knew her secret. Roland had some quality, as Simon had intimated: and it both thrilled and terrified her. She almost wanted to tell him, but he smiled at her, and shook his head strangely. 'If you know Alex well, Lucy, then you know Will. Let's find Simon.' And they retreated from the tiny space, Lucy lost in thought.

Three mugs of coffee were waiting on a low table, up to which Simon had pulled some chairs. Roland produced a knife from the kitchen and handed it to Lucy. She started to cut the tape on the packet while he and Simon talked together, but she was completely immersed in her own thoughts and physical actions, unable to follow their conversation. Her hands were almost trembling when she sliced through the seals, and began to pull back the brown paper and bubble wrapping. She could smell the scent of roses.

25 March 1609, Mortlake

It is near dawn, Kate Dee perceives, as a servant comes in to tease up the fire in the half-empty grate; but she shakes her head gently, waves him away. Her father looks comfortable enough on the cushioned settle, dozing peacefully after a lack of sleep these three nights running. He'd refused to go to his bed chamber at all on this last, feeling, she knew, that he may never come out of it again if he submitted to sleep. The room is panelled and warm enough; she would rather let him rest while he can.

She bends her head away from the light of the candle to avoid the shadow falling across her work. Her fingers are numb from long hours of stitching, though her needle remains sharp: she is hopeful of letting him see her design for the burse progressing as quickly as she may. Neither she nor her brother, Arthur, will speak of it, but both know he should not be with them many days more. And Kate, like Arthur, sees it will be a blessing. Though well past eighty, the marvellous, child-like, learned man is only now becoming scattered in his mind, fretting over the household items he feels he has 'missed'; his precious silver-gilt salt has been worrying him, and his apostle spoons will not be found. She has no heart to tell him Arthur has been obliged to sell them, to meet the expenses for their necessities.

She returns quickly to the design, her needle flashing in and out of the linen at speed, following the form of her under-drawn lines closely with speckling stitch, to create shadows under the roses. She wants to show him this section completed, having copied the pattern from those same carved and painted roses in red and white twining over her head here in this, his favourite chamber. She is to work only the red roses, he has directed her; the time of the white rose is all to come. And she must find place for the pale grey silk-moth, at once the shadow of our mortality and symbol of the transcended state to which we may aspire – 'in your pleasing couching stitch, Kate, taught you by Mistress Goodwin' – he has told her. And so she has assented, and the moth grows under her skilful hand, a rebus for the precious silk of our soul, and the dark-faced angel of Saturn who watches over alchemists. 'And the dark lady,' she whispers.

A book falls to the floor as he rouses himself, and she lights at his side like a bee on a flower. 'Rest longer, Father.' She adjusts a small cushion and replaces the counterpane for him, noticing his dear face shows the colour of parchment; his eyes are looking at her, she thinks, yet not seeing. She is happy when he closes them again, a line at his mouth trying to smile some reassurance at her. And she slips back to her chair in the light, picks up her frame.

'The words will be as the numbers, Kate.' She starts, and pricks a finger on hearing him speak with closed eyes, surprising her. 'Your return journey will retrace the steps through the labyrinth.'

'Yes, Father.' She smiles at him without lifting her head from her work. He would be talking to his last hour. 'You've told me. The numbers must count downwards again, from the end of the Jupiter Tablet; and the first number I use shall be thirteen, as the day of your birth.'

'It is just so, Kate. And your chosen word will be thirteenth in the line, though it is but "and"; and your daughter – God willing you shall have one – must choose lines to give her the proper word in the eighth place, and her daughter in the twelfth.'

'Or if it be not me, Father – for you know I have left it late to marry in this life – the task shall pass to my niece, your granddaughter Margarita. She shall choose lines for me, to render "Adonis" in the eighth place, as you ask.' She looks up at him from her broidery, unable to upbraid fate for demanding she nurse her father as her mother had wished in these last years. Now more than twenty-six, she knows her hopes of marriage are not high.

'My Katherine. Do you not see what is beside you?' The voice has surprising strength, and gentle good humour. 'Master Saunders has loved you these three years past; and he is an honest and well-disposed young man. Do not fight against what is well for you, Kate.' And he turns over, and sleeps again.

25 March 2004, Manhattan

Roland and Simon suddenly broke from their catch-up chatter, and all three of them stared as some outer paper and corrugated cardboard fell away. Lucy pulled free an exquisite, hand-stitched needlepoint object from some tissue paper, which itself had been encased in heavy plastic sheeting. It was an envelope-shaped bag – like a slip case. Made of a base fabric of heavy linen, tasselled at the corners, it was lavishly embroidered with coloured silks, predominantly red, gold, and creamy parchment; and it was buttoned at the centre with a large tear-drop pearl. As she held it up, the light revealed the details.

On the rear side, in coloured cottons, she examined a rendering of the now-familiar mulberry tree, entwined with an odd-shaped, formal symbol of a moon linked through a sun. This was worked in pale coloured silk threads, which

Lucy thought was perhaps satin and seed stitching. But on the front buttoned side, fashioned in silk threads in what Lucy would call raised work, there were two simple red roses in one corner, a red and golden border that reminded her of an ancient folio design, and a depiction of the Chartres labyrinth, which was rendered, as though flat, from the bottom of the case into an open luminescent void beyond. On closer scrutiny she could see some gold-inked script, faded in places, which ran across the face of it. It seemed to have been silk-screened, or even under-painted, in gold leaf or ink upon the linen base fabric, and some of the words stood in bolder relief within the verse lines. She noticed 'seek', and 'sleeps', and 'Lady'; and possibly 'Venus' and 'meeting'. It would take some work to decipher, but what struck her most was the effect of total enchantment, created by the whole piece. This had been a labour of love for someone, and no one would have placed such an object in the ground for long, no matter how well protected from the elements. Had it been one of Diana's final acts to set it there?

The two men, equally, were mesmerised, and time dallied for several minutes; until Roland spoke.

'The moth, or the butterfly, in the top corner, signifies a reincarnated or awakened soul. What have you got here?'

Lucy hadn't noticed this at first, but she nodded at him. The cover seemed to have been repaired and re-embroidered endlessly through eternity, patched and reworked by forgotten fingers – and yet for her, the hand of the original maker was more than evident. Yes, it was for her, she thought. It had been waiting all that time, just for her. The knowledge of this was immense for Lucy. It made her feel tied to Alex in a way that was consuming, exalting, and yet alarming. She was her own person, and always had been. No one had ever really claimed her. Now she belonged to, or with, someone else.

Close to tears, Lucy laid the case flat on the table and unbuttoned the cover with knowing fingers. Inside were the parchment sheets she knew would be there, the top pages exactly like the copies Will had created; but resting loosely in the bag was a single white rose which exhaled its soft old-world fragrance into the modern space around them. Like its twin in L'Aigle, it was perfectly faded.

Lucy was struck by Simon's silence; but Roland leaned forward and touched the embroidered cover with reverence. 'One of the strangest things I've seen. If I believed in God I would say it was his work. But I don't, so tell me you two, where in the world did this come from? And what is it?'

'We hope,' said Simon at last, 'that it's the answer to a lot of complicated questions.'

'And how could you possibly know, Roland,' Lucy asked, looking up at him with watering eyes, 'that it came from a true Garden of Eden?'

30

With the crab apple and magnolia blossoming in the small front garden it was easily the prettiest house in the terrace. A willowy blonde figure came to the door, pecked his cheek, and Alex disappeared inside with an orchid. Lucy watched from his car, felt a small wave of panic, her thoughts as arrhythmic as her pulse. This was his past; and her first taste of what a future could be like.

Terrified of becoming dependent on the unparalleled emotions she was experiencing with Alex, she'd completely run away since her return from New York. She had spent only two nights with him, and those so tightly coiled that she defied physical contact. She needed to let things calm down, and find her single self again, so she'd taken refuge in her obligation to catch up long overdue work in the editing suite. Then came the milestone of her twenty-four-hour test at Harefield the previous Friday, six months on from the transplant. He'd exchanged a shift on a weekend day to drive her, and he'd waited while she had the wires and monitors attached, stayed with her throughout the wearying ordeal. She was brittle, unwell, fractious with him: but he'd been here before, seen it all, and he took it in his stride. At times his patience with her was almost an irritation. Did she want to make him angry?

When Alex dropped her back at Battersea after the tests, his face mildly confused, Grace was a fury. 'Don't play with people's emotions, Lucy. You're not the only person who's ever been hurt. Isn't it time to leave the wounded child behind, and live like a woman?'

That had stung. It was unprecedented from her closest friend, who'd never spoken to her that way before. And, oh God, yes! She felt the blow – knew its truth. Who understood better than she how well Alex hid his own feelings, what a consummate performer he was? Wasn't it his habit to relegate his private pain in the interests of anyone who, he perceived, depended on his strength? Yet the humanity of the man was, for her at least now, always to the fore. Grace had accused her – with justification – of being too selfishly immersed in her own drama. She could see she was repeating the patterns of her past, twisting back on herself in looping coils. But what would lead her out? Nevertheless – or possibly because of this – she'd avoided Alex in the days leading to the Easter break, burying herself in work and knowing he would do the same. She hadn't glanced at the Dee material for the whole fortnight since her return.

In a moment – too quickly for her to prepare – he reappeared at the door with his son and a weekend bag. Lucy saw that Anna was securing back the latch, following her ex-husband towards the car; and she gulped in some air. Alex's voice was incongruously even as he made the introductions and packed the boot; everyone was saying 'hello', Anna commenting cheerfully on their luck with the early April weather for the Easter weekend. Lucy removed her sunglasses, shook hands and even managed a smile, the panic subduing slightly. Alex explained to his son that his brand-new state-of-the-art skateboard had just come to him courtesy of Lucy, from Bloomingdales in New York, and the boy beamed appreciation at her. Love was sent to Henry, Max climbed willingly into the back seat, was thrilled the roof was down, passed Lucy a CD; and they were off. Anna waved them away. It was over; had been absurdly uncomplicated. Alex squeezed her hand knowingly between gear changes; and a few tears escaped quietly behind her glasses.

As they arrived in Longparish – Lucy and Max having sung their hearts into the wind for the whole journey – she greeted Henry with a hug of such feeling that she knew she had transferred the apology due to the son to his father. Alex's smile said he understood her reservations and insecurities better than she. Cloistering herself in the kitchen, she baked treats she couldn't possibly eat on her strict diet, but Max was entranced. She kept occupied spending the early part of Good Friday afternoon reading in the warm, sheltered garden with Henry, while Max and his father went skateboarding.

Alex had handed her a large envelope before taking off with his son, and she now drew out a beautiful A4 illustration. It was of a crystal sphere with mountains depicted at its heart, the whole embraced by the arms of a great tree, like a transparent globe. The text underneath captioned it the *Axis Mundi*, something she'd asked him about before going to New York. She hadn't understood his reference to it, but now became engrossed by the image before her. It was the centre of the world, the place where heaven was believed to meet the earth. On a second, smaller sheet she saw his own pen and ink drawing of the symbol of medicine, the caduceus, with a note in his distinctive hand explaining that the rod was a depiction of the axis itself, and the serpents the channel by which the healer crossed the axis from this world to bring back knowledge from the higher world. Number thirty-four was connected to it according to various attributions, and Alex's note briefly explained how Dante had chosen it to complete his *Inferno* precisely because it represented this crossing point, the middle of the earth, the brush with hell – and then the emergent point for spiritual realisation, 'back to the stars'. Into the centre and out again, she thought, while Henry was pruning some bushes: the road to Jerusalem. The labyrinth.

Late in the day Henry took Alex into the library, and though they didn't at all close her out, she felt they might appreciate some privacy. She went to look for Max, and decided to give this time to him, learning all about the Sims on his computer. She listened to the boy's talk of his adored grandmother – who had taught him some French – and his uncle, whom he missed so much. She was still occupying this special, private space with him when Alex and Henry emerged from the library to check on them. Neither wished to be dislodged from his or her spot at the desk, so, as Simon and Grace were due tomorrow, and Siân would be arriving on Easter Sunday morning, the senior Stafford men departed to rearrange some furniture upstairs.

The latter invitation was rather a sudden one from Alex, Calvin having gone away again unexpectedly – to Jerusalem, no less – altering the plans he'd made quite out of the blue to take Siân back home to meet his family in Nantucket. Very unsatisfactory, Lucy had thought. Siân was unsure what to think. That Alex had lent support to the idea of Siân's going with Calvin at all had surprised Lucy; but it seemed even more strange that he was so non-judgemental about the subsequent change of plan. That had truly amazed her. Perhaps it was the present state of equipoise? Since their return from New York – and Calvin's delivery of Will's documents to his college elders – warfare had ceased. They had been given the originals as before, while Lucy and Alex had privately created double-sided copies for their own investigation. The precious embroidered bag she had not yielded up – not even to Alex's keeping: it remained in her possession. But nothing more was heard from their adversaries, and if Alex felt annoyance that they had something that didn't belong to them, he remained silent. Still, Lucy didn't trust Calvin as far as she could throw him, and she was relieved Siân would be coming to them after visiting her mother in Wales. She should get free of him, Lucy thought, and she struggled with Alex's equanimity. She had learned to respect his judgement in virtually any circumstance, yet she couldn't help feeling he was a bit blind to something in Calvin, perhaps because of their kinship. She couldn't make sense of it any other way.

At the end of an active day Max was drooping, and went up to his attic bedroom without being asked at precisely nine o'clock, leaving the other three to their conversation. Alex had poached a salmon and served it with tarragon hollandaise, leaving Lucy to wonder why he always apologised for his culinary efforts.

'Who are you comparing yourself with, Alex? You've never given me a bad dinner. You're a fine cook, and your hands smell like a herb garden.' She kissed them quickly, and was struck that these were among the first kind words she'd offered him since her trip. She needed to talk, which Henry could see, and he excused himself to his own room with a good book, locking up as he passed. But they had cleaned and cleared everything before either could break the silence with more than a monosyllable. Eventually she laced her arms around his hips, and searched his eyes. It was a holiday, and he hadn't shaved. She loved this face, touched the mild show of stubble – it belonged to *her* Alex, hinted he wasn't always rigidly in control. She relaxed a little, but still felt tongue-tied. He began.

'You were superb today. Max enjoyed being with you.'

'Why didn't you tell me he was so sweet, that it would be that easy?'

Alex laughed. 'You didn't ask me. Don't let him fool you – he's no angel. But I think we're fairly lucky.'

'I've been impossible, Alex.'

'Impossible,' he agreed, with light humour. 'Very guarded.'

'Full retreat.' She was trying to laugh at herself.

'You did warn me . . .' He knew from her resigned smile that she was worn out with her own self-torment. She seemed haunted by the inevitability of a psychological fall from paradise, determined to sacrifice any joy that might blossom in a strong relationship just to avoid the tumults and stresses of the emotional state that she was sure must also be inescapable. Her distress pained him, and he leaned his forehead down to her. 'Lucy, what do you want? Can I help?'

She took a moment, then spoke artlessly. 'Could you take me to bed, and make love to me?'

This time Alex led her to his own room. In France, desire and the frustrations of a long delay had hushed her anxiety, and she'd responded to him as naturally as breathing. But in the intervening weeks there had been time to intellectualise. Even now, while she wanted to trust her senses, she was observing herself from a distance. She saw Alex undressing her quietly, caressing her without a hint of possessiveness, but she was choked by the urge to withhold her feelings. She understood their happiness was at stake, and willed her heart to let go.

Alex read the thoughts darkening her eyes, turning the brown steel-grey. He lay beside her on his back and threaded an arm under the arc of her waist; his other hand stroked her slight, feminine shape for what seemed to her an eternity, until her diaphragm rose and fell evenly. His breath was warm at her temple.

'What word, or colour, describes the feelings you have when I touch you here?' His fingers found her breasts and the raw, scarred tissue between them.

She smiled, turned her face to him. 'Closeness.'

'Mm. And here? On your tummy?'

'Warm. Intimate.' She stretched like a cat, curled her spine slightly.

He raised himself a little to explore the dreamscape of her body – her hips and abdomen, the undulation of her waist, her delicate throat and nipples, the small of her back and the curve of her bottom, using different pressures, his tongue, his fingertips, the mildly abrasive skin of his unshaved face, sometimes a thumb. He didn't rush; and Lucy had to attend closely to the erotic sensations to discern and then articulate her response. There was more gentle laughter than breathy sighing. He leaned up higher, kissed her lips, and placed the flat of his hand delicately inside her thigh, folding her leg back with care, stroking upwards. She caught her breath and stretched her arms above her head. 'Violet, and indigo, and pinprick holes of starlight after a storm.'

'Unfair. That's more than one word. You're allowed one. Concentrate . . .' His fingers had begun to caress her silkiness, then gently pushed inside her; and she could hardly breathe. He heard his name. 'What's this word?' His body was hard but his voice was so soft.

'Sublime . . . Alex, I want you . . .'

He entered her, moving slowly. 'And now?'

'Elysium.' Lucy's breathing was lost as her passions quickly unlocked; and when his kiss blotted all the sound from her mouth she thought her heart might burst. He broke free just long enough to wander to her ear, whisper an enquiry for the word. 'I can't find one,' she cried out and pulled him deeper into her body; and with his gentle movements, his mouth on hers, her breathing came in quicker gasps. No kiss, from any lover, had ever been so demanding, and insistent, and arousing.

'Lucy, what's the word now?' But a soft flush mottled her chest, and he knew she'd let go. From Lucy, this gesture of trust was everything. They were through it.

'Release, Alex. Epopteia.' It was no more than a sigh. She had no breath for words: could only just get air into her lungs. Their bodies were so closely entwined she could feel the tremble, but didn't know which of them was shaking. She locked his eyes, his body, in hers, and their movement and breathing became an unaccompanied plainsong. 'Colours unknown even to the rainbow,' she whispered.

He laughed and kissed her softly, their senses too heightened for more. 'Then you understand. You are a goddess. Celestial.' He kissed her between every phrase.

And she did understand. She was somewhere she'd never been. She was beloved.

She stretched down for the quilt, and they dissolved into each other.

Though it was only the beginning of the second week in

April, Saturday's sunshine held, and the fruits of Lucy's Good Friday baking provided a four o'clock tea where the garden offered a windbreak. Simon and Grace lifted it to a higher epicurean level with an excellent champagne, and the company at The Old Chantry declared an afternoon off. Max was content, having led Lucy and his father around the countryside on bikes in the morning sunshine. The little boy was shocked – but Alex not in the least surprised – to discover Lucy was almost fitter than father or son, and she felt very smug about all the miles she'd notched up on her exercise bike since her operation. She teased Alex that she was planning to run with him and Courtney for the hospital in the next London Marathon.

Max was now playing with a friend from the village, and Simon's impatience took over. He'd fished for explanations about Calvin since hearing of Siân's ordeal, and he wanted the question resolved now, before her arrival tomorrow.

'I'm curious too, Alex. How are you so calm about it?' Lucy knew Alex's style was to weigh all the evidence before making cursory judgements, whereas Simon would act first and think about the repercussions afterwards. But she took Siân's pain very personally. Purely from instinct, she felt protective towards Siân, which made her livid with Calvin.

Alex had filled his father in the day before on the assault, and Henry commented now: 'It does look bad, Alex.'

His son nodded. 'I know. But I was in her flat the morning after with your friend from the Met, and his forensic team, Simon, when Calvin arrived from the airport. Thrust into the maelstrom like that, he was devastated. He had no part in it, and may have been the intended victim.

But whether he realised it before that moment or not, he loves Siân. When he saw her at my flat, he couldn't speak. Then, later – well, he was truly caring. I haven't been his supporter, but he surprised me on this.'

'You can't feel cuddly about him, Alex!' Simon had steam escaping, and clattered his plate on to the table clumsily. 'I've a mind to take Will's part in this and rearrange his expensive dental work, regardless of his affections for Siân. Maybe she *wants* to believe in him, but you're too canny for that. You know the loathsome company he keeps! I wish they'd find what they're looking for, and discover it really has some evil curse on it. My favourite Bible story is about the Ark of the Covenant falling into the hands of the Philistines. They all came down with haemorrhoids! Now *that* would be justice.'

Grace's swallow of champagne hit the lawn, and Alex erupted into laughter. 'A grim punishment in the days before Preparation H! Seriously, though, Simon, I sympathise with your feelings about Calvin, but I think we should give him the benefit of the doubt. For the moment. We talked for a long time when we met at the hospital for lunch. He remedied the situation with the papers as fast as he was able, they haven't breathed a syllable to me since . . .'

'They shouldn't have the damned papers,' Simon broke in heatedly.

'. . . and I hope he's an ally now.' Alex finished his sentence very deliberately, then met his friend's eyes without hesitation. 'Have a little faith in me, Simon. Calvin may be misguided philosophically in my book – his belief system is thoroughly alien to mine – but he's a genuinely spiritual man, which I can't hold against him. It's not my way that he's chosen, but he's a thinker, with a conscience.'

'And you believe he loves Siân? I wasn't altogether convinced he was a committed ladies' man.' Lucy was tense, feeling Alex might be withholding something.

'Interestingly enough, Lucy, I'd wondered that. But I do believe he's in love with her. And that poor girl needs some kind of closure, to let go of the past and move on. She's suffered enough. Let's be as supportive as possible.' Alex exchanged a look with Henry, who nodded.

Grace had been sipping champagne, listening; but she posed a question for all of them. 'Alex, if he cares for her, why drop off the planet without telling her? Was he scared? And why let her down so atrociously over the trip to the States? She was excited about it.'

'I can't answer you, Grace. I agree the cancelled trip is a blow. But Professor Walters and his group are in Jerusalem for a reason – one we might guess at with some distaste – and I'll trust Calvin knows what he's doing in joining them there.' Alex emptied the last of the bottle into the visitors' glasses and changed the subject abruptly. 'Now, where are you sleuths up to with the "Dee-files"? If we're going to race them to the prize, it's time for a reckoning, surely.'

Alex had concealed something, Lucy was certain. But clearly he wasn't going to speak further. She was mulling this over when she realised she'd missed some of what Henry was saying, and tried to pick up the thread.

'. . . amusing dinner this week with John, my friend in the Deanery at Winchester, and he had some very interesting thoughts on these Christian Zionists of Simon's.'

'Good God, Henry!' Simon interjected. 'Please don't call them creatures of mine.'

Henry put up one hand. 'Apologies, Simon – they are odious, it seems. John knew all about them and corroborated your every word. Suffice to say, he doesn't like their Old Testament-dependent ideas, which are prophecy-based much more than being concerned with the person of Jesus. He feels their teachings could lead to all-out war in the whole of the Middle East if they're unchecked – a blood bath. They're shamelessly exploiting the tensions and anxieties of the West's attitudes to Islam. One prays they're being watched by the secret services. This Rapture policy you spoke of, Simon, means they don't care for the rest of humanity – they assume a "join us or perish" platform. And John is nervous that certain elements of the Evangelical movement – particularly in the United States and alarmingly close to the White House – are exporting their violently apocalyptic, but hardly Christian, theology with a strong recruitment incentive. Let's hope your cousin isn't caught up in that, Alex! But now, I'd like to hear about your retrieval of the documents, Lucy. You had trouble getting hold of them?'

'That was peculiar, Henry. Our suspicions ran amok when Alex told us that Calvin was in Boston at the same time as Roland. But it was all a red herring. Will's things were at Roland's loft all along. He couldn't have been more helpful.' Lucy thought afresh of their touching encounter, the emotions it had triggered in her, and she smiled at Alex now with a meaning that was purely personal to her.

'He was distraught to learn of Will's death,' Simon added.

'He had no idea – thought he'd gone away to Mexico or South America for a year. He'll be writing to you.'

Henry nodded sadly at them. It was painful, yet quite a relief to be involved in something that brought his wife and son so close to him again. 'But, he didn't have the key you were looking for?'

'I'm afraid not,' Simon answered. 'He knew nothing of it. He had only the package and a note from Will about holding on to it until it was needed. He enclosed a white rose inside the dossier bag, which Lucy believes came from Diana's garden.'

Alex had been pondering Henry's new interest in the quest with some fascination, but he now looked at Lucy. 'A white rose? The symbol of female secrets. I think the "rose" is as important as the number thirty-four.'

'So are the keys, I believe,' Grace said with enthusiasm. 'Simon and I scoured the sheets while you were editing your documentary, Lucy,' she looked at her friend, 'and we think the first page is about St Peter – "the rock" – holding the keys to heaven. One was gold and the other silver. Also "Martha", two pages later, was Mary Magdalene's sister, and legend says she went to France. Keys were her symbol too.'

Alex opened the folio of copy papers and a blank book on the tea table. 'The keys to heaven are gold and silver? Then our pair must reflect them.' He noted down the ideas, and shuffled the sheets into order. 'That makes it vital to find the second key, Lucy, with the ruby. Perhaps whatever our keys unlock here is an entry point to heaven, and we still need the silver key.' Alex left his champagne largely untouched, his thoughts drifting.

'And we still have it,' she told them. 'They've forgotten about it, and I haven't reminded them!'

Alex was a little worried by this reminder, but he nodded and consulted the papers again. 'Presumably, the "symbol of our union" is in France, like Martha? Chartres, perhaps.'

'Or the knot garden at L'Aigle?' Henry suggested. 'A knot represents either marriage or loyalty.'

'The family motto has something to do with this?' Alex turned to his father.

'"Loyal and True", Alex. Not true for Henry Stafford, Duke of Buckingham, who changed sides during the Wars of the Roses more often than horses. But his cousin Humphrey was our ancestor – ever constant to York. It cost him his life under Henry Tudor. You reminded me last night about the Stafford ambassador to France, Lucy – who knew Giordano Bruno. I had to check our own little family history in the library this morning, but yes, he was our ancestor, Edward. John Calvin was godfather to one of his sons.'

'You see, Henry,' Lucy spoke gently, 'that the Staffords are as much a part of the story as the Dees.' She smiled at him, feeling Diana had surely thought as much.

'But,' he resumed, with a warm look at her, 'a knot with either Cupid, or Venus and Mars, represents the tie of love – "war subdued by love", your mother taught me, Alex. You know after St Martin's she did her diploma in art appreciation at the Sorbonne – where I met her when I was doing a stint for NATO in the Provost Marshal's office,' Henry explained to the others.

Alex was pensive. He remembered his parents' history – and the family fighting on the white rose side at Bosworth.

Did it mean anything? 'The Stafford badge has a knot and a swan?'

'And the cross of St George. But remember the Gordian knot – the cufflinks your mother gave you, in the shape of a knot, when you graduated?'

Alex was thinking that, although she'd given the key to Will at her death, he himself had been written into her family mystery from his birth. He looked at his father without speaking, nibbled some cake, picked up the sheets. 'Siân's white roses. Will was a Yorkist – a knight "loyal and true". A blind? Or a legitimate strand to consider? Lucy?'

Lucy glanced at Alex, caught in her own thoughts. She was considering the roses on Diana's tea service, with a cup in her hands. 'I'm beginning to understand those white roses. Sunflowers track the sun, but white roses come alive under the moonlight. Something different is going to happen, I think, when night is the real day, and a woman has power again – like Queen Elizabeth in John Dee's time. Maybe now, while the second Elizabeth is Queen.'

Lucy had said something which touched everyone, but she went on quickly, 'And I was thinking just now of the second text, about "uxorious Henry" – the too many times married Henry VIII.' She laughed. 'From my research into Elizabeth, I discovered that her mother, Henry's wife number two, wore a "hart" around her neck, and was thought to be able to change into the shape of a hare. The lines, "Maids are May when they are maids" are from *As You Like It*; and Anne Boleyn was executed in May, wearing a grey dress. Do you think that's what this riddle is referring to? "A Lady of Light" was St Lucy, and I was born in February, the time of Candlemas.'

'But the papers also "came to light" on your birthday, February the third, here in the garden – another journey started on the thirty-fourth day of the year.' Alex poured tea into her cup, and left them all briefly to recharge the pot. When he returned a moment later, carrying the fresh tea and an old, yellowing file, he thought it appeared as though Lucy had a spell cast over her.

'What you said, Alex. I hadn't thought of it that way.' She looked at him in slight confusion as he sat again. 'Princess Elizabeth, Dee's patron, was Anne's child. She and I are both "King's daughters", so to speak. My Sicilian grandmother and English grandfather met during the liberation in the war. From him I get my patriality and my English surname.'

Alex's eyes smiled. She rarely said a thing about her family, so such details were a revelation to him. 'Perhaps this quest is simultaneously about them, and us. Her, and you? But I want to throw something else into the mix. Anne's sister, Mary Boleyn, had a son and a daughter almost certainly by Henry VIII – though their surname was Carey. Mary's son was Henry – named for his true father, the King – and he was Elizabeth's Lord Chamberlain, all-important patron to Shakespeare's acting company.'

'Of course – the Lord Chamberlain's Men,' Henry said.

'And Henry Carey was Elizabeth's brother, as much as cousin. But Mary Boleyn's daughter – Shakespeare's patron's sister – was granted all the manor and lands of Longparish. They'd belonged to Wherwell Abbey until the Dissolution. So this house – which has been in our family for generations, and started as a chantry – was on land belonging to her. She was the King's illegitimate daughter.' Alex now opened the small file he'd brought from the house, and drew out some papers with care.

Simon had been holding his glass still. 'This suggests a relationship between your family, Dee's descendants – or even Dee himself – and a group who were possibly connected with Shakespeare through the Lord Chamberlain, Alex.'

'I believe so, Simon. Put simply, Shakespeare's patron's sister owned this land, so I conjecture that she gave this house – or the land it's on – to one of my ancestors. But for what reason . . . ?'

'In Catholic England a chantry was a holy place, don't forget.' Grace looked carefully at the oldest part of the building. 'A chapel dedicated to a soul's passing – a place to keep the soul's spirit safe.'

'True,' Alex said, and he noticed Lucy was staring. 'But there's more.'

He carefully unfolded a tattered document, comprised of several sheets of vellum. 'Dad gave this to me yesterday,' Alex explained, 'and it belongs with the deeds to the house. You can just about make out the name near the top here.' He pointed carefully to a line of the document, close-written in an old-style hand that was demanding for modern eyes to read. Grace was out of her chair in a second.

'"Given by this hand",' she leaned over him to help, and read aloud: '"in the thirty-fourth year of the reign of Elizabeth, by the Grace of God of England, France and Ireland, Queen" . . .' she followed Alex's finger as it skipped several words, '"to Mistress Lanyer."' Grace's eyes were suddenly surprised. 'Thirty-four years of Elizabeth must have been 1592 or '93, Alex. She came to the throne late in 1558.'

Alex noted Grace's comment with interest. 'One of the best candidates for Shakespeare's "dark lady" of the sonnets,' he told them all after a moment, 'was Henry Carey's mistress, Emilia Lannier, whose maiden name was Bassano. She was a musician whose family came from Venice, a brilliant woman of unusual beauty and exoticism, who later published an epic poem exonerating Eve. You'd have liked her, Lucy,' Alex enthused. 'She could have furnished Shakespeare with a strong feminist viewpoint when he needed it – if she did indeed have his ear, and he her sexual favours, as some historians believe.'

'How did you put all this together, Alex?' Lucy asked him, almost in distress.

'It was only yesterday when I realised that one of the books that was taken in the break-in was an early, valuable copy of her published poem. This house may have been connected with her – perhaps a bequest from Henry Carey via his sister, who owned all the lands? The deeds seem to support that, though there are some frustrating blank spaces in them beyond this period.'

'Alex, I thought you were a scientist.' Grace had plopped down back in her chair exhausted with the excitement, and was just cutting a piece of lemon cake for herself and Henry when her humour bubbled up again. 'You're not bad on your history – or literature for that matter.'

He laughed with a hint of embarrassment. 'Not really, Grace. I was the science child in an arts family. I had to at least try to keep up. Mum took Will and me to countless productions of Shakespeare plays as soon as we could sit still. My education was probably a little light when it came to

Winnie-the-Pooh and Alice, but I can get by without programme notes at the Globe. And anyhow,' he added, 'I've been over the ground again in this last couple of weeks, like all of you!'

'Don't listen, Grace,' Lucy teased, suddenly thinking there was a lot of Dr John Dee in his many times great-grandson. 'Alex knows as much poetry as I do. And I know nothing about stem cells.'

Alex's father had sat quietly, closing his eyes in the unseasonably warm sunshine. Now he smiled at her enigmatically. 'In my experience, Lucy, men of science often know more about the arts than we humanities students know about their discipline. But don't put him on a pedestal. Alex isn't keen on heights.'

Henry's expression was opaque, and she was unsure what he meant. Had Anna placed him up too high, so that he would inevitably fall?

Henry continued speaking. 'Each of these interpretations could be valid. Queen Elizabeth, Lucy, and Katherine Carey – and how intriguing if Shakespeare's "dark lady" is connected with the house. Your mother would have enjoyed that, Alex, and she'd have known.' Henry was full of regret that he'd never appreciated the fascination of her family until this time. 'What has "May" to do with the riddle?'

'I believe time will have a part to play,' Alex said. He looked hard into all the pensive faces. 'Simon, you're uncommonly quiet.'

Simon had indeed been strangely mute, but he answered Alex with animation. 'Yes, I've been so absorbed in all of this new information, I almost forgot. Grace and I found a connection with your magic number in the text that begins "Over one arm the lusty coursers rein." It's the thirty-fourth line of Shakespeare's *Venus and Adonis*. Lucy pointed out the references to these lovers in several texts.' Simon paused to read aloud the appropriate page. 'But here's the weird thing. The painting *Venus and Adonis* in the National Gallery – Grace has a copy here with her – is catalogued as NG34. It was the thirty-fourth painting acquired by the Gallery in the early nineteenth century. It represents the waning love between Philip and Mary Tudor, and Mary was Henry VIII's daughter too. Venus begged Adonis not to hunt – which I guess was about her not wanting Philip to stray.'

'To her sister, Elizabeth!' Grace had taken a postcard of the painting from the basket beside her, and showed them an image that Simon passed first to Lucy and Alex, and they in turn gave to Henry.

'The line numbers of the poem could have been counted then, of course,' he was saying, 'but how, in the late sixteenth or early seventeenth century, could they know the painting would become NG34, two hundred years on?'

Four faces stared, and a sceptical laugh escaped Alex. 'You might as well add that Philip's Spain now has a dialling code of thirty-four, when you telephone!' It was an absurd coincidence, but it was none the less wonderful. At some level it spun out various existentialist questions. Was life copying art to an exaggerated degree?

Lucy carried on the idea. 'I love it! But add it to the previous text. "Where did I leave the sweet lady sleeping?" I've developed real empathy for Ariadne, the sleeping lady left on Naxos by Theseus. Titian paints her watching

Theseus disappear, yet also reaching for Dionysus, or Bacchus. His Ariadne doesn't have to die, but gets a new heart from the kindest of the Three Fates – a reprieve. She's elevated to a goddess for rescuing man from the labyrinth. That painting is one of the stars of the National Gallery too, and might solve that text, I feel.'

Alex leafed through the pile of sheets and found the right one, making a point of ticking it with his pencil, and setting it aside with those they'd discussed. 'Is that five down? What about this one, concerning the River Styx? It has another reference to Venus and Adonis, but we renamed the Thames as River Styx for the night of our cruise, Lucy, and we had to pay the ferryman, and pass the grim reaper.' Alex turned to his father to explain. 'For the hospitals' Halloween night.'

'Alex,' Lucy answered him, 'the "celestial goddess of light", and the man who "passes in reality into the Fortunate Isles of the Soul" . . .' They waited for her to explain her ideas, but she couldn't express what she wanted to say. It was too strange to share. She remembered the thud of her heart when they'd seen the strange barge. She suddenly understood that was forty days and nights after her operation, and Will's death. Like Christ in the wilderness, or Moses on Sinai, or the Egyptians' period of purification of the mummy, it was the length of time a soul was thought to wait in limbo. Was his heart staying with her, and his soul departing for Elysium? She only said: 'The whole document is our chronicle.'

And Alex's response astonished her. He smiled softly. 'Yes. It is.'

Lucy found the whole experience rather intense, touching

off as it had some very personal emotions. She needed some space, and while Grace put further questions to Alex about the woman who'd owned the land, she departed for the sanctuary of Diana's kitchen, ostensibly to make more tea and a pot of coffee; but her head was swimming. While the kettle heated on the Rayburn, she stepped into Diana's small study off the main living room, without feeling at all that she was intruding. There on her desk, reinstated to its position of precedence, was the tiny portrait of the sixteenth-century lady with her beautiful bodice of trees, and insects, and stags. Lucy picked it up and confronted the dark beauty, wondering who she was, and what her story would add, if they knew it.

The kettle was not yet singing, so she changed rooms and seated herself at Alex's laptop, where she and Max had got better acquainted the day before. She entered: 'Emilia Lannier, 1592', and was offered alternative spellings, but her eyes danced across the excerpted data that immediately attracted her. Rushing back to the kitchen, she almost burned her hand in her haste to pour the boiling water, then she flew to the garden in an excited state.

'Lucina was the midwife to Adonis,' Henry was telling Grace, his glasses propped on his nose while he read from her chosen page, 'and she liberated him from his confinement in the sacred myrrh tree – just as Prospero does with Ariel from the pine.'

But everyone now looked up at Lucy as she set both pots on the table.

'What is it?' Simon asked her.

'I think,' she told them with a twinkle, 'that the portrait

which was taken from you, and returned, is of the Lord Chamberlain's pretty mistress, Emilia.'

Alex had only recently learned how the painting had come back to them – and at whose behest; but he had told them nothing of it. He eased back into his Lloyd loom chair and folded his arms, puzzled. 'Go on.'

'Dark Lady or no, she was embarrassingly pregnant to the Lord Chamberlain in 1592, and was hastily married off to a musician called "Lannier" – although she called her son Henry, after his real father. Wouldn't that be a perfect time to make a gift of a parcel of out-of-the-way land, that belonged not so tellingly to him, but to his sister?'

'That's the thirty-fourth year of Elizabeth's reign,' Alex nodded. 'But, how did it come after that, to us?'

'Perhaps there's a link between her, and either Shakespeare, or Dee, or one of Dee's children,' Simon said.

'She knew everything,' Lucy asserted. 'And perhaps the "bequest" in that document you were looking at is spiritual – and included the portrait. She was connected to Dee's circle, I believe.'

This prompted Alex to move the discussion to something that intrigued him, and was a little less personal. 'That very text, Lucy, has the clue I mentioned to you and Simon on the phone,' Alex told them. 'The words are about the element of the moon, and the miniatures and enamels,' he passed the sheet back to her. 'The element of the moon is Woman, in one sense, but the riddle concerns the element selenium. It's used to make traffic lights and enamel paints because it has a soft, luminous quality. And it's very important in medicine now, because it seems to play an important role in the prevention of some kinds of cancer, and crucially, for a healthy immune system. We have a long way to go with it, but trials are about to start to see if it could help patients with HIV. The odd thing is,' he said with a slight frown, 'it's the thirty-fourth element in the periodic table, which didn't even exist in Dee's day.'

'Maybe an angel told Dee all about it then?' Lucy raised her eyebrow at him.

Alex laughed. 'That begs a question, doesn't it? Who actually wrote them, these papers? Was it Dee? And should we assume that the second batch have all been added by later hands? Perhaps one generation after another of the women in Mum's family, because she has certainly added this last one. There are seventeen of them, plus the simple tiled number square; just as there were seventeen of the first batch plus the Tablet of Jupiter.'

'That's becoming a resonant total,' Simon added.

'Is it that the time is now "ripe", as Lear would say? After four hundred years, we are approaching the answer at this moment,' Alex suggested.

'And seventeen women and their partners – assuming you're right about one text for each generation, Alex – mean that thirty-four people produced you and Will.' Lucy didn't want to say more than this, but she felt heavy in her head, experienced a feeling of wildness in her heart – a not unpleasant palpitation. The circumstances, she thought, have to be exact; and so they are. Will's death, her life: she was his rescue and resurrection, figuratively speaking, and he hers. It offered a meaning below the obvious one in the texts that only she and Alex could be sensitive to.

But there had to be a present-day correspondence too; a reason why these documents and ideas were arriving in the consciousness of this moment. She was sure it concerned the Rapturists, which meant that they were inevitably involved.

'This is Bab El Rameh, Calvin,' Fitzalan Walters told him as they looked at the golden stone of the ancient structure. The afternoon sun turned a brilliance of colour on its fascia, creating a rose-gold glow over the Roman arches now in-filled with smoother blocks of stone.

'It's also known as the Mercy Gate, I believe, which the old Jewish tradition says is where the Messiah will enter into the city.' Though he had been fêted to holy sites and antiquities galore for two days, Calvin was truly struck by the symmetry and beauty of the ancient gateway. Sacred to three religions, it had watched successive events of human drama unfolding over time. His shirt was too heavy for the location, and sweat was prickling the back of his neck after an oven-hot April day; but the air was marginally cooler now, and the city – filled with Pilgrims for the Passover week and Easter period – offered a comparative stillness in this hour as the faithful walked to the many synagogues and churches around the great city. It made Calvin deeply emotional – a place of such history and beauty, as much as pain and strife.

'But the Golden, or Mercy, Gate is precisely where Jesus made his last entry into Jerusalem. And the next event in God's prophetic plan is going to be the catching away of the Saints, Calvin, in the presence of the Lord. And if the texts from Dee's angels are right, it may be here, tomorrow, Easter Sunday.' FW had that special fervour in his voice that he reserved for the big places and the even bigger occasions; and in his panama hat and immaculate jacket, Calvin noticed his companion didn't seem in the least troubled by sweat or heat.

Guy had stood a little apart from the two of them, to give them space for the experience; but now he stepped forward and said 'Amen' to the professor's assertions. 'Because this is his alpha and omega, FW, right here in Jerusalem. Here he died; here he will come back to us.'

'And all the clues add to an April date,' FW said with gravity. 'My heart thrills at the very idea. Will it be tomorrow that we witness the white horse, and the heavens opening? Jesus coming to get his bride, all of us faithful who are born again?'

Calvin put his sunglasses back on and scanned the edifice again, keeping his eyes from the intense light, but also from the men with him. 'And in the Koran this is the Gate of Mercy, isn't it?' he asked. 'Through which the just will pass on the Day of Judgement?'

But FW was somewhere else. 'He is dressed in a robe that is dripped in blood, and his name is the word of God,' he told them in a stirring voice, taking his text from his beloved Revelations. Calvin shivered in the sun.

The afternoon shrank as they depleted the pile of old riddles in the pages before them, with proffered solutions and shrugged-off confusions. Lucy decided to ask Alex for a reference book. 'There must be a complete Shakespeare here?'

He went to fetch it for her.

'And an atlas,' Simon called after him. Alex broke into a jog.

He took enough time in the house to check on the boys, and bring out jumpers and jackets; but he returned in time to hear Lucy ask his father an interesting question.

'What of Dido, Henry? What was she pleased to see?'

'When Queen Dido was jilted by Aeneas and threw herself on a funeral pyre, Juno took pity on her and sent Iris on a rainbow to release Dido's soul, by cutting a lock of her hair. It was the rainbow she was happy to see. The idea of a person's soul leaving their body as long as it had an object to cleave to was common in classicism; and the rainbow was the bridge to high wisdom, and the initiation into paradise.'

'Newton was musing on an iconic symbol.' Alex's eyes engaged with Lucy's as he helped her into an oversized cardigan. They had been introduced to this symbol of higher wisdom together; and he started to wonder whether anyone's soul was residing in the object she'd retrieved from under the tree.

Everyone was absorbed in their own thoughts and research for some time, when Lucy, who had been busying herself in the Shakespeare volume, looked up excitedly. 'Lines from his thirty-fourth sonnet – the closing couplet – are in several of the texts. "Ah! But those tears are pearl which thy love sheeds".' She spoke to a circle of concentrated faces.

Simon had also struck gold in the atlas, scouring the meridians of longitude and latitude at thirty-four degrees. Something clicked for him, and he talked them through his awareness that the Ancient Mariner, sailing south 'towards the Line', had made Lucy and him first think of Sydney, on their plane trip. 'Sure enough, Botany Bay is a later name for Stingray Bay, and it's situated at thirty-four degrees south latitude. Lucy's birth place.' He looked up and grinned: 'And I've just understood your mother, Alex. "Following in Eve's footsteps" is surely a reference to the fossilised prints found near Cape Town, of the oldest known ancestress of Homo Sapien – "Eve". The whole line, from Cape Town to Port Elizabeth, is an archaeological treasure trove regarded as the cradle of man. At thirty-four degrees south latitude, naturally'.

Lucy, like the others, was hardly surprised any more. But it brought up a problem, which she now voiced. 'Does it suggest a place other than England, do you think, which might house the so-called pot of gold? Could Dee have placed this – whatever it is – on one of his travels abroad?'

'You're right, Lucy. We've got some way to go with this,' Alex said. 'But the number thirty-four underscores every word, every text. If we haven't seen how in all of them, I suspect it's our failure. We have Venus and Adonis, and Ariadne. The month of May could be significant; and roses wind through the puzzles. The first sheet – copied and handed down through every generation – answers "William Shakespeare" to its riddle. And "rose" is, I think, intended as a near-homophone for the Latin "*ros*", or "dew", a prime ingredient in alchemy. In Will's reference books I found the words below Dee's "monas" symbol, "God give you the dew of heaven, and fatness of the earth." Alchemy was a principal interest for Dee.'

'But, Alex,' Henry said, laying aside the page he was reading, 'I think, crucially, roses are about female beauty and strength. The whole shape is suggestive of female allure and sexual regenerative power. I imagine they intend something hopeful and positive concerning women. My own reading this week reminded me that Queen Elizabeth – also a Virgo – was known to Dee's circle and her literate courtiers as Astraea, the goddess of justice from the Golden Age. Then, the gods and heaven itself were on earth. Perhaps – it's a lot to hope – Dee is expecting a new golden age, under a successor to Elizabeth, to come soon.'

He looked directly at his son, and Alex felt this was of major significance; but the discussion was cut short by a phone call, which he took inside on his mobile. When he returned he was preoccupied.

Without any idea how she knew, Lucy guessed the call had come from Calvin, and that Alex would be secretive about it. Was this only because none of them liked him?

It was close to six o'clock and getting cold, so Alex loaded the remnants of their afternoon tea on to a tray and called the boys to arrange walking Max's guest home. Grace and Simon put on warmer layers and wandered in the garden; Henry still had his head in Shakespeare; and Lucy took another path, lost in a goddess' thoughts. She spent a little time around the mulberry tree, completely bare of buds though it was, and felt something pull at her. She kneeled, contemplated, and saw in her mind a lady's gloved hand closed on something beating – like a bird, perhaps? The image disturbed but didn't repel her. She turned back along the path and started gathering flowers. She cut perfumed narcissi for the room she shared with Alex, which recalled the days that followed her transplant; then she hunted for some early anemones for Siân's room. She was picking them when her thoughts suddenly spilled from her mouth in a moment of illumination.

'Alex, I understand!'

The words carried such conviction that everyone came to her. She explained.

'It's not the thirty-fourth degree of latitude or longitude: at least, I don't believe so. But time does have a part to play. Alex realised that my birthday is the thirty-fourth day of the year. So I started thinking, the thirty-fourth degree of the zodiac would be four degrees of Taurus – the sign connected with April and May, and the Minotaur.'

'And the labyrinth,' Alex agreed.

Lucy continued. 'It would fall around April twenty-third or twenty-fourth – depending on the exact degree in any one year. There's a text that asks, what are men when they woo? They're April – and December when they wed – in *As You Like It*. Now consider, the twenty-third would be St George's Day – and it was originally a pagan feast, the day of Green George, or the Green Man. And, in a riddling kind of language, "green" could be the middle name of Iris – as the middle colour of the rainbow.'

All eyes were fixed on Lucy – straining to make her leap of discovery.

'Henry, the St George's Cross is specifically on the Stafford badge?' He confirmed this; and she asked simply, 'Whose "alpha" and "omega" was St George's Day?' Lucy challenged them to catch her.

Alex's head was askew. Lucy's huge brown eyes swam, were hypnotic – and he enjoyed their power. 'William Shakespeare, of course! That's inspirational, Lucy. And that's the very text in Mum's own handwriting – "Taurus four, the pot of gold at the end of the rainbow." It must be a Sabian symbol – Shakespeare's personal Sabian symbol for the degree of his birthday.'

'Sabian symbol, Alex?' Grace was mystified.

'Created by Marc Edmund Jones in the 1920s, Grace. Each of the three-hundred-and-sixty degrees of the zodiac inspires a phrase or a picture, an intuitive approach to that part of the individual sign, and Mum had a copy.'

Everyone was lost in thought, until finally Henry voiced their unspoken question. 'So, where do you need to be, and what will happen, on April the twenty-third?'

But it was nearly two hours later when Max – avoiding laying the table – called in high-pitched excitement to Lucy and his father. At Alex's laptop, he'd been arranging the scanned-in pictures on the reverse of all the documents, marrying images by matching the lines of a maze. When he'd finished, a whole plotted labyrinth swam before them all. And unmistakably, a face watched from within it.

'Well,' Alex grinned, 'I think the man from Stratford is trying to tell us.'

31

Pub closing time was past and the cathedral clock chimed the half of an undisclosed hour. In murky light, two male figures could just be made out emerging through the late April mist from the alley at the back of the abbey of England's first martyr, in St Albans. One was carrying a Gladstone bag, and, like phantoms, they crossed the street known as Holywell Hill. The other drew keys from his coat pocket and opened the door to a pottery shop. Not a soul was in sight and, unwitnessed, they entered the building and switched off the alarm, keeping the interior dark.

In the dimness it was possible to make out that the room was furnished with round tables – each grouped with chairs, a set of paint pots, and brushes for potters to decorate plates or other pieces, before they were fired in the kiln. The door and windows at the front of the shop had been replaced – perhaps in the last hundred years. They admitted a degree of yellowish light, and potentially exposed the room to any passer-by along Holywell Hill.

On the left side of the front door was a desk and cash till, while a door at the rear opened into another passage and, possibly, further rooms behind the wall. Along this wall were three sets of free-standing stripped pine shelves, laden with unglazed pottery awaiting artistic inspiration. And behind these shelves ran an unbroken wall of fine, eighteenth-century wood panelling, which a torch, switched on for a moment, revealed to be of a mellow, honeyed colour. It was this panelling, more than anything else, that attracted the intruders' interest.

The two men turned their full attention to this wall and, working in silence with systematic efficiency, quickly cleared the shelves, neatly piling their contents on to the tables. The street lighting gave an eerie incandescence to their work, throwing strange shadows on to the panels. The shelves cleared, they carefully pulled the dressers back from the panelling and employed them as a screen, so that they appeared unremarkable to the outside world, whilst effectively concealing the movement behind them.

Now they removed their coats and placed them over the backs of the units to block out any light that might throw their movements into relief. A laser torch was switched on again, and a neatly rolled pack of tools was unfurled from the Gladstone. This was placed on the floor along with another small laser torch, and a solid rubber-headed mallet. Both men donned gloves; neither spoke; the taller of the two kept a careful watch on the outside world.

One man now turned his full attention to the panelling. He took a long, slim-bladed knife from the roll and probed the panelling from end to end with his hands, the blade, and the thin stream of torchlight. He hesitated, then slipped the knife into a section of the woodwork and moved it along the join between two sections of panelling, until it hit something hard. He withdrew the blade a fraction until he bypassed the obstruction, then he pushed it in again and continued moving the blade along the line join, until it met another obstruction.

In near blackness he had to whistle softly to his companion, who was at some distance away; then he focused his attention on the panel above that he'd just been working on. He repeated the process. This time the blade found an obstruction in the join, but instead of bypassing it he pressed hard against the knife. The knife suddenly moved in the space, and a loud crash followed. The lower panels fell clear from the wall at his feet. He instantly killed the light and froze. The man nearer the window simultaneously dropped to the floor, and they paused to see if the noise had attracted any interest either from the bedroom in the pub above them, or from the street. They breathed nervously; a car approached and slowed. The noise of someone speaking was followed by the beam of headlights from another car that swung round in the road. The men tensed, waited, heard more voices; then a car door slammed and the vehicle pulled away up the hill. After waiting unmoving for five minutes, the man by the panels bent again, and shone the fine prism of torchlight behind the opening left by the missing section. The uneven line of an old brick wall became visible, and he inhaled audibly. Undeterred, however, he reached his tool-kit and selected the rubber mallet and a bolster chisel along with a small sheet of plastic, which he spread carefully on the floor. As silently as possible, he set about removing a section of the brickwork. He paused now and then to check that he was not overheard. His partner raised a thumb to communicate assurances that everything seemed in order.

The old lime mortar gave way surprisingly quickly and he loosened the bricks, holding on to them to kill the sound, placing them quietly on the plastic sheeting. Through the aperture he had made he could see what looked like a beautifully constructed hiding space, set into the thick wall behind the bricks. It might have been part of the fireplace, or a priest's hole from centuries lost. Prying into the hole once more, with the help of the torch, he beckoned to his accomplice to join him. Among the piles of dust and cobwebs they saw two ageing boxes – the larger square and bound with an elaborately tied rope, and the other with a curved, gold-topped lid bearing a painted inscription.

They now hastened to clear the remaining bricks and haul the boxes into the open area behind the shelves. They gave their immediate attention to the smaller of the two. An exploratory tug proved that it was locked fast, but an elaborate keyhole in each side was revealed in the laser light. One gloved hand streaked away some dust to reveal the words of the inscription. Their heads consulted each other, hesitating; then cautiously they pushed this box aside and concentrated on the larger one. The knot in the cord was stiff and complex, and after a moment's struggle, the taller of the two was handed the knife by his associate. He paused fleetingly, then sliced cleanly through the cord.

Inside the box was a large parchment covered with complex mechanical drawings and notes. Underneath this was a collection of what appeared to be crude, scientific equipment: an odd selection of tarnished brass tubes, some clamps, mirrors, and a prism-shaped piece of what the focused torchlight revealed to be fine clear crystal. Separately wrapped in fragile cloth was an extraordinarily detailed set of lines and shapes etched or drawn on to a piece of glass.

The visitors removed the contents from the box and spread them out carefully on the floor, studying them. Eventually one man spoke, almost the only words uttered within the confines of the shop: '*Non angli, sed angeli*', and he muffled a laugh. Both men nodded, then carefully rolled the paper, wrapped the glass painting back into its cloth, and replaced both objects in their original coffer along with the other pieces of equipment. One man blew through a straw or small pipe, scattering a tilth of dust again on top of the smaller, untried box. After some moments, they returned this one alone to its original hiding place, keeping the second close by them.

What followed was almost an hour of near-silent repair work in dark shadows. When the dust had settled, the first man leaped up on to a table and spent some time tinkering with a screwdriver around the overhead light. The other man squeezed into the area behind the counter and gave his attention to a wall-light above the shelves mounted on the back wall. About ten minutes later, they edged to the door, clutching the corded box between them. One made a final check of the room – which now showed no signs of disturbance.

The road was deserted and, balancing their cargo carefully between them, they reactivated the alarm before securing the door behind them, utterly shrouded in the darkness of the alley.

The carillon had been exuberantly heralding St George's Day for a full fifteen minutes. Lucy, almost inaudible against the complex changes of cascading sound, suddenly squeezed Alex's hand, and pointed in the direction of the river with her head. One of the two figures walking towards them had a confident, exaggerated swagger, the sexy elegance of a catwalk model; and Lucy grinned.

It had been an hour after her arrival on Easter Sunday morning, while everyone else was hunting for eggs, that Lucy had found Siân in Will's bedroom in abject silence, sunk against the headboard. The jacket – rent in two – was laid on the bed. Siân plucked at it.

'I never had a chance to say goodbye,' she'd told Lucy. 'He left in such a rage one night – we put off our goodbyes until we weren't so cross with each other. Then we never got to say those words.'

Lucy had thought of responses she might make, but she'd let the silence speak, allowing Siân to choose a reply, then simply hugged her. After tears and reflections, Lucy gently offered: 'Would you let me repair the jacket for you, Siân? I think I can reconcile the halves with neat stitches so you'll still be able to wear it.' She understood – in ways that would probably have mystified Alex and certainly have infuriated Simon – that the coat would serve as an emblem for that leave-taking between them, a strange *memento mori*. Siân had held on to her.

So, late on that Easter Day, while Alex took Max and the others sightseeing in Winchester, Lucy had remained behind with Henry and Siân, stitching skilfully. She had found the leather-working tools in Diana's studio, and quickly learned her way around them. The soothing motion recaptured her hospital days of waiting, and quilting; and she was sentient to the extraordinary change in her fortunes. The contrast with Siân had bothered her – until Henry spoke, allowing Lucy to hear some simple words that had struck Siân dumb.

'We've discussed what would be the best time to tell you, Siân. Alex assures me that time is now, so I'll trust his judgement.' He broke off for a second to reassure her hesitant face that he was not preparing her for any more bad tidings. 'I don't know if you know – perhaps you do – that Will had an insurance policy to cover him in the unsafe places he so often travelled to?'

Siân closed her magazine and looked up at this, uncomprehending, giving Henry her undivided attention. Henry tried to smile, then continued, 'It's easiest to be plain. I'm the executor of Will's estate, and since the coroner's final verdict a month or so ago established he was in no way culpable in his own death, I've had a letter to the effect that half of the policy he had in place – which he renewed only a short time prior – is to be drawn in your favour. In other words, there's a sizeable legacy to come to you. I should have a cheque within the month. I wanted to be able to pass it to you and explain then; but Alex feels you need a little good news now, so I'm pre-empting its arrival.'

In total shock, Siân hedged at this. 'But, Henry, we'd parted. It's surely an oversight?'

'No. Not at all. He decided in June, when he'd already moved out from the flat you shared. Max is the other beneficiary. I think he wanted you to find some happiness, independence, security – even without him. He obviously cared very much for you, Siân. I don't know the precise figure yet; but it will be a solid start towards a flat. And speaking personally, I couldn't be happier. Nor could Alex.'

The extraordinary disclosure, the knowledge that Will cared enough for her to have thought of this, prompted Siân's heavy flow of tears. Lucy leaped up at once and threw her arms around them both with the jacket and a needle still in her hands, pricking herself slightly into the bargain. Instinctively she clutched at the lining for some fabric to cushion the sting and slow the blood, and in the action her fingers came upon something small and firm that had dropped through from the pocket of Will's coat to the interior lining. She knew that the 'something' would almost certainly be golden, with a ruby inset: and she smiled before she looked.

And so on this April morning, as the tourists and theatre patrons were milling about in the church grounds in the atmosphere of fête day, the striking figure of the lovely young woman in a retro-style Ducati classic jacket returned Lucy's wave. As the couple reached Lucy and Alex outside Stratford's Holy Trinity Church, Siân's smile radiated a new warmth that communicated the first real calm in her. Even Alex was grinning at her sexiness in Will's coat, and Lucy admitted to herself for the first time how handsome Calvin seemed today in a light denim shirt, hair ultra-blond and well cut, his height close to Alex's. He was less restrained than at their first encounter, and though he wasn't the kind of man she was drawn to, she understood Siân's attraction better.

'Good morning, Kitty Fisher.' She greeted her with a hug.

Siân laughed aloud, and returned the embrace. 'Good to see you, Lucy Locket.'

Their physical closeness allowed Alex to enjoy the sharp contrast in their personal styles. He appreciated Siân's pertness in her tight jeans and the leather coat; and he adored Lucy in her single-buttoned, grey bolero silk cardigan and tapering silk-linen trousers. He smiled at them both, and, stifling a yawn, dropped in behind the girls with Calvin at his side.

All four headed into the building. It was Friday, 23 April, and though the main celebration for St George's Day was tomorrow, the nearest Saturday to the date proper, floral tributes were already accumulating as the church played host to the curious and the reverential. Alex bought Lucy a photographic permit, and she backed down the aisle to shoot a frame. Will's Leica was the proverbial rose-tinted glass: it lent a softness to the images which she loved. She focused playfully on Alex in the chancel, and saw Calvin discreetly take Siân's hand and move towards the altar. An expensively dressed man was reading in the front row. He exuded polish even at this distance, and she was riveted by him, tense, but unable to look away. When she located Alex through the lens again she relaxed. He was straining across the iron grille which separated Shakespeare's grave from the public.

She joined Alex at the gravestone. Access was denied by an

iron rail, but it was also buried in flowers which irritated her. She consulted a steward in the side aisle and showed him her accreditation. Moments later he accompanied her back to the chancel, reverently moving the tributes while she photographed the bared grave. Alex shook his head in disbelief; her manner often prompted people to grant her wishes. He read:

> **GOOD FREND FOR JESVS SAKE FORBEARE**
> **TO DIGG THE DVST ENCLOASED HEARE**
> **BLEST BE Y MAN Y SPARES THES STONES**
> **AND CVRST BE HE Y MOVES MY BONES.**

Counting had become a habit: the thirty-fourth letter was 'G' – no help, unless one thought of 'gamma' standing in for Chartres in France. He mocked himself for the idea until Lucy leaned against him and whispered: 'The first thirty-four letters spell out: "Good frend for Jesus' sake forbeare to digg." Which confirms to me that it's not this place we want – that nothing exceptional is going to happen here today. What do you think?' She didn't wait for an answer, but gazed at the bust of the playwright watching from the wall. What was he thinking about them down here, pondering a mystery that might all have been of his making? An Elizabethan gentleman, quill in hand. She felt confounded. Then she noticed the opened Bible on the lectern. She nudged Alex. It was open at Psalms. Number forty-six. His eyes narrowed.

She suddenly looked at him. 'Alex, I've just realised. "Will, I am". The theme of the central document. Just count up the value of the letters numerologically. Five plus nine plus three plus three; "I" is nine, and then one and four at the end.' She was shaking her head as it dawned on her, and Alex could guess the sum instantly.

After a further quarter of an hour thinking of alternative 'beginnings' and 'endings', she walked to the door, still unsure what St George's Day would reveal to them – if anything. She passed through the doorway and waited at the porch.

Calvin reached his cousin at the church crossing and touched his arm. Only Alex noticed him flick his eyes in the direction of the front row. He took in the man indicated, and watched him closely for a moment. They awaited Siân, who was walking back from the altar, then stepped through old wooden doors to rejoin Lucy. Emerging into blinding sunlight, they were instantly aware of two men crowding her, one examining the elaborate door-knocker.

'Dr Stafford.' The familiar voice oozed a Kentucky drawl, and Alex's posture stiffened fractionally. 'Guy Temple. We've spoken on the phone.' Siân saw the heavier man obscuring Lucy and touched her cheek defensively. The other man continued speaking. '*Je suis très content de faire votre connaissance.*'

'That makes one of us then.' Alex had the conviction that one of these men had at least some role in his brother's accident, and Lucy's eyes confirmed that the immaculately dressed, heavy-set man blocking her in was the physical force behind her abduction in France.

'I believe the ladies have had the pleasure of Angelo's company on other occasions,' Guy continued with a cynical, threatening smile.

'Could there possibly be anything further we can do for you, Mr Temple?' Alex struggled to keep his voice level, and only narrowly succeeded. Unusually for him, he experienced a real surge of anger. From the corner of his eye he saw Calvin had circled Siân's waist. They all knew what had to be done, and Alex was relieved that Simon had gone in another direction that morning, as in these circumstances it was unlikely he'd be able to contain himself.

'Just curious,' Temple answered him, 'as to whether you've found what we're all looking for?' He and his henchman were now fully blocking the path down the steps.

'If it's a grave you want, you're going the right way.' Alex leaned across the larger man seeking Lucy's hand, but she was just out of reach. 'Though I'm sure there are no angels waiting for you.'

Guy wouldn't be needled by Alex's sarcasm; he had a job to do, and wanted to demonstrate his capacity to achieve their objective with minimal fuss. They still had no clear idea what might happen today, but he was determined not to give that away.

'Omitting the pleasantries, Doctor, you know why we're here; there's no doubt in my mind you were expecting us. The minute we have what we want, we'll vanish into air – into thin air.' Angelo started to back Lucy against the door. 'You're aware we need you or Miss King. We think she is the key – if not the key-holder. We'd hate to tempt fate and force the locks.'

This Rapture doctrine was nothing if not devout to its message, and superstitious in every detail, Alex realised grimly, understanding they genuinely expected to be caught up in their clouds to meet the Lord, on this very day.

Lucy now swerved to evade her minder, and challenged Temple: 'Have you any idea where this lock will be found?'

'You'll tell me that, Lady of Light. You're the Ariadne who'll lead us out of the labyrinth. When you accept that our interest is both inevitable and legitimate, and that it's in *your* interests to get us through these forthrights and meanders, Angelo will escort you back to your guardian angel here, no strings attached.'

Lucy glowered at him. How could he call their interest 'legitimate'? He read the thought and answered her.

'Oh, yes, Miss King: we've waited our time too. We knew all about Dee's interest in the Apocalypse. And we knew that *that* time and *this* time were carefully measured – that there is an optimum moment for it to come to light. All measurements are open to interpretation; but Dee had angelic advice. What little we've learned from Calvin has only consolidated what we knew already.'

Until this time, Calvin had been hovering between inaction and controlled aggression; but now he spoke to ease the sense of rising hostility that was becoming apparent in the body language of Angelo. He, Calvin realised, was the loose cannon in the group; Alex had quickly come to the same conclusion.

'I believe that FW would want us to find a calm resolution to this, Guy,' he said mildly. He was also tacitly addressing Angelo, the minder.

Lucy flinched when she heard Calvin say Temple's name with a French pronunciation, suggesting a closer relationship between the men than she'd expected; she looked to Alex for direction, but he was thinking quickly on his feet. Coming face to face with Angelo, who had obviously been both Lucy's kidnapper and Siân's assailant – and very probably Max's too, he thought, marrying his son's description with the size of the man here – all previous discussion and conjecture about what to do if they appeared here at Stratford seemed meaningless. He'd been over this with Calvin, who seemed convinced they would avoid violence if they weren't thwarted to their 'find'. But Alex, seeing Angelo for the first time, identified real anger in him. He was definitely unreliable, and surely had been the cause of Will's accident. Temple lacked control over him, he decided, and all bets were off. He was swiftly reworking their plans in his mind. Lucy should not be separated from the group.

Calvin could easily see Alex's thought processes at work and took Temple by the arm, steering him away from the church porch towards the lawn, enabling the others to follow – though trailed by the physical bulk of Angelo. The change of vantage point made Alex notice another man, taller, also immaculately dressed, waiting alone at the bottom of the path, near the roadway. Though still as the grave, he was watching them closely.

'You will have to convince Dr Stafford that Lucy would be safe on her own with you, or lose his help altogether. Which it would appear, from the riddles, you'll need.' Calvin's voice told Lucy nothing about his real feelings for Guy Temple. 'It seems to me,' he was saying, 'that Angelo is the problem.' Calvin was almost appearing to confide in him as they strolled together beside the tranquil, grassy space.

'Calvin,' Temple halted to address him, 'it seems to me that they don't, after all, know where they are headed on this vital date, even if FW believes differently. He's been wrong before.' Temple's response showed Calvin – and Alex, who had almost caught them up – that he was at something of a loss, unsure how to proceed. 'And in any case,' Temple was adding, with one finger raised to still the man at the end of the pathway, 'I'm sure Dr Stafford will flatly refuse his consent to our taking Lucy on her own – with or without Angelo – even if she were willing to go.'

Alex had overheard enough, and now offered himself – without hesitation – to accompany Temple and his pair of shadows. 'As long as Siân and Lucy are allowed to go free immediately. Without conditions,' he added emphatically, in a tone that precluded discussion.

But Temple's response was a flat 'No'. 'She's quite obviously our insurance policy that there'll be no tricks.'

The moment dallied, the impasse deepening as the whole group hovered in the half-sunlight. Angelo was standing far too close to Lucy for Alex's comfort, and he was trying to decide what might happen in such a public location if they simply risked pushing past them. But – his concerns for Max and Anna aside – he knew they had to bring this to an end. These people would keep coming at them, especially if they had a sense of divine permission and an imminent event.

Lucy had watched Alex's expressions subtly changing. His anxieties would be opaque to others, but she could sense them now, and came quickly to a decision. She proposed a new solution: she would go, after all, with Temple and his man Angelo, provided they allowed Alex, Siân and Calvin to leave, without caveat.

'Out of the question,' Alex said in front of Temple and Angelo as if they weren't there. 'These men orchestrated your abduction in France, the break-in at my family home, the strikes on Max and Siân in London. God knows what they did to Will, but I know the police would love to get their hands on them. They've broken faith with every agreement they've made with me. Do you imagine for a second I'm going to trust them now?'

'Alex, they're not after me. You know that,' she said. 'They want whatever there is to be found: and perhaps so do we. Nothing but that discovery will bring a conclusion to all this.' She met him eye to eye and stood her ground, a smile flickering across her face, before turning fully to Temple. 'You've just acknowledged that I'm your Ariadne. You understand from the clues that it's me you need.' She challenged him. 'I'm quite sure now where the final answer will be.' She said the penultimate word with special emphasis. 'Stratford has proved a dead end, but I'm still the one who has the means to open the final lock.' Carefully, she drew an intricate, ruby-inset gold key from under her shirt, and everyone's eyes engaged with it. Calvin's widened, and Alex's eyes burned with questions; there was something unfathomable in them to everyone except Lucy.

'All the more reason not to go alone with them,' Alex stated firmly. 'Whatever it is we're searching for has been hidden and protected for centuries – surely to preserve the wisdom or knowledge it contains from people such as these.'

'There you are wrong, Dr Stafford,' the French-American

broke in. 'The "end of time" scenario is inevitable. It is written and fixed. Nothing you or I can do will hold it back.'

'Which is exactly my reason for not wanting Lucy to go with you.' Alex's voice was resolute. 'We should be looking for ways to make the world a better place, not bent on the destruction of society through your potentially self-fulfilling prophecies. Surely any ideology or philosophy worth listening to is concerned with teaching us how to live successfully, rather than how to die with some kind of assurance of salvation? Hope is the faith that drives us – whether through God, or science, or both. Any group of people who can only advocate the inevitability of an "Armageddon" have abandoned the planet, and all hope. You're dragging us all to an utterly hopeless place, where no just or loving God would want to take his people.'

'As you like, Dr Stafford,' Temple replied wearily. He turned his eyes from Alex, refusing to engage.

Alex knew it was pointless. He was desperate to encourage others to think, but Temple preferred only to bully believers through fear. Nothing would move him. How was it possible to convince anyone so entrenched that the use of fear and violence should have no place in what was, essentially, a debate about faith?

Lucy moved quietly forwards and joined Alex in the sunlight. She smiled at him and took both of his hands, and a secret passed between them. 'You have presented that just as your father would have done, and I agree with you. I'm not sure whether to laugh or cry, Alex, and you're a brilliant advocate for any *reasoning* jury. But I'm going to go with them because, in spite of what you say . . .' She looked straight into his eyes. 'Lucy Locket lost her pocket. Then, Kitty Fisher found it.'

Alex had argued eloquently, from his heart, in front of everyone, to shift her determination to go with them. It had been an impressive performance. But she was as adamant as ever.

They kissed. 'Alex, you're the one person I've met who understands real strength is not only controlled anger, but very often controlled *in*action. Be strong now and trust me to be active in your stead.'

He was silenced, and hugged her.

'And don't worry,' she added. 'You know there's an angel in me.'

She turned to follow Temple towards the roadway. As she did so, another shadow slipped from the church and was hastening to a large, dark grey Lancia Thesis – a car none of them had noticed – parked at the bottom of the path. Lucy turned back briefly, her eyes making contact with Alex alone; then she and her odd 'allies' were gone.

At seven thirty, Simon answered his mobile and the question put to him. 'Grace and I are famished. We're tucking into cod and chips at a pub called The Herne's Oak in Old Windsor. Appropriate, don't you think? Herne's another incarnation of Green George.'

'You're eating a better dinner than we are,' Alex said, looking at the three tense faces opposite him, all hunched over Calvin's laptop. The sandwiches were untouched. No one – least of all Alex – had any appetite. 'Did you find anything?'

'Yes and no. Nothing material to get excited about, Alex. Mortlake was a complete waste of time – just as Lucy thought. That's not the right alpha and omega. So we came straight on to St George's best-known chapel here in Windsor. We had one pair of very dark eyes trained on us all day – he's still trailing us here at the pub somewhere – but you were the main draw. Definitely no treasure chests here, but a lot of carved angels. However,' Simon said with emphasis, 'we have come up with an unexpected prize. Listen to this.' He drew his shorthand pad from his jacket pocket, and looked around quickly to see if anyone were obviously listening. When Grace's nod confirmed that their spy was just about within earshot, Simon began a short, strange saga.

It had been precisely 3.40 p.m. GMT when the ceremonial nature of the day had ebbed away. Grace squeezed Simon's hand in a half-gesture of panic. Completely absorbed in the Garter Stalls at St George's Chapel, they were suddenly alerted to footsteps echoing through the huge building; and Grace's nerves strained at the approach of a robed figure, his eyes fixed on them. When he was close enough for Grace to see the pores of his skin, a smile warmed his face, and a verger introduced himself. Why were they interested in the emblems and banners in the ancient stalls, he wondered. Grace demonstrated her passion for history and heraldry, which delighted him, and a floodgate opened. An alchemist and a self-confessed Rosicrucian, he took them on a tour of the exquisite building, explaining that the white roses – so much in evidence – are a symbol of female in alchemy, and to the

Rosicrucians. The frequently missed message about the white rose of York, he told them proudly, is that they were descended from Edward III through the female line; red Lancaster was male. Answering a stream of Grace's fervent questions, white roses were revealed as the unclouded hopes of a pure heart and good judgement over selfish passion.

'It should be everyone's spiritual goal,' he'd told them.

'I've made notes, Alex.' Simon spoke softly into his phone. 'All initiates of this ancient wisdom strive to be "open to the grace of the rose". That's something Will wrote – remember? The rose is commonly associated with romantic love; but this uncanny messenger today told us it paradoxically encodes purity and passion, earthly desire and heavenly perfection, virginity and fertility, life and death. It was as though he were sent to tell us that the rose itself links the goddesses Isis and Venus with the blood of Osiris, Adonis and Christ. The male red rose, when married to the white – like the Tudor rose – becomes the basis of magic and the metamorphosis of the soul. He called it "the means by which we distil the *divine* in ourselves".'

Alex interrupted: 'That's the metaphor for this whole quest of Dee's, Simon. The message of the rose is common to all spiritual, and even aesthetic philosophies. If we can blend the contrasted characteristics it represents, we become godlike – the best we can aspire to be. Put simply, the white and red roses married represent a celestial wedding – the best expression of "male" and "female" on earth.'

Simon wasn't sure he'd kept pace with Alex, but he nodded, checked his notes, went on. 'The white rose specifically concerns purity and innocence, acceptance, unconditional love. It is about feminine, and sometimes necessarily passive, energy, and it is chosen for the initiation of all new members into the Old Wisdom. The boar slaying Adonis is the winter slaying summer – which is the key philosophy for the Rosicrucians. When Adonis, the Sun, is slain by the boar, the flowers appearing from his blood prompt resurrection – which is very sexual and female too, as Henry said. And you know who was a founding father of the Rosicrucians, Alex?'

There was no need to answer. 'That's a fine piece of unexpected research, Simon. What an other-worldly emissary. And how oddly timed. Your account makes me feel he was waiting for you. Surely his appearance is no coincidence.' But who sent him? Alex was wondering. Did other people know something about this day? 'What about St George?'

'The Rosy Cross brothers took off in Germany early in the seventeenth century, directly after Dee's mission to Prague in the 1580s, which Queen Elizabeth and Leicester encouraged. Dee in person spread the Elizabethan movement of scientific, mystical and poetic ideas. The "Rose Cross" name comes from the St George Cross and English chivalry – the garter was the prestigious medieval honour in Europe, and still is.'

Impatiently, and quite unusually for her, Grace suddenly prised the phone from Simon to speak briefly to Alex, wanting to impart to him the whole of what she had taken from their extraordinary exchange that afternoon, which had made enormous impact on her.

'Alex, about the rose: Dee chose it – as others had before him – because it's *the* symbol that ties us together as a whole brotherhood of mankind. And if we can understand its message, and then we combine the dew, as you said – the divine breath – with the spirit of the rose, it performs some expression of magic to transmute the human soul into gold, and perform an act of healing. That's the theory, and I love the very idea of it.'

Alex had listened to her intently, without judgement, appreciative of the philosophy behind it. 'Thank you, Grace. That's beautifully expressed.'

'Oh, and one final thing, Alex,' Simon had the phone back. 'Cast your mind back to Will's unsent email to you. Our alchemist verger tells me that initiates of alchemy and masonry, and the Rosicrucians – following Bruno and Dee – focus on light as the Divine Source. They attend so-called "light meetings", when adepts of the past and present link together, across time, to share "the light and wisdom of the rose". Can you see the significance of light pouring through a rose window in a great church like Chartres? That's where Will's head was at. I wonder whether he ever managed to make that link with others – across time and space? Anyway, what's happening your end?'

Alex was mesmerised by this flow of extraordinary information, and paused before answering Simon's penultimate question. 'Simon, I rather think he did. But I can't quite explain why I feel this.' He recalled Lucy's words about the light, the rose scent in Chartres, and knew she had experienced something very unusual – that she possibly shared with his brother. It made him feel very privileged to be close to her, and also much less afraid for her. 'They took the bait,' he now resumed his report of the day's events. 'Lucy's with them. I almost couldn't let her go, when it came to it. She's been in their company for hours now.'

'Don't worry about her, Alex. Lucy's unique. She's one of Shakespeare's creatures – a true cross-dressed heroine, like Viola or Rosalind. She'll outwit them.'

Alex reflected that Simon was more right than he knew; but he was comforted by the objective appraisal. 'I know. I've got to go. I'll see you here later. Check if you're still being followed. Those dark eyes belong to an intolerant Israeli whom I ran across in France – Ben Dovid is his name. He's with Temple and Walters because he wants his own Temple in Jerusalem. Calvin got up close and personal with him over Easter. He's very keen on the idea of blowing up the mosques at the Temple Mount. Don't provoke him.'

Alex knew Simon would be wondering why Calvin might have relayed that information, but he made no reply about it, and Alex disconnected, dialling a second number instantly.

Flanked by the yellow-eyed Angelo and the taller, grey Frenchman who had driven Lucy in France – both standing at a short distance – the immaculately attired figure of Professor Fitzalan Walters presided over the private dining table in his hotel suite. He poured the wine for his guest with exaggerated politeness, and stopped at half a glass. 'I know you're not allowed to drink; alcohol inhibits your medication. But a little won't do any harm. This white burgundy is the perfect partner to the monkfish.'

Lucy's posture had been a study in poise, in an effort to

communicate her self-control and independent will; but, chilled by this further implication of how much he knew about her, it was once again tested. The questions he'd asked earlier about how old she'd been when her mother left Sydney had her reeling, but she'd tried to conceal her alarm. Her phone started ringing on the table beside her.

'I'm sure it's Alex. He'll be worried about me. Best to let me answer.' Her dinner companion assented without debate. It was eerie how genteel, intelligent and well-mannered he was.

'I'm all right, Alex. And before you ask, yes, I'm eating. I'm being given a fine dinner, in fact. Eat something yourself. I'm sure I can call you the minute we've completed our business.' Lucy struggled to hide the emotion his voice sparked; she didn't want to show weakness. She rang off and raised her eyes defiantly, noticing that her dinner companion's eyes were intent on the rubied key that peeped from inside her cardigan.

'How fortunate you've been, Miss King, to have had such personal concern from your physician. Could he be disciplined for it? I thought it was acceptable to lose a patient, but never to sleep with one.' Lucy couldn't decide whether this revealed a distaste for sensual relationships, or an understated voyeurism about them. She didn't blink, however, ignoring his impertinence, and he changed tack. 'Why wait until after eleven tonight?' He was softly spoken, and thus more menacing. The panelled door of the Tudor-style hotel suite opened and closed, and Guy Temple rejoined them, without contributing to the conversation.

'Firstly,' she answered him, 'it will be easier if the White Hart has closed, otherwise there'll be too many potentially curious witnesses. Secondly, I believe that the time has to be absolutely precise. If my calculations are correct it will be exactly four degrees of Taurus near midnight tonight. Something is ordained to happen.'

'I see. The hour when Hamlet sees the ghost. Poetic. And this building you've agreed to take us to. You think this is definitely the right one?'

'It has to be. Mortlake was Dee's ending, but not his beginning – he was born in the Tower of London wards. And though Stratford was Shakespeare's beginning and ending, he couldn't have known this prior to his death. I'm sure from the clues that he is the author of the riddles – probably for John Dee. So it must be the inn. It's the only place left where all the clues merge. The white stag, Shakespeare, the rose, Venus and Adonis. It seems to have been their chosen meeting place for esoteric discussions.'

All three together had spent the greater part of the afternoon at the Alveston Manor in Stratford in Walters' suite, conferring over texts. Lucy looked carefully at the originals again, feeling a renewed pleasure in touching them. She was amused that her captors had missed the patterned labyrinth on the reverse of the sheets – and thus failed to notice the face, which was so clear once the lines married. Only a bright seven year old had immediately seen the relevance of that, and she decided not to enlighten them now. But on the other hand, they had possession of Diana's remarkable family Bible, dating from the seventeenth century – an object that had filled Lucy with strength just to hold. It made her feel sick that they had plundered it, pored over it; that it had in fact supplied the thieves with a vast amount of annotation that she and Alex had lacked. But it had kept back several of its secrets from the unfaithful too. Several of the words she had noticed, picked out on the embroidered document case, were written again here: throughout Proverbs, all of the items about wisdom, and pearls, and rubies, were marked, and the lines of verse that concluded each parchment were copied out here, on the half-title page of the Bible, surrounding the mysterious Tablet of Jupiter square, which fired Lucy's thoughts. Did it suggest there was some counting to be done with these words, as with the psalm Alex had decoded? She felt that with study, it would yield up a clear message.

In addition, there was a tiny reproduction of the so-called 'rainbow portrait' of Queen Elizabeth painted by hand into the inside back cover, with references in the margin to 'Astraea', the goddess of justice, as Henry had suggested. It was also dotted with marginalia from Proverbs about the pearls and rubies and Wisdom – always called 'she.' So, it dawned on Lucy, Queen Elizabeth, bedecked in pearls and rubies, had been packaged as the living embodiment of Wisdom, down-playing any negatives about being a female ruler; perhaps Dee was one of her propagandists – the original agent of 'spin'? And, Lucy realised, something significant must have been anticipated by Dee in this, their own current age, under the dominion of another wise and powerful woman to come, just as Henry alluded. Frustratingly, it posed many new riddles, and she thought quietly on this while she sat drinking tea. Not one word about any of it, though, did she share with her present company.

The Bible had got them to Stratford, Shakespeare's 'alpha' and 'omega'. Now, it remained for her to convince them where the 'pot of gold' described in the last text – written by Diana herself – would be found. It was just a week ago, she explained to them, when she had been researching the background to Shakespeare's poem, *Venus and Adonis*, on the web, that she had first found mention of what she believed in her heart must be of major significance. On the professor's expensive notebook, she asked him to enter the relevant data, and they watched together as the images loaded: a magnificent contemporary painting of Shakespeare's published work – the only one in existence, a 'national treasure' according to one enthusiastic source. Uncovered almost by accident as some panelling was stripped to mend an old wall, the narrative mural had only recently seen daylight again for the first time in centuries. What secrets did it conceal about the original purpose of the room? What rituals had it watched over, and why had such an image been painted on the ordinary wall of an unassuming inn in the first place? The data indicated that it seemed to date to the year 1600: so close to Giordano Bruno's death. When she and Alex discussed the possibility that it might be involved in their quest, he had thought it apt that the shrine of England's first martyr could launch the Rapture for the professor's followers. 'Why not?' he'd shrugged. And though she kept this dry comment from them now, she fully enthused the two men at her side with her narrative, and her suggestion of the old White Hart Inn at St Albans, of a room of long-ago predictions, and of a revelation to come.

So now Lucy used her own mobile and made the necessary phone call, to arrange getting some keys for the unused part of the building tonight. 'It must be tonight,' she insisted.

'And the alpha-omega clue?' Guy Temple asked her.

'I imagine the White Hart is the place where they first formed the idea for this quest, and thus, where it will end.' Lucy had a confidence about her that was compelling.

'And, by corollary, something else begins once we find whatever is interred there.' Professor Walters seemed satisfied, and he and Temple agreed with Lucy. 'So the Rapture will begin toward midnight tonight, and no sooner,' Fitzalan pondered, circling his wine in its balloon-shaped glass. 'They have understood the significance of this special date for hundreds of years: the number, the Realisation of Man. It's the number linked with the foundation stone of the entire world, the core of the Temple in Jerusalem. But Dee must have had this application about its timing directly from the angels, and we're in the right place at the right time – or we will be. For now we can linger over dinner,' Walters suggested, 'and you'll follow the fish with a fruit course. What you eat before initiation – it's very important. Like the last supper. A fitting preparation for a convocation of angels and men. Even Prospero fed Ferdinand on mussels and sea water before he was granted a vision of the gods beside his future bride. And we must be prepared for something very extraordinary tonight, Miss King.'

She realised he was warming to his theme and speaking about seemingly desultory ideas. Perhaps they were linked in ways she couldn't yet appreciate. He rattled on: 'Guy never misses his fruit now, you understand. Did you know he'd had open heart surgery too? A bypass. Had a near-death experience, actually. I'm surprised he didn't share this with you while you two were sequestered in France. An angel spoke to him. Just the once.' Lucy detected cynicism. 'And he's a healthy eater now.'

Lucy thought it strange that the man being spoken of made no comment whatsoever. He looked a little anxious, in her opinion.

It was twenty minutes before midnight by the clock inset in the walnut dashboard of Fitzalan Walters' Lancia – a more commodious model than the sleek, smaller coupé that had stolen her in France – when they turned between the arches into the courtyard car park of the White Hart Hotel. Angelo, seated next to her, now opened the car door for Lucy, and Temple lurched from the front passenger seat. She was speechless at the charade of chivalry, until it dawned on her that they really believed they were about to witness a special religious moment.

'I'll be at the front door with Angelo in ten minutes,' Walters told them, relaxing back into the leather as the car pulled away.

The oddly paired Temple and Lucy headed towards the hotel reception desk.

'Lucy King. I work for a television company – I phoned a few hours ago. Is there someone here called Mr McBeath?' Lucy asked this of a girl who wasn't at all interested in latecomers to the hotel, whoever they worked for. She hardly lifted her eyes from the ledger in front of her to look at them. She obviously knew nothing about the Rapture, Lucy thought with a smile.

'Ross!' she called up the stairs; and Lucy and her chaperone were left waiting in poor light.

32

St George's Day, 1608, At the White Hart Inn, near London

The candles sputter, and two large salvers are cleared from the rose-strewn trestle. More wine is passed around, and a toast proposed.

'Now does our project gather to a head. In this last hour of the feast of St George, let us drink: To Berowne!' Seemingly unaffected by the amount he has been drinking, the man at one end of the table springs energetically to his feet, shunting back his chair. The theme of the toast is heartily espoused by all of his companions. Some places at the table are empty, and the room rings out with intoxicated laughter in the smoky light.

'But, Will, you ask of him the labours of a true initiate. How shall he, then, inspire the speechless sick to smile?' A long-limbed man interrupts the release of smoke from a pipe to address his master of ceremonies.

At the other end of the table an old man moves forward. He is clearly the chief of this company. His face is lined and scarred with worry, but alive with interest at the unfolding discussion.

'And what hope has he, Will, besides, to turn the heartless zealots from their course? Those who would bear the sword of heaven should be as holy as they are severe. Into what poverty of spirit these men have fallen, and what they hide inside, though angels on their outmost side.' He pushes a small crystal sphere away from him.

The younger man seats himself again. 'Good Doctor, and Lord Francis, know ye not, love is tutored in a lady's eyes, giving every power an added power. Such love boasts the labours of a Hercules. The poet, indeed, ought not take up his pen until his ink is tempered with love's sighs . . . Oh, he will triumph – for have we not willed it so? The red rose king shall win back his white rose queen, and naught shall go ill. In black his lady's brows are decked, and thus again shall she prove that unfashionable complexion fair. A true angel of melancholy. Her dark beauty is heavenly and her countenance wise – the inspiration to his genius, and a spur to his wit.'

A raven-haired woman, seated at the left of the older man at one end of the table, raises her head and her drink in salute. 'To Rosa Mundi, then, Will – two blent as one. The secret heart of love.' From end to end of the long table their eyes are now fastened on each other. The eroticism is disturbed only by the sound of footsteps on the stairs behind the fireplace, coming from the passageway that leads into the meeting room from the main body of the White Hart Inn.

In a moment a door, flush with the panelling, has opened. All faces turn, scrutinising the latecomers; all eyes seem to challenge them unblinking; until the man who had proposed the toast rises again quietly:

> 'Thou blind fool, Love, what dost thou to mine eyes,
> That they behold, and see not what they see?'

A dark-haired, dark-eyed, fresh-faced beauty is hovering in the doorway; then she spills into the room in semi-darkness, leaving her open-mouthed companion rooted to the spot where he stands. She is aware of the faces in the room fixed on her, the cold silence, broken only by the harsh metallic sound of the keys that suddenly jangle so loudly in her hand. A strange odour pervades the room, which is not altogether a pleasant one. Her emotions are taut, and she can hear her pulse in her ears. She is aware of feeling like a child who has disturbed adults at dinner. She breathes purposefully slowly; then she floats to the opposite doorway, which has been curtained off. The fire is spitting: and she knows that she is 'in' the moment.

'This is it,' she whispers. 'Nothing enraptured, no angel – unless it be me.'

Now she prevaricates, and stares at the man who has spoken to her. His is a strangely familiar face, and he is speaking to her again, and to his friends.

'Gentlemen, and dear ladies. No remedy, when this "lady of light" proves afresh that beauty herself is black.' His gaze shifts from the raven-haired lady at the table, to the equally dark-headed Lucy.

Lucy plucks up the courage to confront him without shrinking. 'Through the wall's chink, poor souls, must we be content to whisper,' she says. The company implode in laughter – everyone other than the oldest man, at the far end of the table. His eyes are restless.

'The lady of light, Will?'

'No other, Your Grace: a vision which, by thine art and mine, we have called to enact our present fancy.'

'Know you, then, lady, that the rose gives us that which is undying.' Dr John Dee looks at the beautiful, welcome intruder. 'And truly, when you understand its meaning, embrace its nature to the very core, a healing of all that is askew shall follow, shall come to the philosopher's child. We each of us seek, everyone here, to possess the Rose in the desert, which blooms at the centre of the labyrinth.'

Riveted by these words and yet unable quite to grasp their meaning, Lucy turns from the man who is clearly their elder, and looks again at the riddler, the man they call Will, and whom she would choose to call Will Shakespeare, if she dared. She is searching for some word, some question: but he is there already, and speaks now to Lucy herself: 'You must remain, decide the ending for our play. And you must do it extempore, for the words are in your characters. So, for now, you that way, we this way.'

The words are crowding Lucy's mind – a din in her ear, inaudible against the noise of her heart. All other sounds are becoming dulled. On the wall behind them she glimpses the painting. She stops suddenly, scouring it for details in the dim light. She is at ease with the images – if not with these strange souls in the room. Her eyes begin absorbing the freshly painted horse, with a rose in its mouth; and she sees also a knight, tumbling at the horse's hoofs. There is a tree with a gaping hole at the base of its trunk. Her head feels tight, and her ears are hollow again. She believes she must be dreaming, but *knows* certainly she is not. Her mind moves to the soft focus of Will's Leica, and of Alex reminding her of the effect of her drugs when taken with a glass of wine, as on that night on the Thames. How many ways of seeing are there? she thought. And is Alex right?

The laughter is now clanging, the sounds close to disturbing, the moment fleeting. She unfastens the front door quickly to the street opposite the passage from which she and Guy Temple have just come. When she turns round again, the other occupants of the room are gone. It has never happened. Using a disused entrance to avoid prying eyes she has caught the room as it once was, when her name was first spoken here by them hundreds of years before. The moment itself, she thinks, was a palindrome.

All the light is now extinguished except for the small shaft thrown by the torch which the manager had given them at the hotel desk to find their way through the old, seldom-used passage to the adjacent pottery shop, which had been a part of the pub's suite of rooms for hundreds of years.

And now Lucy notices that Guy Temple, perhaps nervous and unsettled by what they have just seen, is slumped against the door-frame, looking grey and ill.

As Lucy unlocked the main shop-front door, the compact figure of Fitzalan Walters entered – trailed as usual by the broad-shouldered Lucifer, as he sometimes called Angelo.

He experienced a strange frisson on seeing Lucy's expression and physical being. The atmosphere was charged, and the air dank with an inherent smell of soot. He glanced at Temple, spoke coolly to him: 'Someone trodden on your grave, Guy?' Temple was feeling too ill to argue or explain, and he supported himself against the wall, flashing his torch at the mural, which was now occupying Lucy.

Lucy was discomforted: she noted that the details seemed less vivid, less complete, than they had been a moment ago. Then she saw that the mural was in fact screened by glass, and appeared smaller. But her eyes told Walters nothing about its apparently changed state. 'The final pointer must be here somewhere,' she said with vigour. '"I want to change the Wall, and make my Will," the central text says. This painting is of Adonis slain by the boar – he has an Elizabethan ruff. Perhaps the rose, in the white horse's mouth above, or in the bridle here, marks a spot?'

Walters grappled unproductively with the electricity switches, disappointed to have such poor light to scrutinise the work before him. Water damage from the bathroom above had required them to cut the power, Lucy was telling Walters as he continued flicking switches. He could see the seepage from the top right-hand corner. What a blasphemy for such a valuable and unique work of art.

'So, Miss King, this is Shakespeare's *Venus and Adonis*, painted about the time the poem was published?'

Lucy nodded. 'It must have been a meeting place for a mystical order originally inspired by Dee – the Rosicrucians in their infancy. Shakespeare would have convened here with them, and Bacon was a leading member too. So were

Spenser and John Donne, and Sir Philip Sidney before his early death – all the Elizabethan men of letters.' And maybe a brilliant woman of letters too, she thought. She shone her light over the painting and it danced on a central image of a horse and rider, the Red-Cross Knight, St George. 'Spenser writes about him in *The Faerie Queen*. In the painting here the horse is poised over Adonis, the Oriental "Lord of the Sun".' Lucy broke off to enjoy the mural, identifying the boar on the right of the painting which symbolised winter, whose destructive powers were reversed when Adonis came back to life via the red-blooming flowers in the foreground, springing from his wound. 'Venus' love and grief causes his renewal,' she told Walters defiantly. 'There are clear parallels with the Christian story. In fact, depictions of her holding the dead Adonis were the inspiration for the Pietàs in art.'

She was challenging him to make the simple connection between pagan iconography and Christian myth, but he latched on to the painting instead and ignored any parallels. The professor and Angelo were concentrating, but she noticed that Temple seemed absent and far from self-composed beside them.

'Adonis was a principal figure for Dee.' She focused her torch. 'This rose represents both his soul and his heart. The Rosicrucians were intent on turning darkness into light, winter to summer – a different view of resurrection.' Lucy's words hung in the air, and everything meant something further for her about Will.

'Yes, very different. So, what were the Rosicrucians after?' Walters asked her.

'Religious enlightenment, partially through magic. It gave

them a mathematical approach to the physical world. Mathematics acquainted them with the second world, the celestial world. But above that is a third – supreme heaven, the super-celestial world. This is higher than Paradise, and you could reach it only with the help of angelic conjuration. They imagined that, once they'd reached this higher level through magic, they would be *one* with the angel hierarchy, where all religions were one. Dee believed this, and thought he'd made contact with good angels. Sadly for Dee, only Edward Kelley spoke to them, passing messages, and he was unreliable. But the movement as Dee conceived it included all religious attitudes, Protestant and Catholic, Jewish and Muslim. All were one at the level of the angels.'

If Lucy hoped this message of commonality and greater spiritual aspiration for all would affect these men, she was disappointed. She looked at them – one grasping his middle as though he had crippling indigestion, the other sure of his own rightness and his own messages from his own 'angels', looking back at her unblinking. She grinned, determined to push her luck with him.

'The three worlds are fascinating, don't you agree? In the physical world we use our earthly body, and in the celestial world, we need our spirit and unselfish emotions. But only in higher paradise do we exercise our intellect. Adam and Eve dwelled in demi-paradise, Eden, but when Eve seized the fruit of knowledge, she was asking for access to the highest heaven. Woman it was, who wanted to lift us from ignorance and have true knowledge; and an ignorant man, it surely is, who could still believe true knowledge should be a male preserve.'

Walters looked at her with irritation. He'd heard this claptrap, pro-feminist, pro-humanist heresy before, which argued that man had the capacity to be god if he were enlightened by knowledge; that he was divine himself. Women, by this dictum, were to be congratulated for wanting to be better educated! But female academics had infiltrated the system, upset the balance, caused moral decay and permanent chaos in the home, changed the basis of marital relationships, and decreased in their respect for men. Walters wanted to get to the prize quickly, however, so he decided to indulge her.

'You're a well-read young woman, Miss King. I can see Dee and his circle were drawn to alchemy, which is a pure translation of the realities of a religious life – the transmutation of the soul from base material to gold.'

Lucy knew he wanted to add, '. . . however misguided'. She turned back to Venus and Adonis. It was a shame not to have better light to examine the images, which were bursting with riddles about Dee and Shakespeare's Hermetic philosophy. 'I want to change the wall . . .' she thought. She could see the words in fiery letters from the page that she had carried through the Chartres labyrinth.

She was aware that Temple, standing near her, was still fidgety. He'd been in some physical distress since witnessing the scene they had unwittingly stumbled in upon. He was an ardent believer, she thought, but he undoubtedly couldn't explain what had happened and was extremely nervous that they might be the victims of some kind of demonology at first hand. It would have made her laugh – but compassion prevented such a callous response. She'd been startled by the spirits of the room; he, she felt, had been genuinely frightened. Just now he too had started chanting the text that had come into her own head. Was it some attempt to placate the apparitions, prevent their return?

'"I want to change the Wall, and make my Will",' he said aloud. '"Wondering what I am or what I ever was." Where is our quarry, FW? We're looking for an object or door, Miss King, that the key fits, aren't we? Is there an opening concealed somewhere in the mural?'

Lucy's eyes ranged over the painting, looking to answer him. She was trying to put together the details she and Alex had talked of before, identify the clues he must have identified. Desperate for her not to look well rehearsed, he'd mentioned only some panelling: did he mean the glass protecting the painting? She answered Guy Temple with genuine uncertainty: 'They can't be urging us to desecrate this. Surely, we have to "change the wall" to find what was left in "the will".' By Will, she thought, and 'for Will'. 'It must be another façade, perhaps on a parallel with the rose, or Adonis – as he is the resurrected figure.'

Temple chanted on, like a holy man bereft of sense, as they turned to the other solid walls in the room. Lucy had a flash of insight. 'All that is aflame . . .' 'Every jointed piece . . .' She spoke fervently: 'This wall housed the fireplace. It must be here – behind the fine woodwork. There must be a cranny through which the fearful lovers can uncover the past.'

Walters understood her references from the old text, and wondered only why she thought a fireplace might be somewhere in this wall. Being internal, with room for a chimney above, it was plausible enough. 'Shall we strip this away, then? It would bring your heritage authorities out in a sweat, but you may be right.'

In ten minutes – all four of them groping along the panels – they had found the chink. Walters called to Temple: 'Guy, have you got that Leatherman tool, on your key chain?'

Temple stopped mumbling the strange rosary that was inspired by the texts. 'Yes. Yes, FW.' He responded wanly, feeling coldness in his limbs and chest, wondering if he was sickening like the archaeologists who open up a long-closed tomb and unleash a virus. The atmosphere in the room was claustrophobic, and he recognised from past association that his boss was inappropriately close to a state of elation. He had no energy to join him in that demi-paradise and was wondering every minute whether the demons and the vile smells of smoke and ale, urine and bad food would return.

'Bring it. Loosen some of this panelling.' Walters pointed to a place in the timbers. Temple tried rather ineffectually to prise it apart until Walters handed him the torch scornfully and took the blade himself. He started to probe frantically at the wall. Both were caught in the tension of the moment when the panel gave way without warning, forcing out a loud crash and a billow of dust. A section of wood cladding and a heap of bricks collapsed into the room. Lucy shrieked nervously, caught off guard by the clatter; and in his muddled state Temple dropped the torch, which smashed against the masonry on the floor.

'Miss King, your light please. Guy has left us in the dark.' Walters' sarcasm was icy as he bent in the dim room. Lucy flashed a steady beam into the alcove containing the inscribed box, and Walters whistled softly. 'That'll do. An old oven bricked up for years alongside the main hearth. Angelo, get this coffer out into the room. We're on the edge of greatness. Thomas Brightman told us that the first of the great seven vials was Elizabeth's succession to the throne in 1558. The seventh Trumpet of the Revelation was sounded in 1588 with the destruction of the Armada. It is appropriate that the most happy tranquillity from thence to the end of the world should proceed now from the rediscovery of this lost knowledge from the great men of her reign. Who knows? Perhaps the chests contain the actual seventh vial. This is a truly apocalyptic moment.'

Lucy had pulled back fractionally, observing an unholy colour in her captor's face. Now a strange fever emanated from his apparently senior colleague too. Together they truly frightened her, and she hoped she wasn't far from the end of the whole ordeal. There was no reasoning with either of them from this point. She had read about these so-called 'seven vials' in her research on Dee and Bruno; she knew about Thomas Brightman. He had counted trumpets and vials from Romans and Revelations, and decided upon a date for the 'calling of the Jews to be a Christian nation'. The anticipated date for this was in the 1630s; but when this failed to materialise, dates and numbers and historical events had been shifted and reordered. Lucy thought that honest record-keepers must be up to at least seventy vials by now – and heaven knew how many trumpets – but she thought this was a bad time to dispute Walters' mathematics.

Angelo carefully stepped into the enormous Tudor fireplace and lifted the strongbox from the side, setting it on a low trestle. Temple had taken a few slow steps to witness the greatness, but crumpled alongside the chest, chanting again. Lucy was startled. He chose the words from the Tablet of Jupiter, which was said to protect one and bring the angels: 'Elohim, Elohi, Adonal, Zebaoth.' She looked at him in the strange half-light, and saw with horror that he was seriously ashen. It was a colour she was familiar with from her own days in hospital, and she was about to speak to Walters when she realised he was single-mindedly intent on his conquest. He was blind to everything except the chest, and turned at last to Lucy with barely reined-in excitement.

'Open it.' This was no polite request. He dropped the polished performance as Lucy had known he eventually must. She peered at the ornate lid, which had a single red rose painted upon it and gilt edges around the metal hinges. It was dusty, not over-large, but strongly made and quite beautiful. The inscription made her shiver as she read aloud, with dramatic effect:

> *'Whomsoever would open this, doe so only if you be the Dark Lady of the Light, Sister and Beloved, and her Rose-Cross Knight Loyal and True. A plague be on your houses if this be not soe. The words of Mercury are harsh, after the sweet songs of Apollo.'*

Lucy saw no reference to angels or trumpets, but she felt the power of ideas behind the words written so long ago. She looked at his eager face. 'Dr Walters, I daren't open this. It may be that I am the Lady of Light, but you're not the Red-Cross Knight. Alexander ought to be here, to metaphorically cut the Gordian knot. Because I think two keys are required.'

Walters hadn't reached this point to be put off by niceties; and he flashed the blade of the Leatherman unflinchingly towards Lucy. 'Listen. The first thing to consider is that there is no knot – not a true knot, anyway. The second thing to remember about Alexander's legendary knot is that he cheated with it. We'll do the same. Now don't drop the thread, or let it go to your head. There's no such thing as a curse. You and I both know that – whatever my underlings here believe. This is the twenty-first century. Besides, are you not both the Lady of Light and a Knight of the True Knot? Two as one?' A cynical sneer twisted his mouth.

Lucy felt punched. Was that true? She hadn't understood the words in this utterly plausible light. She was equally afraid to think what he might mean, and know. How was he privy to something she'd discussed only with Alex? And how was she to swallow the extraordinary paradox of his not holding with 'silly beliefs' in the twenty-first century in tandem with his earlier drivel about vials and trumpets. This was anomalous, lacked sense or consistency. Was he a believer, a schizophrenic madman, or just a mountebank exploiting others' gullibility?

Guy Temple, meanwhile, had turned a greyer shade and sweat beaded his forehead: Lucy was aware of an unhealthy, clammy smell that emanated from him. She knew he was in serious trouble and couldn't help her concern, bending to him. He implored Fitzalan Walters to delay, having waited until now. They were so close. 'Get Angelo to find Dr Stafford . . . Please . . . He can't be far. I half expect he's followed us here . . .' His words tailed off as a clock bell chimed just once, an unknown hour, perhaps thirty minutes past midnight.

But Walters was unmoved and ignored him. Plainly fixated on his holy grail, he jerked Lucy upright and rounded on her again with the short, ugly blade. Compelled only by instinct, Lucy switched off her torch and sprang away – a lady of light no longer – leaving the room in stuffy blackness. Angelo made an empty grab for her in the dark but, dressed in pale grey silk, she disappeared into the space like a spirit. Walters also lunged at her, catching fiercely at a hank of her loose hair, but both men then stopped dead.

An overpowering scent of roses suddenly cloyed their senses: stifling, rather than sweet. No one moved a limb. A yellow-green light spread from the middle of the room, and a small, ethereal presence – an angel, with the visage and physical attributes almost of Lucy – was among them. Suspended in midair above the ancient box, she was luminous against the painted horse with its rose bridle, the fallen knight, the gaping tree. Guy Temple, holding his chest, stooped lower to the ground, sighing out a wounded sound. The impact of the apparition was electrifying, wonderful, heart-stopping; he read in it a profound warning.

With her whole being – eyes and mind – intent on the angel, Lucy froze, aware of her own heartbeat, her pulse clouding her eardrums; aware too of Fitzalan Walters leaping from her, laughing, his arms raised, on to the box – up into the arms of the angel. Then all sight and sound fused. There was a deafening 'pop', accompanied by a dense arc of blue light, a curl of smoke, and the clear impression of flight in the black-dark space. Lucy's throat disgorged a sound, between a whisper and a scream.

'Oh God! Alex!'

33

Kneeling behind her on the floor, Siân's arms were clamped firmly around her, rocking her gently; but Lucy said nothing. In her mind Walters' fingers were again at her throat, insistent, squeezing, companion actions to a flash of metal and a manic laugh. Yet her eyes were witness to his slumped body a metre or two away, Alex tending to him. Her nostrils wouldn't let go of the smell of him – his suit, cologne, the breath that had been in her face – and a strange odour of something acrid, smoky. But she gradually became aware of Alex's voice talking to her, without its richness, exactly as she had heard it a dozen times talking her down into anaesthesia. She felt isolated and alone; but he was there.

An interplay of disorienting high-power torch beams had now been succeeded by a more constant light source, and she looked round the room, which in the space of three or four minutes had become peopled with uniformed strangers. Calvin was holding Angelo down, while another man was restraining him with cuffs; a lady handed Alex a blanket, which he spread over the prone figure of Walters in front of him; and a distinctive Scottish voice was talking quietly to Guy Temple a short distance from Alex.

Additional moments seemed foreshortened to seconds when Lucy listened to the doctor hand over to a team of paramedics: 'Patient on the right has angina, but no apparent evidence of a myocardial infarction. Victim on the left has suffered an electric shock from the overhead pendant light. No loss of consciousness I'm aware of, though he's been rambling and laughing for a few moments. His lips are bluish and he has scorch marks on the fingers of his right hand, very slight arrhythmia, but his breathing is regular. I can't find any evidence of an entry or exit wound, but he was thrown several feet clear of the source, so we can't rule out spinal injury.' And in minutes more, they were gone.

Alex's voice, with none of its richness: 'Lucy?'

He crouched beside her, relieving Siân of her watch. When her lovely face had first prompted his smile, almost a year ago, her dark silk hair had been lopped to help her manage it, and her eyes had been enormous in her thin, pale face. In the intervening months her hair had grown past her shoulders, and her gradual gain in weight and healthy colour had reanimated her face, giving a generous prominence to her cheekbones. But looking at her now – her face full of shadow and her eyes smudged with exhaustion – he had never seen her so vulnerable. 'Lucy,' he said; and held her.

Alex's voice: with all of its richness. 'Lucy?'

A door opened softly; floorboards creaked; but she

ignored the intrusion until sunlight flooded the room, and she winced, held her arms over her head, covered her eyes. She felt the clean air, heard the window being secured, then a scraping noise beside her that intrigued her, forcing her eyes open – forcing her to peep from cotton snow. He'd placed a teacup and a perfect white bloom borne on a stem among tight blush-pink buds on the table next to her: 'Madame Hardy.' His hand on her face was warm, his voice not at all hollow. 'The first white rose of the year, from an old English garden. I think it's a week or two early.' He kissed her, and left the room.

She composed her thoughts. She was in Alex's room, in Longparish; had returned to it some time after three o'clock this morning. She had lived in a dream, seen the impish faces, been travelling a long time, trying to get back *to him*, she realised. And now she could stop. She gazed into the erotic shape of the flower beside her: an elegant damask, she thought, a hundred petals around a familiar green 'eye' not fully opened. It would be, later in the day. The scent was very present, but not at all cloying.

She sipped the tea and lifted her watch. It was after ten o'clock, so she slipped on a robe and stepped to the open window. Henry was cutting the grass, and the garden was alive with buds and early flowers, the first pendulous blooms of wisteria just starting to invade the room through the mullioned window.

When she came downstairs to the kitchen she found Alex with a coffee in one hand, Will's silver key in the other, alone with his thoughts. He was staring at the box, now installed on the pale ash-wood table. 'James McPherson brought it this morning, along with Mum's Bible.' He looked up at her. 'He drove all the way down, just to bring them.'

'Has he established we can keep the box? English Heritage doesn't want it?'

'He'd settled that earlier – as long as Suzie at the shop, and the pub landlords, waived any claim on it.' Alex looked at her with a tired smile, put down his cup. 'They all very generously feel we can establish a genuine provenance, though we can't sell it abroad without offering whatever's inside it to a museum here first.'

Lucy looked at the silent shape for some time, without a word. It seemed so innocent, yet had occasioned so much fighting, trouble, curiosity, and pain – however unconsciously. She noticed the dirty print of Fitzalan Walters' shoe, clear in the dust: he'd trampled the painted rose underfoot, making contact with the gold and the iron strapping. Maybe there was a curse attached to it, after all? She turned away, to put the tea kettle on the hob.

'Shall we open it?' he asked her gently.

'The time feels – out of joint. Too much has happened today.' She walked over and placed her hands on his shoulders, still watching the object. 'Is there any word about Walters, and Guy Temple?'

'Oh, the villains are fine,' he let out an ironic laugh. 'McPherson arrested the driver of the car – who refuses to say a word in English. Angelo is at Paddington Green, and looks certain to be charged with abduction and possibly manslaughter. That will be some justice, I suppose. Temple has had another mild attack, in the place where his heart ought to be! But he'll be transferred to the Brompton some time today – where we can keep a proper eye on him.'

'But what about Fitzalan Walters?' Lucy pinched at the muscles in Alex's shoulders unthinking. 'I honestly thought he was dead.'

Alex put his hand up to cover hers. 'Walters is a little the worse for wear, but he was lucky the tool fused to the socket, and threw him clear. It seems they did find an entry wound – through a tiny cut in his wrist. But his ECG and echo are reassuringly clear. When I spoke to Amel this morning about Temple, I mentioned Walters' electric shock, and he's adamant there'll be some serious nerve damage down the line, but I'm not so sure. It seems you can't kill the devil!' Alex tried to joke. 'I think he'll live to fight another day.'

'And be revenged upon the whole pack of us,' Lucy said with a shiver. She looked at Alex, concealing her emotions. He was still holding the silver key, and now she asked him, 'Do you want to open it?'

Alex was affected by her analogy between Fitzalan Walters and Malvolio; it had an aura of truth. But he answered her with his usual soft smile and light humour. 'The others want to be here. They're catching some sleep and coming down later; but perhaps we'd rather not have a cast of thousands, if we're going to unleash the Rapture from our Hampshire kitchen?'

'Is this how Pandora felt?'

She smiled, and they stood, Lucy freeing the small golden key from its place around her neck with just the suggestion of a tremble in her fingers. Alex carefully inspected the box once more; and a little solemnly, they inserted a silver key into a silver lock at one end of the box, and a golden key into the other, at the opposite end. Alex nodded, and they clicked in unison, the mechanism yielding at once.

As Alex lifted the lid, they both breathed. Whatever the contents of the box, everything was a foot deep in densely packed, pale-coloured rose petals – giving up an air of the most overwhelming perfume. It seemed as though the very hour, the very minute of a high-summer garden had been packed into the tidy space. 'The rose,' Lucy told Alex, 'symbolises that which is undying. Dee told me.' And he looked at her, all questions seeming superfluous.

For a while they peered inside without another motion, each separately concluding that though the box was crammed full of flower blooms, it appeared quite loosely packed with any other contents. Cautiously, however, Lucy closed her hand around the one single item that was topmost and central in the box, held in a small piece of vellum. Alex's eyes encouraged her, and she slowly prised the wrapping from the object, taking care to damage neither one. The written scrap she passed across to Alex, and in her open palm she held a small golden jewel of simple beauty, a few centimetres in length, inlaid with perhaps a dozen pearls and as many rubies, with one black-dark sapphire at the centre. It was a shape both of them recognised: a crescent moon, above a sun, above a cross; and viewed another way, alpha at the top, omega at bottom; embracing all, the interwoven symbols of Venus and Mars – woman and man. It was the monas of John Dee.

With the modest emblem – a homage to everyone's faith and religion from antiquity to modernity, and to the continuing hope of a brotherhood of man – resting in her hand, Alex offered the words on the fragment to Lucy. 'It's a quotation – nothing I recognise.'

She read aloud: '"When you make the two into one, and when you make the inner as the outer, and the outer as the inner, and the above as the below; and when you make the male and female into a single one; then shall you enter the kingdom."'

And they looked at each other, understanding perfectly. They should put the rest away, until they could open it on just such a day.

Alex half crushed Lucy in his arms, and for the longest time, neither spoke. She knew his mind and deepest emotions were with his mother, and with Will, and with her. She knew these emotions were fragile, that he wouldn't risk a word; and she knew this because her own thoughts, and feelings, and senses, were so close to his. Then he asked her simply, 'Shall it be midsummer?'

Her eyes answered him first, then her words affirmed: 'In Diana's Garden of Eden.'

34

She'd slept late – had heard the door open and close, the shutters pushed back, in a waking dream, refusing to let it register. Near panic, she sat up so quickly she felt light headed; but the familiar vase beside the less familiar bed made her smile. The italic fountain pen – the truest conduit of Alex's feelings – had inscribed just eight words:

Rosa Mundi: plucked for my love, at midsummer.

Lucy was leaning out of the window of Will's room when a single knock at the door preceded the appearance of Max. She stretched an arm to him, and they stood together for a moment without a word, watching the scene below. A man and two women were carrying boxes and catering equipment through the rear door into the kitchen. She saw Max was already dressed smartly in a jacket and trousers, and flakes of light shone in his hair. He looked his father's son, and she squeezed him.

'Daddy asked me to help you move your things next door into his room, as soon as you're ready. Siân will be here soon, and we've got to leave for Chartres at eleven. Oh – and there's a box for you downstairs.'

Lucy passed him a weekend bag and draped a garment over his arm. 'Thanks, Max. Can you take this for me? But I'll leave my dress and shoes here in Uncle Will's room. It's unlucky for your dad to see them, so I'll get ready here. Siân won't mind helping me.'

'Is it unlucky for me?' He looked at her with a charm beyond that of a child who'd just had his eighth birthday. With a smile and a finger zippering his lips, Lucy wordlessly extracted a pledge from him not to divulge a single detail, and delighted to be initiated into the secret, he peeked with exaggerated conspiracy at the silver silk in the cupboard. He circled his thumb and forefinger, then Lucy patted him away.

It was after ten o'clock French time when the sounds of Simon's voice, and other guests staying at the house, filtered in through the open doors to the garden. They were already finishing their breakfast, but she felt suddenly calmed and very pleased to find Henry alone in the kitchen.

'Don't rush, Lucy. We still have the best part of an hour. These came for you – a little while ago.' He pointed to a box of flowers, and she peeled off the note. They were from her father, the words attempting to make up for his non-appearance with their conventional wishes for her luck and happiness. She showed Henry the card and knotted her arms around him.

'I'm sad for him,' he told her. 'Not to know you would leave an empty space in my life now.'

*

A small boy stood in shadow in the western aisle of the south transept of Chartres Cathedral. Above him was the window of St Apollinaire, and beside him a rectangular flagstone positioned at odds with its neighbours, its whiteness stark against the grey surrounding paving. A gilded pin was in the cusp of the light: it was approaching noon on the eve of the solstice – the day prior to the longest of the year.

His father addressed the select group around him: 'Good friends. We have a little tableau to show you, from the seventeenth century – truly a miracle. How did they do it? My son will now present, "*Non angli, sed angeli.*"'

A handful of tourists paused as Max took the stage. 'In just a few minutes, a beam from the sun will shine through a tiny hole in the window up there,' he raised his finger, 'and hit the floor at this place, as it has every Midsummer's Day.' He gestured at the metal talon, and continued: 'You can see this concave mirror has been placed so it can direct the light through the crystal we have clamped, there.' He squatted to demonstrate the objects with all the esprit of an apprentice television presenter, and Grace and Lucy exchanged amused glances. Max warmed to his task.

'Dr Dee's small crystal will divide the beam,' he said, pointing at it, 'then one section of it will bounce off this mirror and light up the white card – which is here. The other part of the light will bounce from the other mirror, there, on to this plate, which may have been hand-crafted hundreds of years ago by the artist Dürer. It's called "three". We need a bit of luck,' Max laughed, 'but if we've got the measurements right, it should hopefully create an image of the angel, which will float in midair in front of the card.'

Lucy was getting tangled, and laughed aloud – Max's grasp of science almost eclipsing her own. She wondered if a preoccupied Alex had slightly denied the little boy some of his childhood, and made a note to herself to bake with him and ride bikes as often as possible.

'The equipment you can see here has just been found among a collection of things from the sixteenth or seventeenth century. Today a laser beam would be better than the sunlight, and the image would be a photographic hologram. But we want to see if we can get any kind of result from the sunbeam. Watch! It should happen any second.'

The dot of light from the sun moved over the floor in the heavy gloom of the aisle until it struck the refracting mirror. For a fleeting moment – literally seconds – the watery image of the angel, first seen in the former front banqueting room of the White Hart Hotel on St George's Night, two months before, reappeared to the enchantment of the group. It lacked the definition it had attained in its first incarnation, when Alex had used lasers and prisms in pitch-darkness, but the effect was tantalising. 'Lucy as an angel' appeared and disappeared in the south transept of Chartres Cathedral as the sun crossed the meridian and moved on, repeating a journey that had been similarly noted on this spot – sans angel – for hundreds of years. Gentle applause, which was thought not too boisterous for the religious setting, accompanied the vision.

'Not angles, but angels,' Alex repeated.

Unrelated observers left, but Amel Azziz – who had arrived with Zarina Anwar via Eurostar in time to watch –

twinkled at Max. It was obvious that the boy had been brilliantly rehearsed by his father, but nevertheless he was impressed. Now he humorously countered Grace – who had made an offer to the child of an immediate job in television – with a suggestion of his own: that Max come and learn beside him in theatre in the 'proper medical field' of myocardial surgery. Alex laughed at the pair of them.

A tall man with Henry now came to shake Max's hand. 'Max, Alex! A most majestic vision! – as Ferdinand told Prospero.' Richard Proctor, Alex's godfather, had arranged consent for the demonstration with a long-standing friend, Monsignor Jérôme.

Alex laughed. 'Well, despite the constraints with the ambient light and the fact that the solstice is tomorrow, we seem to have raised some spirits – literally. Prospero would have approved, I think: "Spirits, which by mine art I have called to enact my present fancies."'

'Could they really have done this, Alex? Made a hologram in the late sixteenth century?'

Alex, with hands in his pockets, shook his head. 'How shall we know? We found these items together in one of the boxes. Whether this was their intention . . . But Dee was an astute mathematician who could easily have plotted the angles, and he experimented with the mirrors given him by Mercator. Bruno was interested in the sun – very poignantly, I'd guess, when he was in the darkness of his Inquisition cell without paper and ink. He'd worked out so many secrets of the solar system philosophically rather than scientifically. Both men rediscovered how the ancient Greeks and Egyptians had used sunlight to make statues speak. It's pure conjecture, Richard – but Dee created similar illusions for the theatre. I think it's what the accompanying diagram was illustrating – though we have the advantage of hindsight. But it is possible. Whether by design, by accident, or angelic intervention – there's another question.' Alex laughed.

'And whether they made it work themselves?' He pressed his godson.

'Very uncertain. They would have had to come somewhere like this, to control the light source. But the glass engraving is astonishing. Dürer's *Melancholia I* is concerned with Saturnian studies of magic, and *Melancholia II* could be his engraving of St Jerome, the patron saint of alchemists. There's always been a rumour of a lost third engraving. Our glass plate has only a Roman "III" on it. But what if it were Dürer – an apt missing piece of the puzzle? In the three levels of initiation, any means to raise an angel would perfectly illustrate the highest level of attainment. Dürer was unquestionably a student of the Hermetic philosophy. It's Dürer, or it's a hoax: you decide.'

Lucy felt like a disappointed child. To keep her reactions natural, he'd never told her what would happen in the room at the White Hart – only to be prepared. His subsequent explanation had, she felt, left too much out; and like the boat, she'd felt sure there was something further at play. 'Alex, is this really all there was to it – the vision that appeared that night?'

He nodded.

'So, you think Dr Dee never raised an angel? That he was aware it was a trick?'

'I see it differently, Lucy. When a pagan aspirant entered

Paradise he was supposedly granted "Epopteia" – a vision of the gods during the Initiation rite. What we know from various Mysteries tells us the aspirants were granted this vision through some magical evocation from the operator, as Dee was known. Prospero does the same thing for Miranda and Ferdinand – to bless their union. Dee would have called it an "Alchemical Wedding".'

'In other words, it's a swizz,' Lucy interrupted him.

'No, I don't think so. For Dee, science was a way to the magic – part of it. Artificial marvels, achieved through mathematics, proved man could create miracles that were on a level with God. It proved the truth of what Pico said – that every man was potentially higher than the angels, which is close to Amel's philosophy. Manufactured marvels were shadows of a heavenly reality. Even Shakespeare called his actors "shadows" – shadows of the people they reflected. Not quite a trick.'

'But, Alex, I think some people may see angels: just as I think some people may see ghosts, or "feel" God without the need for rationale. It's faith – something found in the darkness itself – outside the reach of enlightenment. Maybe it's like being touched by music. That's what Chartres Cathedral is about. The darkness is mystical, as is the light, like Bruno's infinity. It crystallises something within us, if we allow ourselves to respond to its subtlety.'

Amel had been listening, and put a hand on Lucy's arm. 'You're right, Lucy – or at least, that is my opinion also. T. S. Eliot said we should be still, and let God's infinite darkness come upon us. The stained glass drenches us in exquisite light, and such subtle vibrations are indeed like music. If you see it – hear it – feel it – you do: when we can respond, wc approach our most divine status.'

'I think that's true,' Alex agreed. 'If it is within your cognisance to see angels or ghosts or gods, then you will see them. If they're not part of your thinking, then you won't. Some people seem to project them, make them real. And others seem sensitive to what my mother called the "telluric currents" running beneath us here. You're just like her, Lucy, experiencing them in a sonorous, visible, luminous way. Ultimately, who can decide which way of seeing is truth, and which is only an illusion?'

Lucy kissed him. They each saw the world a little differently, each accepted the other's variance of vision. She was secure in what she saw, keenly sensitive to the world around her since her illness; but not being threatened, she had no need to browbeat others over it, no compulsion to convince Alex of her version of events. On 23 April, Shakespeare's and St George's days, the thirty-fourth degree of the zodiac had allowed her to cross over worlds – had yielded a vision that Temple had shared with her, pushing his health over the edge. She couldn't fully explain it to Alex, nor properly describe the rose scent that haunted her, the light she often saw, which some people might recast as an angel. He respected her intelligence enough to offer her largesse of spirit. He would always listen to her, was intellectually generous enough never to dismiss her perspective. This made him the only truly strong man she'd ever known.

While Max and his grandfather were packing away the instruments, and their other friends toured the cathedral, Alex accompanied Lucy to the labyrinth they'd walked yesterday. Afterwards, Alex's godfather and a monsignor of Chartres had offered them their views on some of its fascinating questions. Lucca had the same labyrinth carved on a pillar, with a Latin inscription which translated as: 'This is the labyrinth built by the Cretan Daedalus. No one has ever found the exit except Theseus, thanks to Ariadne's thread.'

The monsignor had told them its relevance here in Chartres might be a metaphor for the soul struggling against its inner demons through the twisting paths of life, a struggle that began with Adam and Eve, depicted in the window above them. The victory of Theseus, and St George, and Christ in the wilderness, acted out the soul's chance to regain Paradise; and Ariadne with her thread was Divine Grace, the path to human redemption. Still gendered female, Lucy had thought.

For Alex these ideas had linked with Lucy emerging from her maze, with her new potential to find her own paradise; and it had also shown him how she held the thread for him, to lead him out of his long winter. She'd convinced him yesterday that the labyrinth had the power to create alchemy. It could heal the soul, prompt changes of perception and feeling – if you were open to it. It had for her; and she believed it had for Will. Siân's white roses, she told Alex, paid tribute to some nascent female strength in her that she'd not yet discovered, as well as stating Will's unconditional – if not passionate – love. Siân would come to this best part of herself one day: she was starting to now.

The labyrinth embodied a common thread in all belief; and though today seating obscured the beautiful snaking path, its rose-like shape had yesterday filled Alex with an unexpected pleasure. Seeking a mathematical riddle somewhere in this great building, he'd wound along the bends with his love, his feet counting each turn to the middle. And he knew exactly how many there would be: thirty-four turns took them together to the heart of the labyrinth, and thirty-four took them out again. The mysterious church had built in the axis of the sun and moon and the axis of the world. It was the place where they could traverse time and space, and bring knowledge from another sphere: if you believed in it.

Now Alex held Lucy's waist as they looked up at the coloured angels watching them from the beautiful Rose Window of the Last Judgement. Her distinctive perfume made him smile. A conversation suddenly surged and caught their ear, and the now familiar American voice of Alex's cousin spoke emotively to Henry, Max, and Siân, whose hand he held tightly. They too were contemplating the Judgement Window.

'Their ideas are totally self-serving. The Rapture philosophy demands a consistently negative, chauvinist, apocalyptic reading of Old Testament prophecy. Walters and his kind marginalise the Christian message of equal grace, and common justice, for mankind. But as Simon's been telling you, they have credulous ears in high places in my country now, and a president who freely admits his belief in it all. We must find a way to stop them, quarantine their influence, or they'll have a devastating effect not only on the future of Christianity, but on all efforts towards religious harmony in the world.'

Unobserved, Simon had been standing a little away with

Grace. Calvin's words had made him conscious of his own prejudices; and he stepped up to him now, looked at him, and saw eyes closely related to Alex and Will looking back at him. In a move that played down sentimentality, he grasped him by the hand, and shook it firmly, then looked away again, up at the rose glass.

'And we should remember,' Henry added, aware that they were being watched by a silent stranger in the aisle, 'that even if they've gone to ground now, with your professor discharged from his hospital bed and sent packing to his friends in Washington with a host of unfulfilled promises to them, they are still out there. These believers in the Rapture are determined to dig up a "seventh vial" somewhere. They want a war.'

Lucy heard Henry, and shuddered as though someone had walked on her grave. She could feel Alex's firm hold of her, but wondered were they out of their labyrinth, or still trapped in a last, hidden loop?

It was just before two o'clock when Alex and Lucy led a procession of their friends and family to the mairie in the town centre; and by four, they were at L'Aigle. In the garden in broad sunshine, Simon saw a ghost, and called to his hosts. Only Alex was unalarmed by the haunting presence, and he now introduced Lucy to the young woman whose unforgettable face had animated Will's photos from Sicily.

'*Mi dispiace, Laura. Non parlo bene l'Italiano, ma, le presento sua sorella, Lucia* – Lucy.'

In shock, Lucy looked from the man to the girl and back again. The new arrival laughed, assured Alex his Italian was no worse than his brother's, and then switched to good English. An explanation followed from the two of them that stole everyone's imagination – but none more than Lucy's. Consulting hospital records, Alex had telephoned her father in Sydney weeks before to tell him of their plans for mid-summer, and asked him to be here for his daughter. Alex assured her he'd declined with genuine regret; but the gently persuasive Dr Stafford had coaxed some secrets from him for the sake of Lucy's future peace, and an address was surrendered. Working quietly, without raising her hopes, he had tracked down the former Sofia King, living now in San Giuliano Terme in Tuscany and using her maiden name, Sofia Bassano. She had replied emotively to Alex; sent a photograph of herself and of her daughter, Laura, whom she believed must closely resemble her beautiful Lucy. She had been unable to marry Laura's father since her former husband had persistently and maliciously blocked her divorce, and denied her all access to the child they shared. These twin factors had deepened the rift between them.

Alex's reaction to the photo had been profound. He recognised a girl in a boat with tousled tresses of hip-length hair and a face close to Lucy's. Somehow, his brother had briefly met her sister on a sunshine day off the coast of Syracuse. There was no more to the story – no untold tale to reveal besides the mystery of the meeting itself. But in Alex's new landscape, the room for surprises had shrunk.

'Lucy, I promise, the more she tried to get to you, the more angry he became, and she was frightened he will take this out on you.' Laura's words were accented, but distinct and fluent. Lucy felt it must have taken some courage to come alone to them all here; and she quietly embraced her unknown sibling.

The sisters wove languages together without finishing a sentence – too much to fit in for fluency. With Alex's knowledge, Sofia was nervously planning to visit Lucy in London within the month; she had rehearsed the longed-for reunion for years, but didn't want to eclipse her daughter's most important day with tremulous dramas from their past.

Eventually Alex caught Lucy's eye and tapped his watch. It was gone five. She swept past and kissed him without a syllable, utterly astounded by him; he was a deep and secretive soul at times, despite the fine cambric shirt and cream linen suit, and the sunshine that always seemed to emanate from him. She had noted the paradox often. She smiled to herself and disappeared upstairs with Grace and Siân. One hour later, wearing a simple fitted knee-length dress of oyster-grey silk that Alex would describe as 'the colour of moonlight', she joined him in the knot garden, where the sun was almost gone. Her bodice, like the one in the portrait in Longparish, was embroidered with a mulberry tree; her hair was looped up in a braided knot secured by the exceptional Elizabethan jewel; and she carried some gardenias Laura had brought from her mother's garden. Watched by Venus and a hundred roses in full scent, the civil rite at the mairie between Lucy King and Alexander Stafford was blessed by Henry's friend from the Deanery in Winchester.

'War subdued!' Henry hugged his son, and kissed the bride.

*

After an understated ceremony, just over thirty guests gathered in the garden in creeping twilight for pre-dinner champagne. Simon, acting as best man for Alex, somehow managed to curb his usual entertaining loquaciousness. He offered in lieu a few well-chosen words, and the simplest of toasts, to the man who had become such a cherished friend and the extraordinary young woman beside him.

'We all bless the day, Alex, when an angel walked into your life. No hologram, but the real thing.' Simon bowed to Lucy, and she returned him a mock-demure smile which, nevertheless, was full of grace. His raised glass led the chorus of their names. 'Alex and Lucy!'

Calvin stepped forward self-consciously with a questioning look at Simon to gauge whether a contribution from him might not be unwelcome. Simon's nod appeared friendly, so he turned to Alex and Lucy.

'I haven't known anyone here for long, but I hope to know both of you better in time.' Siân looked pleased; but his words also seemed to please Alex and Lucy. He went on, 'Marriage – such a brave step! Such a commitment. But I thought you'd appreciate these words from the Gnostic Gospel of Thomas. I know you're not a believer, Alex, but I think the words will have meaning for you.' He cleared his throat: '"When you make the two into one, and when you make the inner as the outer . . ."'

Alex and Lucy locked hands, listening to Calvin's voice intone the words they had found in the very top of their box from John Dee, wrapped around the jewel. No one else had seen them – not another soul besides themselves. The box had been put by for this hour, this day. It seemed impossible that Calvin should know, and select, the exact words from the secret place. Or perhaps, Alex was thinking, it wasn't.

When Calvin finished the short verse he offered his toast to the 'two as one'; and, after the murmur died down, Amel Azziz too wished to say something, prompted by the atmosphere and the scent of the garden in early evening.

'May I add a toast of my own?' His eyes twinkled in their habitual way, and he looked no less delighted than Henry at the outcome of events. Alex was special to him; and he believed him worthy of Lucy. She had elicited a subtle change in him, and Amel noticed it with pleasure. Raising his own glass, he spoke each word clearly: '"In the driest, whitest stretch of pain's infinite desert, I lost my sanity and found this rose." The words are from the Sufi poet Rumi, Alex. I think they are apposite.'

He made his salutation, 'To Alex and his rose!' and everyone assented.

'Thank you, Amel.' Lucy hugged him with considerable strength.

Oh! The rose, on the box, Grace thought suddenly, and wiped away a tear. She caught her best friend's eye, looked at her imploringly. While chatter broke out a little between the guests, she asked her, 'Lucy, what is in the box after all? Besides the exquisite jewel in your hair? You've made us wait for tonight! Didn't you promise to share it now?'

'I don't know either yet, Grace. I suspect there'll be more questions than answers – many important things for us to think about. That's the real treasure.' She smiled at Alex.

'But as to the material contents – I believe it's almost timc for us to find out, as we promised.'

A lady had crossed from the house and spoken with Henry, who now called the gathering to table in the citrus-scented orangerie. Simon and Grace led the party – asking Alex and Lucy to come in last, befitting tradition. Simon and Grace passed every guest a glowing taper to set before them at the long trestle. A row of lights steadily disappeared into the house and were already doubling and redoubling in the glass of the orangerie. Henry escorted Laura last of all, and the ancient boxes – including that with the severed cord, which had bequeathed Alex his 'angel' – were silhouetted against the windows.

Alex and Lucy lingered a moment in Diana's knot garden with champagne. The new Mrs Stafford spoke.

'It's our own midsummer night's dream, Alex, very near the solstice hour. Just after midnight it will be, in this garden of good over evil where everything is roundabout and upside down.' She leaned against him, looping a finger along the mirrored trail in Venus' fountain. Tonight more than ever, Alex had what Lucy called his 'luminous quality', and a smile played on his mouth.

'Are you getting drunk tonight, Lucy? I've never seen you drunk.'

She laughed and shook her head emphatically. 'Do you think I would? I want to remember every hour of this night – all the night long.'

There was something Alex had wanted to say to her privately since the afternoon; and he spoke now, hoping it wouldn't alter her shining spirits. 'Lucy, I'm so sorry your mother didn't come with Laura. It's one quest I truly wanted to see you follow to its end; to find her.'

Ah yes! Laura, Lucy thought, and she smiled mischievously at him. But she decided now was not the time for those questions, and propped her glass in the fountain. She put a strong hand on either side of his face and shook her head gently. 'Don't you know yet, Alex Stafford? I have found her. Here.' And she watched his smile of relief, his mouthed 'yes', which communicated his understanding. Diana had become that person in her life better than anyone else ever would.

'Here's to Diana,' she continued. 'To the plurality of faiths; and the avoidance of dogma about things we can have no certain knowledge of.' Finding her own glass almost empty, she took over his, and drained it, laughing. 'But can people ever understand this?'

'Can controlling governments afford for them to?'

Lucy leaned her body weight against him. 'Well, that's part of the legacy from the chest, I think. Simon, and Grace, and Calvin, I now realise, and you and I, and everyone like us, should shout from the rooftops about these people's terrifying influence on politics, and laws, and the freedom of our choices. No single religion has a monopoly on bigoted fundamentalism. In Revelation, Jesus is the hero with a "sword in his mouth" – and I hope we can mount a very effective counteroffensive with our own words.'

Lucy touched the beautiful monas jewel in her hair – a wedding gift, as she deemed it, from John Dee and Prospero. Whether or not it had any true magic in it, she embraced all of its meaning with her whole being; had worn it close to her, in one place or another, since that morning at

Longparish. It told her to reconcile whatever was opposite to herself, to embrace what was 'foreign', or 'other'. She'd dwelled on the idea: that the inner should be like the outer, and the female like the male; and she wanted to find a way to make that cerebral idea into a physical truth. And she had.

After long, stubborn discussions and eventual agreement with Alex, she had gone to James Lovell a few days later to discuss an adjustment of her medicines. She was confident that she could prune down her use of immunosuppressants to the barest minimum, because she felt such a complete psychological oneness with Will. It was unconventional, but there were excellent reasons to encourage it for the sake of her ongoing health – especially if she were ever going to try to have a child; so she persuaded them to help her. They had gradually cut out her calcineurin inhibitors and moved her over to the newer sirolimus, which would be kinder to her kidneys and lessen the chance later of coronary artery disease. It was still in trial, and Alex was nervous, but almost two months on, Lucy was radiant. She was convinced she could do entirely without her drugs; but Alex was having none of it, so she accepted her initial victory as a present step and would see what she could do over time. She would never suffer rejection, she believed. She loved Will as a whole part of her.

'What a maze trod indeed. I wish Dee's faith in all of us might be justified – that after four hundred years we were ready for the cryptic messages he left us – which take some work. But, Alex, haven't we learned that if things were hot then, they're almost hotter now? And don't men like Walters want to keep the gods vengeful and jealous, to serve their own power plays?'

'But when Love speaks, Lucy, the gods "make heaven drowsy with the harmony". If the lost labours of love are truly won, perhaps we'll learn the answer.' Alex laughed energetically, and took her hand. 'At least, Ariadne – and I assure you you're a goddess to me, and no angel – you brought us out of it. Although there may be more clues in there waiting for us.' Alex laughed again, but rather unsettlingly.

'"Labyrinth",' she recited from heart, '"a complicated structure with many passages hard to find your way through. An entangled state of affairs".' She kissed him sensuously, then teased: 'But, Alex, does thy firmness make my circle just?'

He recovered his breath: 'And make us end where we begunne?'

Lucy led him by the hand, towards the myriad reflections of light.

EPILOGUE

St George's Day 1609

'And by such means as these, gentlemen – and most beauteous ladies – Love's Lost Labours are at last, Won.' The raconteur takes an exaggerated bow.

Hands applaud, and laughter envelopes the diners at the long trestle. Drinks are replenished in the candlelight. 'We know you love these tight-jammed words, Will; but "New-York"?' one man asks. 'And "Tick Tock"?' adds another. Derision breaks out again, and a man smoking a pipe offers his last word on it. 'In truth, "Rapture ready" is an excellent jest.'

'But, Will, when will it end? Will it ever end?' The dark-haired, dark-eyed beauty, seated at one end of the table, rises to hand him a richly embroidered piece of fabric. He carefully wraps it around a spice-scented Gallica rose, secures it with two locks of hair, one dark and the other fair, and packs them tenderly into what looks like a prop chest.

'And a red rose, plucked at midsummer,' he says to her. His voice wanders for a moment, then he turns to her with a face full of mobility and humour. 'It wants a twelve-month and a day, and then t'will end. It Will, so. Though in this case, the true span of that "twelve-month" is a mystery. A play sees a lifetime in an hour. Nine springs have passed since first we planned our play. Its final compass will defy a man's measurement.'

'And a woman's. For how long is the thread?' she challenges him, then points at an empty space at the head of the table. 'What shall become of his heart? Shall it flourish where it is planted?'

'Mean you the heart? Or the white hart? Or the heart that is hers, that was his? Or the heart that was his . . .' he throws his hand likewise in the direction of the empty chair, '. . . that will tell her where 'twas hid? Or the heart that was mine that you stole? Or the heart that is his, that he gives freely at midsummer? The heart that beats in her chest – or the heart in the chest that no longer beats? Well, truly, the one is a heart with wit and a will; the other a heart of Will, with a wit. And all are one.'

His dark-haired companion admonishes him with a finger, and he picks up. 'Nay, lady. The doctor's heart rests awhile in darkness, seeking only the light, beating apace below Wisdom's breast. Yet it is nourished in repose, never truly lost among riddling words. It will leap once more into passion – its meaning clear. The ripeness is all.'

She deflects his wordplay with another dismissive hand gesture, and addresses him now with intensity. 'Good plier of ink, have you not said already, many men have learned enough religion to hate, not yet enough religion to love. And will it ever be so? Will there be a time when the pedants no longer cant like schoolmasters, but listen with their minds and hearts to fresh ideas, broaden their narrow world?' She yields to him a tiny portrait, with a forlorn look.

'Nay, not this, Mistress Bassano. This must be in jointure with the King's Book, and pass through the family. Your bodice here contains the rebus, contains answers to the riddles. And I almost cannot part with it.' He lays it to one side.

''Tis only a copy, Will. You invest too much in it.'

'My copy,' he emphasises, and returns to his task of packing the chest. 'To this, the jewelled monas he created for the Queen at the alpha of her reign, and which she returned to his keeping at its omega, add only my unwrit playscript, the broken staff, and the show-stone he tells us is from another world. He quite assured us it was given by the angels, with a message of healing that shall be understood when they solve this last riddle he leaves us: when the white rose flourishes in a house of that complexion, in a country that chooses just such a bloom for its device.'

With her gloved hand, she now places these items into the rose-filled casket, and stands it beside the other much heavier corded box. 'Here shall his angel rest . . .'

'But to return to yours,' her companion resumes his discourse. 'Aye, marry. Such a time may yet be. It is here writ. The good doctor decrees it shall come . . .' he breaks off to read a parchment before handing it to her – '"when Astraea rises, East of the West of the West. Lo, she shall be married with one Will – and with one large Will, and that

Will with a large and peaceless will. This bird in the hand is worth two, and thus may the once bright Sun reappear to render power to the gentle Moon. And now our celestial pair walk forth; and as they do so – while the pedants are truly in the coldest month – the January term at Oxford and at the Law – the zealots shall feel a long winter; others, a rite of spring."'

'Good shadow, that's too long for a play. And as you leave them sans words, how shall they con their parts?' Her dark eyes flash at him, and she takes up the parchment he has only a moment since completed writing.

'Yet shall they do it extempore, Mistress Bassano. Their characters are wrought with Wisdom, and they shall live them.'

She reads aloud the few words, in the poor light of the shortening candles.

'She is both sister and bride, and more precious than rubies. All the things thou canst desire are not to be compared unto her. Her ways are ways of pleasantness, and all her paths are peace.'

And they each take a key: and lock opposite ends of the chest.

Author's Note

John Dee buried many of his papers – including those relating to the so-called angel seances – in the fields around his home in Mortlake in the early 1600s. While Sir Robert Cotton dug up a substantial haul of them, it is doubtful that they were ever fully recovered. His sadly scattered book collection remains a mystery to trace and volumes occasionally turn up in unexpected places.

In December 2004, a crystal ball belonging to Dr John Dee was stolen from the Science Museum in South Kensington. During the time of writing this it has been recovered, together with two Renaissance portraits from the Victoria and Albert Museum. The case has not yet come to court, and further information is as yet unavailable.

Giordano Bruno has recently been considered as a possible figure for beatification; and a memorial to his importance stands in the Campo de' Fiori in Rome where he was burned at the stake.

The apocalyptic Rapture fiction, which has created a vast following of believers in its prophecies, is selling in the millions across the world, particularly in the United States where it counts a president among its readers.

'Cellular memory' is undergoing research at a sophisticated level. No consensus has so far been reached as to whether it is an aberration, an explainable phenomenon, or a myth based on misinterpretation of the 'effects'.

STEP INTO THE ROSE LABYRINTH . . .

– Titania Hardie on her inspiration

– The thirty-four riddles

– A bibliography

'In the driest, whitest stretch of pain's infinite desert,
I lost my sanity and found this rose.'

ENTERING *THE ROSE LABYRINTH* BY TITANIA HARDIE

Human beings are naturally curious animals, with lively intellects, as long as we are engaged in something that stimulates our imaginations.

It was some years ago that Umberto Eco's great tale, *The Name of the Rose*, proved to me how much we, as individuals, are fascinated with the retrieval of 'occult' – hidden – messages. We have a natural inclination to want to solve riddles, and to be intrigued by secret information. Katherine Neville's *The Eight*, and more recently Dan Brown's *The Da Vinci Code* and, during the time that I have been writing my own book, Kate Mosse's hugely successful *Labyrinth*, have reminded us that we perhaps feel we have only been given partial information – that there are truths from which we have been excluded, and even greater understandings that we may have lost over time. And this is especially so, I think, for women, the healers and the intuitors of the past.

This was a huge part of the inspiration for *The Rose Labyrinth*. I was absorbed by the fact that Queen Elizabeth's court placed an exceptional woman at the heart of a cohort of powerful men with restless intellects and new ideas who were surviving dangerous times: the Shakespeares and Marlowes, the Drakes and Raleighs, the Spencers and Sidneys, the Walsinghams. One of the most unsung heroes of her age, however, was the great astrologer/philosopher/mathematician, John Dee. We undersell him, I think, as the man who drew up Elizabeth's birth chart and suggested a promising date for her coronation. He was also a great scholar, and an unparalleled bibliophile whose collection of books – bought up from the monasteries across Europe as they were being shut down and looted – formed the reference library for the Queen's scholars and explorers, men of letters, and even her spy network. Dee brought the books and the thoughts that ushered a late-flowering Renaissance into the Elizabethan age; and Shakespeare honoured him as the 'Prospero' of his last play, *The Tempest*.

This was an age of Secrets. During Elizabeth's reign, the Inquisition was casting terror in the Catholic south, and the Reformation was changing the ideology of Northern Europe. Exploration of The New World altered man's conception of the world he inhabited, expanding his philosophical and physical awareness. And these secret ideas, which so strongly concerned the spiritual and political, could and did endanger lives.

It is against this background that I have woven a modern love story. Just as Shakespeare made veiled statements about the political regimes and social problems of his own time and space through histories and comedies and tragedies set in other times and places, *The Rose Labyrinth* explores some parallel strands between Elizabeth's world of social change and religious anxiety, and our own. I wrote it in the style of a Shakespearean comedy: three pairs of lovers entering a labyrinth in which their emotions, awareness, and outlooks will undergo metamorphosis. It is, centrally, a love story, wrapped around a quest to uncover a secret legacy left by John Dee – a man who was said to be able to speak to the angels – to one of his descendants. But it is also, crucially, a quest for the meaning of the Rose, a search for the brotherhood of man. Its hero is Lucy, a gifted young woman, for whom some unusual circumstances provoke an altered response to the world she is living in. While it is a gentle, feminist tale, it also suggests that the greatest good comes from a special blending of those qualities that we regard as 'feminine' with those we think of as 'masculine'. Man and woman come together to discover greater personal realisations. The novel is a romantic mystery, a plea for us to bring different energies and ideas to work together – not only the male and female, but also those which are spiritually diverse.

The route through the labyrinth is fraught with dangers: and here the novel becomes highly political and very modern indeed. There are groups, it seems, who are as entrenched in their religious outlook now, in the twenty-first century, as there were in Shakespeare's day. What I have said – what I suggest – will upset some of them. I wanted, however, to tackle the politics and the religion unflinchingly, as so many tolerant voices are being drowned out now by those who call for extreme solutions and who prey on very real fears. It seemed to me – at the most pessimistic level – that we are teetering on the edge of an Inquistion of our own.

My own background probably demonstrates, at very least, a spiritual unorthodoxy on my side. My father left Italy as a boy in the nineteen thirties as his own family became too vocal in opposition to some of Mussolini's ideas, leaving behind their land and their lives out of a sense of pending danger. My husband's father was also a political exile – forced to flee Hollywood in the nineteen fifties to avoid the McCarthy inquisition. Perhaps, being so personal to me, then, this is why I have used *The Rose Labyrinth* to explore themes of ideological conflict and the dangers of narrow, entrenched thinking.

But it is a love story; and it is about hope. It is about something Robert Frost suggested in his poem, 'Riders': about ideas that we haven't yet tried.

I hope that the tightly woven and many stranded story, along with the riddles and puzzles that form the backbone of the novel, will do justice to your lively curiosity, and stimulate your imagination.

The Riddles

These are the thirty-four riddles which Lucy and Alex unearth. Can you decipher them too? You can also reveal deeper secrets that are not fully explained within the narrative.

There is a carefully worded message hidden across the pages: can you find it, even though the characters never do?

You can find and download all the riddles with their illustrations at www.theroselabyrinth.com. As Max discovers, these images form a puzzle. Assemble them in the right order to create the labyrinth, and you will discover who is at its heart.

+ ELOHIM + ELOHI +

ADONAI					ZEBAOTH
	4	14	15	1	
	9	7	6	12	
	5	11	10	8	
	16	2	3	13	

+ ROGYEL + JOSPHIEL +

'Vexilla Regis prodeunt inferni
verso di noi; però dinanza mira',
disse 'l maestro mio, 'se tu 'l discerni'.

As virtuous men pass mildly away ...

I' faith, trust may exist betwixt a master and his servant. Such hath it been with me. E'en now behold the golden seal in one hand, and to th'other shall ye be given access to truth through the servant o' the master. What shall this symbol be? Of two precious metals is one the gate to the lower world, and the other to the higher. But the grete test must first arise, and the lower world is no demise, but a trial of courage only.

And first to hold this was the Lady of the East. Her weeds are adorned with a walled crown, and she rides i' the grete chariot, drawn by liones. And she bears the sceptre bright, and this trinket of her will, and the grete globe. Her weeds are greene; struck o'er with flowers of the fields. And she is of the element of the Earth. Her being was as a sacred stone carried forth to Rome, looped on a cord to Claudia who drew the boat along the grete river.

A further, later, rock is given the same. Two precious metals, one to the lower dominions and the other above to the Sky. Yet at this time the authority is divided. And they are uncrossed. All the years of his pontificate are fabled to be just so, and goe towards the weaving of our tale. The gift and the decree were chronicled by Matthew, in the eighteenth part of the sixteenth piece of the greater whole: and one anon. And you may seek the sum of all their truth: but how shall ye judge who shall have access, or how?

From whence came that sister of Mary of Bethany, that Martha, she who carries the same; and to what place? Here now grows the symbol of our union. The patroness is Venus and she sways the fiery Mars: and here cometh that union i' the days to come, rich-scented with her flower. This most precious impresa shall be jewelled when it comes again from the underworld unto the light. And the lady shall find him a knight, loyal and true, and strife shall be subdued.

גאל

For trewthe telleth that loue . is triacle of hevene;
May no synne be on him sene . that useth that spise.

And whisper to their souls …

Maids are May when they are Maids, but the sky changes when they are wives.

Alone the first three wives of uxorious Henry bore his children: and taking into our minds all of his status, and thus further into our counting, be it said they had a cumulative effect on him. But you must make twice as much of that as others do, and then take into account the addition of the last as the different entity she undoubtedly was, so you will have arrived at the point that we will all depart together.

We are seeking something from the second of that number, accused of practising the Craft. Yet may she be truly said to have changed form into a ***hare****? Or if the last was changed? Or to have had as many fingers as he wives on one of her hands? She was the daughter of Thomas without doubt, yet is she accused through* ***Time*** *of being the* ***Daughter of the Moon****.*

Whatall else she was, she was in deed the Miranda of her followers: sonnets and songs unfolded under her aegis for whosoever list to hunt the hind. Yet did she but seek the ***hart****, and go too near the Sunne. What she drew from her royal husband was a she that drew forth the* ***tree of silk****. Until her fall from* ***Grace****, in that grave moment when she lost one and all. It all adds to the same.*

And in the faery month she did depart, a Lady in Grey. But here we goe before us in our tale. It shall be in the candle month, that our Lady of Light begins her journey, looping and turning. Who shall feel pity for the motherless King's daughter, 'til that she find her true path?

אהיחוד

to go …

Stolen waters are sweet, and bread eaten in secret is pleasant.

And even the same hath been given to Martha: and where did she goe? You will knowe from the golden thread. The family of Mantua know me. Shall you find your path through? **Forse che si, forse che non**. *Their palace on an island in the marshy land was only for the initiates. But how shall we discover that cycle of Mars with Jupiter when they are conjoined?*

The aspirant takes a Spartan diet before he is admitted to his ceremony. But what of brave Theseus? Look deep into the tale. Once there stood a lady by his side; but she is there no more. And they shall melt, thaw and dissolve. See the spikes of jewel-bright colours? At the great gate at Cumae, you shall find me.

Hence, heart, with her that must depart,
And hald thee with thy soverane!
For I had liever want ane heart
Nor have the heart that dois me pain.

אהיחוד

Take off thy helm, and enter the temple with the Moon and the Sunne. Your journey has only now begun. Plato tells the road is not a plain, a single road; but there are several byways and cross-paths as I conjecture, from the circuits of our sacrifices and religious practices. Each pace may yet be measured by Fibonacci.

WHILST SOME OF THEIR SAD FRIENDS DO SAY,
THE BREATH GOES NOW ...

Western wind, when will thou blow,
The small rain down can rain?
Christ, if my love were in my arms
And I in my bed again!

O Fates! come come;
Cut thread and thrum;
Quail, crush, conclude, and quell.

Three souls. Three choices. Three daughters of Night. Three Fates. Follow Clotho and a lock of hair ... *Long before he may sit to hear the merriment; before he may woo his buskinned mistress; his father sends him to end the third heavy payment and engage with this most important sign. Yet he must remember to return with gallant sail. But the Son who sets sail o'er the Sea must have help from the Daughter of the King. Some say she used glittering jewels. I think their fate was more entwined – or surely would become so. The master draughtsman told her the secret, and she left her embroidery unfinished to fly this place.*

With what beast may she fly it? High on a rocky path it waits.

לבב

We mounted up – he first and I the second ... We then emerged to see the stars again.

True to Clotho, she would weep under the tree, as his imagination failed her. Do not leave her to her own devices, without hope ... Nor consign her to a tree so bare, without leaves of silk. Follow Atropos to Cyprus. This is the Court of no appeal. The green goddess cannot fulfil her promise of fecundity ... Weave a spell and speak to the middle sister: follow her through endless vicissitudes, preserving the power of luck.

Sleeping in marble, just before her kiss. Let us leave her here to rest awhile ... ***T****ime.* ***A****fter the* ***U****nknown.* ***R****ecline.* ***U****nder the* ***S****tars.*

AND SOME SAY, NO:

Vixi Puellis Nuper Idoneus – Sir Thomas Wyatt

They flee from me that sometime did me seek,
With naked foot stalking in my chamber:
Once have I seen them gentle, tame, and meek,
That now are wild, and do not once remember
That sometime they have put themselves in danger
To take bread at my hand.

Why didst thou promise such a beauteous day
And make me travel forth without my cloak?

Video meliora, proboque;
Deteriora sequor.

Heavy labours just have been imposed: unknown to us. They are a test of the will. And what Martin divided, so shall she, and thee, until the rift is made as one again. For all the thoughts upon the nature of the path and the number of ways, and the many roads and many streets and many lanes and byways, on the road to realisation there is no justice in the count.

My brain I'll prove the female to my soul.

אגל

The son of the son of the sea by his buskinned mistress was dragged away, pulled by wild horses to his fate. What joins him with the saint and his keys, with the horses running free? A rose … Then two. Rose-cheeked Adonis hied him to the chase; Hunting he loved, but love he laughed to scorn.

But what are men when they woo, and what when they wed? King Henry knew. Both of them … But such a marriage can only be in that degree … And only, I confess, to such a degree.

SO LET US MELT . . .

Lorenzo: … Within the house, your mistress is at hand; … How sweet the moonlight sleeps upon this bank! …

To what degree do you confer? Greene George shall saye

Ah! but those tears are pearl which thy love sheeds,
And they are rich, and ransom all ill deeds.

'Tis said that bees hovered in his cradle, and that the nectar which came after was the food of god, angels and man – if he be worthy. How comes he in this tale? The Franciscan Brown came once upon a tide/ And three knots hitched about him: one as his guide. A M B R O S I A: but another must be gained.

Non fumum ex fulgore, sed ex fumo dare lucem Cogitat.

His beauty was a byword. The arrow grazes cruelly, and by chance. He follows the Lord Adonae; she follows the weeping goddess. They follow together and come unto the mark where the arrow fell, and here is the key to all.

כ י ד

For every seeker after truth the same remorseless path must be imposed. In an intricate labyrinth, he stays long and painfully amid countless winding paths that lead nowhither. How shall we count the loops in the great house of the Sunne and Moon, where he must seek? He will rise from the passional water, then must the seeker rise through the maze and the wilderness and mount into the clear air of reason; at last the Word of Truth may be spoken as with Anchises. And yet another must be gained, as with Ambrosia.

His virtues will plead like angels, trumpet-tongued; Epopteia. Yet still shall the winter come apace …

AND MAKE NO NOISE …

In life she is Diana chaste,
In troth Penelopey;
In word and eke in deed steadfast
– What will you more we say?

But what should I do in Illyria?
My brother he is in Elysium.

And he hath crossed the Stygian water, and waits. The Light may yet bring him on to greater realms, returning to his original home; or as Anchises hath said, the Soul may return after a time. Of whom do we speak? The lower realm hovers in the air; and from here may the bright soul return. But if it attains to the Celestial sphere, it need not return at all.

I am fire and air: my other elements I give to baser life.

In the candle month, the Lady of Light starts her journey: how many days have passed since the count of our time sprang anew? To the bearded Druids, it is ewe's milk, and shall be again, though not for many days yet.

AND PATCHES BRIGHT AND SHARDS OF LIGHT FAR INTO THE NIGHT DEEP INTO MELANCHOLY.

El Iksandria: the Lord is worshipped since antiquity. His body is set upon the tide; and is resurrected the following day, petals mingled with the waters. She cries blood- red roses for him: and the marriage is celestial. He draws aside his cloak. Now come the darker days: until the light is recovered. Three months and three graces,
Dancing with Flora,
Strewn with my flower,
Ushering in the Primavera,
In that very hour.

לבּב

NO TEAR-FLOODS, NOR SIGH-TEMPESTS MOVE.

… by moonlight. Doth the moon shine that night we play our play?

Where did I leave the sweet lady sleeping?

In the Greater Initiation, after a kinde of death, comes revelation. The journey: from Earth through 'Water to Mist thence Air and, after, Aether. From Elysium the seeker comes to Celestial Paradise, where things divine are glimpsed, just as in the fixed mind Truth is disclosed when the aspirant, closing his eyes to the external world, mounts high from the plane of reason, Air, to that of the Intuitional perceptions: Aether.

Now I am fire and air: my other elements I give to baser life.

Yet when she wakes she pleases Lachesis – by far the best choice of the three. What are his attributes? A book is open before him, laurel is his due, and Minerva sits with him awhile – yet the air is scented with Persephone's flowers. So many years have passed.

Yet while one sleeps, the other weeps. It is her will to **T***ake* **an** **u***nblown* **r***ed rose, and place it* **u***nder a staff cut from a pine tree, as well as a pine cone,* **s***ome ivy, a few drops of* **m***yrrh* **o***il, and two of her own* **n***ewly cried* **t***ears, shed from* **h***arrowing circumstance.*

כּוח

The air is scented sweet. When you wake, Iris sends her messenger. Follow her to Chaucer's great capital. Find Edward's monument to his queen. Move on from this station of the Cross. Penetrate the façade of the man who was king in name.

Two neighbours will keep company. The young knight throws aside his cloak and water. He is the godson of that king. And in the days to come, stop there. And see …

lovers' meeting

Sitting on a bank, Weeping again the King my father's wreck, This music crept by me upon the waters, Allaying both their furie and my passion With its sweet air;

Whan that Aprill with his shoures soote The droghte of March hath perced to the roote
And bathed every veyne in swich licour Of which vertu engendered is the flour; When Zephirus eek with his sweete breeth Inspired hath in every holt and heeth

Who shall steal his sister's book of days? 5933 9 14

'Oh do not run with Diana's hounds ...' asks my neighbour. 'Was he thus when he sued ... for poor Catherine's daughter?' She the first of the six. He the second of the name. It the first of the several?

Was she thus when she sued for his love, the child perfumed with sweet myrrh? Cupid's torch no longer blazes ... and she cannot hold him back. (Cupid's torch no longer blazed, and she could not hold him back.) Perhaps this was why it suited his rooms ...

And in the present instance, alchemy occurs: the colours are transmuted.

בּבּל

He makes a copy. Hold on to the thread. AND MAKE NO NOISE.

Kit Marlowe:

And, as their wealth increaseth, so enclose
Infinite riches in a little room.

S A T O R
A R E P O
T E N E T
O P E R A
R O T A S

Here be the charm of power and mystery, out of old mythologies, the paternoster, alpha and omega. The ancients discovered me before your memory existed, I am everywhere from the Roman cities to the dawning world, I am loyal to all who vest power in me. Embroider me. Keep me. I will keep you. I have powers as yet untried.

For I have given you here a thread of mine own life.

גאל

My troth, is thy lady within?

This music crept by me upon the waters … Yet who shall pay this fearful ferryman?

After forty days of fruitless wanderings the seeker grows aweary.

'Tis all to say sub rosa. On this night is a crack between the worlds. The crossing of the River Styx to Elysium beckons the shedding of Earthly and Watery bodies; and here we see the states of consciousness to which we may attain during life. See on the Fortunate Isles: he who in the present state vanquishes as far as is possible the corporeal life, through the exercise of his cathartic virtues, he may pass in reality into the Fortunate Isles of the Soul.

The Empyrean is a heaven blazing with fire. And the Lower World becomes transformed by the angel, the celestial goddess of light. 'Tis a place of sweet and pleasant air.

אגל

Legend tells that when the beautiful goddess of love was born, ferried to shore by Sweet Zephyr's breath, a shower of roses followed her: and when she is near in any wise, her scent precedes her. Rosa Damascena: the flower should be pressed to counter melancholia and anxiety. and Jupiter's tablet will counter too much power of Saturn. Used in jointure, there is grete remedy.

Swift-footed, thorn-pricked, pure-white, now blood-red, love-stained, heart-rent. In mirror form.

The clock upbraids me with the waste of time.
The clock upbraids me with the waste of time.

To the Lady Lucie

Me thinkes I see faire Virtue readie stand,
T'unlocke the closet of your louely breast,
Holding the key of Knowledge in her hand,
Key of that Cabbine where your selfe doth rest,
To let him in, by whom her youth was blest:
The true-loue of your soule, your heart's delight,
Fairer than all the world in your cleare sight.

I have been asleep too long. I long for the Spanish King's painter to give me a kinder fate ... And it is forty days. A shaft of June sun on an autumn day: an autumn wind disturbs the swell on a June day. So has it been; so shall it be.

She never dies, but lasteth
In life of lover's heart;
He ever dies that wasteth
In love his chiefest part:
Thus is her life still guarded
In never-dying faith;
Thus is his death rewarded,
Since she lives in his death.

NG34 Over one arm the lusty courser's rein/ Under her other was the tender boy,/Who blushed and pouted in a dull disdain,/With leaden appetite, unapt to toy;/ She red and hot as coals of glowing fire,/He red for shame, but frosty in desire.

ידיד

How ill white hairs become a fool and jester!

Witches' trees. Moons in a year. Sacred to Diana. Far above

DULL SUBLUNARY LOVERS' LOVE (WHOSE SOUL IS SENSE)

Yet follow me. For the soul's punishment and subsistence is no more than a continuum of its state for the present, a transmigration from sleep to sleep, and from dream to dream. Indeed, the man whose rational or intellectual faculty doth not enable him to define the idea of good is, in the present life, sunk in sleep, and conversant with the delusions of dreams.

The name of Simon came before another, yet it will be of greater service if you contemplate the time he spent in Rome.

When shall we three meet again?

In the great room of books. Use all of the first sixteen numbers.

לבב

heart thy to music thy Tune

Have you yet grasped the wisdom of the lovers? Wise Nature never put her jewels into a garret four storeys high. Nay, but you must search in the colour of the rose, coupled to the companion of the huntress, near the first saint.

Christ was immersed in the River Jordan. He ascended to wander in the lonely wilderness; and he received the word of Truth from the aerial agents of holy inspiration. As was the aspirant also: immersed in the sea; made to walk in darkness on the seashore. Finally after searching in the wilderness, he receives the word of truth from his oral communication. We come to paradosis. And thus Aeneas crossed the River Styx and came through purgatory, to find Elysium, and heard the words of his father.

גאל

She laid her love on the finest silks and linens. Where did she gather the scent for bringing pure love? From the oldest of cities. Scented with the spices and oils of the sacred flower of love, and thus the love woven into the fabric of its making, it is the pearl of the east.

Ah! but those tears are pearl which thy love sheeds,
And they are rich, and ransom all ill deeds.

To which degree do we remain here? Consult the Queens' eyes map. Keep the degree, and find your element: then let us lay the table … Hold fast the thread … For the day shall be measured. Woe unto you lawyers, for you have taken away the key of knowledge.

Shall I not? Shall I not take mine ease in mine Inn but I shall have my pocket picked?

A grey day. The Winter Solstice. No year. Any year. Every year. Lord Essex's livery. This year.

A Gematria Grammar.

1 א *Aleph* **A** *an ox*
2 ב *Beth* **B** *a house*
3 ג *Gimel* **G** *a camel*
4 ד *Daleth* **D** *a door*
5 ה *He* **H/E** *window*
6 ו *Vau* **V/U/W** *nail*
7 ז *Zain* **Z** *the weapon*
8 ח *Cheth* **H/Ch** *fence or wall*
9 ט *Teth* **T** *a serpent*
10 י *Jod* **J/I/Y** *the hand*
20 כ *Caph* **K/C** *the palm (of the hand)*
30 ל *Lamed* **L** *ox-goad*
40 מ *Mem* **M** *water*
50 נ *Nun* **N** *a fish*
60 ס *Samek* **S/X** *strut or support*
70 ע *Ayin* **O** *he eye*
80 פ *Pe* **P** *mouth*
90 צ *Tzaddi* **Tz/Ts** *fish-hook*
100 ק *Quoph* **Q** *behind the head*
200 ר *Resh* **R** *head*
300 ש *Shin* **Sh** *tooth*
400 ת *Tau* **Th** *the cross.*

AL AB. *'The Father'.* HEVIE. *'From Cheth. 'Angels of the seven paths'. Precursor of Mother.*

כ י ד

A bell rang in the garden on that day in the rain. 6 and 60 = 66.

Peace, ho! I bar confusion;
'Tis I must make conclusion
Of these most strange events.

Under the greenwood tree
Who loves to lie with me,
And turn his merry note
Unto the sweet bird's throat,
Come hither, come hither, come hither:
He shall he see
No enemy
But winter and rough weather.

Once more unto the breach, dear friends,
… Close the wall up

Does the silk-worm expend her yellow labours
For thee? For thee, does she undo herself?

Under the greenwood tree

And they are all his yesterdays, where the abbot was crushed, and the bequest given to the Lord Chamberlain's sister-daughter. Look you carefully on the likeness. Can'st see whose house is blazoned there? A stag and mulberry tree above her hart.

We may draw breath, move to signal a new stage. We may make light together. We may paint in miniature with enamels, in the very element of the Moon. But this road is not a plain united road; there are twisting paths and cross-ways, as I conjecture; and in the snow shall we come to't. Closing his eyes to th'external world he mounts from the plane of reason to that of Intuitional Perception. One must know something of the Underworld to reach to the Sky. How many books of this infernal knowledge were given?

In graceful care of sweet Lucina, the boy struggles myrrh-scented from his mother; each spring the flowers burst once more from the ground to call him back.

Free, upright, and whole, is thy will …

גאל

'Tis fresh morning with me, when you are by at night, are by at night.

Our two souls therefore . . .

All that is ablaze in the Field of Flowers! Pluck forth a bloom, and think on what has been; on centuries of betrayal, and pain, and misunderstanding . . .

I am what I am, and what I am is what I am. I have a will to be what I am, and what I will be is only what I am. If I have a will to be, I will to be no more than what I was. If I was what I am willed to be, yet they ever will be wondering what I am or what I ever was. I want to change the Wall, and make my will.

That I am that same wall; the truth is so;
And this the cranny is, right and sinister,
Through which the fearful lovers are to whisper.

Each pair adds up to every jointed piece; the bottom left is a square; bottom right is a square; top left is a square; top right is a square. The heart is a square too.

Which are one . . .

And I am halfway through the orbit. And if you take half of the whole and make up pairs to equal me, you will soon use up all of the pairs.

Now, look no further than the day. My alpha and my omega. Make of these two halves a whole. Take the song of equal number in the old King's book. Equal number of paces forward from the start. Equal number of paces backwards from the end – omitting only the single exit word. Amen to that.

I am what I am, and what I am is what you will see.
Know you who I am? Count on me very carefully.

Endure not yet a breach, but an expansion

Even as the sun with purple-coloured face Had ta'en his last leave of the weeping morn, Rose-cheeked Adonis hied him to the chase; Hunting he loved, but love he laughed to scorn. Sick-thoughted Venus makes amain unto him, And like a bold-faced suitor gins to woo him.

You have been under the power of the Sunne. Now cometh the time of the Moon.

From the words of Plotinus, to be plunged in matter is to descend into Hades, there to fall into sleep. And *1685 455* fell into sleep at the Equinox; so she shall stir again in Spring.

After a dance in the ring of fire the spirits may hound thee. Terrestrial daemons are the demons of the plane of the Earth, just as Angels are the daemons of the plane of the Air; they may come after thee, after many wanderings, only to bark at the Soul. After the most holy initiations and e'en near to the presence of the god, yet implusive forms of certain terrestrial daemons appear to vie for the attention of the aspirant, tempting him and her from undefiled good, to matter, urging the consciousness down to the terrestrial plane. Yet if the aspirant may remain steadfast and ignore the dogs, he will afterwards soar.

Fain would I climb: yet fear I to fall.
If thy heart fails thee, climb not at all.

כּוח כּיד

'Twixt crimson shame and anger ashy-pale; Being red she loves him best; and being white, her best is bettered with a more delight.

Sir Humphrey Gilbert obtained letters patent from the late Queen; and on the advice of many including her eyes, she granted him and his heirs the lands discovered by him. But he spent his health and fortune in the fruitless labours of settlement in the cold and barren climes around the Cape. Whereupon his half- brother, who writ the words afore, intervened; following the plan with a fresh patent from the Crown.

'And in the reign of our present King and Sovereyne Lord, James, in the fourth
year of his power, the charters named the region Virginia, and the territories
were all that extended from the thirty-fourth degree of northern latitudes unto the forty-fifth. May this yet be the power of the realisation of man when he reaches forth his grasp.'

From this realm, from out the cold and barren time, comes the new Astraea. And where may a new Avalon rise, an island of apples where the goddess shall thrive in a new golden age?

Having ascended through water and mist, she is lifted through air to a ring of fire, where initiation awaits, thence, bliss, monas, intuition.

לבב כדי

Catch to this Thre a d .... like gold to airy thinness beat.

A breeding jennet, lusty, young, and proud,
Adonis' trampling courser doth espy

Dante gave one hundred songs in his Commedia. Four times so many years as songs shall bring Astraea back. And one-third of those songs be given to Purgatory; and one-third of those songs be given to Heaven; but yet more than one third be given to Hades, where we struggle out our lives until the new Golden Age. The number of these songs has resonance. And when the spell be broken, and the riddle answered, a change may be. May be.

The strange creature crouches in the sand. Posing teasing thread-like questions … The day is given to the Roman boy. His is the domain of the beast in the lair. His protégée is the well-born lady.

The day was given to honour vegetation. The man is known by so many names, one of whom is borrowed from the one above. What is released by the midwife from the pine? A sweet scent, and a revelation.

לבּב אהיחוד

A Pedlar

Fine knacks for ladies! Cheap, choice, brave, and new,
Good pennyworths – but money cannot move:
I keep a fair but for the Fair to view –
A beggar may be liberal of love.
Though all my wares be trash, the heart is true,
The heart is true.

THE *King's daughter is all glorious* WITHIN, *her clothing is of wrought gold.*

Where your TREASURE IS, *there will your* HEART *be also.*

THE*re is a garden in her face,*
Where roses and WHITE *lilies grow;*
A heav'nly paradise is that place,
Wherein all pleasant fruits do flow.

'Equal number of paces forward from the start; equal number of paces backwards. Count on me very carefully.'

Friend …

Hold my thread, and seize the middle colour of my belt.

For I testify unto every man that heareth the words of the prophecy of this book, If any man shall add unto these things, God shall add unto him the plagues that are written in this book:

Man of the woods in colour am I.

I am of greater import than some of those who have gone before. With my hand on the golden twine, we return in golden time …

And I am one half of the royal married couple. My bride is dressed in the white tresses of the tree, garlanded with flowers, the goddess of the season of fertility and fruitful passion. Together we stir the senses of the Earth's mantle, and blossoms defeat the powers of winter who durst not chuse to pave our way. In the South, singing and dancing herald my bride's return. In the North her mantle is warmer, and hilaria accompanies her journey.

Yet I, too, have many names: too many to record all. Some call me Jack, some George; but I leap from the wild-woods ready to embrace the flames.

You may embroider my tale, weave my story, return me to the Earth each year at my time. I will sing you songs of love and mystery; will help you find the flame from within. This is the flame that propels you through adversity: this is the fire of love, passion and life. Feed the flame, on this day.

By my God have I leaped over a wall.

And they heard a great voice from heaven saying unto them, Come up hither. And they ascended up to heaven in a cloud; and their enemies beheld them.

בּבּל

Good frend for Jesus' sake forbear

23 date. Twice this. One for the beginning. One for the ending. Two frames so near as neighbours in this place, one from the beginning, one from the unseen ending. Two ladies gaze:

One lady sits with olive eyes. She plays the virginals. Her bodice tells the story, but without this clue, take warning. 'Good frend …' Do as you're bid by careful count. Yet aye, with her nod and sigh, with her say-so, consult her rich-wrought threads and she will lead you on a chase. Th'other watches from the skies. She is as a thing enskied. She is Gloriana, Astraea, Virginia.

Know you the legend of each? Sweet Robin's sweet Robin gave her his sign. She is a spur to his wit, and a wit to his will. She was a spur to his wit and a wit to his will.

So the tablet of Jove hath one scheme; and this, th'other.

בּאלא

... the race that is set before us, Looking unto Jesus, the author and finisher of our faith.

Iam redit et virgo, redeunt saturna regna

Now returns the virgin, now return the ages of Saturn. The choice for Heracles is towards the one who is scented by the laurels, and she is ushered by peace and plenty.

The King's Daughter played by the seashore. Her attention was taken by the great creature's seeming sweetness. Looping wondrous garlands of flowers, she bedecked his horns with the blooms, and climbed on to his back to ride. They set off together into the raging sea.

Shall I not take mine ease in mine inn but I shall have my pocket picked?

What's not devoured by Time's devouring hand?
Where's Troy, and where's the Maypole in the Strand?

You must needs struggle up a hill from whence the well sprang; where the first martyr changed clothes with his priest.

אגל

E'en for his own name's sake.

Lucy Locket lost her pocket,
Kitty Fisher found it.
There was not a penny in it
But a ribbon round it.

Before this another began. Dissipating riches in her glass of wine, just now painted as fisher-queen by the bespectacled man. And before that, another 'he' left his cloak and shed tears of pearl. He said:
'My mind departed the forest. It entered the labyrinthine streets of the city, and settled in the unfashionable quarter, where stewed prunes were a speciality. The badge from my county was tethered beside me. It gave me an idea for a new direction.'

Can you replace the threads – worn bare? Where were we when last we looked? At the beginning, or at the end? I haven't decided yet.

God is jealous, and the Lord revengeth; the Lord revengeth, and is furious; the Lord will take vengeance on his adversaries, and he reserveth wrath for his enemies.

STIFF TWIN COMPASSES ARE TWO.

לד

With shield of proof shield me from out the prease
Of those fierce darts Despair at me doth throw:

Enter the walled city famous for salt. The commerce is in my name. What is the value in such a name?

The last one I composed in this, my native city. There I left my youth behind. I finished it a day late to be perfectly magical, but it came after my return from Paris. Key in C. The trumpets sound the call. The first few bars might suggest opera? But at the finale, it has fire and thunder painted behind a smile. Life is ever onward, never ending, never fading, blossoming ever anew, upward through the elements.

In sequence it fits with all the others – everything, and especially the place where I sat and wrote it down. The whole world harmonises. God geometrises.

Oh – But the king's daughter is in danger of dropping a *stitch.* Losing the thread. Letting it go to her head. One of them was my friend, but she laughed to scorn my proposal of marriage! The Key is in C.

דל

Hold to the thread. O what a tangled web we weave …

The lost maiden has fallen from high degree; she has known the regions of pain and uncertainty, the kingdom of the dead. She figures as the Wisdom the Initiate seeks; but she is more than a prize. She, too, is initiate. Like the fallen and sleeping Soul, it is the object of Initiation to awaken and restore her.

When you face an obstacle willingly, you admit the necessity of raising your capacities. This approach to the infinite requires humility, resourcefulness, the exchange of one way of thinking for another, untried way. Before Greater Initiation, one must walk the Labyrinth. From Luxor. Through Knossos. From Cumae. Through Lucca. To the great Cathedrals of the Virgin. The steps remain, trace the tie.

Will you go hunt, my lord?

What, Curio?

The hart.

Thus have I, Wall, my part discharged so;
And being done, thus Wall away doth go.

The wall is down. I cannot dig; to beg I am ashamed.

Forth? Back? from Dante's Hell?

In an early rose war they fought here. And for Gay, only change th'expiring flame renews. Yet marked I where the bolt of Cupid fell. It fell upon a little western flower – before, milk white; now purple with love's wound –

Even as the sun with purple-coloured face
Had ta'en his last leave of the weeping morn,
Rose-cheeked Adonis hied him to the chase;
Hunting he loved, but love he laughed to scorn.
  Sick-thoughted Venus makes amain unto him,
  And like a bold-faced suitor gins to woo him.

If you allow some latitude in our thinking, we can move to the broader venue for a more contemporary love goddess's opening serve.

But let us all look ahead, too, to the great city, new-named for the white rose. And proudly casting shade upon a square, a building now is heralded, a copy of the great Veronese palazzo.

כדי

Macbeth shall never vanquished be, never until
Great Birnam wood to high Dunsinane Hill
Shall come against him.

James of Whitby was an enlightened man, but his beginning may not be as important as his arrival elsewhere on the coal barge from home. Observing the dance of Venus, the love goddess, dallying with Apollo in the South Sea Islands, he moved abroad, travelling incognito, perfumed with plumeria.

What do you know of Stingray Bay? But pray you, mark the moment when the first flowers were plucked by a gallant botanist, many miles from the May Queen.

Joseph was knighted later. He found so many native herbs and plants that they changed not only his name, but the place where he found them. The first link sent men there later, but the fear of the unknown soon passed. The best measure is made from the north coast – and remember, the inlet is one mile wide.

The labyrinth is a metaphor for life, journey without overview, demanding humour and strength of purpose. There are false paths, end-stopped alleyways, high and low barriers. For a moment, time is outside of us within the winding lanes. A window to a new consciousness, a door opens onto another realm. We trace ancient paths where those who trod before stepped to a ritual dance to appease the Mother, tame the weather, decoy ill luck or an ill wind. If the goddess walks with you, her scent is released. The seven-circuit labyrinth contains the magical number of routes to the bliss of the gods: mortals find new spiritual consciousness.

אגל

– AND SOME SAY, NO.

I am the Alpha and Omega, the first, and the last: and, What thou seest written in the book, and send it unto the seven churches which are in Asia.

To find me? Look in Afghanistan; and Syria; Morocco and Damascus.

And how shall we light our path? Under a Greek Moon, the element is between the metals and the non-metals. Red in a pulver, but black when glassy-eyed. We can make enamels of the colour of the love rose, and measure light. Well, we can do more than this. In the days to come it will SIGNAL changes; it will aid first one brother's work, and then the other's. How strongly it may come to aid that brother's work in healing will not be known when you first read this: not for many years after you read this will it be fully revealed. It is in the domain of the Greek Moon, and will take time to come to light.

For now you need to understand my relationship to the Telluric currents.

And to measure the time for a betrothed couple? Traditionally, I am a compound – of pearl, linen and silk. In the modern world, you would say diamond perhaps, and then electricity or the appliances run by it. But shall anyone stay together for so long?

כ י ד

In the first resurrection: on such the second death hath no power, but they shall be priests of God and of Christ, and shall reign with him a thousand years.

Like Wisdom, the bride of the initiate shares in, imparts, revelation. Persephone was the deity who presided over the quickening of the dead seed. 'The mistress which I serve quickens what's dead.' And she, as the seed buried and sleeping in the earth, is both the divine essence and soul buried and sleeping in the physical self.

Mired in matter, the Soul descends into Hades and sleeps, as Dante tells us in just so many songs. From this sleep the Soul may be fully awakened and initiated. And like the Sleeping Beauty, the princess plays with a spinning frame and pricks her finger, falling into a stupor. Thus was Persephone weaving her tapestry when Aphrodite persuaded her to pluck a narcissus. Yet when the gift comes from the healer and seeker after Truth and Reason, the soul may be quickened.

Zarathustra sought Arduizur: and from the mountain top, after the chill shudder of death passed over him, he perceived a great luminous arch in the sky, and his soul was wrenched from his body, soaring upwards. Beyond this luminous ring he saw the woman draped in light. She told him, 'I am Arduizur, I came to thee in thy solitude, and I am thine own divine soul.' And so they drank the cup of the fountain of light.

And now I: I am the bridge between gods and mortals, the heavens and the earth. I have wings and wear a coat of many colours. I bring the messages of the higher realms. Poor Dido was pleased to catch sight of me. I have a sway over my friends when they are feasting, and when you need a change of weather, ask for me. Green is the middle of my name.

אגל לבּב

The things which I have seen I now can see no more.

Winter's dregs made desolate the weakening eye of day.

Strange symian energy. Plunging upwards to the very tip of the apple tree, we go to the 86th floor. An Art Deco foyer and ten thousand square feet of marble; one must now go downwards to observe what's happening and join the long lines ... You **will** find me waiting for you, quite ready. I have been a star in the moving pictures, stood the test of time. I am taller than my peers, but you could have shopped in the department store for this same information. Why are we here? What could you see – would you see – if you stood on my shoulders? What have I to do with the whole?

My place is so important. My statistics are impressive: 102, 1931, 1453. But other statistics are more helpful. How did you find me here? Hold on to your thread and weave by me, and around me, and up on top of me, your needle in the darkness – embroidering the thread of time. Hold to me and you will find your way out again ...

Before taming the bull, one must catch him. And is this the rainbow's pot of gold?

גאל

SUCH WILT THOU BE TO ME ...

There were some very strong objections against the lady.

It was a cold day for the maiden's return, and the music died that day. To what degree do you agree?

The history of the state is written on the flag - and all begins in the silk of the same hue as the Madonna's robe. The little girl in the path of the twister looked up at the gathering storm - a veritable tempest blew. Without its weather the story would never have taken off. The smell of the orange blossom is like a walk through a field of sunflowers - one of which has been plucked and placed centre stage. The brick-work matches, but the shoes do not! The lady who explained about them defeated her sister in a sizzling final, but it was written by a man, and it's hard to know how much he understood. Did he really feel that there was no place like home, or was that just what the little girl was expected to sing, garlanded with flowers?

Glinda certainly had the good advice, but of course, it was the Wizard's domain. There is a parallel... You might call Spain? Or you might rather, as I would, count the turns you make to reach the centre of the Road to Jerusalem, in the great building of the Lady.

And a few steps back again

דכּי

The Mariner tells of
how the ship
sailed southward
with a good wind
and fair weather,
till it reached the
Line.

Sir Christopher Hatton gave his queen a curious rent. For the garden we know that bears his name once belonged to that Bishop of Ely who had pride in his strawberries, and gave them on request to one of the white-rose kings, the winter king. Sir Christopher's rent
at midsummer was a bloom of another colour, and yours shall be that which tells of the realisation of woman, as well as of man. The chemical wedding. Lucy's claims are strong; yet let us tread in Eve's footsteps from the wet sand, walk the line from Cape Town to Port Elizabeth.

If you have come so far, you know my meaning – and what waits. This is more than I know. And you have gifts beyond those this will leaves. And so:

Taurus 4 The rainbow's pot of gold

Here at last is the true symbol of the best incentives of an outer and a physical world, and the rewards that are guaranteed by an eternal covenant between the least of individuality and the universal matrix of life itself. Here is the promise of a treasure that, at the end, proves to be a gratifying compliment in physical tokens of whatever spirituality the Self has brought into manifestation through its own efforts. The keyword is what it always was: FAITH.

לבב כוח אגל

A Song

Who hath his fancy pleased
With fruits of happy sight,
Let here his eyes be raised
On Nature's sweetest light;
A light which doth dissever
And yet unite the eyes,
A light which, dying never,
Is cause the looker dies.

And makes me end where I began.

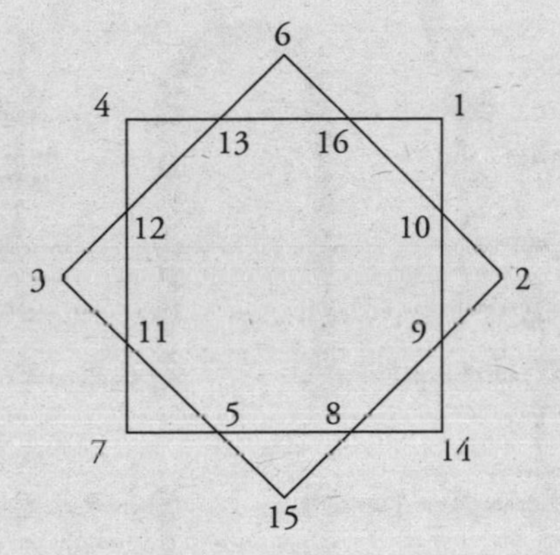

E quindi uscimmo a riveder le stelle.

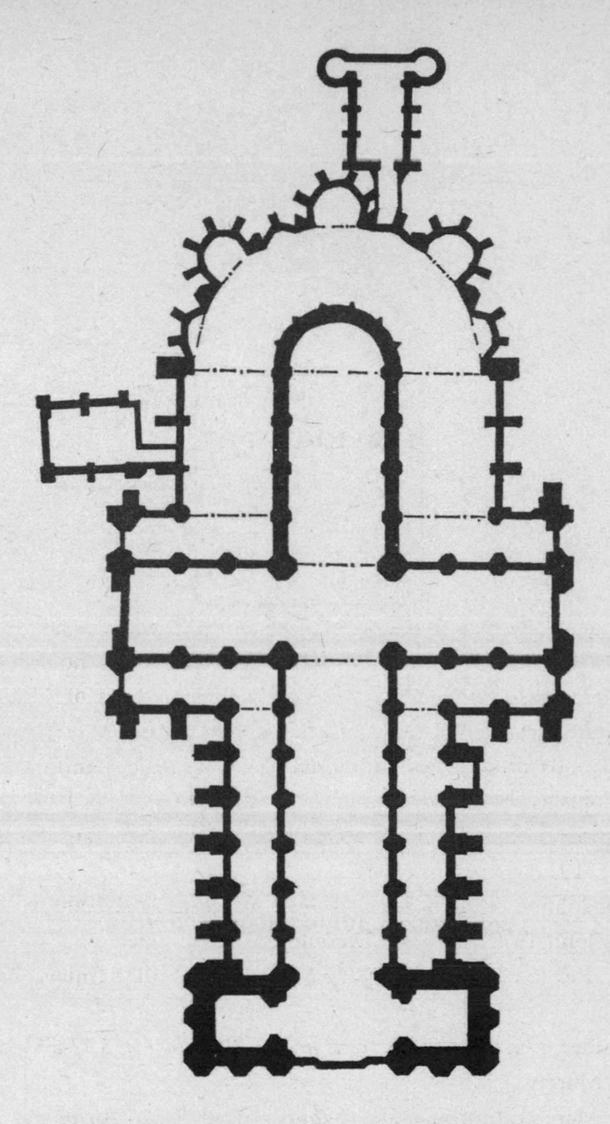

The floor plan of Chartres Cathedral

'The building tilts slightly – you can see it from the great west door if you face east . . . the longer and shorter axis have been twisted, and there's a visible "wiggle" right across the transept. It's deliberate. Every other measure is precise.'

Grace, Chapter 27

BIBLIOGRAPHY

'A Brother of the Fraternity', *Secret Symbols of the Rosicrucians of the 16th and 17th Centuries*, reprinted by Kessinger Publications (no date given).

Bayley, Harold, *The Hidden Symbols of the Rosicrucians*, 1903. Reprinted Sure Fire Press, 1988.

Begg, Ean, *Myth and Today's Consciousness*, Coventure, London, 1984.

Bossy, John, *Giordano Bruno and the Embassy Affair*, Yale, 1991.

Charpentier, Louis, *The Mysteries of Chartres Cathedral*, trans. Sir Ronald Fraser, 1972. Thorsons, 1988.

Dee, Dr John, *The Hieroglyphic Monad*, Weiser Books, 2000.

Donne, John, *Selected Poems*, Everyman, 1997.

Gibson, Rex (ed), *Shakespeare: The Sonnets*, Cambridge University Press, 1997.

Hall, James, *Dictionary of Subjects and Symbols in Art*, 1974. Reprinted John Murray, 1985.

Jones, Marc Edmund, *The Sabian Symbols in Astrology*, 1953. Shambahla, 1978.

Kaplan, Esther, *With God on their Side: George W. Bush and the Christian Right*, The New Press, 2004, 2005.

Márquez, Gabriel García, *One Hundred Years of Solitude*, Penguin, 1998.

Peterson, J. H. (ed), *John Dee's Five Books of Mystery: Original Sourcebook of Enochian Magic*, Weiser, 2003.

Rossing, Barbara R., *The Rapture Exposed: The Message of Hope in the Book of Revelations*, Basic Books, 2005.

Sizer, Stephen, *Christian Zionism*, Inter-Varsity Press, Leicester, England, 2004.

Strachan, Gordon, *Chartres: Sacred Geometry, Sacred Space*, Floris Books, 2003.

Still, Colin, *Shakespeare's Mystery Play: a Study of The Tempest*, first published Cecil Palmer, London, 1921. Reprinted by Kessinger Publishing (undated).

Woolley, Benjamin, *The Queen's Conjuror: The Life and Magic of Dr Dee*, 2001. Reprinted Flamingo, 2002.

Yates, Frances, *The Rosicrucian Enlightenment*, Routledge, 1972.

Yates, Frances, *The Occult Philosophy in the Elizabethan Age*, Routledge, 1979.

Yates, Frances, *Giordano Bruno and the Hermetic Tradition*, 1964. Reprinted University of Chicago Press, 1991.

Articles:

'The American Rapture' Craig Ungar, *Vanity Fair Magazine*, December 2005.

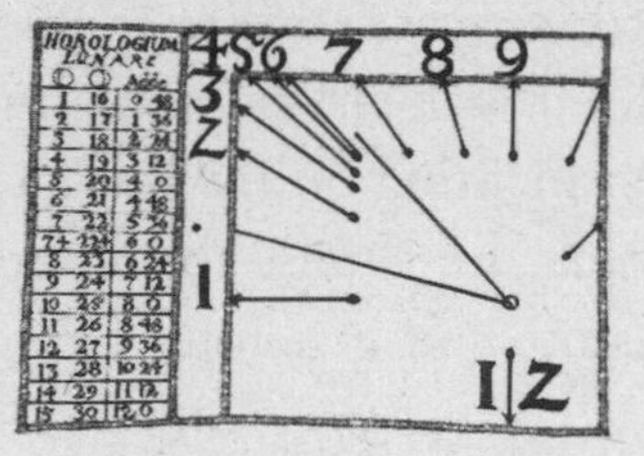

AUTHOR'S ACKNOWLEDGEMENTS

I cannot do proper justice to all the people who helped in the construction and creation of this book. Many have read and made comments on the manuscript, through its variety of stages. From the outset, Janet Opie, Kathryn Toyne and Philip Whelan should be singled out, generously reading it on my terms and enjoying its tricks, while sensitively pointing out its weaknesses. To Philip I owe the clever description of Lucy as a 'cross-dressed heroine' – for you observed this from the first chapters. Thanks to all three of you. Fiona Donaldson also added many clever insights and likewise was willing to read the book in its best light: thanks to you too – and especially for your thoughts on Calvin and Lucy's leather-working tools! My daughter Samantha was invaluable for giving me some modernisms, dressing Siân, defending my observations at crucial moments and, simply, always believing in me. Daughter number two, Zephyrine, taught me all about the Sims on Max's behalf: thank you, darling, especially for the Grim

Reaper, which fitted in so astonishingly! To my dear English mother and friend, Dr Joan Bridgeman, my heartfelt thanks for reading and commenting on the manuscript, and for all your wisdom and insight. I miss the joy of studying with you. And to the astute and generous Carolyn Burdet, very deep thanks.

For just some of the multitude of details that make up the story, but which were outside my areas of knowledge: John Fisher, whose superb website heart-transplant.co.uk was a mainstay for me, as well as John's witty responses to my various (unusual!) questions for Lucy. Thanks, John – you are an amazing person! Russell White, Phil Charter, and Brian Adam at the Museum of St Albans for help regarding the painting at the White Hart Inn; the Paramedics at Shepton Mallet Ambulance Station; Ducati Motor Bikes; Hampshire Primary Care Trust; the London School of Hygiene and Tropical Medicine; the British Heart Foundation; Somerset and Avon, and Wiltshire, Constabularies; Elaine and Steve Mancini at the Cricketers Inn in Longparish (special thanks, Elaine!); Ross and Jane McBeath at the White Hart Hotel in St Albans; and Suzie Vincent. Thanks too, to Liz Foster. Particular thanks to coroner David Billingham, in Cheltenham, for answering so many questions about the protocol and responsibility of the coroner, and to John Harmshaw, solicitor advocate, for his advice and help concerning various legalities – you are a worthy spokesman for Henry Stafford, John. Calvin's voice is supplied by 'Mr Smith', with my profound thanks.

For reading the draft and checking for all kinds of errors: thanks to Jenny de Gex, Valentina Harris, Katie Bayer,

Kate Byrne, Anne Williams, John Jarrold, and Robin Stokoe. Among the first editors, considerable thanks are due to Anna South, who made such a generous appraisal of all that was right with the book while drawing my attention to the most apposite flaws which marred it: I appreciate your comments and help. To Yvonne Holland for a brilliant job of copy-editing. To Claire Peters for working so hard on getting the flavour of the puzzle texts just right. To Edward Bettison for the delicious cover design, and Ami Smithson. Thanks also to Joy FitzSimmons and Michael and Julia at Johnson Banks for their parts in the labyrinth illustration. To my friend from North Sydney Girls High School, Susan 'Maysie' Lyons, in NY: thanks, Sus, for encouraging me and suggesting some gentle sculpting, while never ruffling my feathers with your editing suggestions! Fiona McIntosh at Harper Collins gave me confidence that this book was worth the pain: dearest Fiona, thank you so much. And crucially, though late in the day, enormous thanks to Professor Sebastian Lucas, of Guy's and St Thomas' Hospital, for checking everything from Alex's CV to the drug names and uses. Much research would have been simplified had I been able to consult you from the first!

And the most important group last. Thanks to: my sister, Wendy Charell, who gave me such an expanded Hermetic reading list. I know this book includes in it your own voice, and I am in your debt. My stepmother-in-law and friend, Dorothy Bromiley Losey Phelan: darling Dot, you were nearly the dedicatee of this book, but Gavrik's claims had to come first. Thanks for commenting honestly, and for your vital needlepoint advice: my own Diana! At Quadrille, thanks are due to Anne Furniss, who believed in me and fought for this book from the start – despite labyrinthine turns and delays – and to Alison Cathie, for agreeing to this whole enterprise over lunch. My very deepest thanks to Jane Morpeth, at Headline, initially for saying 'yes' to Anne and Alison, and latterly for continuing support and faith in me. And to my fabulous agents, Andrew Nurnberg and Sarah Nundy at Nurnbergs: joining up with you is a great privilege, in every respect. You got me across the finish line and kept me focused. Thank you.

Outsized bouquets and thanks go to my exceptional editor at Headline, Flora Rees, who coped graciously with my moaning about her interminable notes but taught me, most importantly, how to be a much better writer. You are a true Dark Lady, Flora, in every literary sense. And to my husband, Gavrik Losey, who 'lit' and 'directed' so much of the book. Unpaid researcher, *maître en scène*, and no resident of Dante's ante-hell in any sense. Without you I, quite simply, could never have got through it. You always stood by me. Thank you! TH x

PUBLISHER'S ACKNOWLEDGEMENTS

The Publisher would like to thank the picture researcher Sarah Hopper and the following photographers and agencies for permission to use their images and illustrations: Antiquarian Images, The Bridgeman Art Library, The British Library, London, Collage/City of London, Guildhall Library, Corbis, David Goff Eveleigh, Getty Images, Hatfield House/By courtesy of the Marquess of Salisbury, Mary Evans Picture Library, National Maritime Museum, The New Yorker Hotel, NY, Sonia Halliday Photographs, V&A Images.

Extract from *One Hundred Years of Solitude* by Gabriel García Márquez published by Jonathan Cape. Reprinted by permission of The Random House Group Ltd.

Extract from *He Wishes for the Cloths of Heaven* by W. B. Yeats reprinted by permission of A. P. Watt on behalf of Gráinne Yeats.